P9-DVC-800

DATE DUE

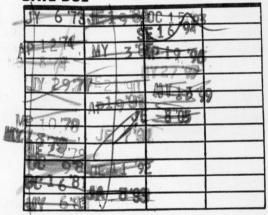

JY 6 '73	JE 19 '9	OC 15 '93
		SE 16 '94
AP 12'74	MY 3'	AP 19 '96
MY 8 '74		
JY 29'77	FE 2 '91	OC 27 98
	AP 19 '91	NV 18 99
MR 10 '78		8 '05
MY 8 '79	JE '91	
JE 29 '79		
OC 9 81	FE 11 '92	
OC 16 81	JA 8 '93	
MY 6 '82		

RIVERSIDE CITY COLLEGE
LIBRARY
Riverside, California

DEMCO

THE COMPLETE SHORT STORIES
OF D. H. LAWRENCE

VOL. II

THE PHOENIX EDITION OF D. H. LAWRENCE

Novels:

THE WHITE PEACOCK
SONS AND LOVERS
THE TRESPASSER
WOMEN IN LOVE
THE RAINBOW

AARON'S ROD
THE LOST GIRL
KANGAROO
THE PLUMED SERPENT
LADY CHATTERLEY'S LOVER

Short Novels:

Two volumes containing:

LOVE AMONG THE HAYSTACKS
THE LADYBIRD
THE FOX
THE CAPTAIN'S DOLL

ST. MAWR
THE VIRGIN AND THE GIPSY
THE MAN WHO DIED

Travel:

Three volumes containing:

TWILIGHT IN ITALY
SEA AND SARDINIA
MORNINGS IN MEXICO and ETRUSCAN PLACES

Short Stories:

The collected short stories in three volumes

Other Writings:

FANTASIA OF THE UNCONSCIOUS and PSYCHOANALYSIS
AND THE UNCONSCIOUS
STUDIES IN CLASSIC AMERICAN LITERATURE

D. H. LAWRENCE

The Complete Short Stories

VOL. II

HEINEMANN : LONDON

Riverside Community College
Library
4800 Magnolia Avenue
Riverside, CA 92506

PR 6023 .A93 A6 1955 v.2

Lawrence, D. H. 1885-1930.

Complete short stories

.td
RONTO
ND

First published 1955
Reprinted 1958, 1960, 1963, 1965, 1968

434 40712 7

Printed and Bound in Great Britain by
Bookprint Limited, Crawley, Sussex

THE COMPLETE SHORT STORIES OF D. H. LAWRENCE
IN THREE VOLUMES

CONTENTS

VOLUME II
(304 *pages*)

ODOUR OF CHRYSANTHEMUMS	283
ENGLAND, MY ENGLAND	303
TICKETS, PLEASE	334
THE BLIND MAN	347
MONKEY NUTS	366
WINTRY PEACOCK	379
YOU TOUCHED ME	394
SAMSON AND DELILAH	411
THE PRIMROSE PATH	427
THE HORSE-DEALER'S DAUGHTER	441
FANNY AND ANNIE	458
THE PRINCESS	473
TWO BLUE BIRDS	513
SUN	528
THE WOMAN WHO RODE AWAY	546
SMILE	582

THE COMPLETE SHORT STORIES OF D. H. LAWRENCE IN THREE VOLUMES

CONTENTS

Volume III
(267 *pages*)

THE BORDER LINE	587
JIMMY AND THE DESPERATE WOMAN	605
THE LAST LAUGH	630
IN LOVE	647
GLAD GHOSTS	661
NONE OF THAT	701
THE MAN WHO LOVED ISLANDS	722
THE OVERTONE	747
THE LOVELY LADY	761
RAWDON'S ROOF	779
THE ROCKING-HORSE WINNER	790
MOTHER AND DAUGHTER	805
THE BLUE MOCCASINS	827
THINGS	844

THE COMPLETE SHORT STORIES OF D. H. LAWRENCE
IN THREE VOLUMES

CONTENTS

VOLUME I
282 *pages*)

A MODERN LOVER	I
THE OLD ADAM	23
HER TURN	39
STRIKE-PAY	45
THE WITCH A LA MODE	54
NEW EVE AND OLD ADAM	71
THE PRUSSIAN OFFICER	95
THE THORN IN THE FLESH	117
DAUGHTERS OF THE VICAR	136
A FRAGMENT OF STAINED GLASS	187
THE SHADES OF SPRING	197
SECOND BEST	212
THE SHADOW IN THE ROSE GARDEN	221
GOOSE FAIR	234
THE WHITE STOCKING	244
A SICK COLLIER	267
THE CHRISTENING	274

ODOUR OF CHRYSANTHEMUMS

I

THE small locomotive engine, Number 4, came clanking, stumbling down from Selston with seven full wagons. It appeared round the corner with loud threats of speed, but the colt that it startled from among the gorse, which still flickered indistinctly in the raw afternoon, out-distanced it at a canter. A woman, walking up the railway line to Underwood, drew back into the hedge, held her basket aside, and watched the footplate of the engine advancing. The trucks thumped heavily past, one by one, with slow inevitable movement, as she stood insignificantly trapped between the jolting black wagons and the hedge; then they curved away towards the coppice where the withered oak leaves dropped noiselessly, while the birds, pulling at the scarlet hips beside the track, made off into the dusk that had already crept into the spinney. In the open, the smoke from the engine sank and cleaved to the rough grass. The fields were dreary and forsaken, and in the marshy strip that led to the whimsey, a reedy pit-pond, the fowls had already abandoned their run among the alders, to roost in the tarred fowl-house. The pit-bank loomed up beyond the pond, flames like red sores licking its ashy sides, in the afternoon's stagnant light. Just beyond rose the tapering chimneys and the clumsy black headstocks of Brinsley Colliery. The two wheels were spinning fast up against the sky, and the winding engine rapped out its little spasms. The miners were being turned up.

The engine whistled as it came into the wide bay of railway lines beside the colliery, where rows of trucks stood in harbour.

Miners, single, trailing and in groups, passed like shadows diverging home. At the edge of the ribbed level of sidings squat a low cottage, three steps down from the cinder track. A large bony vine clutched at the house, as if to claw down the tiled roof. Round the bricked yard grew a few wintry primroses. Beyond, the long garden sloped down to a bush-covered brook course. There were some twiggy apple trees,

winter-crack trees, and ragged cabbages. Beside the path hung
dishevelled pink chrysanthemums, like pink cloths hung on
bushes. A woman came stooping out of the felt-covered fowl-
house, half-way down the garden. She closed and padlocked
the door, then drew herself erect, having brushed some bits
from her white apron.

She was a tall woman of imperious mien, handsome, with
definite black eyebrows. Her smooth black hair was parted
exactly. For a few moments she stood steadily watching
the miners as they passed along the railway: then she turned
towards the brook course. Her face was calm and set, her
mouth was closed with disillusionment. After a moment she
called:

"John!" There was no answer. She waited, and then said
distinctly:

"Where are you?"

"Here!" replied a child's sulky voice from among the
bushes. The woman looked piercingly through the dusk.

"Are you at that brook?" she asked sternly.

For answer the child showed himself before the raspberry-
canes that rose like whips. He was a small, sturdy boy of five.
He stood quite still, defiantly.

"Oh!" said the mother, conciliated. "I thought you were
down at that wet brook—and you remember what I told
you——"

The boy did not move or answer.

"Come, come on in," she said more gently, "it's getting dark.
There's your grandfather's engine coming down the line!"

The lad advanced slowly, with resentful, taciturn movement.
He was dressed in trousers and waistcoat of cloth that was too
thick and hard for the size of the garments. They were
evidently cut down from a man's clothes.

As they went slowly towards the house he tore at the ragged
wisps of chrysanthemums and dropped the petals in handfuls
among the path.

"Don't do that—it does look nasty," said his mother. He
refrained, and she, suddenly pitiful, broke off a twig with
three or four wan flowers and held them against her face.
When mother and son reached the yard her hand hesitated,
and instead of laying the flower aside, she pushed it in her
apron-band. The mother and son stood at the foot of the
three steps looking across the bay of lines at the passing home

of the miners. The trundle of the small train was imminent. Suddenly the engine loomed past the house and came to a stop opposite the gate.

The engine-driver, a short man with round grey beard, leaned out of the cab high above the woman.

"Have you got a cup of tea?" he said in a cheery, hearty fashion.

It was her father. She went in, saying she would mash. Directly, she returned.

"I didn't come to see you on Sunday," began the little grey-bearded man.

"I didn't expect you," said his daughter.

The engine-driver winced; then, reassuming his cheery, airy manner, he said:

"Oh, have you heard then? Well, and what do you think——?"

"I think it is soon enough," she replied.

At her brief censure the little man made an impatient gesture, and said coaxingly, yet with dangerous coldness:

"Well, what's a man to do? It's no sort of life for a man of my years, to sit at my own hearth like a stranger. And if I'm going to marry again it may as well be soon as late—what does it matter to anybody?"

The woman did not reply, but turned and went into the house. The man in the engine-cab stood assertive, till she returned with a cup of tea and a piece of bread and butter on a plate. She went up the steps and stood near the footplate of the hissing engine.

"You needn't 'a' brought me bread an' butter," said her father. "But a cup of tea"—he sipped appreciatively—"it's very nice." He sipped for a moment or two, then: "I hear as Walter's got another bout on," he said.

"When hasn't he?" said the woman bitterly.

"I heerd tell of him in the 'Lord Nelson' braggin' as he was going to spend that b—— afore he went: half a sovereign that was."

"When?" asked the woman.

"A' Sat'day night—I know that's true."

"Very likely," she laughed bitterly. "He gives me twenty-three shillings."

"Aye, it's a nice thing, when a man can do nothing with his money but make a beast of himself!' said the grey-whiskered man. The woman turned her head away. Her father swallowed the last of his tea and handed her the cup.

"Aye," he sighed, wiping his mouth. "It's a settler, it is——"

He put his hand on the lever. The little engine strained and groaned, and the train rumbled towards the crossing. The woman again looked across the metals. Darkness was settling over the spaces of the railway and trucks: the miners, in grey sombre groups, were still passing home. The winding engine pulsed hurriedly, with brief pauses. Elizabeth Bates looked at the dreary flow of men, then she went indoors. Her husband did not come.

The kitchen was small and full of firelight; red coals piled glowing up the chimney mouth. All the life of the room seemed in the white, warm hearth and the steel fender reflecting the red fire. The cloth was laid for tea; cups glinted in the shadows. At the back, where the lowest stairs protruded into the room, the boy sat struggling with a knife and a piece of white wood. He was almost hidden in the shadow. It was half-past four. They had but to await the father's coming to begin tea. As the mother watched her son's sullen little struggle with the wood, she saw herself in his silence and pertinacity; she saw the father in her child's indifference to all but himself. She seemed to be occupied by her husband. He had probably gone past his home, slung past his own door, to drink before he came in, while his dinner spoiled and wasted in waiting. She glanced at the clock, then took the potatoes to strain them in the yard. The garden and fields beyond the brook were closed in uncertain darkness. When she rose with the saucepan, leaving the drain steaming into the night behind her, she saw the yellow lamps were lit along the high road that went up the hill away beyond the space of the railway lines and the field.

Then again she watched the men trooping home, fewer now and fewer.

Indoors the fire was sinking and the room was dark red. The woman put her saucepan on the hob, and set a batter-pudding near the mouth of the oven. Then she stood unmoving. Directly, gratefully, came quick young steps to the door. Someone hung on the latch a moment, then a little girl entered and began pulling off her outdoor things, dragging a mass of curls, just ripening from gold to brown, over her eyes with her hat.

Her mother chid her for coming late from school, and said she would have to keep her at home the dark winter days.

"Why, mother, it's hardly a bit dark yet. The lamp's not lighted, and my father's not home."

"No, he isn't. But it's a quarter to five! Did you see anything of him?"

The child became serious. She looked at her mother with large, wistful blue eyes.

"No, mother, I've never seen him. Why? Has he come up an' gone past, to Old Brinsley? He hasn't, mother, 'cos I never saw him."

"He'd watch that," said the mother bitterly, "he'd take care as you didn't see him. But you may depend upon it, he's seated in the 'Prince o' Wales.' He wouldn't be this late."

The girl looked at her mother piteously.

"Let's have our teas, mother, should we?" said she.

The mother called John to table. She opened the door once more and looked out across the darkness of the lines. All was deserted: she could not hear the winding-engines.

"Perhaps," she said to herself, "he's stopped to get some ripping done."

They sat down to tea. John, at the end of the table near the door, was almost lost in the darkness. Their faces were hidden from each other. The girl crouched against the fender slowly moving a thick piece of bread before the fire. The lad, his face a dusky mark on the shadow, sat watching her who was transfigured in the red glow.

"I do think it's beautiful to look in the fire," said the child.

"Do you?" said her mother. "Why?"

"It's so red, and full of little caves—and it feels so nice, and you can fair smell it."

"It'll want mending directly," replied her mother, "and then if your father comes he'll carry on and say there never is a fire when a man comes home sweating from the pit. A public-house is always warm enough."

There was silence till the boy said complainingly: "Make haste, our Annie."

"Well, I am doing! I can't make the fire do it no faster, can I?"

"She keeps wafflin' it about so's to make 'er slow," grumbled the boy.

"Don't have such an evil imagination, child," replied the mother.

Soon the room was busy in the darkness with the crisp sound of crunching. The mother ate very little. She drank her tea determinedly, and sat thinking. When she rose her anger was evident in the stern unbending of her head. She looked at the pudding in the fender, and broke out:

"It is a scandalous thing as a man can't even come home to his dinner! If it's crozzled up to a cinder I don't see why I should care. Past his very door he goes to get to a public-house, and here I sit with his dinner waiting for him——"

She went out. As she dropped piece after piece of coal on the red fire, the shadows fell on the walls, till the room was almost in total darkness.

"I canna see," grumbled the invisible John. In spite of herself, the mother laughed.

"You know the way to your mouth," she said. She set the dust-pan outside the door. When she came again like a shadow on the hearth, the lad repeated, complaining sulkily:

"I canna see."

"Good gracious!" cried the mother irritably, "you're as bad as your father if it's a bit dusk!"

Nevertheless, she took a paper spill from a sheaf on the mantelpiece and proceeded to light the lamp that hung from the ceiling in the middle of the room. As she reached up, her figure displayed itself just rounding with maternity.

"Oh, mother——!" exclaimed the girl.

"What?" said the woman, suspended in the act of putting the lamp-glass over the flame. The copper reflector shone hand-somely on her, as she stood with uplifted arm, turning to face her daughter.

"You've got a flower in your apron!" said the child, in a little rapture at this unusual event.

"Goodness me!" exclaimed the woman, relieved. "One would think the house was afire." She replaced the glass and waited a moment before turning up the wick. A pale shadow was seen floating vaguely on the floor.

"Let me smell!" said the child, still rapturously, coming forward and putting her face to her mother's waist.

"Go along, silly!" said the mother, turning up the lamp. The light revealed their suspense so that the woman felt it almost unbearable. Annie was still bending at her waist.

Irritably, the mother took the flowers out from her apron-band.

"Oh, mother—don't take them out!" Annie cried, catching her hand and trying to replace the sprig.

"Such nonsense!" said the mother, turning away. The child put the pale chrysanthemums to her lips, murmuring:

"Don't they smell beautiful!"

Her mother gave a short laugh.

"No," she said, "not to me. It was chrysanthemums when I married him, and chrysanthemums when you were born, and the first time they ever brought him home drunk, he'd got brown chrysanthemums in his button-hole."

She looked at the children. Their eyes and their parted lips were wondering. The mother sat rocking in silence for some time. Then she looked at the clock.

"Twenty minutes to six!" In a tone of fine bitter careless-ness she continued: "Eh, he'll not come now till they bring him. There he'll stick! But he needn't come rolling in here in his pit-dirt, for I won't wash him. He can lie on the floor—— Eh, what a fool I've been, what a fool! And this is what I came here for, to this dirty hole, rats and all, for him to slink past his very door. Twice last week—he's begun now——"

She silenced herself, and rose to clear the table.

While for an hour or more the children played, subduedly intent, fertile of imagination, united in fear of the mother's wrath, and in dread of their father's home-coming, Mrs. Bates sat in her rocking-chair making a 'singlet' of thick cream-coloured flannel, which gave a dull wounded sound as she tore off the grey edge. She worked at her sewing with energy, listening to the children, and her anger wearied itself, lay down to rest, opening its eyes from time to time and steadily watch-ing, its ears raised to listen. Sometimes even her anger quailed and shrank, and the mother suspended her sewing, tracing the footsteps that thudded along the sleepers outside; she would lift her head sharply to bid the children 'hush', but she recovered herself in time, and the footsteps went past the gate, and the children were not flung out of their play-world.

But at last Annie sighed, and gave in. She glanced at her wagon of slippers, and loathed the game. She turned plain-tively to her mother.

"Mother!"—but she was inarticulate.

John crept out like a frog from under the sofa. His mother glanced up.

"Yes," she said, "just look at those shirt-sleeves!"

The boy held them out to survey them, saying nothing. Then somebody called in a hoarse voice away down the line, and suspense bristled in the room, till two people had gone by outside, talking.

"It is time for bed," said the mother.

"My father hasn't come," wailed Annie plaintively. But her mother was primed with courage.

"Never mind. They'll bring him when he does come—like a log." She meant there would be no scene. "And he may sleep on the floor till he wakes himself. I know he'll not go to work to-morrow after this!"

The children had their hands and faces wiped with a flannel. They were very quiet. When they had put on their night-dresses, they said their prayers, the boy mumbling. The mother looked down at them, at the brown silken bush of intertwining curls in the nape of the girl's neck, at the little black head of the lad, and her heart burst with anger at their father, who caused all three such distress. The children hid their faces in her skirts for comfort.

When Mrs. Bates came down, the room was strangely empty, with a tension of expectancy. She took up her sewing and stitched for some time without raising her head. Mean-time her anger was tinged with fear.

II

The clock struck eight and she rose suddenly, dropping her sewing on her chair. She went to the stair-foot door, opened it, listening. Then she went out, locking the door behind her.

Something scuffled in the yard, and she started, though she knew it was only the rats with which the place was over-run. The night was very dark. In the great bay of railway lines, bulked with trucks, there was no trace of light, only away back she could see a few yellow lamps at the pit-top, and the red smear of the burning pit-bank on the night. She hurried along the edge of the track, then, crossing the converging lines, came to the stile by the white gates, whence she emerged on the road. Then the fear which had led her shrank.

People were walking up to New Brinsley; she saw the lights in the houses; twenty yards farther on were the broad windows of the 'Prince of Wales', very warm and bright, and the loud voices of men could be heard distinctly. What a fool she had been to imagine that anything had happened to him! He was merely drinking over there at the 'Prince of Wales'. She faltered. She had never yet been to fetch him, and she never would go. So she continued her walk towards the long straggling line of houses, standing back on the highway. She entered a passage between the dwellings.

"Mr. Rigley?—Yes! Did you want him? No, he's not in at this minute."

The raw-boned woman leaned forward from her dark scullery and peered at the other, upon whom fell a dim light through the blind of the kitchen window.

"Is it Mrs. Bates?" she asked in a tone tinged with respect.

"Yes. I wondered if your Master was at home. Mine hasn't come yet."

"'Asn't 'e! Oh, Jack's been 'ome an' 'ad 'is dinner an' gone out. 'E's just gone for 'alf an hour afore bed-time. Did you call at the 'Prince of Wales'?"

"No——"

"No, you didn't like——! It's not very nice." The other woman was indulgent. There was an awkward pause. "Jack never said nothink about—about your Master," she said.

"No!—I expect he's stuck in there!"

Elizabeth Bates said this bitterly, and with recklessness. She knew that the woman across the yard was standing at her door listening, but she did not care. As she turned:

"Stop a minute! I'll just go an' ask Jack if 'e knows anythink," said Mrs. Rigley.

"Oh no—I wouldn't like to put——!"

"Yes, I will, if you'll just step inside an' see as th' childer doesn't come downstairs and set theirselves afire."

Elizabeth Bates, murmuring a remonstrance, stepped inside. The other woman apologised for the state of the room.

The kitchen needed apology. There were little frocks and trousers and childish undergarments on the squab and on the floor, and a litter of playthings everywhere. On the black American cloth of the table were pieces of bread and cake, crusts, slops, and a teapot with cold tea.

"Eh, ours is just as bad," said Elizabeth Bates, looking at the

B

woman, not at the house. Mrs. Rigley put a shawl over her head and hurried out, saying:

"I shanna be a minute."

The other sat, noting with faint disapproval the general untidiness of the room. Then she fell to counting the shoes of various sizes scattered over the floor. There were twelve. She sighed and said to herself: "No wonder!"—glancing at the litter. There came the scratching of two pairs of feet on the yard, and the Rigleys entered. Elizabeth Bates rose. Rigley was a big man, with very large bones. His head looked particularly bony. Across his temple was a blue scar, caused by a wound got in the pit, a wound in which the coal-dust remained blue like tattooing.

"'Asna 'e come whoam yit?" asked the man, without any form of greeting, but with deference and sympathy. "I couldna say wheer he is—'e's non ower theer!"—he jerked his head to signify the 'Prince of Wales'.

"'E's 'appen gone up to th' 'Yew'," said Mrs. Rigley.

There was another pause. Rigley had evidently something to get off his mind.

"Ah left 'im finishin' a stint," he began. "Loose-all 'ad bin gone about ten minutes when we com'n away, an' I shouted: 'Are ter comin', Walt?' an' 'e said: 'Go on, Ah shanna be but a'ef a minnit,' so we com'n ter th' bottom, me an' Bowers, thinkin' as 'e wor just behint, an' 'ud come up i' th' next bantle——"

He stood perplexed, as if answering a charge of deserting his mate. Elizabeth Bates, now again certain of disaster, hastened to reassure him:

"I expect 'e's gone up to th' 'Yew Tree', as you say. It's not the first time. I've fretted myself into a fever before now. He'll come home when they carry him."

"Ay, isn't it too bad!" deplored the other woman.

"I'll just step up to Dick's an' see if 'e is theer," offered the man, afraid of appearing alarmed, afraid of taking liberties.

"Oh, I wouldn't think of bothering you that far," said Elizabeth Bates, with emphasis, but he knew she was glad of his offer.

As they stumbled up the entry, Elizabeth Bates heard Rigley's wife run across the yard and open her neighbour's door. At this, suddenly all the blood in her body seemed to switch away from her heart.

"Mind!" warned Rigley. "Ah've said many a time as Ah'd fill up them ruts in this entry, sumb'dy 'll be breakin' their legs yit."

She recovered herself and walked quickly along with the miner.

"I don't like leaving the children in bed, and nobody in the house," she said.

"No, you dunna!" he replied courteously. They were soon at the gate of the cottage.

"Well, I shanna be many minnits. Dunna you be frettin' now, 'e'll be all right," said the butty.

"Thank you very much, Mr. Rigley," she replied.

"You're welcome!" he stammered, moving away. "I shanna be many minnits."

The house was quiet. Elizabeth Bates took off her hat and shawl, and rolled back the rug. When she had finished, she sat down. It was a few minutes past nine. She was startled by the rapid chuff of the winding-engine at the pit, and the sharp whirr of the brakes on the rope as it descended. Again she felt the painful sweep of her blood, and she put her hand to her side, saying aloud: "Good gracious!—it's only the nine o'clock deputy going down," rebuking herself.

She sat still, listening. Half an hour of this, and she was wearied out.

"What am I working myself up like this for?" she said pitiably to herself, "I s'll only be doing myself some damage."

She took out her sewing again.

At a quarter to ten there were footsteps. One person! She watched for the door to open. It was an elderly woman, in a black bonnet and a black woollen shawl—his mother. She was about sixty years old, pale, with blue eyes, and her face all wrinkled and lamentable. She shut the door and turned to her daughter-in-law peevishly.

"Eh, Lizzie, whatever shall we do, whatever shall we do!" she cried.

Elizabeth drew back a little, sharply.

"What is it, mother?" she said.

The elder woman seated herself on the sofa.

"I don't know, child, I can't tell you!"—she shook her head slowly. Elizabeth sat watching her, anxious and vexed.

"I don't know," replied the grandmother, sighing very deeply. "There's no end to my troubles, there isn't. The things

I've gone through, I'm sure it's enough——!" She wept without wiping her eyes, the tears running.

"But, mother," interrupted Elizabeth, "what do you mean? What is it?"

The grandmother slowly wiped her eyes. The fountains of her tears were stopped by Elizabeth's directness. She wiped her eyes slowly.

"Poor child! Eh, you poor thing!" she moaned. "I don't know what we're going to do, I don't—and you as you are—it's a thing, it is indeed!"

Elizabeth waited.

"Is he dead?" she asked, and at the words her heart swung violently, though she felt a slight flush of shame at the ultimate extravagance of the question. Her words sufficiently frightened the old lady, almost brought her to herself.

"Don't say so, Elizabeth! We'll hope it's not as bad as that; no, may the Lord spare us that, Elizabeth. Jack Rigley came just as I was sittin' down to a glass afore going to bed, an' 'e said: ''Appen you'll go down th' line, Mrs. Bates. Walt's had an accident. 'Appen you'll go an' sit wi' 'er till we can get him home.' I hadn't time to ask him a word afore he was gone. An' I put my bonnet on an' come straight down, Lizzie. I thought to myself: 'Eh, that poor blessed child, if anybody should come an' tell her of a sudden, there's no knowin' what'll 'appen to 'er.' You mustn't let it upset you, Lizzie—or you know what to expect. How long is it, six months—or is it five, Lizzie? Ay!"—the old woman shook her head—"time slips on, it slips on! Ay!"

Elizabeth's thoughts were busy elsewhere. If he was killed—would she be able to manage on the little pension and what she could earn?—she counted up rapidly. If he was hurt—they wouldn't take him to the hospital—how tiresome he would be to nurse!—but perhaps she'd be able to get him away from the drink and his hateful ways. She would—while he was ill. The tears offered to come to her eyes at the picture. But what sentimental luxury was this she was beginning? She turned to consider the children. At any rate she was absolutely necessary for them. They were her business.

"Ay!" repeated the old woman, "it seems but a week or two since he brought me his first wages. Ay—he was a good lad, Elizabeth, he was, in his way. I don't know why he got to be such a trouble, I don't. He was a happy lad at home, only

full of spirits. But there's no mistake he's been a handful of
trouble, he has! I hope the Lord'll spare him to mend his ways.
I hope so, I hope so. You've had a sight o' trouble with him,
Elizabeth, you have indeed. But he was a jolly enough lad wi'
me, he was, I can assure you. I don't know how it is. . . ."

The old woman continued to muse aloud, a monotonous
irritating sound, while Elizabeth thought concentratedly,
startled once, when she heard the winding-engine chuff
quickly, and the brakes skirr with a shriek. Then she heard the
engine more slowly, and the brakes made no sound. The old
woman did not notice. Elizabeth waited in suspense. The
mother-in-law talked, with lapses into silence.

"But he wasn't your son, Lizzie, an' it makes a difference
Whatever he was, I remember him when he was little, an' I
learned to understand him and to make allowances. You've
got to make allowances for them——"

It was half-past ten, and the old woman was saying: "But
it's trouble from beginning to end; you're never too old for
trouble, never too old for that——" when the gate banged
back, and there were heavy feet on the steps.

"I'll go, Lizzie, let me go," cried the old woman, rising. But
Elizabeth was at the door. It was a man in pit-clothes.

"They're bringin' 'im, Missis," he said. Elizabeth's heart
halted a moment. Then it surged on again, almost suffocating
her.

"Is he—is it bad?" she asked.

The man turned away, looking at the darkness:

"The doctor says 'e'd been dead hours. 'E saw 'im i' th' lamp-
cabin."

The old woman, who stood just behind Elizabeth, dropped
into a chair, and folded her hands, crying: "Oh, my boy, my
boy!"

"Hush!" said Elizabeth, with a sharp twitch of a frown.
"Be still, mother, don't waken th' children: I wouldn't have
them down for anything!"

The old woman moaned softly, rocking herself. The man
was drawing away. Elizabeth took a step forward.

"How was it?" she asked.

"Well, I couldn't say for sure," the man replied, very ill at
ease. " 'E wor finishin' a stint an' th' butties 'ad gone, an' a
lot o' stuff come down atop 'n 'im."

"And crushed him?" cried the widow, with a shudder.

"No," said the man, "it fell at th' back of 'im. 'E wor under th' face, an' it niver touched 'im. It shut 'im in. It seems 'e wor smothered."

Elizabeth shrank back. She heard the old woman behind her cry:

"What?—what did 'e say it was?"

The man replied, more loudly: "'E wor smothered!"

Then the old woman wailed aloud, and this relieved Elizabeth.

"Oh, mother," she said, putting her hand on the old woman, "don't waken th' children, don't waken th' children."

She wept a little, unknowing, while the old mother rocked herself and moaned. Elizabeth remembered that they were bringing him home, and she must be ready. "They'll lay him in the parlour," she said to herself, standing a moment pale and perplexed.

Then she lighted a candle and went into the tiny room. The air was cold and damp, but she could not make a fire, there was no fireplace. She set down the candle and looked round. The candlelight glittered on the lustre-glasses, on the two vases that held some of the pink chrysanthemums, and on the dark mahogany. There was a cold, deathly smell of chrysanthemums in the room. Elizabeth stood looking at the flowers. She turned away, and calculated whether there would be room to lay him on the floor, between the couch and the chiffonier. She pushed the chairs aside. There would be room to lay him down and to step round him. Then she fetched the old red tablecloth, and another old cloth, spreading them down to save her bit of carpet. She shivered on leaving the parlour; so, from the dresser drawer she took a clean shirt and put it at the fire to air. All the time her mother-in-law was rocking herself in the chair and moaning.

"You'll have to move from there, mother," said Elizabeth. "They'll be bringing him in. Come in the rocker."

The old mother rose mechanically, and seated herself by the fire, continuing to lament. Elizabeth went into the pantry for another candle, and there, in the little pent-house under the naked tiles, she heard them coming. She stood still in the pantry doorway, listening. She heard them pass the end of the house, and come awkwardly down the three steps, a jumble of shuffling footsteps and muttering voices. The old woman was silent. The men were in the yard.

Then Elizabeth heard Matthews, the manager of the pit, say:
"You go in first, Jim. Mind!"

The door came open, and the two women saw a collier backing into the room, holding one end of a stretcher, on which
they could see the nailed pit-boots of the dead man. The two
carriers halted, the man at the head stooping to the lintel of
the door.

"Wheer will you have him?" asked the manager, a short,
white-bearded man.

Elizabeth roused herself and came from the pantry carrying
the unlighted candle.

"In the parlour," she said.

"In there, Jim!" pointed the manager, and the carriers
backed round into the tiny room. The coat with which they
had covered the body fell off as they awkwardly turned
through the two doorways, and the women saw their man,
naked to the waist, lying stripped for work. The old woman
began to moan in a low voice of horror.

"Lay th' stretcher at th' side," snapped the manager, "an'
put 'im on th' cloths. Mind now, mind! Look you now——!"

One of the men had knocked off a vase of chrysanthemums.
He stared awkwardly, then they set down the stretcher.
Elizabeth did not look at her husband. As soon as she could
get in the room, she went and picked up the broken vase and
the flowers.

"Wait a minute!" she said.

The three men waited in silence while she mopped up the
water with a duster.

"Eh, what a job, what a job, to be sure!" the manager was
saying, rubbing his brow with trouble and perplexity. "Never
knew such a thing in my life, never! He'd no business to ha'
been left. I never knew such a thing in my life! Fell over him
clean as a whistle, an' shut him in. Not four foot of space,
there wasn't—yet it scarce bruised him."

He looked down at the dead man, lying prone, half naked, all
grimed with coal-dust.

" ' 'Sphyxiated', the doctor said. It *is* the most terrible job
I've ever known. Seems as if it was done o' purpose. Clean
over him, an' shut 'im in, like a mouse-trap"—he made a sharp,
descending gesture with his hand.

The colliers standing by jerked aside their heads in hopeless
comment.

The horror of the thing bristled upon them all.

Then they heard the girl's voice upstairs calling shrilly: "Mother, mother—who is it? Mother, who is it?"

Elizabeth hurried to the foot of the stairs and opened the door:

"Go to sleep!" she commanded sharply. "What are you shouting about? Go to sleep at once—there's nothing——"

Then she began to mount the stairs. They could hear her on the boards, and on the plaster floor of the little bedroom. They could hear her distinctly:

"What's the matter now?—what's the matter with you, silly thing?"—her voice was much agitated, with an unreal gentleness.

"I thought it was some men come," said the plaintive voice of the child. "Has he come?"

"Yes, they've brought him. There's nothing to make a fuss about. Go to sleep now, like a good child."

They could hear her voice in the bedroom, they waited whilst she covered the children under the bedclothes.

"Is he drunk?" asked the girl, timidly, faintly.

"No! No—he's not! He—he's asleep."

"Is he asleep downstairs?"

"Yes—and don't make a noise."

There was silence for a moment, then the men heard the frightened child again:

"What's that noise?"

"It's nothing, I tell you, what are you bothering for?"

The noise was the grandmother moaning. She was oblivious of everything, sitting on her chair rocking and moaning. The manager put his hand on her arm and bade her "Sh—sh!!"

The old woman opened her eyes and looked at him. She was shocked by this interruption, and seemed to wonder.

"What time is it?" the plaintive thin voice of the child, sinking back unhappily into sleep, asked this last question.

"Ten o'clock," answered the mother more softly. Then she must have bent down and kissed the children.

Matthews beckoned to the men to come away. They put on their caps and took up the stretcher. Stepping over the body, they tiptoed out of the house. None of them spoke till they were far from the wakeful children.

When Elizabeth came down she found her mother alone on

the parlour floor, leaning over the dead man, the tears dropping on him.

"We must lay him out," the wife said. She put on the kettle, then returning knelt at the feet, and began to unfasten the knotted leather laces. The room was clammy and dim with only one candle, so that she had to bend her face almost to the floor. At last she got off the heavy boots and put them away.

"You must help me now," she whispered to the old woman. Together they stripped the man.

When they arose, saw him lying in the naïve dignity of death, the woman stood arrested in fear and respect. For a few moments they remained still, looking down, the old mother whimpering. Elizabeth felt countermanded. She saw him, how utterly inviolable he lay in himself. She had nothing to do with him. She could not accept it. Stooping, she laid her hand on him, in claim. He was still warm, for the mine was hot where he had died. His mother had his face between her hands, and was murmuring incoherently. The old tears fell in succession as drops from wet leaves; the mother was not weeping, merely her tears flowed. Elizabeth embraced the body of her husband, with cheek and lips. She seemed to be listening, inquiring, trying to get some connection. But she could not. She was driven away. He was impregnable.

She rose, went into the kitchen, where she poured warm water into a bowl, brought soap and flannel and a soft towel. "I must wash him," she said.

Then the old mother rose stiffly, and watched Elizabeth as she carefully washed his face, carefully brushing the big blond moustache from his mouth with the flannel. She was afraid with a bottomless fear, so she ministered to him. The old woman, jealous, said:

"Let me wipe him!"—and she kneeled on the other side drying slowly as Elizabeth washed, her big black bonnet sometimes brushing the dark head of her daughter-in-law. They worked thus in silence for a long time. They never forgot it was death, and the touch of the man's dead body gave them strange emotions, different in each of the women; a great dread possessed them both, the mother felt the lie was given to her womb, she was denied; the wife felt the utter isolation of the human soul, the child within her was a weight apart from her.

At last it was finished. He was a man of handsome body,

and his face showed no traces of drink. He was blond, full-fleshed, with fine limbs. But he was dead.

"Bless him," whispered his mother, looking always at his face, and speaking out of sheer terror. "Dear lad—bless him!" She spoke in a faint, sibilant ecstasy of fear and mother love.

Elizabeth sank down again to the floor, and put her face against his neck, and trembled and shuddered. But she had to draw away again. He was dead, and her living flesh had no place against his. A great dread and weariness held her: she was so unavailing. Her life was gone like this.

"White as milk he is, clear as a twelve-month baby, bless him, the darling!" the old mother murmured to herself. "Not a mark on him, clear and clean and white, beautiful as ever a child was made," she murmured with pride. Elizabeth kept her face hidden.

"He went peaceful, Lizzie—peaceful as sleep. Isn't he beautiful, the lamb? Ay—he must ha' made his peace, Lizzie. 'Appen he made it all right, Lizzie, shut in there. He'd have time. He wouldn't look like this if he hadn't made his peace. The lamb, the dear lamb. Eh, but he had a hearty laugh. I loved to hear it. He had the heartiest laugh, Lizzie, as a lad——"

Elizabeth looked up. The man's mouth was fallen back, slightly open under the cover of the moustache. The eyes, half shut, did not show glazed in the obscurity. Life with its smoky burning gone from him, had left him apart and utterly alien to her. And she knew what a stranger he was to her. In her womb was ice of fear, because of this separate stranger with whom she had been living as one flesh. Was this what it all meant—utter, intact separateness, obscured by heat of living? In dread she turned her face away. The fact was too deadly. There had been nothing between them, and yet they had come together, exchanging their nakedness repeatedly. Each time he had taken her, they had been two isolated beings, far apart as now. He was no more responsible than she. The child was like ice in her womb. For as she looked at the dead man, her mind, cold and detached, said clearly: "Who am I? What have I been doing? I have been fighting a husband who did not exist. He existed all the time. What wrong have I done? What was that I have been living with? There lies the reality, this man." And her soul died in her for fear: she knew she had never seen him, he had never seen her, they had met in the dark and had fought in the dark, not knowing whom they met nor whom they fought. And now she saw, and turned silent in seeing. For she had been wrong. She had said he was something he was not; she had felt familiar with him. Whereas he was apart all the while, living as she never lived, feeling as she never felt. In fear and shame she looked at his naked body, that she had known falsely. And he was the father of her children. Her soul was torn from her body and stood apart. She looked at his naked body and was ashamed, as if she had denied it. After all, it was itself. It seemed awful to her. She looked at his face, and she turned her own face to the wall. For his look was other than hers, his way was not her way. She had denied him what he was—she saw it now. She had refused him as himself. And this had been her life, and his life. She was grateful to death, which restored the truth. And she knew she was not dead.

And all the while her heart was bursting with grief and pity for him. What had he suffered? What stretch of horror for this helpless man! She was rigid with agony. She had not been able to help him. He had been cruelly injured, this naked man, this other being, and she could make no reparation. There were the children—but the children belonged to life. This dead man had nothing to do with them. He and she were only channels through which life had flowed to issue in the children. She was a mother—but how awful she knew it now to have been a wife. And he, dead now, how awful he must have felt it to be a husband. She felt that in the next world he would be a stranger to her. If they met there, in the beyond, they would only be ashamed of what had been before. The children had come, for some mysterious reason, out of both of them. But the children did not unite them. Now he was dead, she knew how eternally he was apart from her, how eternally he had nothing more to do with her. She saw this episode of her life closed. They had denied each other in life. Now he had withdrawn. An anguish came over her. It was finished then: it had become hopeless between them long before he died. Yet he had been her husband. But how little!

"Have you got his shirt, 'Lizabeth?"

Elizabeth turned without answering, though she strove to weep and behave as her mother-in-law expected. But she could not, she was silenced. She went into the kitchen and returned with the garment.

"It is aired," she said, grasping the cotton shirt here and there to try. She was almost ashamed to handle him; what right had she or anyone to lay hands on him; but her touch was humble on his body. It was hard work to clothe him. He was so heavy and inert. A terrible dread gripped her all the while: that he could be so heavy and utterly inert, unresponsive, apart. The horror of the distance between them was almost too much for her—it was so infinite a gap she must look across.

At last it was finished. They covered him with a sheet and left him lying, with his face bound. And she fastened the door of the little parlour, lest the children should see what was lying there. Then, with peace sunk heavy on her heart, she went about making tidy the kitchen. She knew she submitted to life, which was her immediate master. But from death, her ultimate master, she winced with fear and shame.

ENGLAND, MY ENGLAND

HE was working on the edge of the common, beyond the small brook that ran in the dip at the bottom of the garden, carrying the garden path in continuation from the plank bridge on to the common. He had cut the rough turf and bracken, leaving the grey, dryish soil bare. But he was worried because he could not get the path straight, there was a pleat between his brows. He had set up his sticks, and taken the sights between the big pine trees, but for some reason everything seemed wrong. He looked again, straining his keen blue eyes, that had a touch of the Viking in them, through the shadowy pine trees as through a doorway, at the green-grassed garden path rising from the shadow of alders by the log bridge up to the sunlit flowers. Tall white and purple columbines, and the butt-end of the old Hampshire cottage that crouched near the earth amid flowers, blossoming in the bit of shaggy wildness round about.

There was a sound of children's voices calling and talking: high, childish, girlish voices, slightly didactic and tinged with domineering: "If you don't come quick, nurse, I shall run out there to where there are snakes." And nobody had the sang-froid to reply: "Run then, little fool." It was always: "No, darling. Very well, darling. In a moment, darling. Darling, you *must* be patient."

His heart was hard with disillusion: a continual gnawing and resistance. But he worked on. What was there to do but submit!

The sunlight blazed down upon the earth, there was a vivid-ness of flamy vegetation, of fierce seclusion amid the savage peace of the commons. Strange how the savage England lingers in patches: as here, amid these shaggy gorse commons, and marshy, snake-infested places near the foot of the South Downs. The spirit of place lingering on primeval, as when the Saxons came, so long ago.

Ah, how he had loved it! The green garden path, the tufts of flowers, purple and white columbines, and great Oriental red poppies with their black chaps and mulleins tall and yellow: this flamy garden which had been a garden for a thousand years, scooped out in the little hollow among the snake-infested commons. He had made it flame with flowers, in a sun-cup under its hedges and trees. So old, so old a place! And yet he had re-created it.

The timbered cottage with its sloping, cloak-like roof was old and forgotten. It belonged to the old England of hamlets and yeomen. Lost all alone on the edge of the common, at the end of a wide, grassy, briar-entangled lane shaded with oak, it had never known the world of to-day. Not till Egbert came with his bride. And he had come to fill it with flowers.

The house was ancient and very uncomfortable. But he did not want to alter it. Ah, marvellous to sit there in the wide, black, time-old chimney, at night when the wind roared overhead, and the wood which he had chopped himself sputtered on the hearth! Himself on one side the angle, and Winifred on the other.

Ah, how he had wanted her: Winifred! She was young and beautiful and strong with life, like a flame in sunshine. She moved with a slow grace of energy like a blossoming, red-flowered bush in motion. She, too, seemed to come out of the old England, ruddy, strong, with a certain crude, passionate quiescence and a hawthorn robustness. And he, he was tall and slim and agile, like an English archer with his long supple legs and fine movements. Her hair was nut-brown and all in energic curls and tendrils. Her eyes were nut-brown, too, like a robin's for brightness. And he was white-skinned with fine, silky hair that had darkened from fair, and a slightly arched nose of an old country family. They were a beautiful couple.

The house was Winifred's. Her father was a man of energy, too. He had come from the north poor. Now he was moderately rich. He had bought this fair stretch of inexpensive land, down in Hampshire. Not far from the tiny church of the almost extinct hamlet stood his own house, a commodious old farmhouse standing back from the road across a bare grassed yard. On one side of this quadrangle was the long, long barn or shed which he had made into a cottage for his youngest daughter Priscilla. One saw little blue-and-white check curtains at the long windows, and inside, overhead, the grand old timbers of the high-pitched shed. This was Prissy's house. Fifty yards away was the pretty little new cottage which he had built for his daughter Magdalen, with the vegetable garden stretching away to the oak copse. And then away beyond the lawns and rose trees of the house-garden went the track across a shaggy, wild grass space, towards the ridge of tall black pines that grew on a dyke-bank, through the pines and above the sloping little bog, under the wide, desolate oak trees, till there was Winifred's cottage crouching unexpectedly in front, so much alone, and so primitive.

It was Winifred's own house, and the gardens and the bit of common and the boggy slope were hers: her tiny domain. She had married just at the time when her father had bought the estate, about ten years before the war, so she had been able to come to Egbert with this for a marriage portion. And who was more delighted, he or she, it would be hard to say. She was only twenty at the time, and he was only twenty-one. He had about a hundred and fifty pounds a year of his own—and nothing else but his very considerable personal attractions. He had no profession: he earned nothing. But he talked of literature and music, he had a passion for old folk-music, collecting folk-songs and folk-dances, studying the Morris-dance and the old customs. Of course, in time he would make money in these ways.

Meanwhile youth and health and passion and promise. Winifred's father was always generous: but still, he was a man from the north with a hard head and a hard skin too, having received a good many knocks. At home he kept the hard head out of sight, and played at poetry and romance with his literary wife and his sturdy, passionate girls. He was a man of courage, not given to complaining, bearing his burdens by himself. No, he did not let the world intrude far into his home. He had a delicate, sensitive wife whose poetry won some fame in the narrow world of letters. He himself, with his tough old barbarian fighting spirit, had an almost child-like delight in verse, in sweet poetry, and in the delightful game of a cultured home. His blood was strong even to coarseness. But that only made the home more vigorous, more robust and Christmassy. There was always a touch of Christmas about him, now he was well off. If there was poetry after dinner, there were also chocolates, and nuts, and good little out-of-the-way things to be munching.

Well then, into this family came Egbert. He was made of quite a different paste. The girls and the father were strong-limbed, thick-blooded people, true English, as holly trees and hawthorn are English. Their culture was grafted on to them, as one might perhaps graft a common pink rose on to a thorn stem. It flowered oddly enough, but it did not alter their blood.

And Egbert was a born rose. The age-long breeding had left him with a delightful spontaneous passion. He was not clever, nor even "literary". No, but the intonation of his voice, and the movement of his supple, handsome body, and the fine texture of his flesh and his hair, the slight arch of his nose, the quickness of his blue eyes would easily take the place of poetry. Winifred loved him, loved him, this southerner, as a higher being. A *higher* being, mind you. Not a deeper. And as for him, he loved her in passion with every fibre of him. She was the very warm stuff of life to him.

Wonderful then, those days at Crockham Cottage, the first days, all alone save for the woman who came to work in the mornings. Marvellous days, when she had all his tall, supple, fine-fleshed youth to herself, for herself, and he had her like a ruddy fire into which he could cast himself for rejuvenation. Ah, that it might never end, this passion, this marriage! The flame of their two bodies burnt again into that old cottage, that was haunted already by so much bygone, physical desire. You could not be in the dark room for an hour without the influences coming over you. The hot blood-desire of bygone yeomen, there in this old den where they had lusted and bred for so many generations. The silent house, dark, with thick, timbered walls, and the big black chimney-place, and the sense of secrecy. Dark, with low, little windows, sunk into the earth. Dark, like a lair where strong beasts had lurked and mated, lonely at night and lonely by day, left to themselves and their own intensity for so many generations. It seemed to cast a spell on the two young people. They became different. There was a curious secret glow about them, a certain slumbering flame hard to understand, that enveloped them both. They too felt that they did not belong to the London world any more. Crockham had changed their blood: the sense of the snakes that lived and slept even in their own garden, in the sun, so that he, going forward with the spade, would see a curious coiled brownish pile on the black soil, which suddenly would start up, hiss, and dazzle rapidly away, hissing. One day Winifred heard the strangest scream from the flower-bed under the low window of the living-room: ah, the strangest scream, like the very soul of the dark past crying aloud. She ran out, and saw a long brown snake on the flower-bed, and in its flat mouth the one hind leg of a frog was striving to escape, and screaming its strange, tiny, bellowing scream. She looked at the snake, and from its sullen flat head it looked at her, obstinately. She gave a cry, and it released the frog and slid angrily away.

That was Crockham. The spear of modern invention had not passed through it, and it lay there secret, primitive, savage as when the Saxons first came. And Egbert and she were caught there, caught out of the world.

He was not idle, nor was she. There were plenty of things to be done, the house to be put into final repair after the workmen had gone, cushions and curtains to sew, the paths to make, the water to fetch and attend to, and then the slope of the deep-soiled, neglected garden to level, to terrace with little terraces and paths, and to fill with flowers. He worked away, in his shirt-sleves, worked all day intermittently doing this thing and the other. And she, quiet and rich in herself, seeing him stooping and labouring away by himself, would come to help him, to be near him. He of course was an amateur—a born amateur. He worked so hard, and did so little, and nothing he ever did would hold together for long. If he terraced the garden, he held up the earth with a couple of long narrow planks that soon began to bend with the pressure from behind, and would not need many years to rot through and break and let the soil slither all down again in a heap towards the stream-bed. But there you are. He had not been brought up to come to grips with anything, and he thought it would do. Nay, he did not think there was anything else except little temporary contrivances possible, he who had such a passion for his old enduring cottage, and for the old enduring things of the bygone England. Curious that the sense of permanency in the past had such a hold over him, whilst in the present he was all amateurish and sketchy.

Winifred would not criticise him. Town-bred, everything seemed to her splendid, and the very digging and shovelling itself seemed romantic. But neither Egbert nor she yet realised the difference between work and romance.

Godfrey Marshall, her father, was at first perfectly pleased with the *ménage* down at Crockham Cottage. He thought Egbert was wonderful, the many things he accomplished, and he was gratified by the glow of physical passion between the two young people. To the man who in London still worked hard to keep steady his modest fortune, the thought of this young couple digging away and loving one another down at Crockham Cottage, buried deep among the commons and marshes, near the pale-showing bulk of the downs, was like a chapter of living romance. And they drew the sustenance for their fire of passion from him, from the old man. It was he who fed their flame. He triumphed secretly in the thought. And it was to her father that Winifred still turned, as the one source of all surety and life and support. She loved Egbert with passion. But behind her was the power of her father. It was the power of her father she referred to, whenever she needed to refer. It never occurred to her to refer to Egbert, if she were in difficulty or doubt. No, in all ·the *serious* matters she depended on her father.

For Egbert had no intention of coming to grips with life. He had no ambition whatsoever. He came from a decent family, from a pleasant country home, from delightful surroundings. He should, of course, have had a profession. He should have studied law or entered business in some way. But no—that fatal three pounds a week would keep him from starving as long as he lived, and he did not want to give himself into bondage. It was not that he was idle. He was always doing something, in his amateurish way. But he had no desire to give himself to the world, and still less had he any desire to fight his way in the world. No, no, the world wasn't worth it. He wanted to ignore it, to go his own way apart, like a casual pilgrim down the forsaken side-tracks. He loved his wife, his cottage and garden. He would make his life there, as a sort of epicurean hermit. He loved the past, the old music and dances and customs of old England. He would try and live in the spirit of these, not in the spirit of the world of business.

But often Winifred's father called her to London: for he loved to have his children round him. So Egbert and she must have a tiny flat in town, and the young couple must transfer themselves from time to time from the country to the city. In town Egbert had plenty of friends, of the same ineffectual sort as himself, tampering with the arts, literature, painting, sculpture, music. He was not bored.

Three pounds a week, however, would not pay for all this. Winifred's father paid. He liked paying. He made her only a very small allowance, but he often gave her ten pounds—or gave Egbert ten pounds. So they both looked on the old man as the mainstay. Egbert didn't mind being patronised and paid for. Only when he felt the family was a little *too* condescending, on account of money, he began to get huffy.

Then of course children came: a lovely little blonde daughter with a head of thistle-down. Everybody adored the child. It was the first exquisite blonde thing that had come into the family, a little mite with the white, slim, beautiful limbs of its father, and as it grew up the dancing, dainty movement of a wild little daisy-spirit. No wonder the Marshalls all loved the child: they called her Joyce. They themselves had their own grace, but it was slow, rather heavy. They had every one of them strong, heavy limbs and darkish skins, and they were short in stature. And now they had for one of their own this light little cowslip child. She was like a little poem in herself.

But nevertheless, she brought a new difficulty. Winifred must have a nurse for her. Yes, yes, there must be a nurse. It was the family decree. Who was to pay for the nurse? The grandfather—seeing the father himself earned no money. Yes, the grandfather would pay, as he had paid all the lying-in expenses. There came a slight sense of money-strain. Egbert was living on his father-in-law.

After the child was born, it was never quite the same between him and Winifred. The difference was at first hardly perceptible. But it was there. In the first place Winifred had a new centre of interest. She was not going to adore her child. But she had what the modern mother so often has in the place of spontaneous love: a profound sense of duty towards her child. Winifred appreciated her darling little girl, and felt a deep sense of duty towards her. Strange, that this sense of duty should go deeper than the love for her husband. But so it was. And so it often is. The responsibility of motherhood was the prime responsibility in Winifred's heart: the responsibility of wifehood came a long way second.

Her child seemed to link her up again in a circuit with her own family. Her father and mother, herself, and her child, that was the human trinity for her. Her husband——? Yes, she loved him still. But that was like play. She had an almost barbaric sense of duty and of family. Till she married, her first human duty had been towards her father: he was the pillar, the source of life, the everlasting support. Now another link was added to the chain of duty: her father, herself, and her child.

Egbert was out of it. Without anything happening, he was

gradually, unconsciously excluded from the circle. His wife still loved him, physically. But, but—he was *almost* the unnecessary party in the affair. He could not complain of Winifred. She still did her duty towards him. She still had physical passion for him, that physical passion on which he had put all his life and soul. But—but——

It was for a long while an ever-recurring *but*. And then, after the second child, another blonde, winsome touching little thing, not so proud and flame-like as Joyce—after Annabel came, then Egbert began truly to realise how it was. His wife still loved him. But—and now the but had grown enormous—her physical love for him was of secondary importance to her. It became ever less important. After all, she had had it, this physical passion, for two years now. It was not this that one lived from. No, no—something sterner, realer.

She began to resent her own passion for Egbert—just a little she began to despise it. For after all there he was, he was charming, he was lovable, he was terribly desirable. But—but —oh, the awful looming cloud of that *but*!—he did not stand firm in the landscape of her life like a tower of strength, like a great pillar of significance. No, he was like a cat one has about the house, which will one day disappear and leave no trace. He was like a flower in the garden, trembling in the wind of life, and then gone, leaving nothing to show. As an adjunct, as an accessory, he was perfect. Many a woman would have adored to have him about her all her life, the most beautiful and desirable of all her possessions. But Winifred belonged to another school.

The years went by, and instead of coming more to grips with life, he relaxed more. He was of a subtle, sensitive, passionate nature. But he simply *would* not give himself to what Winifred called life, *Work*. No, he would not go into the world and work for money. No, he just would not. If Winifred liked to live beyond their small income—well, it was her look-out.

And Winifred did not really want him to go out into the world to work for money. Money became, alas, a word like a firebrand between them, setting them both aflame with anger. But that is because we must talk in symbols. Winifred did not really care about money. She did not care whether he earned or did not earn anything. Only she knew she was dependent on her father for three-fourths of the money spent for herself and her children, that she let that be the *casus belli*, the drawn weapon between herself and Egbert.

What did she want—what did she want? Her mother once said to her, with that characteristic touch of irony: "Well, dear, if it is your fate to consider the lilies, that toil not, neither do they spin, that is one destiny among many others, and perhaps not so unpleasant as most. Why do you take it amiss, my child?"

The mother was subtler than her children, they very rarely knew how to answer her. So Winifred was only more confused. It was not a question of lilies. At least, if it were a question of lilies, then her children were the little blossoms. They at least *grew*. Doesn't Jesus say: "Consider the lilies *how they grow*." Good then, she had her growing babies. But as for that other tall, handsome flower of a father of theirs, he was full grown already, so she did not want to spend her life considering him in the flower of his days.

No, it was not that he didn't earn money. It was not that he was idle. He was *not* idle. He was always doing something, always working away, down at Crockham, doing little jobs. But, oh dear, the little jobs—the garden paths—the gorgeous flowers—the chairs to mend, old chairs to mend!

It was that he stood for nothing. If he had done something unsuccesfully, and *lost* what money they had! If he had but striven with something. Nay, even if he had been wicked, a waster, she would have been more free. She would have had something to resist, at least. A waster stands for something, really. He says: "No, I will not aid and abet society in this business of increase and hanging together, I will upset the apple-cart as much as I can, in my small way." Or else he says: "No, I will *not* bother about others. I have lusts, they are my own, and I prefer them to other people's virtues." So, a waster, a scamp, takes a sort of stand. He exposes himself to opposition and final castigation: at any rate in story-books.

But Egbert! What are you to do with a man like Egbert? He had no vices. He was really kind, nay, generous. And he was not weak. If he had been weak Winifred could have been kind to him. But he did not even give her that consolation. He was not weak, and he did not want her consolation or her kindness. No, thank you. He was of a fine passionate temper, and of a rarer steel than she. He knew it, and she knew it. Hence she was only the more baffled and maddened, poor thing. He, the higher, the finer, in his way the stronger, played with his garden, and his old folk-songs and Morris dances, just played, and let her support the pillars of the future on her own heart.

And he began to get bitter, and a wicked look began to come on his face. He did not give in to her; not he. There were seven devils inside his long, slim, white body. He was healthy, full of restrained life. Yes, even he himself had to lock up his own vivid life inside himself, now she would not take it from him. Or rather, now that she only took it occasionally. For she had to yield at times. She loved him so, she desired him so, he was so exquisite to her, the fine creature that he was, finer than herself. Yes, with a groan she had to give in to her own un-quenched passion for him. And he came to her then—ah, terrible, ah, wonderful, sometimes she wondered how either of them could live after the terror of the passion that swept between them. It was to her as if pure lightning, flash after flash, went through every fibre of her, till extinction came.

But it is the fate of human beings to live on. And it is the fate of clouds that seem nothing but bits of vapour slowly to pile up, to pile up and fill the heavens and blacken the sun entirely.

So it was. The love came back, the lightning of passion flashed tremendously between them. And there was blue sky and gorgeousness for a little while. And then, as inevitably, as inevitably, slowly the clouds began to edge up again above the horizon, slowly, slowly to lurk about the heavens, throwing an occasional cold and hateful shadow: slowly, slowly to congre-gate, to fill the empyrean space.

And as the years passed, the lightning cleared the sky more and more rarely, less and less the blue showed. Gradually the grey lid sank down upon them, as if it would be permanent.

Why didn't Egbert do something, then? Why didn't he come to grips with life? Why wasn't he like Winifred's father, a pillar of society, even if a slender, exquisite column? Why didn't he go into harness of some sort? Why didn't he take *some* direction?

Well, you can bring an ass to the water, but you cannot make him drink. The world was the water and Egbert was the ass. And he wasn't having any. He couldn't: he just couldn't. Since necessity did not force him to work for his bread and butter, he would not work for work's sake. You can't make the columbine flowers nod in January, nor make the cuckoo sing in England at Christmas. Why? It isn't his season. He doesn't want to. Nay, he *can't* want to.

And there it was with Egbert. He couldn't link up with the world's work, because the basic desire was absent from him. Nay, at the bottom of him he had an even stronger desire: to hold aloof. To hold aloof. To do nobody any damage. But to hold aloof. It was not his season.

Perhaps he should not have married and had children. But you can't stop the waters flowing.

Which held true for Winifred, too. She was not made to endure aloof. Her family tree was a robust vegetation that had to be stirring and believing. In one direction or another her life *had* to go. In her own home she had known nothing of this diffidence which she found in Egbert, and which she could not understand, and which threw her into such dismay. What was she to do, what was she to do, in face of this terrible diffidence?

It was all so different in her own home. Her father may have had his own misgivings, but he kept them to himself. Perhaps he had no very profound belief in this world of ours, this society which we have elaborated with so much effort, only to find ourselves elaborated to death at last. But Godfrey Marshall was of tough, rough fibre, not without a vein of healthy cunning through it all. It was for him a question of winning through, and leaving the rest to heaven. Without having many illusions to grace him, he still *did* believe in heaven. In a dark and unquestioning way, he had a sort of faith: an acrid faith like the sap of some not-to-be-exterminated tree. Just a blind acrid faith as sap is blind and acrid, and yet pushes on in growth and in faith. Perhaps he was unscrupulous, but only as a striving tree is unscrupulous, pushing its single way in a jungle of others.

In the end, it is only this robust, sap-like faith which keeps man going. He may live on for many generations inside the shelter of the social establishment which he has erected for himself, as pear trees and currant bushes would go on bearing fruit for many seasons, inside a walled garden, even if the race of man were suddenly exterminated. But bit by bit the wall fruit trees would gradually pull down the very walls that sustained them. Bit by bit every establishment collapses, unless it is renewed or restored by living hands, all the while.

Egbert could not bring himself to any more of this restoring or renewing business. He was not aware of the fact: but awareness doesn't help much, anyhow. He just couldn't. He had the stoic and epicurean quality of his old, fine breeding. His father-in-law, however, though he was not one bit more of a fool than Egbert, realised that since we are here we may as well live. And so he applied himself to his own tiny section of the social work, and to doing the best for his family, and to leaving the rest to the ultimate will of heaven. A certain robustness of blood made him able to go on. But sometimes even from him spurted a sudden gall of bitterness against the world and its make-up. And yet—he had his own will-to-succeed, and this carried him through. He refused to ask himself what the success would amount to. It amounted to the estate down in Hampshire, and his children lacking for nothing, and himself of some importance in the world: *and basta!*—Basta! Basta!

Nevertheless, do not let us imagine that he was a common pusher. He was not. He knew as well as Egbert what disillusion meant. Perhaps in his soul he had the same estimation of success. But he had a certain acrid courage, and a certain will-to-power. In his own small circle he would emanate power, the single power of his own blind self. With all his spoiling of his children, he was still the father of the old English type. He was too wise to make laws and to domineer in the abstract. But he had kept, and all honour to him, a certain primitive dominion over the souls of his children, the old, almost magic prestige of paternity. There it was, still burning in him, the old smoky torch of paternal godhead.

And in the sacred glare of this torch his children had been brought up. He had given the girls every liberty, at last. But he had never really let them go beyond his power. And they, venturing out into the hard white light of our fatherless world, learned to see with the eyes of the world. They learned to criticise their father, even, from some effulgence of worldly white light, to see him as inferior. But this was all very well in the head. The moment they forgot their tricks of criticism, the old red glow of his authority came over them again. He was not to be quenched.

Let the psycho-analyst talk about father complex. It is just a word invented. Here was a man who had kept alive the old red flame of fatherhood, fatherhood that had even the right to sacrifice the child to God, like Isaac. Fatherhood that had life-and-death authority over the children: a great natural power. And till his children could be brought under some other great authority as girls; or could arrive at manhood and become themselves centres of the same power, continuing the same male mystery as men; until such time, willy-nilly, Godfrey Marshall would keep his children.

It had seemed as if he might lose Winifred. Winifred had *adored* her husband, and looked up to him as to something wonderful. Perhaps she had expected in him another great authority, a male authority greater, finer than her father's. For having once known the glow of male power, she would not easily turn to the cold white light of feminine independence. She would hunger, hunger all her life for the warmth and shelter of true male strength.

And hunger she might, for Egbert's power lay in the abnegation of power. He was himself the living negative of power. Even of responsibility. For the negation of power at last means the negation of responsibility. As far as these things went, he would confine himself to himself. He would try to confine his own *influence* even to himself. He would try, as far as possible, to abstain from influencing his children by assuming any responsibility for them. "A little child shall lead them——" His child should lead, then. He would try not to make it go in any direction whatever. He would abstain from influencing it. Liberty!——

Poor Winifred was like a fish out of water in this liberty, gasping for the denser element which should contain her. Till her child came. And then she knew that she must be responsible for it, that she must have authority over it.

But here Egbert, silently and negatively, stepped in. Silently, negatively, but fatally he neutralised her authority over her children.

There was a third little girl born. And after this Winifred wanted no more children. Her soul was turning to salt.

So she had charge of the children, they were her responsibility. The money for them had come from her father. She would do her very best for them, and have command over their life and death. But no! Egbert would not take the responsibility. He would not even provide the money. But he would not let her have her way. Her dark, silent, passionate authority he would not allow. It was a battle between them, the battle between liberty and the old blood-power. And of course he won. The little girls loved him and adored him. "Daddy! Daddy!" They could do as they liked with him. Their mother would have ruled them. She would have ruled them passionately, with indulgence, with the old dark magic of parental authority, something looming and unquestioned and, after all, divine: if we believe in divine authority. The Marshalls did, being Catholic.

And Egbert, he turned her old dark, Catholic blood-authority into a sort of tyranny. He would not leave her her children. He stole them from her, and yet without assuming responsibility for them. He stole them from her, in emotion and spirit, and left her only to command their behaviour. A thankless lot for a mother. And her children adored him, adored him, little knowing the empty bitterness they were preparing for themselves when they too grew up to have husbands: husbands such as Egbert, adorable and null.

Joyce, the eldest, was still his favourite. She was now a quicksilver little thing of six years old. Barbara, the youngest, was a toddler of two years. They spent most of their time down at Crockham, because he wanted to be there. And even Winifred loved the place really. But now, in her frustrated and blinded state, it was full of menace for her children. The adders, the poison-berries, the brook, the marsh, the water that might not be pure—one thing and another. From mother and nurse it was a guerilla gunfire of commands, and blithe, quick-silver disobedience from the three blonde, never-still little girls. Behind the girls was the father, against mother and nurse. And so it was.

"If you don't come quick, nurse, I shall run out there to where there are snakes."

"Joyce, you *must* be patient. I'm just changing Annabel!"

There you are. There it was: always the same. Working away on the common across the brook he heard it. And he worked on, just the same.

Suddenly he heard a shriek, and he flung the spade from him and started for the bridge, looking up like a startled deer. Ah, there was Winifred—Joyce had hurt himself. He went on up the garden.

"What is it?"

The child was still screaming—now it was—"Daddy! Daddy! Oh—oh, Daddy!" And the mother was saying:

"Don't be frightened, darling. Let mother look."

But the child only cried:

"Oh, Daddy, Daddy, Daddy!"

She was terrified by the sight of the blood running from her own knee. Winifred crouched down, with her child of six in her lap, to examine the knee. Egbert bent over also.

"Don't make such a noise, Joyce," he said irritably. "How did she do it?"

"She fell on that sickle thing which you left lying about after cutting the grass," said Winifred, looking into his face with bitter accusation as he bent near.

He had taken his handkerchief and tied it round the knee. Then he lifted the still sobbing child in his arms, and carried her into the house and upstairs to her bed. In his arms she became quiet. But his heart was burning with pain and with guilt. He had left the sickle there lying on the edge of the grass, and so his first-born child whom he loved so dearly had come to hurt. But then it was an accident—it was an accident. Why should he feel guilty? It would probably be nothing, better in two or three days. Why take it to heart, why worry? He put it aside.

The child lay on the bed in her little summer frock, her face very white now after the shock. Nurse had come carrying the youngest child: and little Annabel stood holding her skirt. Winifred, terribly serious and wooden-seeming, was bending over the knee, from which she had taken his blood-soaked handkerchief. Egbert bent forward, too, keeping more sang-froid in his face than in his heart. Winifred went all of a lump of seriousness, so he had to keep some reserve. The child moaned and whimpered.

The knee was still bleeding profusely—it was a deep cut right in the joint.

"You'd better go for the doctor, Egbert," said Winifred bitterly.

"Oh no! Oh no!" cried Joyce in a panic.

"Joyce, my darling, don't cry!" said Winifred, suddenly catching the little girl to her breast in a strange tragic anguish, the *Mater Dolorata*. Even the child was frightened into silence. Egbert looked at the tragic figure of his wife with the child at her breast, and turned away. Only Annabel started suddenly to cry: "Joycey, Joycey, don't have your leg bleeding!"

Egbert rode four miles to the village for the doctor. He

could not help feeling that Winifred was laying it on rather. Surely the knee itself wasn't hurt! Surely not. It was only a surface cut.

The doctor was out. Egbert left the message and came cycling swiftly home, his heart pinched with anxiety. He dropped sweating off his bicycle and went into the house, looking rather small, like a man who is at fault. Winifred was upstairs sitting by Joyce, who was looking pale and important in bed, and was eating some tapioca pudding. The pale, small, scared face of his child went to Egbert's heart.

"Doctor Wing was out. He'll be here about half-past two," said Egbert.

"I don't want him to come," whimpered Joyce.

"Joyce, dear, you must be patient and quiet," said Winifred. "He won't hurt you. But he will tell us what to do to make your knee better quickly. That is why he must come."

Winifred always explained carefully to her little girls: and it always took the words off their lips for the moment.

"Does it bleed yet?" said Egbert.

Winifred moved the bedclothes carefully aside.

"I think not," she said.

Egbert stooped also to look.

"No, it doesn't," he said. Then he stood up with a relieved look on his face. He turned to the child.

"Eat your pudding, Joyce," he said. "It won't be anything. You've only got to keep still for a few days."

"You haven't had your dinner, have you, Daddy?"

"Not yet."

"Nurse will give it to you," said Winifred.

"You'll be all right, Joyce," he said, smiling to the child and pushing the blonde hair aside off her brow. She smiled back winsomely into his face.

He went downstairs and ate his meal alone. Nurse served him. She liked waiting on him. All women liked him and liked to do things for him.

The doctor came—a fat country practitioner, pleasant and kind.

"What, little girl, been tumbling down, have you? There's a thing to be doing, for a smart little lady like you! What! And cutting your knee! Tut-tut-tut! That *wasn't* clever of you, now was it? Never mind, never mind, soon be better. Let us look at it. Won't hurt you. Not the least in life. Bring a bowl with a little warm water, nurse. Soon have it all right again, soon have it all right."

Joyce smiled at him with a pale smile of faint superiority. This was *not* the way in which she was used to being talked to.

He bent down, carefully looking at the little, thin, wounded knee of the child. Egbert bent over him.

"Oh, dear, oh, dear! Quite a deep little cut. Nasty little cut. Nasty little cut. But, never mind. Never mind, little lady. What's your name?"

"My name is Joyce," said the child distinctly.

"Oh, really!" he replied. "Oh, really! Well, that's a fine name too, in my opinion. Joyce, eh?—And how old might Miss Joyce be? Can she tell me that?"

"I'm six," said the child, slightly amused and very condescending.

"Six! There now. Add up and count as far as six, can you? Well, that's a clever little girl, a clever little girl. And if she has to drink a spoonful of medicine, she won't make a murmur, I'll be bound. Not like *some* little girls. What? Eh?"

"I take it if mother wishes me to," said Joyce.

"Ah, there now! That's the style! That's what I like to hear from a little lady in bed because she's cut her knee. That's the style——"

The comfortable and prolix doctor dressed and bandaged the knee and recommended bed and a light diet for the little lady. He thought a week or a fortnight would put it right. No bones or ligatures damaged—fortunately. Only a flesh cut. He would come again in a day or two.

So Joyce was reassured and stayed in bed and had all her toys up. Her father often played with her. The doctor came the third day. He was fairly pleased with the knee. It was healing. It was healing—yes—yes. Let the child continue in bed. He came again after a day or two. Winifred was a trifle uneasy. The wound seemed to be healing on the top, but it hurt the child too much. It didn't look quite right. She said so to Egbert.

"Egbert, I'm sure Joyce's knee isn't healing properly."

"I think it is," he said. "I think it's all right."

"I'd rather Doctor Wing came again—I don't feel satisfied."

"Aren't you trying to imagine it worse than it really is?"

"You would say so, of course. But I shall write a post-card to Doctor Wing now."

The doctor came next day. He examined the knee. Yes, there was inflammation. Yes, there *might* be a little septic poisoning—there might. There might. Was the child feverish?

So a fortnight passed by, and the child *was* feverish, and the knee was more inflamed and grew worse and was painful, painful. She cried in the night, and her mother had to sit up with her. Egbert still insisted it was nothing, really—it would pass. But in his heart he was anxious.

Winifred wrote again to her father. On Saturday the elderly man appeared. And no sooner did Winifred see the thick, rather short figure in its grey suit than a great yearning came over her.

"Father, I'm not satisfied with Joyce. I'm not satisfied with Doctor Wing."

"Well, Winnie, dear, if you're not satisfied we must have further advice, that is all."

The sturdy, powerful, elderly man went upstairs, his voice sounding rather grating through the house, as if it cut upon the tense atmosphere.

"How are you, Joyce, darling?" he said to the child. "Does your knee hurt you? Does it hurt you, dear?"

"It does sometimes." The child was shy of him, cold towards him.

"Well, dear, I'm sorry for that. I hope you try to bear it, and not trouble mother too much."

There was no answer. He looked at the knee. It was red and stiff.

"Of course," he said, "I think we must have another doctor's opinion. And if we're going to have it, we had better have it at once. Egbert, do you think you might cycle in to Bingham for Doctor Wayne? I found him *very* satisfactory for Winnie's mother."

"I can go if you think it necessary," said Egbert.

"Certainly I think it necessary. Even if there *is* nothing, we can have peace of mind. Certainly I think it necessary. I should like Doctor Wayne to come this evening if possible."

So Egbert set off on his bicycle through the wind, like a boy sent on an errand, leaving his father-in-law a pillar of assurance, with Winifred.

Doctor Wayne came, and looked grave. Yes, the knee was certainly taking the wrong way. The child might be lame for life.

Up went the fire of fear and anger in every heart. Doctor Wayne came again the next day for a proper examination. And, yes, the knee had really taken bad ways. It should be X-rayed. It was very important.

Godfrey Marshall walked up and down the lane with the doctor, beside the standing motor-car: up and down, up and down in one of those consultations of which he had had so many in his life.

As a result he came indoors to Winifred.

"Well, Winnie, dear, the best thing to do is to take Joyce up to London, to a nursing home where she can have proper treatment. Of course this knee has been allowed to go wrong. And apparently there is a risk that the child may even lose her leg. What do you think, dear? You agree to our taking her up to town and putting her under the best care?"

"Oh, father, you *know* I would do anything on earth for her."

"I know you would, Winnie darling. The pity is that there has been this unfortunate delay already. I can't think what Doctor Wing was doing. Apparently the child is in danger of losing her leg. Well then, if you will have everything ready, we will take her up to town to-morrow. I will order the large car from Denley's to be here at ten. Egbert, will you take a telegram at once to Doctor Jackson? It is a small nursing home for children and for surgical cases, not far from Baker Street. I'm sure Joyce will be all right there."

"Oh, father, can't I nurse her myself?"

"Well, darling, if she is to have proper treatment, she had best be in a home. The X-ray treatment, and the electric treatment, and whatever is necessary."

"It will cost a great deal——" said Winifred.

"We can't think of cost, if the child's leg is in danger—or even her life. No use speaking of cost," said the elder man impatiently.

And so it was. Poor Joyce, stretched out on a bed in the big closed motor-car—the mother sitting by her head, the grandfather in his short grey beard and a bowler hat, sitting by her feet, thick, and implacable in his responsibility—they rolled slowly away from Crockham, and from Egbert, who stood there bareheaded and a little ignominious, left behind. He was to shut up the house and bring the rest of the family back to town, by train, the next day.

Followed a dark and bitter time. The poor child. The poor, poor child, how she suffered, an agony and a long crucifixion in that nursing home. It was a bitter six weeks which changed the soul of Winifred for ever. As she sat by the bed of her poor, tortured little child, tortured with the agony of the knee, and the still worse agony of these diabolic, but perhaps necessary modern treatments, she felt her heart killed and going cold in her breast. Her little Joyce, her frail, brave, wonderful, little Joyce, frail and small and pale as a white flower! Ah, how had she, Winifred, dared to be so wicked, so wicked, so careless, so sensual.

"Let my heart die! Let my woman's heart of flesh die! Saviour, let my heart die. And save my child. Let my heart die from the world and from the flesh. Oh, destroy my heart that is so wayward. Let my heart of pride die. Let my heart die."

She prayed beside the bed of her child. And like the Mother with the seven swords in her breast, slowly her heart of pride and passion died in her breast, bleeding away. Slowly it died, bleeding away, and she turned to the Church for comfort, to Jesus, to the Mother of God, but most of all, to that great and enduring institution, the Roman Catholic Church. She withdrew into the shadow of the Church. She was a mother with three children. But in her soul she died, her heart of pride and passion and desire bled to death, her soul belonged to her Church, her body belonged to her duty as a mother.

Her duty as a wife did not enter. As a wife she had no sense of duty: only a certain bitterness towards the man with whom she had known such sensuality and distraction. She was purely the *Mater Dolorata*. To the man she was closed as a tomb.

Egbert came to see his child. But Winifred seemed to be always seated there, like the tomb of his manhood and his fatherhood. Poor Winifred: she was still young, still strong and ruddy and beautiful like a ruddy hard flower of the field. Strange—her ruddy, healthy face, so sombre, and her strong, heavy, full-blooded body, so still. She, a nun! Never. And yet the gates of her heart and soul had shut in his face with a slow, resonant clang, shutting him out for ever. There was no need for her to go into a convent. Her will had done it.

And between this young mother and this young father lay the crippled child, like a bit of pale silk floss on the pillow, and a little white pain-quenched face. He could not bear it. He just could not bear it. He turned aside. There was nothing to do but to turn aside. He turned aside, and went hither and thither, desultory. He was still attractive and desirable. But there was a little frown between his brow as if he had been cleft there with a hatchet: cleft right in, for ever, and that was the stigma.

The child's leg was saved: but the knee was locked stiff. The fear now was lest the lower leg should wither, or cease to grow. There must be long-continued massage and treatment, daily treatment, even when the child left the nursing home. And the whole of the expense was borne by the grandfather.

Egbert now had no real home. Winifred with the children and nurse was tied to the little flat in London. He could not live there: he could not contain himself. The cottage was shut up—or lent to friends. He went down sometimes to work in his garden and keep the place in order. Then with the empty house around him at night, all the empty rooms, he felt his heart go wicked. The sense of frustration and futility, like some slow, torpid snake, slowly bit right through his heart. Futility, futility, futility: the horrible marsh-poison went through his veins and killed him.

As he worked in the garden in the silence of day he would listen for a sound. No sound. No sound of Winifred from the dark inside of the cottage: no sound of children's voices from the air, from the common, from the near distance. No sound, nothing but the old dark marsh-venomous atmosphere of the place. So he worked spasmodically through the day, and at night made a fire and cooked some food alone.

He was alone. He himself cleaned the cottage and made his bed. But his mending he did not do. His shirts were slit on the shoulders, when he had been working, and the white flesh showed through. He would feel the air and the spots of rain on his exposed flesh. And he would look again across the common, where the dark, tufted gorse was dying to seed, and the bits of cat-heather were coming pink in tufts, like a sprinkling of sacrificial blood.

His heart went back to the savage old spirit of the place: the desire for old gods, old, lost passions, the passion of the cold-blooded, darting snakes that hissed and shot away from him, the mystery of blood-sacrifices, all the lost, intense sensations of the primeval people of the place, whose passions

c

seethed in the air still, from those long days before the Romans came. The seethe of a lost, dark passion in the air. The presence of unseen snakes.

A queer, baffled, half-wicked look came on his face. He could not stay long at the cottage. Suddenly he must swing on to his bicycle and go—anywhere. Anywhere, away from the place. He would stay a few days with his mother in the old home. His mother adored him and grieved as a mother would. But the little, baffled, half-wicked smile curled on his face, and he swung away from his mother's solicitude as from everything else.

Always moving on—from place to place, friend to friend: and always swinging away from sympathy. As soon as sympathy, like a soft hand, was reached out to touch him, away he swerved, instinctively, as a harmless snake swerves and swerves and swerves away from an outstretched hand. Away he must go. And periodically he went back to Winifred.

He was terrible to her now, like a temptation. She had devoted herself to her children and her Church. Joyce was once more on her feet; but, alas! lame, with iron supports to her leg, and a little crutch. It was strange how she had grown into a long, pallid, wild little thing. Strange that the pain had not made her soft and docile, but had brought out a wild, almost mænad temper in the child. She was seven, and long and white and thin, but by no means subdued. Her blonde hair was darkening. She still had long sufferings to face, and, in her own childish consciousness, the stigma of her lameness to bear.

And she bore it. An almost mænad courage seemed to possess her, as if she were a long, thin, young weapon of life. She acknowledged all her mother's care. She would stand by her mother for ever. But some of her father's fine-tempered desperation flashed in her.

When Egbert saw his little girl limping horribly—not only limping but lurching horribly in crippled, childish way, his heart again hardened with chagrin, like steel that is tempered again. There was a tacit understanding between him and his little girl: not what we would call love, but a weapon-like kinship. There was a tiny touch of irony in his manner towards her, contrasting sharply with Winifred's heavy, unleavened solicitude and care. The child flickered back to him with an answering little smile of irony and recklessness: an odd flippancy which made Winifred only the more sombre and earnest.

The Marshalls took endless thought and trouble for the child, searching out every means to save her limb and her active freedom. They spared no effort and no money, they spared no strength of will. With all their slow, heavy power of will they willed that Joyce should have her liberty of move-ment, should win back her wild, free grace. Even if it took a long time to recover, it should be recovered.

So the situation stood. And Joyce submitted, week after week, month after month, to the tyranny and pain of the treat-ment. She acknowledged the honourable effort on her behalf. But her flamy reckless spirit was her father's. It was he who had all the glamour for her. He and she were like members of some forbidden secret society who know one another but may not recognise one another. Knowledge they had in common, the same secret of life, the father and the child. But the child stayed in the camp of her mother, honourably, and the father wandered outside like Ishmael, only coming sometimes to sit in the home for an hour or two, an evening or two beside the camp-fire, like Ishmael, in a curious silence and tension, with the mocking answer of the desert speaking out of his silence, and annulling the whole convention of the domestic home.

His presence was almost an anguish to Winifred. She prayed against it. That little cleft between his brow, that flickering, wicked little smile that seemed to haunt his face, and above all, the triumphant loneliness, the Ishmael quality. And then the erectness of his supple body, like a symbol. The very way he stood, so quiet, so insidious, like an erect, supple symbol of life, the living body, confronting her downcast soul, was torture to her. He was like a supple living idol moving before her eyes, and she felt if she watched him she was damned.

And he came and made himself at home in her little home. When he was there, moving in his own quiet way, she felt as if the whole great law of sacrifice, by which she had elected to live, were annulled. He annulled by his very presence the laws of her life. And what did he substitute? Ah, against that question she hardened herself in recoil.

It was awful to her to have to have him about—moving about in his shirt-sleeves, speaking in his tenor, throaty voice to the children. Annabel simply adored him, and he teased the little girl. The baby, Barbara, was not sure of him. She had been born a stranger to him. But even the nurse, when she saw his white shoulder of flesh through the slits of his torn shirt, thought it a shame.

Winifred felt it was only another weapon of his against her.

"You have other shirts—why do you wear that old one that is all torn, Egbert?" she said.

"I may as well wear it out," he said subtly.

He knew she would not offer to mend it for him. She *could* not. And no, she would not. Had she not her own gods to honour? And could she betray them, submitting to his Baal and Ashtaroth? And it was terrible to her, his unsheathed presence, that seemed to annul her and her faith, like another revelation. Like a gleaming idol evoked against her, a vivid life-idol that might triumph.

He came and he went—and she persisted. And then the Great War broke out. He was a man who could not go to the dogs. He could not dissipate himself. He was pure-bred in his Englishness, and even when he would have liked to be vicious, he could not.

So when the war broke out his whole instinct was against it: against war. He had not the faintest desire to overcome any foreigners or to help in their death. He had no conception of Imperial England, and Rule Britannia was just a joke to him. He was a pure-blooded Englishman, perfect in his race, and when he was truly himself he could no more have been aggressive on the score of his Englishness than a rose can be aggressive on the score of its rosiness.

No, he had no desire to defy Germany and to exalt England. The distinction between German and English was not for him the distinction between good and bad. It was the distinction between blue water-flowers and red or white bush-blossoms: just difference. The difference between the wild boar and the wild bear. And a man was good or bad according to his nature, not according to his nationality.

Egbert was well-bred, and this was part of his natural understanding. It was merely unnatural to him to hate a nation *en bloc*. Certain individuals he disliked, and others he liked, and the mass he knew nothing about. Certain deeds he disliked, certain deeds seemed natural to him, and about most deeds he had no particular feeling.

He had, however, the one deepest pure-bred instinct. He re-coiled inevitably from having his feelings dictated to him by the mass feeling. His feelings were his own, his understanding was his own, and he would never go back on either, willingly. Shall a man become inferior to his own true knowledge and self, just because the mob expects it of him?

What Egbert felt subtly and without question, his father-in-law felt also in a rough, more combative way. Different as the two men were, they were two real Englishmen, and their instincts were almost the same.

And Godfrey Marshall had the world to reckon with. There was German military aggression, and the English non-military idea of liberty and the 'conquests of peace'—meaning indus-trialism. Even if the choice between militarism and indus-trialism were a choice of evils, the elderly man asserted his choice of the latter, perforce. He whose soul was quick with the instinct of power.

Egbert just refused to reckon with the world. He just re-fused even to decide between German militarism and British industrialism. He chose neither. As for atrocities, he despised the people who committed them, as inferior criminal types. There was nothing national about crime.

And yet, war! War! Just war! Not right or wrong, but just war itself. Should he join? Should he give himself over to war? The question was in his mind for some weeks. Not because he thought England was right and Germany wrong. Probably Germany was wrong, but he refused to make a choice. Not because he felt inspired. No. But just—war.

The deterrent was the giving himself over into the power of other men, and into the power of the mob-spirit of a demo-cratic army. Should he give himself over? Should he make over his own life and body to the control of something which he *knew* was inferior, in spirit, to his own self? Should he commit himself into the power of an inferior control? Should he? Should he betray himself?

He was going to put himself into the power of his inferiors, and he knew it. He was going to subjugate himself. He was going to be ordered about by petty *canaille* of non-com-missioned officers—and even commissioned officers. He who was born and bred free. Should he do it?

He went to his wife, to speak to her.

"Shall I join up, Winifred?"

She was silent. Her instinct also was dead against it. And yet a certain profound resentment made her answer:

"You have three children dependent on you. I don't know whether you have thought of that."

It was still only the third month of the war, and the old pre-war ideas were still alive.

"Of course. But it won't make much difference to them. I shall be earning a shilling a day, at least."

"You'd better speak to father, I think," she replied heavily.

Egbert went to his father-in-law. The elderly man's heart was full of resentment.

"I should say," he said rather sourly, "it is the best thing you could do."

Egbert went and joined up immediately, as a private soldier. He was drafted into the light artillery.

Winifred now had a new duty towards him: the duty of a wife towards a husband who is himself performing his duty towards the world. She loved him still. She would always love him, as far as earthly love went. But it was duty she now lived by. When he came back to her in khaki, a soldier, she submitted to him as a wife. It was her duty. But to his passion she could never again fully submit. Something prevented her, for ever: even her own deepest choice.

He went back again to camp. It did not suit him to be a modern soldier. In the thick, gritty, hideous khaki his subtle physique was extinguished as if he had been killed. In the ugly intimacy of the camp his thoroughbred sensibilities were just degraded. But he had chosen, so he accepted. An ugly little look came on to his face, of a man who has accepted his own degradation.

In the early spring Winifred went down to Crockham to be there when primroses were out, and the tassels hanging on the hazel-bushes. She felt something like a reconciliation towards Egbert, now he was a prisoner in camp most of his days. Joyce was wild with delight at seeing the garden and the common again, after the eight or nine months of London and misery. She was still lame. She still had the irons up her leg. But she lurched about with a wild, crippled agility.

Egbert came for a week-end, in his gritty, thick, sandpaper khaki and puttees and the hideous cap. Nay, he looked terrible. And on his face a slightly impure look, a little sore on his lip, as if he had eaten too much or drunk too much or let his blood become a little unclean. He was almost uglily healthy, with the camp life. It did not suit him.

Winifred waited for him in a little passion of duty and sacrifice, willing to serve the soldier, if not the man. It only made him feel a little more ugly inside. The week-end was torment to him: the memory of the camp, the knowledge of the life he led there; even the sight of his own legs in that abhorrent khaki. He felt as if the hideous cloth went into his blood and made it gritty and dirty. Then Winifred so ready to serve the *soldier*, when she repudiated the man. And this made the grit worse between his teeth. And the children running around praying and calling in the rather mincing fashion of children who have nurses and governesses and literature in the family. And Joyce so lame! It had all become unreal to him, after the camp. It only set his soul on edge. He left at dawn on the Monday morning, glad to get back to the realness and vulgarity of the camp.

Winifred would never meet him again at the cottage—only in London, where the world was with them. But sometimes he came alone to Crockham, perhaps when friends were staying there. And then he would work a while in his garden. This summer still it would flame with blue anchusas and big red poppies, the mulleins would sway their soft, downy erections in the air: he loved mulleins: and the honeysuckle would stream out scent like memory, when the owl was whooing. Then he sat by the fire with the friends and with Winifred's sisters, and they sang the folk-songs. He put on thin civilian clothes and his charm and his beauty and the supple dominancy of his body glowed out again. But Winifred was not there.

At the end of the summer he went to Flanders, into action. He seemed already to have gone out of life, beyond the pale of life. He hardly remembered his life any more, being like a man who is going to take a jump from a height, and is only looking to where he must land.

He was twice slightly wounded, in two months. But not enough to put him off duty for more than a day or two. They were retiring again, holding the enemy back. He was in the rear—three machine-guns. The country was all pleasant, war had not yet trampled it. Only the air seemed shattered, and the land awaiting death. It was a small, unimportant action in which he was engaged.

The guns were stationed on a little bushy hillock just out-side a village. But occasionally, it was difficult to say from which direction came the sharp crackle of rifle-fire, and beyond, the far-off thud of cannon. The afternoon was wintry and cold.

A lieutenant stood on a little iron platform at the top of the ladders, taking the sights and giving the aim, calling in a high, tense, mechanical voice. Out of the sky came the sharp cry of the directions, then the warning numbers, then "Fire!" The shot went, the piston of the gun sprang back, there was a sharp explosion, and a very faint film of smoke in the air. Then the other two guns fired, and there was a lull. The officer was un-certain of the enemy's position. The thick clump of horse-chestnut trees below was without change. Only in the far distance the sound of heavy firing continued, so far off as to give a sense of peace.

The gorse bushes on either hand were dark, but a few sparks of flowers showed yellow. He noticed them almost uncon-sciously as he waited in the lull. He was in his shirt-sleeves, and the air came chill on his arms. Again his shirt was slit on the shoulders, and the flesh showed through. He was dirty and unkempt. But his face was quiet. So many things go out of consciousness before we come to the end of consciousness.

Before him, below, was the highroad, running between high banks of grass and gorse. He saw the whitish, muddy tracks and deep scores in the road, where the part of the regiment had retired. Now all was still. Sounds that came, came from the outside. The place where he stood was still silent, chill, serene: the white church among the trees beyond seemed like a thought only.

He moved into a lightning-like mechanical response at the sharp cry from the officer overhead. Mechanism, the pure mechanical action of obedience at the guns. Pure mechanical action at the guns. It left the soul unburdened, brooding in dark nakedness. In the end, the soul is alone, brooding on the face of the uncreated flux, as a bird on a dark sea.

Nothing could be seen but the road, and a crucifix knocked slanting and the dark, autumnal fields and woods. There appeared three horsemen on a little eminence, very small, on the crest of a ploughed field. They were our own men. Of the enemy, nothing.

The lull continued. Then suddenly came sharp orders, and a

new direction of the guns, and an intense, exciting activity. Yet at the centre the soul remained dark and aloof, alone.

But even so, it was the soul that heard the new sound: the new, deep 'papp!' of a gun that seemed to touch right upon the soul. He kept up the rapid activity at the machine-gun, sweating. But in his soul was the echo of the new, deep sound, deeper than life.

And in confirmation came the awful faint whistling of a shell, advancing almost suddenly into a piercing, tearing shriek that would tear through the membrance of life. He heard it in his ears, but he heard it also in his soul, in tension. There was relief when the thing had swung by and struck, away beyond. He heard the hoarseness of its explosion, and the voice of the soldier calling to the horses. But he did not turn round to look. He only noticed a twig of holly with red berries fall like a gift on to the road below.

Not this time, not this time. Whither thou goest I will go. Did he say it to the shell, or to whom? Whither thou goest I will go. Then, the faint whistling of another shell dawned, and his blood became small and still to receive it. It drew nearer, like some horrible blast of wind; his blood lost consciousness. But in the second of suspension he saw the heavy shell swoop to earth, into the rocky bushes on the right, and earth and stones poured up into the sky. It was as if he heard no sound. The earth and stones and fragments of bush fell to earth again, and there was the same unchanging peace. The Germans had got the aim.

Would they move now? Would they retire? Yes. The officer was giving the last lightning-rapid orders to fire before withdrawing. A shell passed unnoticed in the rapidity of action. And then, into the silence, into the suspense where the soul brooded, finally crashed a noise and a darkness and a moment's flaming agony and horror. Ah, he had seen the dark bird flying towards him, flying home this time. In one instant life and eternity went up in a conflagration of agony, then there was a weight of darkness.

When faintly something began to struggle in the darkness, a consciousness of himself, he was aware of a great load and a clanging sound. To have known the moment of death! And to be forced, before dying, to review it. So, fate, even in death.

There was a resounding of pain. It seemed to sound from the outside of his consciousness: like a loud bell clanging very

near. Yet he knew it was himself. He must associate himself
with it. After a lapse and a new effort, he identified a pain in
his hand, a large pain that clanged and resounded. So far he
could identify himself with himself. Then there was a lapse.

After a time he seemed to wake up again, and waking, to
know that he was at the front, and that he was killed. He did
not open his eyes. Light was not yet his. The clanging pain in
his head rang out the rest of his consciousness. So he lapsed
away from consciousness, in unutterable sick abandon of life.

Bit by bit, like a doom, came the necessity to know. He was
hit in the head. It was only a vague surmise at first. But in the
swinging of the pendulum of pain, swinging ever nearer and
nearer, to touch him into an agony of consciousness and a
consciousness of agony, gradually the knowledge emerged—
he must be hit in the head—hit on the left brow; if so, there
would be blood—was there blood?—could he feel blood in his
left eye? Then the clanging seemed to burst the membrance of
his brain, like death-madness.

Was there blood on his face? Was hot blood flowing? Or
was it dry blood congealing down his cheek? It took him
hours even to ask the question: time being no more than an
agony in darkness, without measurement.

A long time after he had opened his eyes he realised he was
seeing something—something, something, but the effort to recall what was too great. No, no; no recall!

Were they the stars in the dark sky? Was it possible it was
stars in the dark sky? Stars? The world? Ah, no, he could
not know it! Stars and the world were gone for him, he closed
his eyes. No stars, no sky, no world. No, no! The thick darkness of blood alone. It should be one great lapse into the thick
darkness of blood in agony.

Death, oh, death! The world all blood, and the blood all
writhing with death. The soul like the tiniest little light out
on a dark sea, the sea of blood. And the light guttering, beating, pulsing in a windless storm, wishing it could go out, yet
unable.

There had been life. There had been Winifred and his
children. But the frail death-agony effort to catch at straws
of memory, straws of life from the past, brought on too great
a nausea. No, no! No Winifred, no children. No world, no
people. Better the agony of dissolution ahead than the nausea
of the effort backwards. Better the terrible work should go

forward, the dissolving into the black sea of death, in the extremity of dissolution, than that there should be any reaching back towards life. To forget! To forget! Utterly, utterly to forget, in the great forgetting of death. To break the core and the unit of life, and to lapse out on the great darkness. Only that. To break the clue, and mingle and commingle with the one darkness, without afterwards or forwards. Let the black sea of death itself solve the problem of futurity. Let the will of man break and give up.

What was that? A light! A terrible light! Was it figures? Was it legs of a horse colossal—colossal above him: huge, huge?

The Germans heard a slight noise, and started. Then, in the glare of a light-bomb, by the side of the heap of earth thrown up by the shell, they saw the dead face.

THERE is in the Midlands a single-line tramway system which boldly leaves the county town and plunges off into the black, industrial country-side, up hill and down dale, through the long ugly villages of workmen's houses, over canals and railways, past churches perched high and nobly over the smoke and shadows, through stark, grimy cold little market-places, tilting away in a rush past cinemas and shops down to the hollow where the collieries are, then up again, past a little rural church, under the ash trees, on in a rush to the terminus, the last little ugly place of industry, the cold little town that shivers on the edge of the wild, gloomy country beyond. There the green and creamy coloured tram-cars seems to pause and purr with curious satisfaction. But in a few minutes—the clock on the turret of the Co-operative Wholesale Society's shops gives the time—away it starts once more on the adventure. Again there are the reckless swoops downhill, bouncing the loops: again the chilly wait in the hill-top market-place: again the breathless slithering round the precipitous drop under the church: again the patient halts at the loops, waiting for the outcoming car: so on and on, for two long hours, till at last the city looms beyond the fat gas-works, the narrow factories draw near, we are in the sordid streets of the great town, once more we sidle to a standstill at our terminus, abashed by the great crimson and cream-coloured city cars, but still perky, jaunty, somewhat dare-devil, green as a jaunty spring of parsley out of a black colliery garden.

To ride on these cars is always an adventure. Since we are in war-time, the drivers are men unfit for active service: cripples and hunchbacks. So they have the spirit of the devil in them. The ride becomes a steeplechase. Hurray! we have leapt in a clear jump over the canal bridge—now for the four-lane corner. With a shriek and a trail of sparks we are clear again. To be sure, a tram often leaps the rails—but what matter! It sits in a ditch till other trams come to haul it out. It is quite common for a car, parked with one solid mass of living people, to come to a dead halt in the midst of unbroken blackness, the heart of nowhere on a dark night, and for the driver and the girl conductor to call: "All get off—car's on fire!" Instead, however, of rushing out in a panic, the passengers stolidly reply: "Get on—get on! We're not coming out. We're stopping where we are. Push on, George." So till flames actually appear.

The reason for this reluctance to dismount is that the nights are howlingly cold, black, and windswept, and a car is a haven of refuge. From village to village the miners travel, for a change of cinema, of girl, of pub. The trams are desperately packed. Who is going to risk himself in the black gulf outside, to wait perhaps an hour for another tram, then to see the forlorn notice 'Depot Only', because there is something wrong! Or to greet a unit of three bright cars all so tight with people that they sail past with a howl of derision. Trams that pass in the night.

This, the most dangerous tram-service in England, as the authorities themselves declare, with pride, is entirely conducted by girls, and driven by rash young men, a little crippled, or by delicate young men, who creep forward in terror. The girls are fearless young hussies. In their ugly blue uniform, skirts up to their knees, shapeless old peaked caps on their heads, they have all the *sang-froid* of an old non-commissioned officer. With a tram packed with howling colliers, roaring hymns downstairs and a sort of antiphony of obscenities upstairs, the lasses are perfectly at their ease. They pounce on the youths who try to evade their ticket-machine. They push off the men at the end of their distance. They are not going to be done in the eye—not they. They fear nobody—and everybody fears them.

"Hello, Annie!"

"Hello, Ted!"

"Oh, mind my corn, Miss Stone. It's my belief you've got a heart of stone, for you've trod on it again."

"You should keep it in your pocket," replies Miss Stone, and she goes sturdily upstairs in her high boots.

"Tickets, please."

She is peremptory, suspicious, and ready to hit first. She can hold her own against ten thousand. The step of that tramcar is her Thermopylæ.

Therefore, there is a certain wild romance aboard these cars —and in the sturdy bosom of Annie herself. The time for soft romance is in the morning, between ten o'clock and one, when things are rather slack: that is, except market-day and Saturday. Thus Annie has time to look about her. Then she often hops off her car and into a shop where she has spied something, while the driver chats in the main road. There is very good feeling between the girls and the drivers. Are they not companions in peril, shipments aboard this careering vessel of a tram-car, for ever rocking on the waves of a stormy land.

Then, also, during the easy hours, the inspectors are most in evidence. For some reason, everybody employed in this tram-service is young: there are no grey heads. It would not do. Therefore the inspectors are of the right age, and one, the chief, is also good-looking. See him stand on a wet, gloomy morning, in his long oilskin, his peaked cap well down over his eyes, waiting to board a car. His face ruddy, his small brown moustache is weathered, he has a faint impudent smile. Fairly tall and agile, even in his waterproof, he springs aboard a car and greets Annie.

"Hello, Annie! Keeping the wet out?"

"Trying to."

There are only two people in the car. Inspecting is soon over. Then for a long and impudent chat on the foot-board, a good, easy, twelve-mile chat.

The inspector's name is John Thomas Raynor—always called John Thomas, except sometimes, in malice, Coddy. His face sets in fury when he is addressed, from a distance, with this abbreviation. There is considerable scandal about John Thomas in half a dozen villages. He flirts with the girl conductors in the morning, and walks out with them in the dark night, when they leave their tram-car at the depôt. Of course, the girls quit the service frequently. Then he flirts and walks out with the newcomer: always providing she is sufficiently attractive, and that she will consent to walk. It is remarkable, however, that most of the girls are quite comely, they are all young, and this roving life aboard the car gives them a sailor's dash and recklessness. What matter how they behave when the ship is in port? To-morrow they will be aboard again.

Annie, however, was something of a Tartar, and her sharp tongue had kept John Thomas at arm's length for many months. Perhaps, therefore, she liked him all the more: for he always came up smiling, with impudence. She watched him vanquish one girl, then another. She could tell by the movement of his mouth and eyes, when he flirted with her in the morning, that he had been walking out with this lass, or the other, the night before. A fine cock-of-the-walk he was. She could sum him up pretty well.

In this subtle antagonism they knew each other like old friends, they were as shrewd with one another almost as man and wife. But Annie had always kept him sufficiently at arm's length. Besides, she had a boy of her own.

The Statutes fair, however, came in November, at Bestwood. It happened that Annie had the Monday night off. It was a drizzling ugly night, yet she dressed herself up and went to the fair-ground. She was alone, but she expected soon to find a pal of some sort.

The roundabouts were veering round and grinding out their music, the side-shows were making as much commotion as possible. In the coconut shies there were no coconuts, but artificial war-time substitutes, which the lads declared were fastened into the irons. There was a sad decline in brilliance and luxury. None the less, the ground was muddy as ever, there was the same crush, the press of faces lighted up by the flares and the electric lights, the same smell of naphtha and a few potatoes, and of electricity.

Who should be the first to greet Miss Annie on the show-ground but John Thomas. He had a black overcoat buttoned up to his chin, and a tweed cap pulled down over his brows, his face between was ruddy and smiling and handy as ever. She knew so well the way his mouth moved.

She was very glad to have a 'boy'. To be at the Statutes without a fellow was no fun. Instantly, like the gallant he was, he took her on the Dragons, grim-toothed, roundabout switchbacks. It was not nearly so exciting as a tram-car actually. But, then, to be seated in a shaking, green dragon, uplifted above the sea of bubble faces, careering in a rickety fashion in the lower heavens, whilst John Thomas leaned over her, his cigarette in his mouth, was after all the right style. She was a plump, quick, alive little creature. So she was quite excited and happy.

John Thomas made her stay on for the next round. And therefore she could hardly for shame repulse him when he put his arm round her and drew her a little nearer to him, in a very warm and cuddly manner. Besides, he was fairly discreet, he kept his movement as hidden as possible. She looked down, and saw that his red, clean hand was out of sight of the crowd.

And they knew each other so well. So they warmed up to the fair.

After the dragons they went on the horses. John Thomas paid each time, so she could but be complaisant. He, of course, sat astride on the outer horse—named 'Black Bess'—and she sat sideways, towards him, on the inner horse—named 'Wildfire'. But of course John Thomas was not going to sit discreetly on 'Black Bess', holding the brass bar. Round they spun and heaved, in the light. And round he swung on his wooden steed, flinging one leg across her mount, and perilously tipping up and down, across the space, half lying back, laughing at her. He was perfectly happy; she was afraid her hat was on one side, but she was excited.

He threw quoits on a table, and won for her two large, pale blue hat-pins. And then, hearing the noise of the cinemas, announcing another performance, they climbed the boards and went in.

Of course, during these performances pitch darkness falls from time to time, when the machine goes wrong. Then there is a wild whooping, and a loud smacking of simulated kisses. In these moments John Thomas drew Anne towards him. After all, he had a wonderfully warm, cosy way of holding a girl with his arm, he seemed to make such a nice fit. And, after all, it was pleasant to be so held : so very comforting and cosy and nice. He leaned over her and she felt his breath on her hair; she knew he wanted to kiss her on the lips. And, after all, he was so warm and she fitted in to him so softly. After all, she wanted him to touch her lips.

But the light sprang up; she also started electrically, and put her hat straight. He left his arm lying nonchalantly behind her. Well, it was fun, it was exciting to be at the Statutes with John Thomas.

When the cinema was over they went for a walk across the dark, damp fields. He had all the arts of love-making. He was especially good at holding a girl, when he sat with her on a stile in the black, drizzling darkness. He seemed to be holding her in space, against his own warmth and gratification. And his kisses were soft and slow and searching.

So Annie walked out with John Thomas, though she kept her own boy dangling in the distance. Some of the tram-girls chose to be huffy. But there, you must take things as you find them, in this life.

There was no mistake about it, Annie liked John Thomas a good deal. She felt so rich and warm in herself whenever he was near. And John Thomas really liked Annie, more than usual. The soft, melting way in which she could flow into a fellow, as if she melted into his very bones, was something rare and good. He fully appreciated this.

But with a developing acquaintance there began a developing intimacy. Annie wanted to consider him a person, a man: she wanted to take an intelligent interest in him, and to have an intelligent response. She did not want a mere nocturnal presence, which was what he was so far. And she prided herself that he could not leave her.

Here she made a mistake. John Thomas intended to remain a nocturnal presence; he had no idea of becoming an all-round individual to her. When she started to take an intelligent interest in him and his life and his character, he sheered off. He hated intelligent interest. And he knew that the only way to stop it was to avoid it. The possessive female was aroused in Annie. So he left her.

It is no use saying she was not surprised. She was at first startled, thrown out of her count. For she had been so *very* sure of holding him. For a while she was staggered, and everything became uncertain to her. Then she wept with fury, indignation, desolation, and misery. Then she had a spasm of despair. And then, when he came, still impudently, on to her car, still familiar, but letting her see by the movement of his head that he had gone away to somebody else for the time being, and was enjoying pastures new, then she determined to have her own back.

She had a very shrewd idea what girls John Thomas had taken out. She went to Nora Purdy. Nora was a tall, rather pale, but well-built girl, with beautiful yellow hair. She was rather secretive.

"Hey!" said Annie, accosting her; then softly: "Who's John Thomas on with now?"

"I don't know," said Nora.

"Why, tha does," said Annie, ironically lapsing into dialect. "Tha knows as well as I do."

"Well, I do, then," said Nora. "It isn't me, so don't bother."

"It's Cissy Meakin, isn't it?"

"It is, for all I know."

"Hasn't he got a face on him!" said Annie. "I don't half

like his cheek. I could knock him off the foot-board when he comes round at me."

"He'll get dropped on one of these days," said Nora.

"Ay, he will, when somebody makes up their mind to drop it on him. I should like to see him taken down a peg or two, shouldn't you?"

"I shouldn't mind," said Nora.

"You've got quite as much cause to as I have," said Annie. "But we'll drop on him one of these days, my girl. What? Don't you want to?"

"I don't mind," said Nora.

But as a matter of fact, Nora was much more vindictive than Annie.

One by one Annie went the round of the old flames. It so happened that Cissy Meakin left the tramway service in quite a short time. Her mother made her leave. Then John Thomas was on the *qui vive*. He cast his eyes over his old flock. And his eyes lighted on Annie. He thought she would be safe now. Besides, he liked her.

She arranged to walk home with him on Sunday night. It so happened that her car would be in the depôt at half-past nine: the last car would come in at 10.15. So John Thomas was to wait for her there.

At the depôt the girls had a little waiting-room of their own. It was quite rough, but cosy, with a fire and an oven and a mirror, and table and wooden chairs. The half-dozen girls who knew John Thomas only too well had arranged to take service this Sunday afternoon. So, as the cars began to come in, early, the girls dropped into the waiting-room. And instead of hurrying off home, they sat around the fire and had a cup of tea. Outside was the darkness and lawlessness of war-time.

John Thomas came on the car after Annie, at about a quarter to ten. He poked his head easily into the girls' waiting-room.

"Prayer-meeting?" he asked.

"Ay," said Laura Sharp. "Ladies only."

"That's me!" said John Thomas. It was one of his favourite exclamations.

"Shut the door, boy," said Muriel Baggaley.

"Oh, which side of me?" said John Thomas.

"Which tha likes," said Polly Birkin.

He had come in and closed the door behind him. The girls

moved in their circle, to make a place for him near the fire.
He took off his great-coat and pushed back his hat.

"Who handles the teapot?" he said.

Nora Purdy silently poured him out a cup of tea.

"Want a bit o' my bread and drippin'?" said Muriel Baggaley
to him.

"Ay, give us a bit."

And he began to eat his piece of bread.

"There's no place like home, girls," he said.

They all looked at him as he uttered this piece of impudence.
He seemed to be sunning himself in the presence of so many
damsels.

"Especially if you're not afraid to go home in the dark," said
Laura Sharp.

"Me! By myself I am."

They sat till they heard the last tram come in. In a few
minutes Emma Houselay entered.

"Come on, my old duck!" cried Polly Birkin.

"It *is* perishing," said Emma, holding her fingers to the fire.

"But—I'm afraid to, go home in, the dark," sang Laura
Sharp, the tune having got into her mind.

"Who're you going with to-night, John Thomas?" asked
Muriel Baggaley coolly.

"To-night?" said John Thomas. "Oh, I'm going home by
myself to-night—all on my lonely-o."

"That's me!" said Nora Purdy, using his own ejaculation.

The girls laughed shrilly.

"Me as well, Nora," said John Thomas.

"Don't know what you mean," said Laura.

"Yes, I'm toddling," said he, rising and reaching for his
overcoat.

"Nay," said Polly. "We're all here waiting for you."

"We've got to be up in good time in the morning," he said,
in the benevolent official manner.

They all laughed.

"Nay," said Muriel. "Don't leave us all lonely, John Thomas.
Take one!"

"I'll take the lot, if you like," he responded gallantly.

"That you won't, either," said Muriel. "Two's company;
seven's too much of a good thing."

"Nay—take one," said Laura. "Fair and square, all above
board and say which."

"Ay," cried Annie, speaking for the first time. "Pick, John Thomas; let's hear thee."

"Nay," he said. "I'm going home quiet to-night. Feeling good, for once."

"Whereabouts?" said Annie. "Take a good 'un, then. But tha's got to take one of us!"

"Nay, how can I take one," he said, laughing uneasily. "I don't want to make enemies."

"You'd only make *one*," said Annie.

"The chosen *one*," added Laura.

"Oh, my! Who said girls!" exclaimed John Thomas, again turning, as if to escape. "Well—good-night."

"Nay, you've got to make your pick," said Muriel. "Turn your face to the wall, and say which one touches you. Go on—we shall only just touch your back—one of us. Go on—turn your face to the wall, and don't look, and say which one touches you."

He was uneasy, mistrusting them. Yet he had not the courage to break away. They pushed him to a wall and stood him there with his face to it. Behind his back they all grimaced, tittering. He looked so comical. He looked around uneasily.

"Go on!" he cried.

"You're looking—you're looking!" they shouted.

He turned his head away. And suddenly, with a movement like a swift cat, Annie went forward and fetched him a box on the side of the head that sent his cap flying and himself staggering. He started round.

But at Annie's signal they all flew at him, slapping him, pinching him, pulling his hair, though more in fun than in spite or anger. He, however, saw red. His blue eyes flamed with strange fear as well as fury, and he butted through the girls to the door. It was locked. He wrenched at it. Roused, alert, the girls stood round and looked at him. He faced them, at bay. At that moment they were rather horrifying to him, as they stood in their short uniforms. He was distinctly afraid.

"Come on, John Thomas! Come on! Choose!" said Annie.

"What are you after? Open the door," he said.

"We shan't—not till you've chosen!" said Muriel.

"Chosen what?" he said.

"Chosen the one you're going to marry," she replied.

He hesitated a moment.

"Open the blasted door," he said, "and get back to your senses." He spoke with official authority.

"You've got to choose!" cried the girls.

"Come on!" cried Annie, looking him in the eye. "Come on! Come on!"

He went forward, rather vaguely. She had taken off her belt, and swinging it, she fetched him a sharp blow over the head with the buckle end. He sprang and seized her. But immediately the other girls rushed upon him, pulling and tearing and beating him. Their blood was now thoroughly up. He was their sport now. They were going to have their own back, out of him. Strange, wild creatures, they hung on him and rushed at him to bear him down. His tunic was torn right up the back, Nora had hold at the back of his collar, and was actually strangling him. Luckily the button burst. He struggled in a wild frenzy of fury and terror, almost mad terror. His tunic was simply torn off his back, his shirt-sleeves were torn away, his arms were naked. The girls rushed at him, clenched their hands on him and pulled at him: or they rushed at him and pushed him, butted him with all their might: or they struck him wild blows. He ducked and cringed and struck sideways. They became more intense.

At last he was down. They rushed on him, kneeling on him. He had neither breath nor strength to move. His face was bleeding with a long scratch, his brow was bruised.

Annie knelt on him, the other girls knelt and hung on to him. Their faces were flushed, their hair wild, their eyes were all glittering strangely. He lay at last quite still, with face averted, as an animal lies when it is defeated and at the mercy of the captor. Sometimes his eye glanced back at the wild faces of the girls. His breast rose heavily, his wrists were torn.

"Now, then, my fellow!" gasped Annie at length. "Now then—now——"

At the sound of her terrifying, cold triumph, he suddenly started to struggle as an animal might, but the girls threw themselves upon him with unnatural strength and power, forcing him down.

"Yes—now, then!" gasped Annie at length.

And there was a dead silence, in which the thud of heart-beating was to be heard. It was a suspense of pure silence in every soul.

"Now you know where you are," said Annie.

The sight of his white, bare arm maddened the girls. He lay in a kind of trance of fear and antagonism. They felt themselves filled with supernatural strength.

Suddenly Polly started to laugh—to giggle wildly—helplessly—and Emma and Muriel joined in. But Annie and Nora and Laura remained the same, tense, watchful, with gleaming eyes. He winced away from these eyes.

"Yes," said Annie, in a curious low tone, secret and deadly. "Yes! You've got it now. You know what you've done, don't you? You know what you've done."

He made no sound nor sign, but lay with bright, averted eyes, and averted, bleeding face.

"You ought to be *killed*, that's what you ought," said Annie, tensely. "You ought to be *killed*." And there was a terrifying lust in her voice.

Polly was ceasing to laugh, and giving long-drawn Oh-h-hs and sighs as she came to herself.

"He's got to choose," she said vaguely.

"Oh, yes, he has," said Laura, with vindictive decision.

"Do you hear—do you hear?" said Annie. And with a sharp movement, that made him wince, she turned his face to her.

"Do you hear?" she repeated, shaking him.

But he was quite dumb. She fetched him a sharp slap on the face. He started, and his eyes widened. Then his face darkened with defiance, after all.

"Do you hear?" she repeated.

He only looked at her with hostile eyes.

"Speak!" she said, putting her face devilishly near his.

"What?" he said, almost overcome.

"You've got to *choose*!" she cried, as if it were some terrible menace, and as if it hurt her that she could not exact more.

"What?" he said, in fear.

"Choose your girl, Coddy. You've got to choose her now. And you'll get your neck broken if you play any more of your tricks, my boy. You're settled now."

There was a pause. Again he averted his face. He was cunning in his overthrow. He did not give in to them really—no, not if they tore him to bits.

"All right, then," he said, "I choose Annie." His voice was strange and full of malice. Annie let go of him as if he had been a hot coal.

"He's chosen Annie!" said the girls in chorus.

"Me!" cried Annie. She was still kneeling, but away from him. He was still lying prostrate, with averted face. The girls grouped uneasily around.

"Me!" repeated Annie, with a terrible bitter accent.

Then she got up, drawing away from him with strange disgust and bitterness.

"I wouldn't touch him," she said.

But her face quivered with a kind of agony, she seemed as if she would fall. The other girls turned aside. He remained lying on the floor, with his torn clothes and bleeding, averted face.

"Oh, if he's chosen——" said Polly.

"I don't want him—he can choose again," said Annie, with the same rather bitter hopelessness.

"Get up," said Polly, lifting his shoulder. "Get up."

He rose slowly, a strange, ragged, dazed creature. The girls eyed him from a distance, curiously, furtively, dangerously.

"Who wants him?" cried Laura, roughly.

"Nobody," they answered, with contempt. Yet each one of them waited for him to look at her, hoped he would look at her. All except Annie, and something was broken in her.

He, however, kept his face closed and averted from them all. There was a silence of the end. He picked up the torn pieces of his tunic, without knowing what to do with them. The girls stood about uneasily, flushed, panting, tidying their hair and their dress unconsciously, and watching him. He looked at none of them. He espied his cap in a corner, and went and picked it up. He put it on his head, and one of the girls burst into a shrill, hysteric laugh at the sight he presented. He, however, took no heed, but went straight to where his overcoat hung on a peg. The girls moved away from contact with him as if he had been an electric wire. He put on his coat and buttoned it down. Then he rolled his tunic-rags into a bundle, and stood before the locked door, dumbly.

"Open the door, somebody," said Laura.

"Annie's got the key," said one.

Annie silently offered the key to the girls. Nora unlocked the door.

"Tit for tat, old man," she said. "Show yourself a man, and don't bear a grudge."

But without a word or sign he had opened the door and gone, his face closed, his head dropped.

"That'll learn him," said Laura.

"Coddy!" said Nora.

"Shut up, for God's sake!" cried Annie fiercely, as if in torture.

"Well, I'm about ready to go, Polly. Look sharp!" said Muriel.

The girls were all anxious to be off. They were tidying themselves hurriedly, with mute, stupefied faces.

THE BLIND MAN

ISABEL PERVIN was listening for two sounds—for the sound of wheels on the drive outside and for the noise of her husband's footsteps in the hall. Her dearest and oldest friend, a man who seemed almost indispensable to her living, would drive up in the rainy dusk of the closing November day. The trap had gone to fetch him from the station. And her husband, who had been blinded in Flanders, and who had a disfiguring mark on his brow, would be coming in from the out-houses.

He had been home for a year now. He was totally blind. Yet they had been very happy. The Grange was Maurice's own place. The back was a farmstead, and the Wernhams, who occupied the rear premises, acted as farmers. Isabel lived with her husband in the handsome rooms in front. She and he had been almost entirely alone together since he was wounded. They talked and sang and read together in a wonderful and unspeakable intimacy. Then she reviewed books for a Scottish newspaper, carrying on her old interest, and he occupied himself a good deal with the farm. Sightless, he could still discuss everything with Wernham, and he could also do a good deal of work about the place—menial work, it is true, but it gave him satisfaction. He milked the cows, carried in the pails, turned the separator, attended to the pigs and horses. Life was still very full and strangely serene for the blind man, peaceful with the almost incomprehensible peace of immediate contact in darkness. With his wife he had a whole world, rich and real and invisible.

They were newly and remotely happy. He did not even regret the loss of his sight in these times of dark, palpable joy. A certain exultance swelled his soul.

But as time wore on, sometimes the rich glamour would leave them. Sometimes, after months of this intensity, a sense of burden overcame Isabel, a weariness, a terrible ennui, in that silent house approached between a colonnade of tall-shafted pines. Then she felt she would go mad, for she could not bear it. And sometimes he had devastating fits of depression, which seemed to lay waste his whole being. It was worse than depression—a black misery, when his own life was a torture to him, and when his presence was unbearable to his wife. The dread went down to the roots of her soul as these black days recurred. In a kind of panic she tried to wrap herself up still further in her husband. She forced the old spontaneous cheerfulness and joy to continue. But the effort it cost her was almost too much. She knew she could not keep it up. She felt she would scream with the strain, and would give anything, anything, to escape. She longed to possess her husband utterly; it gave her inordinate joy to have him entirely to herself. And yet, when again he was gone in a black and massive misery, she could not bear him, she could not bear herself; she wished she could be snatched away off the earth altogether, anything rather than live at this cost.

Dazed, she schemed for a way out. She invited friends, she tried to give him some further connection with the outer world. But it was no good. After all their joy and suffering, after their dark, great year of blindness and solitude and unspeakable nearness, other people seemed to them both shallow, prattling, rather impertinent. Shallow prattle seemed presumptuous. He became impatient and irritated, she was wearied. And so they lapsed into their solitude again. For they preferred it.

But now, in a few weeks' time, her second baby would be born. The first had died, an infant, when her husband first went out to France. She looked with joy and relief to the coming of the second. It would be her salvation. But also she felt some anxiety. She was thirty years old, her husband was a year younger. They both wanted the child very much. Yet she could not help feeling afraid. She had her husband on her hands, a terrible joy to her, and a terrifying burden. The child would occupy her love and attention. And then, what of Maurice? What would he do? If only she could feel that he, too, would be at peace and happy when the child came! She did so want to luxuriate in a rich, physical satisfaction of maternity. But the man, what would he do? How could she provide for him, how avert those shattering black moods of his, which destroyed them both?

She sighed with fear. But at this time Bertie Reid wrote to Isabel. He was her old friend, a second or third cousin, a Scotsman, as she was a Scotswoman. They had been brought up near to one another, and all her life he had been her friend, like a brother, but better than her own brothers. She loved him —though not in the marrying sense. There was a sort of kinship between them, an affinity. They understood one another instinctively. But Isabel would never have thought of marrying Bertie. It would have seemed like marrying in her own family.

Bertie was a barrister and a man of letters, a Scotsman of the intellectual type, quick, ironical, sentimental, and on his knees before the women he adored but did not want to marry. Maurice Pervin was different. He came of a good old country family—the Grange was not a very great distance from Oxford. He was passionate, sensitive, perhaps over-sensitive, wincing— a big fellow with heavy limbs and a forehead that flushed painfully. For his mind was slow, as if drugged by the strong provincial blood that beat in his veins. He was very sensitive to his own mental slowness, his feelings being quick and acute. So that he was just the opposite to Bertie, whose mind was much quicker than his emotions, which were not so very fine.

From the first the two men did not like each other. Isabel felt that they *ought* to get on together. But they did not. She felt that if only each could have the clue to the other there would be such a rare understanding between them. It did not come off, however. Bertie adopted a slightly ironical attitude, very offensive to Maurice, who returned the Scotch irony with English resentment, a resentment which deepened sometimes into stupid hatred.

This was a little puzzling to Isabel. However, she accepted it in the course of things. Men were made freakish and unreasonable. Therefore, when Maurice was going out to France for the second time, she felt that, for her husband's sake, she must discontinue her friendship with Bertie. She wrote to the barrister to this effect. Bertram Reid simply replied that in this, as in all other matters, he must obey her wishes, if these were indeed her wishes.

For nearly two years nothing had passed between the two friends. Isabel rather gloried in the fact; she had no compunction. She had one great article of faith, which was, that husband and wife should be so important to one another, that the rest of the world simply did not count. She and Maurice were husband and wife. They loved one another. They would have children. Then let everybody and everything else fade into insignificance outside this connubial felicity. She professed herself quite happy and ready to receive Maurice's friends. She was happy and ready: the happy wife, the ready woman

in possession. Without knowing why, the friends retired
abashed, and came no more. Maurice, of course, took as much
satisfaction in this connubial absorption as Isabel did.

He shared in Isabel's literary activities, she cultivated a real
interest in agriculture and cattle-raising. For she, being at
heart perhaps an emotional enthusiast, always cultivated the
practical side of life, and prided herself on her mastery of
practical affairs. Thus the husband and wife had spent the
five years of their married life. The last had been one of blindness and unspeakable intimacy. And now Isabel felt a great
indifference coming over her, a sort of lethargy. She wanted
to be allowed to bear her child in peace, to nod by the fire and
drift vaguely, physically, from day to day. Maurice was like
an ominous thunder-cloud. She had to keep waking up to
remember him.

When a little note came from Bertie, asking if he were to put
up a tombstone to their dead friendship, and speaking of the
real pain he felt on account of her husband's loss of sight, she
felt a pang, a fluttering agitation of re-awakening. And she
read the letter to Maurice.

"Ask him to come down," he said.

"Ask Bertie to come here!" she re-echoed.

"Yes—if he wants to."

Isabel paused for a few moments.

"I know he wants to—he'd only be too glad," she replied.
"But what about you, Maurice? How would you like it?"

"I should like it."

"Well—in that case—— But I thought you didn't care for
him——"

"Oh, I don't know. I might think differently of him now,"
the blind man replied. It was rather abstruse to Isabel.

"Well, dear," she said, "if you're quite sure——"

"I'm sure enough. Let him come," said Maurice.

So Bertie was coming, coming this evening, in the November
rain and darkness. Isabel was agitated, racked with her old
restlessness and indecision. She had always suffered from this
pain of doubt, just an agonising sense of uncertainty. It had
begun to pass off, in the lethargy of maternity. Now it
returned, and she resented it. She struggled as usual to main-
tain her calm, composed, friendly bearing, a sort of mask she
wore over all her body.

A woman had lighted a tall lamp beside the table, and spread the cloth. The long dining-room was dim, with its elegant but rather severe piece of old furniture. Only the round table glowed softly under the light. It had a rich, beautiful effect. The white cloth glistened and dropped its heavy, pointed lace corners almost to the carpet, the china was old and handsome, creamy-yellow, with a blotched pattern of harsh red and deep blue, the cups large and bell-shaped, the teapot gallant. Isabel looked at it with superficial appreciation.

Her nerves were hurting her. She looked automatically again at the high, uncurtained windows. In the last dusk she could just perceive outside a huge fir tree swaying its boughs: it was as if she thought it rather than saw it. The rain came flying on the window panes. Ah, why had she no peace? These two men, why did they tear at her? Why did they not come— why was there this suspense?

She sat in a lassitude that was really suspense and irritation. Maurice, at least, might come in—there was nothing to keep him out. She rose to her feet. Catching sight of her reflection in a mirror, she glanced at herself with a slight smile of recognition, as if she were an old friend to herself. Her face was oval and calm, her nose a little arched. Her neck made a beautiful line down to her shoulder. With hair knotted loosely behind, she had something of a warm, maternal look. Thinking this of herself, she arched her eyebrows and her rather heavy eyelids, with a little flicker of a smile, and for a moment her grey eyes looked amused and wicked, a little sardonic, out of her transfigured Madonna face.

Then, resuming her air of womanly patience—she was really fatally self-determined—she went with a little jerk towards the door. Her eyes were slightly reddened.

She passed down the wide hall, and through a door at the end. Then she was in the farm premises. The scent of dairy, and of farm-kitchen, and of farmyard and of leather almost overcame her: but particularly the scent of dairy. They had been scalding out the pans. The flagged passage in front of her was dark, puddled and wet. Light came out from the open kitchen door. She went forward and stood in the doorway. The farm-people were at tea, seated at a little distance from her, round a long, narrow table, in the centre of which stood a white lamp. Ruddy faces, ruddy hands holding food, red mouths working, heads bent over the tea-cups: men, land-girls, boys: it was tea-time, feeding-time. Some faces caught sight

of her. Mrs. Wernham, going round behind the chairs with a
large black teapot, halting slightly in her walk, was not aware
of her for a moment. Then she turned suddenly.

"Oh, is it Madame!" she exclaimed. "Come in, then, come
in! We're at tea." And she dragged forward a chair.

"No, I won't come in," said Isabel. "I'm afraid I interrupt
your meal."

"No—no—not likely, Madame, not likely."

"Hasn't Mr. Pervin come in, do you know?"

"I'm sure I couldn't say! Missed him, have you, Madame?"

"No, I only wanted him to come in," laughed Isabel, as if
shyly.

"Wanted him, did ye? Get up, boy—get up, now———"

Mrs. Wernham knocked one of the boys on the shoulder.
He began to scrape to his feet, chewing largely.

"I believe he's in top stable," said another face from the
table.

"Ah! No, don't get up. I'm going myself," said Isabel.

"Don't you go out of a dirty night like this. Let the lad go.
Get along wi' ye, boy," said Mrs. Wernham.

"No, no," said Isabel, with a decision that was always
obeyed. "Go on with your tea, Tom. I'd like to go across to
the stable, Mrs. Wernham."

"Did ever you hear tell!" exclaimed the woman.

"Isn't the trap late?" asked Isabel.

"Why, no," said Mrs. Wernham, peering into the distance at
the tall, dim clock. "No, Madame—we can give it another
quarter or twenty minutes yet, good—yes, every bit of a
quarter."

"Ah! It seems late when darkness falls so early," said Isabel.

"It do, that it do. Bother the days, that they draw in so,"
answered Mrs. Wernham. "Proper miserable!"

"They are," said Isabel, withdrawing.

She pulled on her over-shoes, wrapped a large tartan shawl
around her, put on a man's felt hat, and ventured out along
the causeways of the first yard. It was very dark. The wind
was roaring in the great elms behind the out-houses. When
she came to the second yard the darkness seemed deeper. She
was unsure of her footing. She wished she had brought a
lantern. Rain blew against her. Half she liked it, half she felt
unwilling to battle.

She reached at last the just visible door of the stable. There was no sign of a light anywhere. Opening the upper half, she looked in: Into a simple well of darkness. The smell of horses, ammonia, and of warmth was startling to her, in that full night. She listened with all her ears, but could hear nothing save the night, and the stirring of a horse.

"Maurice!" she called, softly and musically, though she was afraid. "Maurice—are you there?"

Nothing came from the darkness. She knew the rain and wind blew in upon the horses, the hot animal life. Feeling it wrong, she entered the stable, and draw the lower half of the door shut, holding the upper part close. She did not stir, because she was aware of the presence of the dark hind-quarters of the horses, though she could not see them, and she was afraid. Something wild stirred in her heart.

She listened intensely. Then she heard a small noise in the distance—far away, it seemed—the chink of a pan, and a man's voice speaking a brief word. It would be Maurice, in the other part of the stable. She stood motionless, waiting for him to come through the partition door. The horses were so terrifyingly near to her, in the invisible.

The loud jarring of the inner door-latch made her start; the door was opened. She could hear and feel her husband entering and invisibly passing among the horses near to her, in darkness as they were, actively intermingled. The rather low sound of his voice as he spoke to the horses came velvety to her nerves. How near he was, and how invisible! The darkness seemed to be in a strange swirl of violent life, just upon her. She turned giddy.

Her presence of mind made her call, quietly and musically: "Maurice! Maurice—dea-ar!"

"Yes," he answered. "Isabel?"

She saw nothing, and the sound of his voice seemed to touch her.

"Hello!" she answered cheerfully, straining her eyes to see him. He was still busy, attending to the horses near her, but she saw only darkness. It made her almost desperate.

"Won't you come in, dear?" she said.

"Yes, I'm coming. Just half a minute. *Stand over—now!* Trap's not come, has it?"

"Not yet," said Isabel.

His voice was pleasant and ordinary, but it had a slight sug-gestion of the stable to her. She wished he would come away.

While he was so utterly invisible she was afraid of him.

"How's the time" he asked.

"Not yet six," she replied. She disliked to answer into the dark. Presently he came very near to her, and she retreated out of doors.

"The weather blows in here," he said, coming steadily forward, feeling for the doors. She shrank away. At last she could dimly see him.

"Bertie won't have much of a drive," he said, as he closed the doors.

"He won't indeed!" said Isabel calmly, watching the dark shape at the door.

"Give me your arm, dear," she said.

She pressed his arm close to her, as she went. But she longed to see him, to look at him. She was nervous. He walked erect, with face rather lifted, but with a curious tentative movement of his powerful, muscular legs. She could feel the clever, careful, strong contact of his feet with the earth, as she balanced against him. For a moment he was a tower of darkness to her, as if he rose out of the earth.

In the house-passage he wavered, and went cautiously, with a curious look of silence about him as he felt for the bench. Then he sat down heavily. He was a man with rather sloping shoulders, but with heavy limbs, powerful legs that seemed to know the earth. His head was small, usually carried high and light. As he bent down to unfasten his gaiters and boots he did not look blind. His hair was brown and crisp, his hands were large, reddish, intelligent, the veins stood out in the wrists; and his thighs and knees seemed massive. When he stood up his face and neck were surcharged with blood, the veins stood out out on his temples. She did not look at his blindness.

Isabel was always glad when they had passed through the dividing door into their own regions of repose and beauty. She was a little afraid of him, out there in the animal grossness of the back. His bearing also changed, as he smelt the familiar, indefinable odour that pervaded his wife's surroundings, a delicate, refined scent, very faintly spicy. Perhaps it came from the pot-pourri bowls.

He stood at the foot of the stairs, arrested, listening. She watched him, and her heart sickened. He seemed to be listening to fate.

"He's not here yet," he said. "I'll go up and change."

"Maurice," she said, "you're not wishing he wouldn't come, are you?"

"I couldn't quite say," he answered. "I feel myself rather on the *qui vive*."

"I can see you are," she answered. And she reached up and kissed his cheek. She saw his mouth relax into a slow smile.

"What are you laughing at?" she said roguishly.

"You consoling me," he answered.

"Nay," she answered. "Why should I console you? You know we love each other—you know *how* married we are! What does anything else matter?"

"Nothing at all, my dear."

He felt for her face, and touched it, smiling.

"*You're* all right, aren't you?" he asked, anxiously.

"I'm wonderfully all right, love," she answered. "It's you I am a little troubled about, at times."

"Why me?" he said, touching her cheeks delicately with the tips of his fingers. The touch had an almost hypnotising effect on her.

He went away upstairs. She saw him mount into the darkness, unseeing and unchanging. He did not know that the lamps on the upper corridor were unlighted. He went on into the darkness with unchanging step. She heard him in the bathroom.

Pervin moved about almost unconsciously in his familiar surroundings, dark though everything was. He seemed to know the presence of objects before he touched them. It was a pleasure to him to rock thus through a world of things, carried on the flood in a sort of blood-prescience. He did not think much or trouble much. So long as he kept this sheer immediacy of blood-contact with the substantial world he was happy, he wanted no intervention of visual consciousness. In this state there was a certain rich positivity, bordering sometimes on rapture. Life seemed to move in him like a tide lapping, lapping, and advancing, enveloping all things darkly. It was a pleasure to stretch forth the hand and meet the unseen object, clasp it, and possess it in pure contact. He did not try to remember, to visualise. He did not want to. The new way of consciousness substituted itself in him.

The rich suffusion of this state generally kept him happy, reaching its culmination in the consuming passion for his wife. But at times the flow would seem to be checked and thrown back. Then it would beat inside him like a tangled sea, and he was tortured in the shattered chaos of his own blood. He grew to dread this arrest, this throw-back, this chaos inside himself, when he seemed merely at the mercy of his own powerful and conflicting elements. How to get some measure of control or surety, this was the question. And when the question rose maddening in him, he would clench his fists as if he would *compel* the whole universe to submit to him. But it was in vain. He could not even compel himself.

To-night, however, he was still serene, though little tremors of unreasonable exasperation ran through him. He had to handle the razor very carefully, as he shaved, for it was not at one with him, he was afraid of it. His hearing also was too much sharpened. He heard the woman lighting the lamps on the corridor, and attending to the fire in the visitor's room. And then, as he went to his room he heard the trap arrive. Then came Isabel's voice, lifted and calling, like a bell ringing:

"Is it you, Bertie? Have you come?"

And a man's voice answered out of the wind:

"Hello, Isabel! There you are."

"Have you had a miserable drive? I'm so sorry we couldn't send a closed carriage. I can't see you at all, you know."

"I'm coming. No, I liked the drive—it was like Perthshire. Well, how are you? You're looking fit as ever, as far as I can see."

"Oh, yes," said Isabel. "I'm wonderfully well. How are you? Rather thin, I think——"

"Worked to death—everybody's old cry. But I'm all right, Ciss. How's Pervin?—isn't he here?"

"Oh, yes, he's upstairs changing. Yes, he's awfully well. Take off your wet things; I'll send them to be dried."

"And how are you both, in spirits? He doesn't fret?"

"No—no, not at all. No, on the contrary, really. We've been wonderfully happy, incredibly. It's more than I can understand—so wonderful: the nearness, and the peace——"

"Ah! Well, that's awfully good news——"

They moved away. Pervin heard no more. But a childish sense of desolation had come over him, as he heard their brisk voices. He seemed shut out—like a child that is left out. He was aimless and excluded, he did not know what to do with himself. The helpless desolation came over him. He fumbled nervously as he dressed himself, in a state almost of childish-

ness. He disliked the Scotch accent in Bertie's speech, and the
slight response it found on Isabel's tongue. He disliked the
slight purr of complacency in the Scottish speech. He disliked
intensely the glib way in which Isabel spoke of their happiness
and nearness. It made him recoil. He was fretful and beside
himself like a child, he had almost a childish nostalgia to be
included in the life circle. And at the same time he was a
man, dark and powerful and infuriated by his own weakness.
By some fatal flaw, he could not be by himself, he had to
depend on the support of another. And this very dependence
enraged him. He hated Bertie Reid, and at the same time he
knew the hatred was nonsense, he knew it was the outcome
of his own weakness.

He went downstairs. Isabel was alone in the dining-room.
She watched him enter, head erect, his feet tentative. He
looked so strong-blooded and healthy, and, at the same time,
cancelled. Cancelled—that was the word that flew across her
mind. Perhaps it was his scars suggested it.

"You heard Bertie come, Maurice?" she said.

"Yes—isn't he here?"

"He's in his room. He looks very thin and worn."

"I suppose he works himself to death."

A woman came in with a tray—and after a few minutes
Bertie came down. He was a little dark man, with a very
big forehead, thin, wispy hair, and sad, large eyes. His expression was inordinately sad—almost funny. He had odd,
short legs

Isabel watched him hesitate under the door, and glance
nervously at her husband. Pervin heard him and turned.

"Here you are, now," said Isabel. "Come, let us eat."

Bertie went across to Maurice.

"How are you, Pervin?" he said, as he advanced.

The blind man stuck his hand out into space, and Bertie
took it.

"Very fit. Glad you've come," said Maurice.

Isabel glanced at them, and glanced away, as if she could
not bear to see them.

"Come," she said. "Come to table. Aren't you both awfully
hungry? I am, tremendously."

"I'm afraid you waited for me," said Bertie, as they sat
down.

Maurice had a curious monolithic way of sitting in a chair,

erect and distant. Isabel's heart always beat when she caught
sight of him thus.

"No," she replied to Bertie. "We're very little later than
usual. We're having a sort of high tea, not dinner. Do you
mind? It gives us such a nice long evening uninterrupted."

"I like it," said Bertie.

Maurice was feeling, with curious little movements, almost
like a cat kneading her bed, for his place, his knife and fork,
his napkin. He was getting the whole geography of his cover
into his consciousness. He sat erect and inscrutable, remote-
seeming. Bertie watched the static figure of the blind man, the
delicate tactile discernment of the large, ruddy hands, and the
curious mindless silence of the brow, above the scar. With
difficulty he looked away, and without knowing what he did,
picked up a little crystal bowl of violets from the table, and
held them to his nose.

"They are sweet-scented," he said. "Where do they come
from?"

"From the garden—under the windows," said Isabel.

"So late in the year—and so fragrant! Do you remember
the violets under Aunt Bell's south wall?"

The two friends looked at each other and exchanged a smile,
Isabel's eyes lighting up.

"Don't I?" she replied. "*Wasn't* she queer!"

"A curious old girl," laughed Bertie. "There's a streak of
freakishness in the family, Isabel."

"Ah—but not in you and me, Bertie," said Isabel. "Give
them to Maurice, will you?" she added, as Bertie was putting
down the flowers. "Have you smelled the violets, dear? Do!—
they are so scented."

Maurice held out his hand, and Bertice placed the tiny bowl
against his large, warm-looking fingers. Maurice's hand closed
over the thin white fingers of the barrister. Bertie carefully
extricated himself. Then the two watched the blind man smelling the violets. He bent his head and seemed to be thinking.
Isabel waited.

"Aren't they sweet, Maurice?" she said at last, anxiously.

"Very," he said. And he held out the bowl. Bertie took it.
Both he and Isabel were a little afraid, and deeply disturbed.

The meal continued. Isabel and Bertie chatted spasmodically. The blind man was silent. He touched his food repeatedly,
with quick, delicate touches of his knife-point, then cut

irregular bits. He could not bear to be helped. Both Isabel and Bertie suffered: Isabel wondered why. She did not suffer when she was alone with Maurice. Bertie made her conscious of a strangeness.

After the meal the three drew their chairs to the fire, and sat down to talk. The decanters were put on a table near at hand. Isabel knocked the logs on the fire, and clouds of brilliant sparks went up the chimney. Bertie noticed a slight weariness in her bearing.

"You will be glad when your child comes now, Isabel?" he said.

She looked up to him with a quick wan smile.

"Yes, I shall be glad," she answered. "It begins to seem long. Yes, I shall be very glad. So will you, Maurice, won't you?" she added.

"Yes, I shall," replied her husband.

"We are both looking forward so much to having it," she said.

"Yes, of course," said Bertie.

He was a bachelor, three or four years older than Isabel. He lived in beautiful rooms overlooking the river, guarded by a faithful Scottish manservant. And he had his friends among the fair sex—not lovers, friends. So long as he could avoid any danger of courtship or marriage, he adored a few good women with constant and unfailing homage, and he was chivalrously fond of quite a number. But if they seemed to encroach on him, he withdrew and detested them.

Isabel knew him very well, knew his beautiful constancy, and kindness, also his incurable weakness, which made him unable ever to enter into close contact of any sort. He was ashamed of himself, because he could not marry, could not approach women physically. He wanted to do so. But he could not. At the centre of him he was afraid, helplessly and even brutally afraid. He had given up hope, had ceased to expect any more that he could escape his own weakness. Hence he was a brilliant and successful barrister, also *littérateur* of high repute, a rich man, and a great social success. At the centre he felt himself neuter, nothing.

Isabel knew him well. She despised him even while she admired him. She looked at his sad face, his little short legs, and felt contempt of him. She looked at his dark grey eyes, with their uncanny, almost child-like intuition, and she loved him. He understood amazingly—but she had no fear of his understanding. As a man she patronised him.

And she turned to the impassive, silent figure of her husband. He sat leaning back, with folded arms, and face a little up-tilted. His knees were straight and massive. She sighed, picked up the poker, and again began to prod the fire, to rouse the clouds of soft, brilliant sparks.

"Isabel tells me," Bertie began suddenly, "that you have not suffered unbearably from the loss of sight."

Maurice straightened himself to attend, but kept his arms folded.

"No," he said, "not unbearably. Now and again one struggles against it, you know. But there are compensations."

"They say it is much worse to be stone deaf," said Isabel.

"I believe it is," said Bertie. "Are there compensations?" he added, to Maurice.

"Yes. You cease to bother about a great many things." Again Maurice stretched his figure, stretched the strong muscles of his back, and leaned backwards, with uplifted face.

"And that is a relief," said Bertie. "But what is there in place of the bothering? What replaces the activity?"

There was a pause. At length the blind man replied, as out of a negligent, unattentive thinking:

"Oh, I don't know. There's a good deal when you're not active."

"Is there?" said Bertie. "What, exactly? It always seems to me that when there is no thought and no action, there is nothing."

Again Maurice was slow in replying.

"There is something," he replied. "I couldn't tell you what it is."

And the talk lapsed once more, Isabel and Bertie chatting gossip and reminiscence, the blind man silent.

At length Maurice rose restlessly, a big, obtrusive figure. He felt tight and hampered. He wanted to go away.

"Do you mind," he said, "if I go and speak to Wernham?"

"No—go along, dear," said Isabel.

And he went out. A silence came over the two friends. At length Bertie said:

"Nevertheless, it is a great deprivation, Cissie."

"It is, Bertie. I know it is."

"Something lacking all the time," said Bertie.

"Yes, I know. And yet—and yet—Maurice is right. There is something else, something *there*, which you never knew was there, and which you can't express."

"What is there?" asked Bertie.

"I don't know—it's awfully hard to define it—but something strong and immediate. There's something strange in Maurice's presence—indefinable—but I couldn't do without it. I agree that it seems to put one's mind to sleep. But when we're alone I miss nothing; it seems awfully rich, almost splendid, you know."

"I'm afraid I don't follow," said Bertie.

They talked desultorily. The wind blew loudly outside, rain chattered on the window-panes, making a sharp drum-sound, because of the closed, mellow-golden shutters inside. The logs burned slowly, with hot, almost invisible small flames. Bertie seemed uneasy, there were dark circles round his eyes. Isabel, rich with her approaching maternity, leaned looking into the fire. Her hair curled in odd, loose strands, very pleasing to the man. But she had a curious feeling of old woe in her heart, old, timeless night-woe.

"I suppose we're all deficient somewhere," said Bertie.

"I suppose so," said Isabel wearily.

"Damned, sooner or later."

"I don't know," she said, rousing herself. "I feel quite all right, you know. The child coming seems to make me indifferent to everything, just placid. I can't feel that there's anything to trouble about, you know."

"A good thing, I should say," he replied slowly.

"Well, there it is. I suppose it's just Nature. If only I felt I needn't trouble about Maurice, I should be perfectly content——"

"But you feel you must trouble about him?"

"Well—I don't know——" She even resented this much effort.

The evening passed slowly. Isabel looked at the clock. "I say," she said. "It's nearly ten o'clock. Where can Maurice be? I'm sure they're all in bed at the back. Excuse me a moment."

She went out, returning almost immediately.

"It's all shut up and in darkness," she said. "I wonder where he is. He must have gone out to the farm——"

Bertie looked at her.

"I suppose he'll come in," he said.

"I suppose so," she said. "But it's unusual for him to be out now."

"Would you like me to go out and see?"

"Well—if you wouldn't mind. I'd go, but——" She did not want to make the physical effort.

Bertie put on an old overcoat and took a lantern. He went out from the side door. He shrank from the wet and roaring night. Such weather had a nervous effect on him: too much moisture everywhere made him feel almost imbecile. Unwilling, he went through it all. A dog barked violently at him. He peered in all the buildings. At last, as he opened the upper door of a sort of intermediate barn, he heard a grinding noise, and looking in, holding up his lantern, saw Maurice, in his shirt-sleeves, standing listening, holding the handle of a turnip-pulper. He had been pulping sweet roots, a pile of which lay dimly heaped in a corner behind him.

"That you, Wernham?" said Maurice, listening.

"No, it's me," said Bertie.

A large, half-wild grey cat was rubbing at Maurice's leg. The blind man stooped to rub its sides. Bertie watched the scene, then unconsciously entered and shut the door behind him. He was in a high sort of barn-place, from which, right and left, ran off the corridors in front of the stalled cattle. He watched the slow, stooping motion of the other man, as he caressed the great cat.

Maurice straightened himself.

"You came to look for me?" he said.

"Isabel was a little uneasy," said Bertie.

"I'll come in. I like messing about doing these jobs."

The cat had reared her sinister, feline length against his leg, clawing at his thigh affectionately. He lifted her claws out of his flesh.

"I hope I'm not in your way at all at the Grange here," said Bertie, rather shy and stiff.

"My way? No, not a bit. I'm glad Isabel has somebody to talk to. I'm afraid it's I who am in the way. I know I'm not very lively company. Isabel's all right, don't you think? She's not unhappy, is she?"

"I don't think so."

"What does she say?"

"She says she's very content—only a little troubled about you."

"Why me?"

"Perhaps afraid that you might brood," said Bertie cautiously.

"She needn't be afraid of that." He continued to caress the flattened grey head of the cat with his fingers. "What I am a bit afraid of," he resumed, "is that she'll find me a dead weight, always alone with me down here."

"I don't think you need think that," said Bertie, though this was what he feared himself.

"I don't know," said Maurice. "Sometimes I feel it isn't fair that she's saddled with me." Then he dropped his voice curiously. "I say," he asked, secretly struggling, "is my face much disfigured? Do you mind telling me?"

"There is the scar," said Bertie, wondering. "Yes, it is a disfigurement. But more pitiable than shocking."

"A pretty bad scar, though," said Maurice.

"Oh yes."

There was a pause.

"Sometimes I feel I am horrible," said Maurice, in a low voice, talking as if to himself. And Bertie actually felt a quiver of horror.

"That's nonsense," he said.

Maurice again straightened himself, leaving the cat.

"There's no telling," he said. Then again, in an odd tone, he added: "I don't really know you, do I?"

"Probably not," said Bertie.

"Do you mind if I touch you?"

The lawyer shrank away instinctively. And yet, out of very philanthropy, he said, in a small voice: "Not at all."

But he suffered as the blind man stretched out a strong, naked hand to him. Maurice accidentally knocked off Bertie's hat.

"I thought you were taller," he said, starting. Then he laid his hand on Bertie Reid's head, closing the dome of the skull in a soft, firm grasp, gathering it, as it were; then, shifting his grasp and softly closing again, with a fine, close pressure, till he had covered the skull and the face of the smaller man, tracing the brows, and touching the full, closed eyes, touching the small nose and the nostrils, the rough, short moustache, the mouth, the rather strong chin. The hand of the blind man grasped the shoulder, the arm, the hand of the other man. He seemed to take him, in the soft, travelling grasp.

"You seem young," he said quietly, at last.

The lawyer stood almost annihilated, unable to answer.

"Your head seems tender, as if you were young," Maurice repeated. "So do your hands. Touch my eyes, will you?— touch my scar."

Now Bertie quivered with revulsion. Yet he was under the power of the blind man, as if hypnotised. He lifted his hand, and laid the fingers on the scar, on the scarred eyes. Maurice suddenly covered them with his own hand, pressed the fingers of the other man upon his disfigured eye-sockets, trembling in every fibre, and rocking slightly, slowly, from side to side. He remained thus for a minute or more, whilst Bertie stood as if in a swoon, unconscious, imprisoned.

Then suddenly Maurice removed the hand of the other man from his brow, and stood holding it in his own.

"Oh, my God," he said, "we shall know each other now, shan't we? We shall know each other now."

Bertie could not answer. He gazed mute and terror-struck, overcome by his own weakness. He knew he could not answer. He had an unreasonable fear, lest the other man should suddenly destroy him. Whereas Maurice was actually filled with hot, poignant love, the passion of friendship. Perhaps it was this very passion of friendship which Bertie shrank from most.

"We're all right together now, aren't we?" said Maurice. "It's all right now, as long as we live, so far as we're concerned."

"Yes," said Bertie, trying by any means to escape.

Maurice stood with head lifted, as if listening. The new delicate fulfilment of mortal friendship had come as a revelation and surprise to him, something exquisite and unhoped-for. He seemed to be listening to hear if it were real.

Then he turned for his coat.

"Come," he said, "we'll go to Isabel."

Bertie took the lantern and opened the door. The cat disappeared. The two men went in silence along the causeways. Isabel, as they came, thought their footsteps sounded strange. She looked up pathetically and anxiously for their entrance. There seemed a curious elation about Maurice. Bertie was haggard, with sunken eyes.

"What is it?" she asked.

"We've become friends," said Maurice, standing with his feet apart, like a strange colossus.

"Friends!" re-echoed Isabel. And she looked again at Bertie. He met her eyes with a furtive, haggard look; his eyes were as if glazed with misery.

"I'm so glad," she said, in sheer perplexity.

"Yes," said Maurice.

He was indeed so glad. Isabel took his hand with both hers, and held it fast.

"You'll be happier now, dear," she said.

But she was watching Bertie. She knew that he had one desire—to escape from this intimacy, this friendship, which had been thrust upon him. He could not bear it that he had been touched by the blind man, his insane reserve broken in. He was like a mollusc whose shell is broken.

MONKEY NUTS

At first Joe thought the job O.K. He was loading hay on the trucks, along with Albert, the corporal. The two men were pleasantly billeted in a cottage not far from the station: they were their own masters, for Joe never thought of Albert as a master. And the little sidings of the tiny village station was as pleasant a place as you could wish for. On one side, beyond the line, stretched the woods: on the other, the near side, across a green smooth field, red houses were dotted among flowering apple trees. The weather being sunny, work being easy, Albert, a real good pal, what life could be better! After Flanders, it was heaven itself.

Albert, the corporal, was a clean-shaven, shrewd-looking fellow of about forty. He seemed to think his one aim in life was to be full of fun and nonsense. In repose, his face looked a little withered, old. He was a very good pal to Joe, steady decent and grave under all his 'mischief'; for his mischief was only his laborious way of skirting his own ennui.

Joe was much younger than Albert—only twenty-three. He was a tallish, quiet youth, pleasant-looking. He was of a slightly better class than his corporal, more personable. Careful about his appearance, he shaved every day. "I haven't got much of a face," said Albert. "If I was to shave every day like you, Joe, I should have none."

There was plenty of life in the little goods-yard: three porter youths, a continual come and go of farm wagons bringing hay, wagons with timber from the woods, coal-carts loading at the trucks. The black coal seemed to make the place sleepier, hotter. Round the big white gate the station-master's children played and his white chickens walked, whilst the station-master himself, a young man getting too fat, helped his wife to peg out the washing on the clothes-line in the meadow.

The great boat-shaped wagons came up from Playcross with the hay. At first the farm-men wagoned it. On the third day one of the land-girls appeared with the first load, drawing to a standstill easily at the head of her two great horses. She was a buxom girl, young, in linen overalls and gaiters. Her face was ruddy, she had large blue eyes.

"Now that's the wagoner for us, boys," said the corporal loudly.

"Whoa!" she said to her horses; and then to the corporal: "Which boys do you mean?"

"We are the pick of the bunch. That's Joe, my pal. Don't you let on that my name's Albert," said the corporal to his private. "I'm the corporal."

"And I'm Miss Stokes," said the land-girl coolly, "if that's all the boys you are."

"You know you couldn't want more, Miss Stokes," said Albert politely. Joe, who was bare-headed, whose grey flannel sleeves were rolled up to the elbow, and whose shirt was open at the breast, looked modestly aside as if he had no part in the affair.

"Are you on this job regular then?" said the corporal to Miss Stokes.

"I don't know for sure," she said, pushing a piece of hair under her hat, and attending to her splendid horses.

"Oh, make it a certainty," said Albert.

She did not reply. She turned and looked over the two men coolly. She was pretty, moderately blonde, with crisp hair, a good skin, and large blue eyes. She was strong, too, and the work went on leisurely and easily.

"Now!" said the corporal, stopping as usual to look round, "pleasant company makes work a pleasure—don't hurry it, boys." He stood on the truck surveying the world. That was one of his great and absorbing occupations: to stand and look out on things in general. Joe, also standing on the truck, also turned round to look what was to be seen. But he could not become blankly absorbed, as Albert could.

Miss Stokes watched the two men from under her broad felt hat. She had seen hundreds of Alberts, khaki soldiers standing in loose attitudes, absorbed in watching nothing in particular. She had seen also a good many Joes, quiet, good-looking young soldiers with half-averted faces. But there was something in the turn of Joe's head, and something in his quiet, tender-looking form, young and fresh—which attracted her eye. As she watched him closely from below, he turned as if he felt her, and his dark-blue eye met her straight, light-blue gaze. He faltered and turned aside again and looked as if he were going to fall off the truck. A slight flush mounted under the girl's full, ruddy face. She liked him.

Always, after this, when she came into the sidings with her team, it was Joe she looked for. She acknowledged to herself that she was sweet on him. But Albert did all the talking. He was so full of fun and nonsense. Joe was a very shy bird, very brief and remote in his answers. Miss Stokes was driven to indulge in repartee with Albert, but she fixed her magnetic attention on the younger fellow. Joe would talk with Albert, and laugh at his jokes. But Miss Stokes could get little out of him. She had to depend on her silent forces. They were more effective than might be imagined.

Suddenly, on Saturday afternoon, at about two o'clock, Joe received a bolt from the blue—a telegram: "Meet me Belbury Station 6.00 p.m. to-day. M.S." He knew at once who M.S. was. His heart melted, he felt weak as if he had had a blow.

"What's the trouble, boy?" asked Albert anxiously.

"No—no trouble—it's to meet somebody." Joe lifted his dark, blue eyes in confusion towards his corporal.

"Meet somebody!" repeated the corporal, watching his young pal with keen blue eyes. "It's all right, then; nothing wrong?"

"No—nothing wrong. I'm not going," said Joe.

Albert was old and shrewd enough to see that nothing more should be said before the housewife. He also saw that Joe did not want to take him into confidence. So he held his peace, though he was piqued.

The two soldiers went into town, smartened up. Albert knew a fair number of the boys round about; there would be plenty of gossip in the market-place, plenty of lounging in groups on the Bath Road, watching the Saturday evening shoppers. Then a modest drink or two, and the movies. They passed an agreeable, casual, nothing-in-particular evening, with which Joe was quite satisfied. He thought of Belbury Station, and of M.S. waiting there. He had not the faintest intention of meeting her. And he had not the faintest intention of telling Albert.

And yet, when the two men were in their bedroom, half undressed, Joe suddenly held out the telegram to his corporal, saying: "What d'you think of that?"

Albert was just unbuttoning his braces. He desisted, took the telegram form, and turned towards the candle to read it.

"Meet me Belbury Station 6.00 p.m. to-day. M.S.," he read, *sotto voce.* His face took on its fun-and-nonsense look.

"Who's M.S.?" he asked, looking shrewdly at Joe.

"You know as well as I do," said Joe, non-committal.

"*M.S.,*" repeated Albert. "Blamed if I know, boy. Is it a woman?"

The conversation was carried on in tiny voices, for fear of disturbing the householders.

"I don't know," said Joe, turning. He looked full at Albert, the two men looked straight into each other's eyes. There was a lurking grin in each of them.

"Well, I'm—*blamed!*" said Albert at last, throwing the telegram down emphatically on the bed.

"Wha—at?" said Joe, grinning rather sheepishly, his eyes clouded, none the less.

Albert sat on the bed and proceeded to undress, nodding his head with mock gravity all the while. Joe watched him foolishly.

"What?" he repeated faintly.

Albert looked up at him with a knowing look.

"If that isn't coming it quick, boy!" he said. "What the blazes! What ha' you bin doing?"

"Nothing!" said Joe.

Albert slowly shook his head as he sat on the side of the bed.

"Don't happen to me when *I've* bin doin' nothing," he said. And he proceeded to pull off his stockings.

Joe turned away, looking at himself in the mirror as he unbuttoned his tunic.

"You didn't want to keep the appointment?" Albert asked, in a changed voice, from the bedside.

Joe did not answer for a moment. Then he said:

"I made no appointment."

"I'm not saying you did, boy. Don't be nasty about it. I mean you didn't want to answer the—unknown person's summons—shall I put it that way?"

"No," said Joe.

"What was the deterring motive?" asked Albert, who was now lying on his back in bed.

"Oh," said Joe, suddenly looking round rather haughtily. "I didn't want to." He had a well-balanced head, and could take on a sudden distant bearing.

"Didn't want to—didn't cotton on, like. Well—*they be art-*

ful, the women——" he mimicked his landlord. "Come on into bed, boy. Don't loiter about as if you'd lost something."

Albert turned over, to sleep.

On Monday Miss Stokes turned up as usual, striding beside her team. Her 'whoa!' was resonant and challenging, she looked up at the truck as her steeds came to a standstill. Joe had turned aside, and had his face averted from her. She glanced him over—save for his slender succulent tenderness she would have despised him. She sized him up in a steady look. Then she turned to Albert, who was looking down at her and smiling in his mischievous turn. She knew his aspects by now. She looked straight back at him, though her eyes were hot. He saluted her.

"Beautiful morning, Miss Stokes."

"Very!" she replied.

"Handsome is as handsome looks," said Albert.

Which produced no response.

"Now, Joe, come on here," said the corporal. "Don't keep the ladies waiting—it's the sign of a weak heart."

Joe turned and the work began. Nothing more was said for the time being. As the week went on all parties became more comfortable. Joe remained silent, averted, neutral, a little on his dignity. Miss Stokes was off-hand and masterful. Albert was full of mischief,

The great theme was a circus, which was coming to the market town on the following Saturday.

"You'll go to the circus, Miss Stokes?" said Albert.

"I may go. Are you going?"

"Certainly. Give us the pleasure of escorting you."

"No, thanks."

"That's what I call a flat refusal—what, Joe? You don't mean that you have no liking for our company, Miss Stokes?"

"Oh, I don't know," said Miss Stokes. "How many are there of you?"

"Only me and Joe."

"Oh, is that all?" she said satirically.

Albert was a little nonplussed.

"Isn't that enough for you?" he asked.

"Too many by half," blurted out Joe, jeeringly, in a sudden fit of uncouth rudeness that made both the others stare.

"Oh, I'll stand out of the way, boy, if that's it," said Albert to Joe. Then he turned mischievously to Miss Stokes. "He wants to know what M. stands for," he said confidentially.

"Monkeys," she replied, turning to her horses.

"What's M.S.?" said Albert.

"Monkey-nuts," she retorted, leading off her team.

Albert looked after her a little discomfited. Joe had flushed dark, and cursed Albert in his heart.

On the Saturday afternoon the two soldiers took the train into town. They would have to walk home. They had tea at six o'clock, and lounged about till half-past seven. The circus was in a meadow near the river—a great red-and-white striped tent. Caravans stood at the side. A great crowd of people was gathered round the ticket-caravan.

Inside the tent the lamps were lighted, shining on a ring of faces, a great circular bank of faces round the green grassy centre. Along with some comrades, the two soldiers packed themselves on a thin plank seat, rather high. They were delighted with the flaring lights, the wild effect. But the circus performance did not affect them deeply. They admired the lady in black velvet with rose-purple legs who leapt so neatly on to the galloping horse; they watched the feats of strength, and laughed at the clown. But they felt a little patronising, they missed the sensational drama of the cinema.

Half-way through the performance Joe was electrified to see the face of Miss Stokes not very far from him. There she was, in her khaki and her felt hat, as usual; he pretended not to see her. She was laughing at the clown; she also pretended not to see him. It was a blow to him, and it made him angry. He would not even mention it to Albert. Least said, soonest mended. He liked to believe she had not seen him. But he knew, fatally, that she had.

When they came out it was nearly eleven o'clock; a lovely night, with a moon and tall, dark, noble trees: a magnificent May night. Joe and Albert laughed and chaffed with the boys. Joe looked round frequently to see if he were safe from Miss Stokes. It seemed so.

But there were six miles to walk home. At last the two soldiers set off, swinging their canes. The road was white between tall hedges, other stragglers were passing out of the town towards the villages; the air was full of pleased excitement.

They were drawing near to the village when they saw a dark figure ahead. Joe's heart sank with pure fear. It was a figure wheeling a bicycle; a land-girl; Miss Stokes. Albert was ready with his nonsense. Miss Stokes had a puncture.

"Let me wheel the rattler," said Albert.

"Thank you," said Miss Stokes. "You *are* kind."

"Oh, I'd be kinder than that, if you'd show me how," said Albert.

"Are you sure?" said Miss Stokes.

"Doubt my words?" said Albert. "That's cruel of you, Miss Stokes."

Miss Stokes walked between them, close to Joe.

"Have you been to the circus?" she asked him.

"Yes," he replied mildly.

"Have *you* been?" Albert asked her.

"Yes. I didn't see you," she replied.

"What!—you say so! Didn't see us! Didn't think us worth looking at," began Albert. "Aren't I as handsome as the clown, now? And you didn't as much as glance in our direction? I call it a downright oversight."

"I never *saw* you," reiterated Miss Stokes. "I didn't know you saw me."

"That makes it worse," said Albert.

The road passed through a belt of dark pine-wood. The village, and the branch road, was very near. Miss Stokes put out her fingers and felt for Joe's hand as it swung at his side. To say he was staggered is to put it mildly. Yet he allowed her softly to clasp his fingers for a few moments. But he was a mortified youth.

At the cross-road they stopped—Miss Stokes should turn off. She had another mile to go.

"You'll let us see you home," said Albert.

"Do me a kindness," she said. "Put my bike in your shed, and take it to Baker's on Monday, will you?"

"I'll sit up all night and mend it for you, if you like."

"No, thanks. And Joe and I'll walk on."

"Oh—ho! Oh—ho!" sang Albert. "Joe! Joe! What do you say to that, boy? Aren't you in luck's way? And I get the bloomin' old bike for my pal. Consider it again, Miss Stokes."

Joe turned aside his face, and did not speak.

"Oh, well! I wheel the grid, do I? I leave you, boy——"

"I'm not keen on going any farther," barked out Joe, in an uncouth voice. "She bain't my choice."

The girl stood silent, and watched the two men.

"There now!" said Albert. "Think o' that! If it was *me* now——" But he was uncomfortable. "Well, Miss Stokes, have me," he added.

Miss Stokes stood quite still, neither moved nor spoke. And so the three remained for some time at the lane end. At last Joe began kicking the ground—then he suddenly lifted his face. At that moment Miss Stokes was at his side. She put her arm delicately round his waist.

"Seems I'm the one extra, don't you think?" Albert inquired of the high bland moon.

Joe had dropped his head and did not answer. Miss Stokes stood with her arm lightly round his waist. Albert bowed, saluted, and bade good night. He walked away, leaving the two standing.

Miss Stokes put a light pressure on Joe's waist, and drew him down the road. They walked in silence. The night was full of scent—wild cherry, the first bluebells. Still they walked in silence. A nightingale was singing. They approached nearer and nearer, till they stood close by his dark bush. The powerful notes sounded from the cover, almost like flashes of light— then the interval of silence—then the moaning notes, almost like a dog faintly howling, followed by the long, rich trill, and flashing notes. Then a short silence again.

Miss Stokes turned at last to Joe. She looked up at him, and in the moonlight he saw her faintly smiling. He felt maddened, but helpless. Her arm was round his waist, she drew him closely to her with a soft pressure that made all his bones rotten.

Meanwhile Albert was waiting at home. He put on his overcoat, for the fire was out, and he had had malarial fever. He looked fitfully at the *Daily Mirror* and the *Daily Sketch*, but he saw nothing. It seemed a long time. He began to yawn widely, even to nod. At last Joe came in.

Albert looked at him keenly. The young man's brow was black, his face sullen.

"All right, boy?" asked Albert.

Joe merely grunted for a reply. There was nothing more to be got out of him. So they went to bed.

Next day Joe was silent, sullen. Albert could make nothing of him. He proposed a walk after tea.

"I'm going somewhere." said Joe.

"Where—Monkey-nuts?" asked the corporal. But Joe's brow only became darker.

So the days went by. Almost every evening Joe went off alone, returning late. He was sullen, taciturn and had a hang-dog look, a curious way of dropping his head and looking dangerously from under his brows. And he and Albert did not get on so well any more with one another. For all his fun and nonsense, Albert was really irritable, soon made angry. And Joe's stand-offish sulkiness and complete lack of confidence riled him, got on his nerves. His fun and nonsense took a biting, sarcastic turn, at which Joe's eyes glittered occasionally, though the young man turned unheeding aside. Then again Joe would be full of odd, whimsical fun, out-shining Albert himself.

Miss Stokes still came to the station with the wain: Monkey-nuts, Albert called her, though not to her face. For she was very clear and good-looking, almost she seemed to gleam. And Albert was a tiny bit afraid of her. She very rarely addressed Joe whilst the hay-loading was going on, and that young man always turned his back to her. He seemed thinner, and his limber figure looked more slouching. But still it had the tender, attractive appearance, especially from behind. His tanned face, a little thinned and darkened, took a handsome, slightly sinister look.

"Come on, Joe!" the corporal urged sharply one day. "What're you doing, boy? Looking for beetles on the bank?"

Joe turned round swiftly, almost menacing, to work.

"He's a different fellow these days, Miss Stokes," said Albert to the young woman. "What's got him? Is it Monkey-nuts that don't suit him, do you think?"

"Choked with chaff, more like," she retorted. "It's as bad as feeding a threshing machine, to have to listen to some folks."

"As bad as what?" said Albert. "You don't mean *me*, do you, Miss Stokes?"

"No," she cried. "I don't mean you."

Joe's face became dark red during these sallies, but he said nothing. He would eye the young woman curiously, as she swung so easily at the work, and he had some of the look of a dog which is going to bite.

Albert, with his nerves on edge, began to find the strain rather severe. The next Saturday evening, when Joe came in more black-browed than ever, he watched him, determined to have it out with him.

When the boy went upstairs to bed, the corporal followed him. He closed the door behind him carefully, sat on the bed and watched the younger man undressing. And for once he spoke in a natural voice, neither chaffing nor commanding.

"What's gone wrong, boy?"

Joe stopped a moment as if he had been shot. Then he went on unwinding his puttees, and did not answer or look up.

"You can hear, can't you?" said Albert, nettled.

"Yes, I can hear," said Joe, stooping over his puttees till his face was purple.

"Then why don't you answer?"

Joe sat up. He gave a long, sideways look at the corporal. Then he lifted his eyes and stared at a crack in the ceiling.

The corporal watched these movements shrewdly.

"And *then* what?" he asked ironically.

Again Joe turned and stared him in the face. The corporal smiled very slightly, but kindly.

"There'll be murder done one of these days," said Joe, in a quiet, unimpassioned voice.

"So long as it's by daylight——" replied Albert. Then he went over, sat down by Joe, put his hand on his shoulder affectionately, and continued: "What is it, boy? What's gone wrong? You can trust me, can't you?"

Joe turned and looked curiously at the face so near to his.

"It's nothing, that's all," he said laconically.

Albert frowned.

"Then who's going to be murdered?—and who's going to do the murdering?—me or you—which is it, boy?" He smiled gently at the stupid youth, looking straight at him all the while, into his eyes. Gradually the stupid, hunted, glowering look died out of Joe's eyes. He turned his head aside, gently, as one rousing from a spell.

"I don't want her," he said, with fierce resentment.

"Then you needn't have her," said Albert. "What do you go for, boy?"

But it wasn't as simple as all that. Joe made no remark.

"She's a smart-looking girl. What's wrong with her, my boy? I should have thought you were a lucky chap, myself."

"I don't want 'er," Joe barked, with ferocity and resentment.

"Then tell her so and have done," said Albert. He waited a

while. There was no response. "Why don't you?" he added.

"Because I don't," confessed Joe sulkily.

Albert pondered—rubbed his head.

"You're too soft-hearted, that's where it is, boy. You want your mettle dipping in cold water, to temper it. You're too soft-hearted——"

He laid his arm affectionately across the shoulders of the younger man. Joe seemed to yield a little towards him.

"When are you going to see her again?" Albert asked. For a long time there was no answer.

"When is it, boy?" persisted the softened voice of the corporal.

"To-morrow," confessed Joe.

"Then let me go," said Albert. "Let me go, will you?"

The morrow was Sunday, a sunny day, but a cold evening. The sky was grey, the new foliage very green, but the air was chill and depressing. Albert walked briskly down the white road towards Beeley. He crossed a larch plantation, and followed a narrow by-road, where blue speedwell flowers fell from the banks into the dust. He walked swinging his cane, with mixed sensations. Then having gone a certain length, he turned and began to walk in the opposite direction.

So he saw a young woman approaching him. She was wearing a wide hat of grey straw, and a loose, swinging dress of nigger-grey velvet. She walked with slow inevitability. Albert faltered a little as he approached her. Then he saluted her, and his roguish, slightly withered skin flushed. She was staring straight into his face.

He fell in by her side, saying impudently:

"Not so nice for a walk as it was, is it?"

She only stared at him. He looked back at her.

"You've seen me before, you know," he said, grinning slightly. "Perhaps you never noticed me. Oh, I'm quite nice-looking, in a quiet way, you know. What——?"

But Miss Stokes did not speak: she only stared with large, icy blue eyes at him. He became self-conscious, lifted up his chin, walked with his nose in the air, and whistled at random. So they went down the quiet, deserted grey lane. He was whistling the air: "I'm Gilbert, the filbert, the colonel of the nuts."

At last she found her voice:

"Where's Joe?"

"He thought you'd like a change: they say variety's the salt of life—that's why I'm mostly in pickle."

"Where is he?"

"Am I my brother's keeper? He's gone his own ways."

"Where?"

"Nay, how am I to know? Not so far but he'll be back for supper."

She stopped in the middle of the lane. He stopped facing her.

"Where's Joe?" she asked.

He struck a careless attitude, looked down the road this way and that, lifted his eyebrows, pushed his khaki cap on one side, and answered:

"He is not conducting the service to-night: he asked me if I'd officiate."

"Why hasn't he come?"

"Didn't want to, I expect. *I* wanted to."

She stared him up and down, and he felt uncomfortable in his spine, but maintained his air of nonchalance. Then she turned slowly on her heel, and started to walk back. The corporal went at her side.

"You're not going back, are you?" he pleaded. "Why, me and you, we should get on like a house on fire."

She took no need, but walked on. He went uncomfortably at her side, making his funny remarks from time to time. But she was as if stone deaf. He glanced at her, and to his dismay saw the tears running down her cheeks. He stopped suddenly, and pushed back his cap.

"I say, you know——" he began.

But she was walking on like an automaton, and he had to hurry after her.

She never spoke to him. At the gate of her farm she walked straight in, as if he were not there. He watched her disappear. Then he turned on his heel, cursing silently, puzzled, lifting off his cap to scratch his head.

That night, when they were in bed, he remarked:

"Say, Joe, boy; strikes me you're well off without Monkeynuts. Gord love us, beans ain't in it."

So they slept in amity. But they waited with some anxiety for the morrow.

It was a cold morning, a grey sky shifting in a cold wind, and threatening rain. They watched the wagon come up the road and through the yard gates. Miss Stokes was with her team as usual; her "Whoa!" rang out like a war-whoop.

She faced up at the truck where the two men stood.

"Joe!" she called, to the averted figure which stood up in the wind.

"What?" he turned unwillingly.

She made a queer movement, lifting her head slightly in a sipping, half-inviting, half-commanding gesture. And Joe was crouching already to jump off the truck to obey her, when Albert put his hand on his shoulder.

"Half a minute, boy! Where are you off? Work's work, and nuts is nuts. You stop here."

Joe slowly straightened himself.

"Joe?" came the woman's clear call from below.

Again Joe looked at her. But Albert's hand was on his shoulder, detaining him. He stood half averted, with his tail between his legs.

"Take your hand off him, you!" said Miss Stokes.

"Yes, Major," retorted Albert satirically.

She stood and watched.

"Joe!" Her voice rang for the third time.

Joe turned and looked at her, and a slow, jeering smile gathered on his face.

"Monkey-nuts!" he replied, in a tone mocking her call.

She turned white—dead white. The men thought she would fall. Albert began yelling to the porters up the line to come and help with the load. He could yell like any non-commissioned officer upon occasion.

Some way or other the wagon was unloaded, the girl was gone. Joe and his corporal looked at one another and smiled slowly. But they had a weight on their minds, they were afraid.

They were reassured, however, when they found that Miss Stokes came no more with the hay. As far as they were concerned, she had vanished into oblivion. And Joe felt more relieved even than he had felt when he heard the firing cease, after the news had come that the armistice was signed.

WINTRY PEACOCK

THERE was thin, crisp snow on the ground, the sky was blue, the wind very cold, the air clear. Farmers were just turning out the cows for an hour or so in the midday, and the smell of cowsheds was unendurable as I entered Tible. I noticed the ash-twigs up in the sky were pale and luminous, passing into the blue. And then I saw the peacocks. There they were in the road before me, three of them, and tailless, brown, speckled birds, with dark-blue necks and ragged crests. They stepped archly over the filigree snow, and their bodies moved with slow motion, like small, light, flat-bottomed boats. I admired them, they were curious. Then a gust of wind caught them, heeled them over as if they were three frail boats, opening their feathers like ragged sails. They hopped and skipped with discomfort, to get out of the draught of the wind. And then, in the lee of the walls, they resumed their arch, wintry motion, light and unballasted now their tails were gone, indifferent. They were indifferent to my presence. I might have touched them. They turned off to the shelter of an open shed.

As I passed the end of the upper house, I saw a young woman just coming out of the back door. I had spoken to her in the summer. She recognised me at once, and waved to me. She was carrying a pail, wearing a white apron that was longer than her preposterously short skirt, and she had on the cotton bonnet. I took off my hat to her and was going on. But she put down her pail and darted with a swift, furtive movement after me.

"Do you mind waiting a minute?" she said. "I'll be out in a minute."

She gave me a slight, odd smile, and ran back. Her face was long and sallow and her nose rather red. But her gloomy black eyes softened caressively to me for a moment, with that momentary humility which makes a man lord of the earth.

I stood in the road, looking at the fluffy, dark-red young cattle that mooed and seemed to bark at me. They seemed happy, frisky cattle, a little impudent, and either determined to go back into the warm shed, or determined not to go back. I could not decide which.

Presently the woman came forward again, her head rather ducked. But she looked up at me and smiled, with that odd, immediate intimacy, something witch-like and impossible.

"Sorry to keep you waiting," she said. "Shall we stand in this cart-shed—it will be more out of the wind."

So we stood among the shafts of the open cart-shed that faced the road. Then she looked down at the ground, a little sideways, and I noticed a small black frown on her brows. She seemed to brood for a moment. Then she looked straight into my eyes, so that I blinked and wanted to turn my face aside. She was searching me for something and her look was too near. The frown was still on her keen, sallow brow.

"Can you speak French?" she asked me abruptly.

"More or less," I replied.

"I was supposed to learn it at school," she said. "But I don't know a word." She ducked her head and laughed, with a slightly ugly grimace and a rolling of her black eyes.

"No good keeping your mind full of scraps," I answered.

But she had turned aside her sallow, long face, and did not hear what I said. Suddenly again she looked at me. She was searching. And at the same time she smiled at me, and her eyes looked softly darkly, with infinite trustful humility into mine. I was being cajoled.

"Would you mind reading a letter for me, in French," she said, her face immediately black and bitter-looking. She glanced at me, frowning.

"No at all," I said.

"It's a letter to my husband," she said, still scrutinising.

I looked at her, and didn't quite realise. She looked too far into me, my wits were gone. She glanced round. Then she looked at me shrewdly. She drew a letter from her pocket, and handed it to me. It was addressed from France to Lance-Corporal Goyte, at Tible. I took out the letter and began to read it, as mere words. *Mon chère* Alfred"—it might have been a bit of a torn newspaper. So I followed the script: the trite phrases of a letter from a French-speaking girl to an English soldier. "I think of you always, always. Do you think sometimes of me?" And then I vaguely realised that I was reading a man's private correspondence. And yet, how could one consider these trivial, facile French phrases private! Nothing more trite and vulgar in the world, than such a love-letter—no newspaper more obvious.

Therefore I read with a callous heart the effusions of the Belgian damsel. But then I gathered my attention. For the letter went on: *"Notre chère petit bébé*—our dear little baby was born a week ago. Almost I died, knowing you were far away, and perhaps forgetting the fruit of our perfect love. But the child comforted me. He has the smiling eyes and virile air of his English father. I pray to the Mother of Jesus to send me the dear father of my child, that I may see him with my child in his arms, and that we may be united in holy family love. Ah, my Alfred, can I tell you how I miss you, how I weep for you. My thoughts are with you always, I think of nothing but you, I live for nothing but you and our dear baby. If you do not come back to me soon, I shall die, and our child will die. But no, you cannot come back to me. But I can come to you, come to England with our child. If you do not wish to present me to your good mother and father, you can meet me in some town, some city, for I shall be so frightened to be alone in England with my child, and no one to take care of us. Yet I must come to you, I must bring my child, my little Alfred to his father, the big, beautiful Alfred that I love so much. Oh, write and tell me where I shall come. I have some money, I am not a penniless creature. I have money for myself and my dear baby——"

I read to the end. It was signed: "Your very happy and still more unhappy Elise." I suppose I must have been smiling.

"I can see it makes you laugh," said Mrs. Goyte, sardonically. I looked up at her.

"It's a love-letter, I know that," she said. "There's too many 'Alfreds' in it."

"One too many," I said.

"Oh, yes—— And what does she say—Eliza? We know her name's Eliza, that's another thing." She grimaced a little, looking up at me with a mocking laugh.

"Where did you get this letter?" I said.

"Postman gave it me last week."

"And is your husband at home?"

"I expect him home to-night. He's been wounded, you know, and we've been applying for him home. He was home about six weeks ago— he's been in Scotland since then. Oh, he was wounded in the leg. Yes, he's all right, a great strapping fellow. But he's lame, he limps a bit. He expects he'll get his discharge—but I don't think he will. We married? We've been married six years—and he joined up the first day of the war. Oh, he thought he'd like the life. He's been through the South African War. No, he was sick of it, fed up. I'm living with his father and mother—I've no home of my own now. My people had a big farm—over a thousand acres—in Oxfordshire. Not like here—no. Oh, they're very good to me, his father and mother. Oh, yes, they couldn't be better. They think more of me than of their own daughters. But it's not like being in a place of your own, is it? You can't *really* do as you like. No, there's only me and his father and mother at home. Before the war? Oh, he was anything. He had a good education—but he liked the farming better. Then he was a chauffeur. That's how he knew French. He was driving in France for a long time——"

At this point the peacocks came round the corner on a puff of wind.

"Hello, Joey!" she called, and one of the birds came forward, on delicate legs. Its grey speckled back was very elegant, it rolled its full, dark-blue neck as it moved to her. She crouched down. "Joey, dear," she said, in an odd, saturnine caressive voice, "you're bound to find me, aren't you?" She put her face forward, and the bird rolled his neck, almost touching her face with his beak, as if kissing her.

"He loves you," I said.

She twisted her face up at me with a laugh.

"Yes," she said, "he loves me, Joey does,"—then, to the bird —"and I love Joey, don't I. I *do* love Joey." And she smoothed his feathers for a moment. Then she rose, saying: "He's an affectionate bird."

I smiled at the roll of her "bir-rrd".

"Oh, yes, he is," she protested. "He came with me from my home seven years ago. Those others are his descendants—but they're not like Joey—*are they, dee-urr?*" Her voice rose at the end with a witch-like cry.

Then she forgot the bird in the cart-shed and turned to business again.

"Won't you read that letter?" she said. "Read it, so that I know what it says."

"It's rather behind his back," I said.

"Oh, never mind him," she cried. "He's been behind my back long enough—all these four years. If he never did no worse things behind my back than I do behind his, he wouldn't have cause to grumble. You read me what it says."

Now I felt a distinct reluctance to do as she bid, and yet I began—"My dear Alfred."

"I guessed that much," she said. "Eliza's dear Alfred." She laughed. "How do you say it in French? *Eliza?*"

I told her, and she repeated the name with great contempt—*Elise.*

"Go on," she said. "You're not reading."

So I began—"I have been thinking of you sometimes—have you been thinking of me——?"

"Of several others as well, beside her, I'll wager," said Mrs. Goyte.

"Probably not," said I, and continued. "A dear little baby was born here a week ago. Ah, can I tell you my feelings when I take my darling little brother into my arms——"

"I'll bet it's *his,*" cried Mrs. Goyte.

"No," I said. "It's her mother's."

"Don't you believe it," she cried. "It's a blind. You mark, it's her own right enough—and his."

"No," I said, "it's her mother's." "He has sweet smiling eyes, but not like your beautiful English eyes——"

She suddenly struck her hand on her skirt with a wild motion, and bent down, doubled with laughter. Then she rose and covered her face with her hand.

"I'm forced to laugh at the beautiful English eyes," she said.

"Aren't his eyes beautiful?" I asked.

"Oh, yes—*very!* Go on!—*Joey, dear, dee-urr, Joey!*"—this to the peacock.

—"Er—We miss you very much. We all miss you. We wish you were here to see the darling baby. Ah, Alfred, how happy we were when you stayed with us. We all loved you so much. My mother will call the baby Alfred so that we shall never forget you——"

"Of course it's his right enough," cried Mrs. Goyte.

"No," I said. "It's the mother's." Er—"My mother is very well. My father came home yesterday—on leave. He is delighted with his son, my little brother, and wishes to have him named after you, because you were so good to us all in that terrible time, which I shall never forget. I must weep now when I think of it. Well, you are far away in England, and perhaps I shall never see you again. How did you find your

dear mother and father? I am so happy that your wound is
better, and that you can nearly walk——"

"How did he find his dear *wife*?" cried Mrs. Goyte. "He
never told her he had one. Think of taking the poor girl in
like that!"

"We are so pleased when you write to us. Yet now you are
in England you will forget the family you served so well——"

"A bit too well—eh, *Joey*?" cried the wife.

"If it had not been for you we should not be alive now, to
grieve and to rejoice in this life, that is so hard for us. But
we have recovered some of our losses, and no longer feel the
burden of poverty. The little Alfred is a great comfort to me.
I hold him to my breast and think of the big, good Alfred, and
I weep to think that those times of suffering were perhaps the
times of a great happiness that is gone for ever."

"Oh, but isn't it a shame, to take a poor girl in like that!"
cried Mrs. Goyte. "Never to let on that he was married, and
raise her hopes—I call it beastly, I do."

"You don't know," I said. "You know how anxious women
are to fall in love, wife or no wife. How could he help it, if
she was determined to fall in love with him?"

"He could have helped it if he'd wanted."

"Well," I said, "we aren't all heroes."

"Oh, but that's different! The big, good Alfred!—did ever
you hear such tommy-rot in your life! Go on—what does she
say at the end?"

"Er—We shall be pleased to hear of your life in England.
We all send many kind regards to your good parents. I wish
you all happiness for your future days. Your very affectionate
and ever-grateful, Elise."

There was silence for a moment, during which Mrs. Goyte
remained with her head dropped, sinister and abstracted.
Suddenly she lifted her face, and her eyes flashed.

"Oh, but I call it beastly, I call it mean, to take a girl in
like that."

"Nay," I said. "Probably he hasn't taken her in at all. Do
you think those French girls are such poor innocent things? I
guess she's a great deal more downy than he."

"Oh, he's one of the biggest fools that ever walked," she
cried.

"There you are!" said I.

"But it's his child right enough," she said.

"I don't think so," said I.

"I'm sure of it."

"Oh, well," I said, "if you prefer to think that way."

"What other reason has she for writing like that——?"

I went out into the road and looked at the cattle.

"Who is this driving the cows?" I said. She too came out.

"It's the boy from the next farm," she said.

"Oh, well," said I, "those Belgian girls! You never know where their letters will end. And, after all, it's his affair—you needn't bother."

"Oh——!" she cried with scorn—"it's not *me* that bothers. But it's the nasty meanness of it—me writing him such loving letters"—she put her hand before her face and laughed malevolently—"and sending him parcels all the time. You bet he fed that gurrl on my parcels—I know he did. It's just like him. I'll bet they laughed together over my letters. I'll bet anything they did——"

"Nay," said I. "He'd burn your letters for fear they'd give him away."

There was a black look on her yellow face. Suddenly a voice was heard calling. She poked her head out of the shed, and answered coolly:

"All right!" Then turning to me: "That's his mother looking after me."

She laughed into my face, witch-like, and we turned down the road.

When I awoke, the morning after this episode, I found the house darkened with deep, soft snow, which had blown against the large west windows, covering them with a screen. I went outside, and saw the valley all white and ghastly below me, the trees beneath black and thin-looking like wire, the rock-faces dark between the glistening shroud, and the sky above sombre, heavy, yellowish-dark, much too heavy for this world below of hollow bluey whiteness figured with black. I felt I was in a valley of the dead. And I sensed I was a prisoner, for the snow was everywhere deep, and drifted in places. So all the morning I remained indoors, looking up the drive at the shrubs so heavily plumed with snow, at the gate-posts raised high with a foot or more of extra whiteness. Or I looked down into the white-and-black valley that was utterly motionless and beyond life, a hollow sarcophagus.

Nothing stirred the whole day—no plume fell off the shrubs,

the valley was as abstracted as a grove of death. I looked over
at the tiny, half-buried farms away on the bare uplands beyond
the valley hollow, and I thought of Tible in the snow, of the
black witch-like little Mrs. Goyte. And the snow seemed to
lay me bare to influences I wanted to escape.

In the faint glow of the half-clear light that came about four
o'clock in the afternoon, I was roused to see a motion in the
snow away below, near where the thorn trees stood very black
and dwarfed, like a little savage group, in the dismal white. I
watched closely. Yes, there was a flapping and a struggle—a
big bird, it must be, labouring in the snow. I wondered. Our
biggest birds, in the valley, were the large hawks that often
hung flickering opposite my windows, level with me, but high
above some prey on the steep valley-side. This was much too
big for a hawk—too big for any known bird. I searched in my
mind for the largest English wild bird, geese, buzzards.

Still it laboured and strove, then was still, a dark spot, then
struggled again. I went out of the house and down the steep
slope, at risk of breaking my leg between the rocks. I knew
the ground so well—and yet I got well shaken before I drew
near the thorn trees.

Yes, it was a bird. It was Joey. It was the grey-brown peacock with a blue neck. He was snow-wet and spent.

"Joey—Joey, de-urr!" I said, staggering unevenly towards
him. He looked so pathetic, rowing and struggling in the
snow, too spent to rise, his blue neck stretching out and lying
sometimes on the snow, his eye closing and opening quickly,
his crest all battered.

"Joey dee-urr!" I said caressingly to him. And at last he lay
still, blinking, in the surged and furrowed snow, whilst I came
near and touched him, stroked him, gathering him under my
arm. He stretched his long, wetted neck away from me as I
held him, none the less he was quiet in my arm, too tired,
perhaps, to struggle. Still he held his poor, crested head away
from me, and seemed sometimes to droop, to wilt, as if he
might suddenly die.

He was not so heavy as I expected, yet it was a struggle to
get up to the house with him again. We set him down, not
too near the fire, and gently wiped him with cloths. He submitted, only now and then stretched his soft neck away from
us, avoiding us helplessly. Then we set warm food by him. I
put it to his beak, tried to make him eat. But he ignored it.

He seemed to be ignorant of what we were doing, recoiled inside himself inexplicably. So we put him in a basket with cloths, and left him crouching oblivious. His food we put near him. The blinds were drawn, the house was warm, it was night. Sometimes he stirred, but mostly he huddled still, leaning his queer crested head on one side. He touched no food, and took no heed of sounds or movements. We talked of brandy or stimulants. But I realised we had best leave him alone.

In the night, however, we heard him thumping about. I got up anxiously with a candle. He had eaten some food, and scattered more, making a mess. And he was perched on the back of a heavy arm-chair. So I concluded he was recovered, or recovering.

The next day was clear, and the snow had frozen, so I decided to carry him back to Tible. He consented, after various flappings, to sit in a big fish-bag with his battered head peeping out with wild uneasiness. And so I set off with him slithering down into the valley, making good progress down in the pale shadow beside the rushing waters, then climbing painfully up the arrested white valley-side, plumed with clusters of young pine trees, into the paler white radiance of the snowy, upper regions, where the wind cut fine. Joey seemed to watch all the time with wide, anxious, unseeing eye, brilliant and inscrutable. As I drew near to Tible township he stirred violently in the bag, though I do not know if he recognised the place. Then, as I came to the sheds, he looked sharply from side to side, and stretched his neck out long. I was a little afraid of him. He gave a loud, vehement yell, opening his sinister beak, and I stood still, looking at him as he struggled in the bag, shaken myself by his struggles, yet not thinking to release him.

Mrs. Goyte came darting past the end of the house, her head sticking forward in sharp scrutiny. She saw me, and came forward.

"Have you got Joey!" she cried sharply, as if I were a thief.

I opened the bag, and he flopped out, flapping as if he hated the touch of the snow now. She gathered him up, and put her lips to his beak. She was flushed and handsome, her eyes bright, her hair slack, thick, but more witch-like than ever. She did not speak.

She had been followed by a grey-haired woman with a

E

round, rather sallow face and a slightly hostile bearing.

"Did you bring him with you, then?" she asked sharply. I answered that I had rescued him the previous evening.

From the background slowly approached a slender man with a grey moustache and large patches on his trousers.

"You've got 'im back 'gain, ah see," he said to his daughter-in-law. His wife explained how I had found Joey.

"Ah," went on the grey man. "It wor our Alfred scarred him off, back your life. He must'a flyed ower t'valley. Tha ma' thank thy stars as 'e wor fun, Maggie. 'E'd a bin froze. They a bit nesh, you know," he concluded to me.

"They are," I answered. "This isn't their country."

"No, it isna," replied Mr. Goyte. He spoke very slowly and deliberately, quietly, as if the soft pedal were always down in his voice. He looked at his daughter-in-law as she crouched, flushed and dark, before the peacock, which would lay its long blue neck for a moment along her lap. In spite of his grey moustache and thin grey hair, the elderly man had a face young and almost delicate, like a young man's. His blue eyes twinkled with some inscrutable source of pleasure, his skin was fine and tender, his nose delicately arched. His grey hair being slightly ruffled, he had a debonair look, as of a youth who is in love.

"We mun tell 'im it's come," he said slowly, and turning he called: "Alfred—Alfred! Wheer's ter gotten to?"

Then he turned again to the group.

"Get up then, Maggie, lass, get up wi' thee. Tha ma'es too much o' th' bod."

A young man approached, wearing rough khaki and knee-breeches. He was Danish-looking, broad at the loins.

"I's come back then," said the father to the son; "leastwise, he's bin browt back, flyed ower the Griff Low."

The son looked at me. He had a devil-may-care bearing, his cap on one side, his hands stuck in the front pockets of his breeches. But he said nothing.

"Shall you come in a minute, Master," said the elderly woman, to me.

"Ay, come in an' ha'e a cup o' tea or summat. You'll do wi' summat, carrin' that bod. Come on, Maggie wench, let's go in."

So we went indoors, into the rather stuffy, overcrowded living-room, that was too cosy, and too warm. The son followed last, standing in the doorway. The father talked to me. Maggie put out the tea-cups. The mother went into the dairy again.

"Tha'lt rouse thysen up a bit again, now, Maggie," the father-in-law said—and then to me: "'Ers not bin very bright sin' Alfred come whoam, an' the bod flyed awee. 'E come whoam a Wednesday night, Alfred did. But ay, you knowed, didna yer. Ay, 'e comed 'a Wednesday—an' I reckon there wor a bit of a to-do between 'em worn't there, Maggie?"

He twinkled maliciously to his daughter-in-law, who flushed, brilliant and handsome.

"Oh, be quiet, father. You're wound up, by the sound of you," she said to him, as if crossly. But she could never be cross with him.

"'Ers got 'er colour back this mornin'," continued the father-in-law slowly. "It's bin heavy weather wi' 'er this last two days. Ay—'er's bin north-east sin' 'er seed you a Wednesday."

"Father, do stop talking. You'd wear the leg off an iron pot. I can't think where you've found your tongue, all of a sudden," said Maggie, with caressive sharpness.

"Ah've found it wheer I lost it. Aren't goin' ter come in an' sit thee down, Alfred?"

But Alfred turned and disappeared.

"'E's got th' monkey on 'is back ower this letter job," said the father secretly to me. "Mother, 'er knows nowt about it. Lot o' tom-foolery, isn't it? Ay! What's good o' makkin' a peck o' trouble over what's far enough off, an' ned niver come no nigher. No—not a smite o' use. That's what I tell 'er. 'Er should ta'e no notice on't. Ty, what can y' expect."

The mother came in again, and the talk became general. Maggie flashed her eyes at me from time to time, complacent and satisfied, moving among the men. I paid her little compliments, which she did not seem to hear. She attended to me with a kind of sinister witch-like graciousness, her dark head ducked between her shoulders, at once humble and powerful. She was happy as a child attending to her father-in-law and to me. But there was something ominous between her eyebrows, as if a dark moth were settled there—and something ominous in her bent, hulking bearing.

She sat on a low stool by the fire, near her father-in-law. Her head was dropped, she seemed in a state of abstraction. From time to time she would suddenly recover, and look up

at us, laughing and chatting. Then she would forget again.
Yet in her hulked black forgetting she seemed very near to us.

The door having been opened, the peacock came slowly in,
prancing calmly. He went near to her and crouched down,
coiling his blue neck. She glanced at him, but almost as if she
did not observe him. The bird sat silent, seeming to sleep, and
the woman also sat hulked and silent, seemingly oblivious.
Then once more there was a heavy step, and Alfred entered.
He looked at his wife, and he looked at the peacock crouching
by her. He stood large in the doorway, his hands stuck in
front of him, in his breeches pockets. Nobody spoke. He
turned on his heel and went out again.

I rose also to go. Maggie started as if coming to herself.

"Must you go?" she asked, rising and coming near to me,
standing in front of me, twisting her head sideways and looking up at me. "Can't you stop a bit longer? We can all be
cosy to-day, there's nothing to do outdoors." And she laughed,
showing her teeth oddly. She had a long chin.

I said I must go. The peacock uncoiled and coiled again his
long blue neck, as he lay on the hearth. Maggie still stood close
in front of me, so that I was acutely aware of my waistcoat
buttons.

"Oh, well," she said, "you'll come again, won't you? Do
come again."

I promised.

"Come to tea one day—yes, do!"

I promised—one day.

The moment I went out of her presence I ceased utterly to
exist for her—as utterly as I ceased to exist for Joey. With
her curious abstractedness she forgot me again immediately.
I knew it as I left her. Yet she seemed almost in physical contact with me while I was with her.

The sky was all pallid again, yellowish. When I went out
there was no sun; the snow was blue and cold. I hurried away
down the hill, musing on Maggie. The road made a loop down
the sharp face of the slope. As I went crunching over the
laborious snow I became aware of a figure striding down the
steep scarp to intercept me. It was a man with his hands in
front of him, half stuck in his breeches pockets, and his
shoulders square—a real farmer of the hills; Alfred, of course.
He waited for me by the stone fence.

"Excuse me," he said as I came up.

I came to a halt in front of him and looked into his sullen blue eyes. He had a certain odd haughtiness on his brows. But his blue eyes stared insolently at me.

"Do you know anything about a letter—in French—that my wife opened—a letter of mine——?"

"Yes," said I. "She asked me to read it to her."

He looked square at me. He did not know exactly how to feel.

"What was there in it?" he asked.

"Why?" I said. "Don't you know?"

"She makes out she's burnt it," he said.

"Without showing it you?" I asked.

He nodded slightly. He seemed to be meditating as to what line of action he should take. He wanted to know the contents of the letter: he must know: and therefore he must ask me, for evidently his wife had taunted him. At the same time, no doubt, he would like to wreak untold vengeance on my unfortunate person. So he eyed me, and I eyed him, and neither of us spoke. He did not want to repeat his request to me. And yet I only looked at him, and considered.

Suddenly he threw back his head and glanced down the valley. Then he changed his position—he was a horse-soldier. Then he looked at me more confidentially.

"She burnt the blasted thing before I saw it," he said.

"Well," I answered slowly, "she doesn't know herself what was in it."

He continued to watch me narrowly. I grinned to myself.

"I didn't like to read her out what there was in it," I continued.

He suddenly flushed so that the veins in his neck stood out, and he stirred again uncomfortably.

"The Belgian girl said her baby had been born a week ago, and that they were going to call it Alfred," I told him.

He met my eyes. I was grinning. He began to grin, too.

"Good luck to her," he said.

"Best of luck," said I.

"And what did you tell *her*?" he asked.

"That the baby belonged to the old mother—that it was brother to your girl, who was writing to you as a friend of the family."

He stood smiling, with the long, subtle malice of a farmer.

"And did she take it in?" he asked.

"As much as she took anything else."

He stood grinning fixedly. Then he broke into a short laugh. "Good for *her*!" he exclaimed cryptically.

And then he laughed aloud once more, evidently feeling he had won a big move in his contest with his wife.

"What about the other woman?" I asked.

"Who?"

"Elise."

"Oh"—he shifted uneasily—"she was all right——"

"You'll be getting back to her," I said.

He looked at me. Then he made a grimace with his mouth. "Not me," he said. "Back your life it's a plant."

"You don't think the *cher petit bébé* is a little Alfred?"

"It might be," he said.

"Only might?"

"Yes—an' there's lots of mites in a pound of cheese." He laughed boisterously but uneasily.

"What did she say, exactly?" he asked.

I began to repeat, as well as I could, the phrases of the letter: "*Mon cher Alfred— Figure-toi comme je suis desolée——*"

He listened with some confusion. When I had finished all I could remember, he said:

"They know how to pitch you out a letter, those Belgian lasses."

"Practice," said I.

"They get plenty," he said.

There was a pause.

"Oh, well," he said. "I've never got that letter, anyhow."

The wind blew fine and keen, in the sunshine, across the snow. I blew my nose and prepared to depart.

"And *she* doesn't know anything?" he continued, jerking his head up the hill in the direction of Tible.

"She knows nothing but what I've said—that is, if she really burnt the letter."

"I believe she burnt it," he said, "for spite. She's a little devil, she is. But I shall have it out with her." His jaw was stubborn and sullen. Then suddenly he turned to me with a new note.

"Why?" he said. "Why didn't you wring that b—— peacock's neck—that b—— Joey?"

"Why?" I said. "What for?"

"I hate the brute," he said. "I had a shot at him——"
I laughed. He stood and mused.

"Poor little Elise," he murmured.

"Was she small—petite?" I asked. He jerked up his head.

"No," he said. "Rather tall."

"Taller than your wife, I suppose."

Again he looked into my eyes. And then once more he went
into a loud burst of laughter that made the still, snow-deserted
valley clap again.

"God, it's a knock-out!" he said, thoroughly amused. Then
he stood at ease, one foot out, his hands in his breeches
pockets, in front of him, his head thrown back, a handsome
figure of a man.

"But I'll do that blasted Joey in——" he mused.

I ran down the hill, shouting with laughter.

YOU TOUCHED ME

THE Pottery House was a square, ugly, brick house girt in by the wall that enclosed the whole grounds of the pottery itself. To be sure, a privet hedge partly masked the house and its ground from the pottery-yard and works: but only partly. Through the hedge could be seen the desolate yard, and the many-windowed, factory-like pottery, over the hedge could be seen the chimneys and the out-houses. But inside the hedge, a pleasant garden and lawn sloped down to a willow pool, which had once supplied the works.

The Pottery itself was now closed, the great doors of the yard permanently shut. No more the great crates with yellow straw showing through stood in stacks by the packing-shed. No more the drays drawn by great horses rolled down the hill with a high load. No more the pottery-lasses in their clay-coloured overalls, their faces and hair splashed with grey fine mud, shrieked and larked with the men. All that was over.

"We like it much better—oh, much better—quieter," said Matilda Rockley.

"Oh, yes," assented Emmie Rockley, her sister.

"I'm sure you do," agreed the visitor.

But whether the two Rockley girls really like it better, or whether they only imagined they did, is a question. Certainly their lives were much more grey and dreary now that the grey clay had ceased to spatter its mud and silt its dust over the premises. They did not quite realise how they missed the shrieking, shouting lasses, whom they had known all their lives and disliked so much.

Matilda and Emmie were already old maids. In a thorough industrial district, it is not easy for the girls who have expectations above the common to find husbands. The ugly industrial town was full of men, young men who were ready to marry. But they were all colliers or pottery-hands, mere workmen. The Rockley girls would have about ten thousand pounds each when their father died: ten thousand pounds' worth of profitable house-property. It was not to be sneezed at: they felt so themselves, and refrained from sneezing away such a fortune on any mere member of the proletariat. Consequently, bank-clerks or non-conformist clergymen or even school-teachers having failed to come forward, Matilda had begun to give up all idea of ever leaving the Pottery House.

Matilda was a tall, thin, graceful, fair girl, with a rather large nose. She was the Mary to Emmie's Martha: that is, Matilda loved painting and music, and read a good many novels, whilst Emmie looked after the housekeeping. Emmie was shorter, plumper than her sister, and she had no accomplishments. She looked up to Matilda, whose mind was naturally refined and sensible.

In their quiet, melancholy way, the two girls were happy. Their mother was dead. Their father was ill also. He was an intelligent man who had had some education, but preferred to remain as if he were one with the rest of the working people. He had a passion for music and played the violin pretty well. But now he was getting old, he was very ill, dying of a kidney disease. He had been rather a heavy whisky-drinker.

This quiet household, with one servant-maid, lived on year after year in the Pottery House. Friends came in, the girls went out, the father drank himself more and more ill. Outside in the street there was a continual racket of the colliers and their dogs and children. But inside the pottery wall was a deserted quiet.

In all this ointment there was one little fly. Ted Rockley, the father of the girls, had had four daughters, and no son. As his girls grew, he felt angry at finding himself always in a household of women. He went off to London and adopted a boy out of a Charity Institution. Emmie was fourteen years old, and Matilda sixteen, when their father arrived home with his prodigy, the boy of six, Hadrian.

Hadrian was just an ordinary boy from a Charity Home, with ordinary brownish hair and ordinary bluish eyes and of ordinary rather Cockney speech. The Rockley girls—there were three at home at the time of his arrival—had resented his being sprung on them. He, with his watchful, charity-institution instinct, knew this at once. Though he was only six years old, Hadrian had a subtle, jeering look on his face when he regarded the three young women. They insisted he should address them as Cousin: Cousin Flora, Cousin Matilda, Cousin Emmie. He complied, but there seemed a mockery in his tone.

The girls, however, were kind-hearted by nature. Flora married and left home. Hadrian did very much as he pleased with Matilda and Emmie, though they had certain strictnesses. He grew up in the Pottery House and about the Pottery premises, went to an elementary school, and was invariably called Hadrian Rockley. He regarded Cousin Matilda and Cousin Emmie with a certain laconic indifference, was quiet and reticent in his ways. The girls called him sly, but that was unjust. He was merely cautious, and without frankness. His uncle, Ted Rockley, understood him tacitly, their natures were somewhat akin. Hadrian and the elderly man had a real but unemotional regard for one another.

When he was thirteen years old the boy was sent to a High School in the County town. He did not like it. His Cousin Matilda had longed to make a little gentleman of him, but he refused to be made. He would give a little contemptuous curve to his lip, and take on a shy, charity-boy grin, when refinement was thrust upon him. He played truant from the High School, sold his books, his cap with its badge, even his very scarf and pocket-handkerchief, to his school-fellows, and went raking off heaven knows where with the money. So he spent two very unsatisfactory years.

When he was fifteen he announced that he wanted to leave England to go to the Colonies. He had kept touch with the Home. The Rockleys knew that, when Hadrian made a declaration, in his quiet, half-jeering manner, it was worse than useless to oppose him. So at last the boy departed, going to Canada under the protection of the Institution to which he had belonged. He said good-bye to the Rockleys, without a word of thanks, and parted, it seemed, without a pang. Matilda and Emmie wept often to think of how he left them: even on their father's face a queer look came. But Hadrian wrote fairly regularly from Canada. He had entered some electricity works near Montreal, and was doing well.

At last, however, the war came. In his turn, Hadrian joined up and came to Europe. The Rockleys saw nothing of him. They lived on, just the same, in the Pottery House. Ted Rockley was dying of a sort of dropsy, and in his heart he wanted to see the boy. When the Armistice was signed, Hadrian had a long leave, and wrote that he was coming home to the Pottery House.

The girls were terribly fluttered. To tell the truth, they were a little afraid of Hadrian. Matilda, tall and thin, was frail in her health, both girls were worn with nursing their father. To have Hadrian, a young man of twenty-one, in the house with them, after he had left them so coldly five years before, was a trying circumstance.

They were in a flutter. Emmie persuaded her father to have his bed made finally in the morning-room downstairs, whilst his room upstairs was prepared for Hadrian. This was done, and preparations were going on for the arrival, when, at ten o'clock in the morning, the young man suddenly turned up, quite unexpectedly. Cousin Emmie, with her hair bobbed up in absurd little bobs round her forehead, was busily polishing the stair-rods, while Cousin Matilda was in the kitchen washing the drawing-room ornaments in a lather, her sleeves rolled back on her thin arms, and her head tied up oddly and coquettishly in a duster.

Cousin Matilda blushed deep with mortification when the self-possessed young man walked in with his kit-bag, and put his cap on the sewing-machine. He was little and self-confident, with a curious neatness about him that still suggested the Charity Institution. His face was brown, he had a small moustache, he was vigorous enough in his smallness.

"Well, is it Hadrian!" exclaimed Cousin Matilda, wringing the lather off her hand. "We didn't expect you till to-morrow."

"I got off Monday night," said Hadrian, glancing round the room.

"Fancy!" said Cousin Matilda. Then, having dried her hands, she went forward, held out her hand, and said:

"How are you?"

"Quite well, thank you," said Hadrian.

"You're quite a man," said Cousin Matilda.

Hadrian glanced at her. She did not look her best: so thin, so large-nosed, with that pink-and-white checked duster tied round her head. She felt her disadvantage. But she had had a good deal of suffering and sorrow, she did not mind any more.

The servant entered—one that did not know Hadrian.

"Come and see my father," said Cousin Matilda.

In the hall they roused Cousin Emmie like a partridge from cover. She was on the stairs pushing the bright stair-rods into place. Instinctively her hand went to the little knobs, her front hair bobbed on her forehead.

"Why!" she exclaimed, crossly. "What have you come to-day for?"

"I got off a day earlier," said Hadrian, and his man's voice so deep and unexpected was like a blow to Cousin Emmie.

"Well, you've caught us in the midst of it," she said, with resentment. Then all three went into the middle room.

Mr. Rockley was dressed—that is, he had on his trousers and socks—but he was resting on the bed, propped up just under the window, from whence he could see his beloved and resplendent garden, where tulips and apple trees were ablaze. He did not look as ill as he was, for the water puffed him up, and his face kept its colour. His stomach was much swollen.

He glanced round swiftly, turning his eyes without turning his head. He was the wreck of a handsome, well-built man.

Seeing Hadrian, a queer, unwilling smile went over his face. The young man greeted him sheepishly.

"You wouldn't make a life-guardsman," he said. "Do you want something to eat?"

Hadrian looked round—as if for the meal.

"I don't mind," he said.

"What shall you have—egg and bacon?" asked Emmie shortly.

"Yes, I don't mind," said Hadrian.

The sisters went down to the kitchen, and sent the servant to finish the stairs.

"Isn't he *altered*?" said Matilda, *sotto voce*.

"Isn't he!" said Cousin Emmie. "*What* a little man!"

They both made a grimace, and laughed nervously.

"Get the frying-pan," said Emmie to Matilda.

"But he's as cocky as ever," said Matilda, narrowing her eyes and shaking her head knowingly, as she handed the frying-pan.

"Mannie!" said Emmie sarcastically. Hadrian's new-fledged, cocksure manliness evidently found no favour in her eyes.

"Oh, he's not bad," said Matilda. "You don't want to be prejudiced against him."

"I'm not prejudiced against him, I think he's all right for looks," said Emmie, "but there's too much of the little mannie about him."

"Fancy catching us like this," said Matilda.

"They've no thought for anything," said Emmie with contempt. "You go up and get dressed, our Matilda. I don't care about him. I can see to things, and you can talk to him. I shan't."

"He'll talk to my father," said Matilda, meaningful.

"*Sly*——!" exclaimed Emmie, with a grimace.

The sister believed that Hadrian had come hoping to get something out of their father—hoping for a legacy. And they were not at all sure he would not get it.

Matilda went upstairs to change. She had thought it all out how she would receive Hadrian, and impress him. And he had caught her with her head tied up in a duster, and her thin arms in a basin of lather. But she did not care. She now dressed herself most scrupulously, carefully folded her long, beautiful, blonde hair, touched her pallor with a little rouge, and put her long string of exquisite crystal beads over her soft green dress. Now she looked elegant, like a heroine in a magazine illustration, and almost as unreal.

She found Hadrian and her father talking away. The young man was short of speech as a rule, but he could find his tongue with his 'uncle'. They were both sipping a glass of brandy, and smoking, and chatting like a pair of old cronies. Hadrian was telling about Canada. He was going back there when his leave was up.

"You wouldn't like to stop in England, then?" said Mr. Rockley.

"No, I wouldn't stop in England," said Hadrian.

"How's that? There's plenty of electricians here," said Mr. Rockley.

"Yes. But there's too much difference between the men and the employers over here—too much of that for me," said Hadrian.

The sick man looked at him narrowly, with oddly smiling eyes.

"That's it, is it?" he replied.

Matilda heard and understood. "So that's your big idea, is it, my little man," she said to herself. She had always said of Hadrian that he had no proper *respect* for anybody or anything, that he was sly and *common*. She went down to the kitchen for a *sotto voce* confab with Emmie.

"He thinks a rare lot of himself!" she whispered.

"He's somebody, he is!" said Emmie with contempt.

"He thinks there's too much difference between masters and men over here," said Matilda.

"Is it any different in Canada?" asked Emmie.

"Oh yes—democratic," replied Matilda. "He thinks they're all on a level over there."

"Ay, well, he's over here now," said Emmie dryly, "so he can keep his place."

As they talked they saw the young man sauntering down the garden, looking casually at the flowers. He had his hands in his pockets, and his soldier's cap neatly on his head. He looked quite at his ease, as if in possession. The two women, fluttered, watched him through the window.

"We know what he's come for," said Emmie, churlishly. Matilda looked a long time at the neat khaki figure. It had something of the charity-box about it still; but now it was a man's figure, laconic, charged with plebeian energy. She thought of a derisive passion in his voice as he had declaimed against the propertied classes, to her father.

"You don't know, Emmie. Perhaps he's not come for that," she rebuked her sister. They were both thinking of the money.

They were still watching the young soldier. He stood away at the bottom of the garden, with his back to them, his hands in his pockets, looking into the water of the willow pond. Matilda's dark blue eyes had a strange, full look in them, the lids, with the faint blue veins showing, dropped rather low. She carried her head light and high, but she had a look of pain. The young man at the bottom of the garden turned and looked up the path. Perhaps he saw them through the window. Matilda moved into shadow.

That afternoon their father seemed weak and ill. He was easily exhausted. The doctor came, and told Matilda that the sick man might die suddenly at any moment—but then he might not. They must be prepared.

So the day passed, and the next. Hadrian made himself at home. He went about in the morning in his brownish jersey and his khaki trousers, collarless, his bare neck showing. He explored the pottery premises, as if he had some secret purpose in so doing, he talked with Mr. Rockley, when the sick man had strength. The two girls were always angry when the two men sat talking together like cronies. Yet it was chiefly a kind of politics they talked.

On the second day after Hadrian's arrival, Matilda sat with her father in the evening. She was drawing a picture which she wanted to copy. It was very still, Hadrian was gone out somewhere, no one knew where, and Emmie was busy. Mr. Rockley reclined on his bed, looking out in silence over his evening-sunny garden.

"If anything happens to me, Matilda," he said, "you won't sell this house—you'll stop here——"

Matilda's eyes took their slightly haggard look as she stared at her father.

"Well, we couldn't do anything else," she said.

"You don't know what you might do," he said. "Everything is left to you and Emmie, equally. You do as you like with it—only don't sell this house, don't part with it."

"No," she said.

"And give Hadrian my watch and chain, and a hundred pounds out of what's in the bank—and help him if he ever wants helping. I haven't put his name in the will."

"Your watch and chain, and a hundred pounds—yes. But you'll be here when he goes back to Canada, father."

"You never know what'll happen," said her father.

Matilda sat and watched him, with her full, haggard eyes, for a long time, as if tranced. She saw that he knew he must go soon—she saw like a clairvoyant.

Later on she told Emmie what her father had said about the watch and chain and the money.

"What right has *he*"—he—meaning Hadrian—"to *my* father's watch and chain—what has it to do with him? Let him have the money, and get off," said Emmie. She loved her father.

That night Matilda sat late in her room. Her heart was anxious and breaking, her mind seemed entranced. She was too much entranced even to weep, and all the time she thought of her father, only her father. At last she felt she must go to him.

It was near midnight. She went along the passage and to his room. There was a faint light from the moon outside. She listened at his door. Then she softly opened and entered. The room was faintly dark. She heard a movement on the bed.

"Are you asleep?" she said softly, advancing to the side of the bed.

"Are you asleep?" she repeated gently, as she stood at the side of the bed. And she reached her hand in the darkness to touch his forehead. Delicately, her fingers met the nose and the eyebrows, she laid her fine, delicate hand on his brow. It seemed fresh and smooth—very fresh and smooth. A sort of surprise stirred her, in her entranced state. But it could not waken her. Gently, she leaned over the bed and stirred her fingers over the low-growing hair on his brow.

"Can't you sleep to-night?" she said.

There was a quick stirring in the bed. "Yes, I can," a voice answered. It was Hadrian's voice. She started away. Instantly she was wakened from her late-at-night trance. She remembered that her father was downstairs, that Hadrian had his room. She stood in the darkness as if stung.

"Is it you, Hadrian?" she said. "I thought it was my father." She was so startled, so shocked, that she could not move. The young man gave an uncomfortable laugh, and turned in his bed.

At last she got out of the room. When she was back in her own room, in the light, and her door was closed, she stood holding up her hand that had touched him, as if it were hurt. She was almost too shocked, she could not endure.

"Well," said her calm and weary mind, "it was only a mistake, why take any notice of it."

But she could not reason her feelings so easily. She suffered, feeling herself in a false position. Her right hand, which she had laid so gently on his face, on his fresh skin, ached now, as if it were really injured. She could not forgive Hadrian for the mistake: it made her dislike him deeply.

Hadrian too slept badly. He had been awakened by the opening of the door, and had not realised what the question meant. But the soft, straying tenderness of her hand on his face startled something out of his soul. He was a charity boy, aloof and more or less at bay. The fragile exquisiteness of her caress startled him most, revealed unknown things to him.

In the morning she could feel the consciousness in his eyes, when she came downstairs. She tried to bear herself as if nothing at all had happened, and she succeeded. She had the calm self-control, self-indifference, of one who has suffered and borne her suffering. She looked at him from her darkish, almost drugged blue eyes, she met the spark of consciousness in his eyes, and quenched it. And with her long, fine hand she put the sugar in his coffee.

But she could not control him as she thought she could. He had a keen memory stinging his mind, a new set of sensations working in his consciousness. Something new was alert in him. At the back of his reticent, guarded mind he kept his secret alive and vivid. She was at his mercy, for he was un-scrupulous, his standard was not her standard.

He looked at her curiously. She was not beautiful, her nose was too large, her chin was too small, her neck was too thin. But her skin was clear and fine, she had a high-bred sensitive-ness. This queer, brave, high-bred quality she shared with her father. The charity boy could see it in her tapering fingers, which were white and ringed. The same glamour that he knew in the elderly man he now saw in the woman. And he wanted to possess himself of it, he wanted to make himself master of it. As he went about through the old pottery-yard, his secretive mind schemed and worked. To be master of that strange soft delicacy such as he had felt in her hand upon his face—this was what he set himself towards. He was secretly plotting.

He watched Matilda as she went about, and she became aware of his attention, as of some shadow following her. But her pride made her ignore it. When he sauntered near her, his hands in his pockets, she received him with that same common-place kindliness which mastered him more than any contempt. Her superior breeding seemed to control him. She made her-self feel towards him exactly as she had always felt: he was a young boy who lived in the house with them, but was a stranger. Only, she dared not remember his face under her hand. When she remembered that, she was bewildered. Her hand had offended her, she wanted to cut it off. And she wanted, fiercely, to cut off the memory in him. She assumed she had done so.

One day, when he sat talking with his 'uncle', he looked straight into the eyes of the sick man, and said:

"But I shouldn't like to live and die here in Rawsley."

"No—well—you needn't," said the sick man.

"Do you think Cousin Matilda likes it?"

"I should think so."

"I don't call it much of a life," said the youth. "How much older is she than me, Uncle?"

The sick man looked at the young soldier.

"A good bit," he said.

"Over thirty?" said Hadrian.

"Well, not so much. She's thirty-two."

Hadrian considered a while.

"She doesn't look it," he said.

Again the sick father looked at him.

"Do you think she'd like to leave here?" said Hadrian.

"Nay, I don't know," replied the father, restive.

Hadrian sat still, having his own thoughts. Then in a small, quiet voice, as if he were speaking from inside himself, he said:

"I'd marry her if you wanted me to."

The sick man raised his eyes suddenly and stared. He stared for a long time. The youth looked inscrutably out of the window.

"*You!*" said the sick man, mocking, with some contempt. Hadrian turned and met his eyes. The two men had an inexplicable understanding.

"If you wasn't against it," said Hadrian.

"Nay," said the father, turning aside, "I don't think I'm against it. I've never thought of it. But—but Emmie's the youngest."

He had flushed, and looked suddenly more alive. Secretly he loved the boy.

"You might ask her," said Hadrian.

The elder man considered.

"Hadn't you better ask her yourself?" he said.

"She'd take more notice of you," said Hadrian.

They were both silent. Then Emmie came in.

For two days Mr. Rockley was excited and thoughtful. Hadrian went about quietly, secretly, unquestioning. At last the father and daughter were alone together. It was very early morning, the father had been in much pain. As the pain abated, he lay still thinking.

"Matilda!" he said suddenly, looking at his daughter.

"Yes, I'm here," she said.

"Ay! I want you to do something——"

She rose in anticipation.

"Nay, sit still. I want you to marry Hadrian——"

She thought he was raving. She rose, bewildered and frightened.

"Nay, sit you still, sit you still. You hear what I tell you."

"But you don't know what you're saying, father."

"Ay, I know well enough. I want you to marry Hadrian, I tell you."

She was dumbfounded. He was a man of few words.

"You'll do what I tell you," he said.

She looked at him slowly.

"What put such an idea in your mind?" she said proudly.

"He did."

Matilda almost looked her father down, her pride was so offended.

"Why, it's disgraceful," she said.

"Why?"

She watched him slowly.

"What do you ask me for?" she said. "It's disgusting."

"The lad's sound enough," he replied testily.

"You'd better tell him to clear out," she said coldly.

He turned and looked out of the window. She sat flushed and erect for a long time. At length her father turned to her, looking really malevolent.

"If you won't," he said, "you're a fool, and I'll make you pay for your foolishness, do you see?"

Suddenly a cold fear gripped her. She could not believe her senses. She was terrified and bewildered. She stared at her father, believing him to be delirious, or mad, or drunk. What could she do?

"I tell you," he said. "I'll send for Whittle to-morrow if you don't. You shall neither of you have anything of mine."

Whittle was the solicitor. She understood her father well enough: he would send for his solicitor, and make a will leaving all his property to Hadrian: neither she nor Emmie should have anything. It was too much. She rose and went out of the room, up to her own room, where she locked herself in.

She did not come out for some hours. At last, late at night, she confided in Emmie.

"The sliving demon, he wants the money," said Emmie. "My father's out of his mind."

The thought that Hadrian merely wanted the money was another blow to Matilda. She did not love the impossible youth—but she had not yet learned to think of him as a thing of evil. He now became hideous to her mind.

Emmie had a little scene with her father next day.

"You don't mean what you said to our Matilda yesterday, do you, father?" she asked aggressively.

"Yes," he replied.

"What, that you'll alter your will?"

"Yes."

"You won't," said his angry daughter.

But he looked at her with a malevolent little smile.

"Annie!" he shouted. "Annie!"

He had still power to make his voice carry. The servant maid came in from the kitchen.

"Put your things on, and go down to Whittle's office, and say I want to see Mr. Whittle as soon as he can, and will he bring a will-form."

The sick man lay back a little—he could not lie down. His daughter sat as if she had been struck. Then she left the room.

Hadrian was pottering about in the garden. She went straight down to him.

"Here," she said. "You'd better get off. You'd better take your things and go from here, quick."

Hadrian looked slowly at the infuriated girl.

"Who says so?" he asked.

"*We* say so—get off, you've done enough mischief and damage."

"Does Uncle say so?"

"Yes, he does."

"I'll go and ask him."

But like a fury Emmie barred his way.

"No, you needn't. You needn't ask him nothing at all. We don't want you, so you can go."

"Uncle's boss here."

"A man that's dying, and you crawling round and working on him for his money!—you're not fit to live."

"Oh!" he said. "Who says I'm working for his money?"

"I say. But my father told our Matilda, and *she* knows what you are. *She* knows what you're after. So you might as well clear out, for all you'll get—guttersnipe!"

He turned his back on her, to think. It had not occurred to him that they would think he was after the money. He *did* want the money—badly. He badly wanted to be an employer himself, not one of the employed. But he knew, in his subtle, calculating way, that it was not for money he wanted Matilda. He wanted both the money and Matilda. But he told himself the two desires were separate, not one. He could not do with Matilda, *without* the money. But he did not want her *for* the money.

When he got this clear in his mind, he sought for an opportunity to tell it her, lurking and watching. But she avoided him. In the evening the lawyer came. Mr. Rockley seemed to have a new access of strength—a will was drawn up, making the previous arrangements wholly conditional. The old will held good, if Matilda would consent to marry Hadrian. If she refused then at the end of six months the whole property passed to Hadrian.

Mr. Rockley told this to the young man, with malevolent satisfaction. He seemed to have a strange desire, quite unreasonable, for revenge upon the women who had surrounded him for so long, and served him so carefully.

"Tell her in front of me," said Hadrian.

So Mr. Rockley sent for his daughters.

At last they came, pale, mute, stubborn. Matilda seemed to have retired far off, Emmie seemed like a fighter ready to fight to the death. The sick man reclined on the bed, his eyes bright, his puffed hand trembling. But his face had again some of its old, bright handsomeness. Hadrian sat quiet, a little aside: the indomitable, dangerous charity boy.

"There's the will," said their father, pointing them to the paper.

The two women sat mute and immovable, they took no notice.

"Either you marry Hadrian, or he has everything," said the father with satisfaction.

"Then let him have everything," said Matilda coldly.

"He's not! He's not!" cried Emmie fiercely. "He's not going to have it. The guttersnipe!"

An amused look came on her father's face.

"You hear that, Hadrian," he said.

"I didn't offer to marry Cousin Matilda for the money," said Hadrian, flushing and moving on his seat.

Matilda looked at him slowly, with her dark blue, drugged eyes. He seemed a strange little monster to her.

"Why, you liar, you know you did," cried Emmie.

The sick man laughed. Matilda continued to gaze strangely at the young man.

"She knows I didn't," said Hadrian.

He too had his courage, as a rat has indomitable courage in the end. Hadrian had some of the neatness, the reserve, the underground quality of the rat. But he had perhaps the ultimate courage, the most unquenched courage of all.

Emmie looked at her sister.

"Oh, well," she said. "Matilda—don't you bother. Let him have everything, we can look after ourselves."

"I know he'll take everything," said Matilda, abstractedly.

Hadrian did not answer. He knew in fact that if Matilda refused him he would take everything, and go off with it.

"A clever little mannie——!" said Emmie, with a jeering grimace.

The father laughed noiselessly to himself. But he was tired. . . .

"Go on, then," he said. "Go on, let me be quiet."

Emmie turned and looked at him.

"You deserve what you've got," she said to her father bluntly.

"Go on," he answered mildly. "Go on."

Another night passed—a night nurse sat up with Mr. Rockley. Another day came. Hadrian was there as ever, in his woollen jersey and coarse khaki trousers and bare neck. Matilda went about, frail and distant, Emmie black-browed in spite of her blondness. They were all quiet, for they did not intend the mystified servant to learn anything.

Mr. Rockley had very bad attacks of pain, he could not breathe. The end seemed near. They all went about quiet and stoical, all unyielding. Hadrian pondered within himself. If he did not marry Matilda he would go to Canada with twenty thousand pounds. This was itself a very satisfactory prospect. If Matilda consented he would have nothing—she would have her own money.

Emmie was the one to act. She went off in search of the solicitor and brought him home with her. There was an interview, and Whittle tried to frighten the youth into withdrawal—but without avail. The clergyman and relatives were summoned—but Hadrian stared at them and took no notice. It made him angry, however.

He wanted to catch Matilda alone. Many days went by, and he was not successful: she avoided him. At last, lurking, he surprised her one day as she came to pick gooseberries, and he cut off her retreat. He came to the point at once.

"You don't want me, then?" he said, in his subtle, insinuating voice.

"I don't want to speak to you," she said, averting her face.

"You put your hand on me, though," he said. "You shouldn't have done that, and then I should never have thought of it. You shouldn't have touched me."

"If you were anything decent, you'd know that was a mistake, and forget it," she said.

"I know it was a mistake—but I shan't forget it. If you wake a man up, he can't go to sleep again because he's told to."

"If you had any decent feeling in you, you'd have gone away," she replied.

"I didn't want to," he replied.

She looked away into the distance. At last she asked:

"What do you persecute me for, if it isn't for the money? I'm old enough to be your mother. In a way I've been your mother."

"Doesn't matter," he said. "You've been no mother to me. Let us marry and go out to Canada—you might as well—you've touched me."

She was white and trembling. Suddenly she flushed with anger.

"It's so *indecent*," she said.

"How?" he retorted. "You touched me."

But she walked away from him. She felt as if he had trapped her. He was angry and depressed, he felt again despised.

That same evening she went into her father's room.

"Yes," she said suddenly. "I'll marry him."

Her father looked up at her. He was in pain, and very ill.

"You like him now, do you?" he said, with a faint smile.

She looked down into his face, and saw death not far off. She turned and went coldly out of the room.

The solicitor was sent for, preparations were hastily made. In all the interval Matilda did not speak to Hadrian, never answered him if he addressed her. He approached her in the morning.

"You've come round to it, then?" he said, giving her a pleasant look from his twinkling, almost kindly eyes. She looked down at him and turned aside. She looked down on him both literally and figuratively. Still he persisted, and triumphed.

Emmie raved and wept, the secret flew abroad. But Matilda was silent and unmoved, Hadrian was quiet and satisfied, and nipped with fear also. But he held out against his fear. Mr. Rockley was very ill, but unchanged.

On the third day the marriage took place. Matilda and Hadrian drove straight home from the registrar, and went straight into the room of the dying man. His face lit up with a clear twinkling smile.

"Hadrian—you've got her?" he said, a little hoarsely.

"Yes," said Hadrian, who was pale round the gills.

"Ay, my lad, I'm glad you're mine," replied the dying man. Then he turned his eyes closely on Matilda.

"Let's look at you, Matilda," he said. Then his voice went strange and unrecognisable. "Kiss me," he said.

She stooped and kissed him. She had never kissed him before, not since she was a tiny child. But she was quiet, very still.

"Kiss him," the dying man said.

Obediently, Matilda put forward her mouth and kissed the young husband.

"That's right! That's right!" murmured the dying man.

SAMSON AND DELILAH

A MAN got down from the motor-omnibus that runs from
Penzance to St. Just-in-Penwith, and turned northwards, up-
hill towards the Polestar. It was only half-past six, but already
the stars were out, a cold little wind was blowing from the
sea, and the crystalline, three-pulse flash of the lighthouse
below the cliffs beat rhythmically in the first darkness.

The man was alone. He went his way unhesitating, but
looked from side to side with cautious curiosity. Tall, ruined
power-houses of tin-mines loomed in the darkness from time
to time, like remnants of some by-gone civilisation. The lights
of many miners' cottages scattered on the hilly darkness
twinkled desolate in their disorder, yet twinkled with the
lonely homeliness of the Celtic night.

He tramped steadily on, always watchful with curiosity. He
was a tall, well-built man, apparently in the prime of life. His
shoulders were square and rather stiff, he leaned forwards a
little as he went, from the hips, like a man who must stoop to
lower his height. But he did not stoop his shoulders: he bent
his straight back from the hips.

Now and again short, stump, thick-legged figures of Cornish
miners passed him, and he invariably gave them good night, as
if to insist that he was on his own ground. He spoke with the
West Cornish intonation. And as he went along the dreary
road, looking now at the lights of the dwellings on land, now
at the lights away to sea, vessels veering round in sight of the
Longships Lighthouse, the whole of the Atlantic Ocean in darkness and space between him and America, he seemed a little
excited and pleased with himself, watchful, thrilled, veering
along in a sense of mastery and of power in conflict.

The houses began to close on the road, he was entering the
straggling, formless, desolate mining village, that he knew of
old. On the left was a little space set back from the road, and
cosy lights of an inn. There it was. He peered up at the sign:
'The Tinners' Rest'. But he could not make out the name of
the proprietor. He listened. There was excited talking and
laughing, a woman's voice laughing shrilly among the men's.

Stooping a little, he entered the warmly-lit bar. The lamp was burning, a buxom woman rose from the white-scrubbed deal table where the black and white and red cards were scattered, and several men, miners, lifted their faces from the game.

The stranger went to the counter, averting his face. His cap was pulled down over his brow.

"Good evening!" said the landlady, in her rather ingratiating voice.

"Good evening. A glass of ale."

"A glass of ale," repeated the landlady suavely. "Cold night—but bright."

"Yes," the man assented, laconically. Then he added, when nobody expected him to say any more: "Seasonable weather."

"Quite seasonable, quite," said the landlady. "Thank you."

The man lifted his glass straight to his lips, and emptied it. He put it down again on the zinc counter with a click.

"Let's have another," he said.

The woman drew the beer, and the man went away with his glass to the second table, near the fire. The woman, after a moment's hesitation, took her seat again at the table with the card-players. She had noticed the man: a big fine fellow, well dressed, a stranger.

But he spoke with that Cornish–Yankee accent she accepted as the natural twang among the miners.

The stranger put his foot on the fender and looked into the fire. He was handsome, well coloured, with well-drawn Cornish eyebrows, and the usual dark, bright, mindless Cornish eyes. He seemed abstracted in thought. Then he watched the card-party.

The woman was buxom and healthy, with dark hair and small, quick brown eyes. She was bursting with life and vigour, the energy she threw into the game of cards excited all the men, they shouted, and laughed, and the woman held her breast, shrieking with laughter.

"Oh, my, it'll be the death o' me," she panted. "Now, come on, Mr. Trevorrow, play fair. Play fair, I say, or I s'll put the cards down."

"Play fair! Why, who's played unfair?" ejaculated Mr. Trevorrow. "Do you mean t'accuse me, as I haven't played fair, Mrs. Nankervis?"

"I do. I say it, and I mean it. Haven't you got the Queen of

Spades? Now, come on, no dodging round me. *I* know you've got that Queen, as well as I know my name's Alice."

"Well—if your name's Alice, you'll have to have it——"

"Ay, now—what did I say? Did ever you see such a man? My word, but your missus must be easy took in, by the looks of things."

And off she went into peals of laughter. She was interrupted by the entrance of four men in khaki, a short, stumpy sergeant of middle age, a young corporal, and two young privates. The woman leaned back in her chair.

"Oh, my!" she cried. "If there isn't the boys back: looking perished, I believe——"

"Perished, Ma!" exclaimed the sergeant. "Not yet."

"Near enough," said a young private uncouthly.

The woman got up.

"I'm sure you are, my dears. You'll be wanting your suppers, I'll be bound."

"We could do with 'em."

"Let's have a wet first," said the sergeant.

The woman bustled about getting the drinks. The soldiers moved to the fire, spreading out their hands.

"Have your suppers in here, will you?" she said. "Or in the kitchen?"

"Let's have it here," said the sergeant. "More cosier—*if* you don't mind."

"You shall have it where you like, boys, where you like."

She disappeared. In a minute a girl of about sixteen came in. She was tall and fresh, with dark, young, expressionless eyes, and well-drawn brows, and the immature softness and mindlessness of the sensuous Celtic type.

"Ho, Maryann! Evenin', Maryann! How's Maryann, now?" came the multiple greeting.

She replied to everybody in a soft voice, a strange, soft aplomb that was very attractive. And she moved round with rather mechanical, attractive movements, as if her thoughts were elsewhere. But she had always this dim far-awayness in her bearing: a sort of modesty. The strange man by the fire watched her curiously. There was an alert, inquisitive, mindless curiosity on his well-coloured face.

"I'll have a bit of supper with you, if I might," he said.

She looked at him with her clear, unreasoning eyes, just like the eyes of some non-human creature.

"I'll ask mother," she said. Her voice was soft-breathing, gently sing-song.

When she came in again:

"Yes," she said, almost whispering. "What will you have?"

"What have you got?" he said, looking up into her face.

"There's cold meat——"

"That's for me, then."

The stranger sat at the end of the table, and ate with the tired, quiet soldiers. Now the landlady was interested in him. Her brow was knit rather tense, there was a look of panic in her large, healthy face, but her small brown eyes were fixed most dangerously. She was a big woman, but her eyes were small and tense. She drew near the stranger. She wore a rather loud-patterned flannelette blouse and a dark skirt.

"What will you have to drink with your supper?" she asked, and there was a new, dangerous note in her voice.

He moved uneasily.

"Oh, I'll go on with ale."

She drew him another glass. Then she sat down on the bench at the table with him and the soldiers, and fixed him with her attention.

"You've come from St. Just, have you?" she said.

He looked at her with those clear, dark, inscrutable Cornish eyes, and answered at length:

"No, from Penzance."

"Penzance!—but you're not thinking of going back there to-night?"

"No—no."

He still looked at her with those wide, clear eyes that seemed like very bright agate. Her anger began to rise. It was seen on her brow. Yet her voice was still suave and deprecating.

"I *thought* not—but you're not living in these parts, are you?"

"No—no, I'm not living here." He was always slow in answering, as if something intervened between him and any outside question.

"Oh, I see," she said. "You've got relations down here."

Again he looked straight into her eyes, as if looking her into silence.

"Yes," he said.

He did not say any more. She rose with a flounce. The anger was tight on her brow. There was no more laughing and card-playing that evening, though she kept up her motherly, suave, good-humoured way with the men. But they knew her, they were all afraid of her.

The supper was finished, the table cleared, the stranger did not go. Two of the young soldiers went off to bed, with their cheery:

"Good night, Ma. Good night, Maryann."

The stranger talked a little to the sergeant about the war, which was in its first year, about the new army, a fragment of which was quartered in this district, about America.

The landlady darted looks at him from her small eyes, minute by minute the electric storm welled in her bosom, as still he did not go. She was quivering with suppressed, violent passion, something frightening and abnormal. She could not sit still for a moment. Her heavy form seemed to flash with sudden, involuntary movements as the minutes passed by, and still he sat there, and the tension on her heart grew unbearable. She watched the hands of the clock move on. Three of the soldiers had gone to bed, only the crop-headed, terrier-like old sergeant remained.

The landlady sat behind the bar fidgeting spasmodically with the newspaper. She looked again at the clock. At last it was five minutes to ten.

"Gentlemen—the enemy!" she said in her diminished, furious voice. "Time, please. Time, my dears. And good night, all!"

The men began to drop out, with a brief good night. It was a minute to ten. The landlady rose.

"Come," she said. "I'm shutting the door."

The last of the miners passed out. She stood, stout and menacing, holding the door. Still the stranger sat on by the fire, his black overcoat opened, smoking.

"We're closed now, sir," came the perilous, narrowed voice of the landlady.

The little, dog-like, hard-headed sergeant touched the arm of the stranger.

"Closing time," he said.

The stranger turned round in his seat, and his quick-moving, dark, jewel-like eyes went from the sergeant to the landlady.

"I'm stopping here to-night," he said, in his laconic Cornish–Yankee accent.

The landlady seemed to tower. Her eyes lifted strangely, frightening.

"Oh, indeed!" she cried. "Oh, indeed! And whose orders are those, may I ask?"

He looked at her again.

"My orders," he said.

Involuntarily she shut the door, and advanced like a great, dangerous bird. Her voice rose, there was a touch of hoarseness in it.

"And what might *your* orders be, if you please?" she cried. "Who might *you* be, to give orders, in the house?"

He sat still, watching her.

"You know who I am," he said. "At least, I know who you are."

"Oh, do you? Oh, do you? And who am *I* then, if you'll be so good as to tell me?"

He stared at her with his bright, dark eyes.

"You're my Missis, you are," he said. "And you know it, as well as I do."

She started as if something had exploded in her.

Her eyes lifted and flared madly.

"*Do* I know it, indeed!" she cried. "I know no such thing! I know no such thing! Do you think a man's going to walk into this bar, and tell me off-hand I'm his Missis, and I'm going to believe him? I say to you, whoever you may be, you're mistaken. I know myself for no Missis of yours, and I'll thank you to go out of this house, this minute, before I get those that will put you out."

The man rose to his feet, stretching his head towards her a little. He was a handsomely built Cornishman in the prime of life.

"What you say, eh? You don't know me?" he said in his sing-song voice, emotionless, but rather smothered and pressing: it reminded one of the girl's. "I should know you anywhere, you see. I should! I shouldn't have to look twice to know you, you see. You see, now, don't you?"

The woman was baffled.

"So you may say," she replied, staccato. "So you may say. That's easy enough. My name's known, and respected, by most people for ten miles round. But I don't know *you*."

Her voice ran to sarcasm. "I can't say I know *you*. You're

a *perfect* stranger to me, and I don't believe I've ever set eyes on you before to-night."

Her voice was very flexible and sarcastic.

"Yes, you have," replied the man, in his reasonable way. "Yes, you have. Your name's my name, and that girl Maryann is my girl; she's my daughter. You're my Missis right enough. As sure as I'm Willie Nankervis."

He spoke as if it were an accepted fact. His face was handsome, with a strange, watchful alertness and a fundamental fixity of intention that maddened her.

"You villain!" she cried. "You villain, to come to this house and dare to speak to me. You villain, you downright rascal!"

He looked at her.

"Ay," he said, unmoved. "All that." He was uneasy before her. Only he was not afraid of her. There was something impenetrable about him, like his eyes, which were as bright as agate.

She towered, and drew near to him menacingly.

"You're going out of this house, aren't you?" She stamped her foot in sudden madness. *"This minute!"*

He watched her. He knew she wanted to strike him.

"No," he said, with suppressed emphasis. "I've told you, I'm stopping here."

He was afraid of her personality, but it did not alter him. She wavered. Her small, tawny-brown eyes concentrated in a point of vivid, sightless fury, like a tiger's. The man was wincing, but he stood his ground. Then she bethought herself. She would gather her forces.

"We'll see whether you're stopping here," she said. And she turned, with a curious, frightening lifting of her eyes, and surged out of the room. The man, listening, heard her go upstairs, heard her tapping at a bedroom door, heard her saying: "Do you mind coming down a minute, boys? I want you. I'm in trouble."

The man in the bar took off his cap and his black overcoat, and threw them on the seat behind him. His black hair was short and touched with grey at the temples. He wore a well-cut, well-fitting suit of dark grey, American in style, and a turn-down collar. He looked well-to-do, a fine, solid figure of a man. The rather rigid look of the shoulders came from his having had his collar-bone twice broken in the mines.

The little terrier of a sergeant, in dirty khaki, looked at him furtively.

"She's your Missis?" he asked, jerking his head in the direction of the departed woman.

"Yes, she is," barked the man. "She's that, sure enough."

"Not seen her for a long time, haven't ye?"

"Sixteen years come March month."

"Hm!"

And the sergeant laconically resumed his smoking.

The landlady was coming back, followed by the three young soldiers, who entered rather sheepishly, in trousers and shirt and stocking-feet. The woman stood histrionically at the end of the bar, and exclaimed:

"That man refuses to leave the house, claims he's stopping the night here. You know very well I have no bed, don't you? And this house doesn't accommodate travellers. Yet he's going to stop in spite of all! But not while I've a drop of blood in my body, that I declare with my dying breath. And not if you men are worth the name of men, and will help a woman as has no one to help her."

Her eyes sparkled, her face was flushed pink. She was drawn up like an Amazon.

The young soldier looked on in delight, the sergeant smoked looked at the man, they looked at the sergeant, one of them looked down and fastened his braces on the second button.

"What say, sergeant?" asked one whose face twinkled for a little devilment.

"Man says he's husband to Mrs. Nankervis," said the sergeant.

"He's no husband of mine. I declare I never set eyes on him before this night. It's a dirty trick, nothing else, it's a dirty trick."

"Why, you're a liar, saying you never set eyes on me before," barked the man near the hearth. "You're married to me, and that girl Maryann you had by me—well enough you know it."

The young soldier looked on in delight, the sergeant smoked imperturbed.

"Yes," sang the landlady, slowly shaking her head in supreme sarcasm, "it sounds very pretty, doesn't it? But you see we don't believe a word of it, and *how* are you going to prove it?" She smiled nastily.

The man watched in silence for a moment, then he said:
"It wants no proof."

"Oh, yes, but it does! Oh, yes, but it does, sir, it wants a lot
of proving!" sang the lady's sarcasm. "We're not such gulls
as all that, to swallow your words whole."

But he stood unmoved near the fire. She stood with one
hand resting on the zinc-covered bar, the sergeant sat with legs
crossed, smoking, on the seat half-way between them, the
three young soldiers in their shirts and braces stood wavering
in the gloom behind the bar. There was silence.

"Do you know anything of the whereabouts of your
husband, Mrs. Nankervis? Is he still living?" asked the
sergeant, in his judicious fashion.

Suddenly the landlady began to cry, great scalding tears, that
left the young men aghast.

"I know nothing of him," she sobbed, feeling for her pocket
handkerchief. "He left me when Maryann was a baby, went
mining to America, and after about six months never wrote a
line nor sent me a penny bit. I can't say whether he's alive or
dead, the villain. All I've heard of him's the bad—and I've
heard nothing for years an' all, now." She sobbed violently.

The golden-skinned, handsome man near the fire watched
her as she wept. He was frightened, he was troubled, he was
bewildered, but none of his emotions altered him underneath.

There was no sound in the room but the violent sobbing of
the landlady. The men, one and all, were overcome.

"Don't you think as you'd better go, for to-night?" said the
sergeant to the man, with sweet reasonableness. "You'd better
leave it a bit, and arrange something between you. You can't
have much claim on a woman, I should imagine, if it's how
she says. And you've come down on her a bit too sudden-like."

The landlady sobbed heart-brokenly. The man watched her
large breasts shaken. They seemed to cast a spell over his mind.

"How I've treated her, that's no matter," he replied. "I've
come back, and I'm going to stop in my own home—for a bit,
anyhow. There you've got it."

"A dirty action," said the sergeant, his face flushing dark.
"A dirty action, to come, after deserting a woman for that
number of years, and want to force yourself on her! A dirty
action—as isn't allowed by the law."

The landlady wiped her eyes.

"Never you mind about law nor nothing," cried the man, in

a strange, strong voice. "I'm not moving out of this public to-night."

The woman turned to the soldiers behind her, and said in a wheedling, sarcastic tone:

"Are we going to stand it, boys? Are we going to be done like this, Sergeant Thomas, by a scoundrel and a bully as has led a life beyond *mention* in those American mining-camps, and then wants to come back and make havoc of a poor woman's life and savings, after having left her with a baby in arms to struggle as best she might? It's a crying shame if nobody will stand up for me—a crying shame——!"

The soldiers and the little sergeant were bristling. The woman stooped and rummaged under the counter for a minute. Then, unseen to the man away near the fire, she threw out a plaited grass rope, such as is used for binding bales, and left it lying near the feet of the young soldiers, in the gloom at the back of the bar.

Then she rose and fronted the situation.

"Come now," she said to the man, in a reasonable, coldly-coaxing tone, "put your coat on and leave us alone. Be a man, and not worse than a brute of a German. You can get a bed easy enough in St. Just, and if you've nothing to pay for it, sergeant would lend you a couple of shillings, I'm sure he would."

All eyes were fixed on the man. He was looking down at the woman like a creature spell-bound or possessed by some devil's own intention.

"I've got money of my own," he said. "Don't you be frightened for your money, I've plenty of that, for the time."

"Well, then," she coaxed, in a cold, almost sneering propitiation, "put your coat on and go where you're wanted—be a *man*, not a brute of a German."

She had drawn quite near to him, in her challenging coaxing intentness. He looked down at her with his bewitched face.

"No, I shan't," he said. "I shan't do no such thing. *You'll* put me up for to-night."

"Shall I?" she cried. And suddenly she flung her arms round him, hung on to him with all her powerful weight, calling to the soldiers: "Get the rope, boys, and fasten him up. Alfred—John, quick now——"

The man reared, looked round with maddened eyes, and heaved his powerful body. But the woman was powerful also, and very heavy, and was clenched with the determination of death. Her face, with its exulting, horribly vindictive look, was turned up to him from his own breast; he reached back his head frantically, to get away from it. Meanwhile the young soldiers, after having watched this frightful Laocoon swaying for a moment, stirred, and the malicious one darted swiftly with the rope. It was tangled a little.

"Give me the end here," cried the sergeant.

Meanwhile the big man heaved and struggled, swung the woman round against the seat and the table, in his convulsive effort to get free. But she pinned down his arms like a cuttle-fish wreathed heavily upon him. And he heaved and swayed, and they crashed about the room, the soldiers hopping, the furniture bumping.

The young soldier had got the rope once round, the brisk sergeant helping him. The woman sank heavily lower, they got the rope round several times. In the struggle the victim fell over against the table. The ropes tightened till they cut his arms. The woman clung to his knees. Another soldier ran in a flash of genius, and fastened the strange man's feet with the pair of braces. Seats had crashed over, the table was thrown against the wall, but the man was bound, his arms pinned against his sides, his feet tied. He lay half-fallen, sunk against the table, still for a moment.

The woman rose, and sank, faint, on to the seat against the wall. Her breast heaved, she could not speak, she thought she was going to die. The bound man lay against the overturned table, his coat all twisted and pulled up beneath the ropes, leaving the loins exposed. The soldiers stood around, a little dazed, but excited with the row.

The man began to struggle again, heaving instinctively against the ropes, taking great, deep breaths. His face, with its golden skin, flushed dark and surcharged. He heaved again. The great veins in his neck stood out. But it was no good, he went relaxed. Then again, suddenly, he jerked his feet.

"Another pair of braces, William," cried the excited soldier. He threw himself on the legs of the bound man, and managed to fasten the knees. Then again there was stillness. They could hear the clock tick.

The woman looked at the prostrate figure, the strong, straight limbs, the strong back bound in subjection, the wide-eyed face that reminded her of a calf tied in a sack in a cart, only its head stretched dumbly backwards. And she triumphed.

The bound-up body began to struggle again. She watched fascinated the muscles working, the shoulders, the hips, the large, clean thighs. Even now he might break the ropes. She was afraid. But the lively young soldier sat on the shoulders of the bound man, and after a few perilous moments, there was stillness again.

"Now," said the judicious sergeant to the bound man, "if we untie you, will you promise to go off and make no more trouble?"

"You'll not untie him in here," cried the woman. "I wouldn't trust him as far as I could blow him."

There was silence.

"We might carry him outside, and undo him there," said the soldier. "Then we could get the policeman, if he made any more bother."

"Yes," said the sergeant. "We could do that." Then again, in an altered, almost severe tone, to the prisioner: "If we undo you outside, will you take your coat and go without creating any more disturbance?"

But the prisoner would not answer, he only lay with wide, dark, bright eyes, like a bound animal. There was a space of perplexed silence.

"Well, then, do as you say," said the woman irritably. "Carry him out amongst you, and let us shut up the house."

They did so. Picking up the bound man, the four soldiers staggered clumsily into the silent square in front of the inn, the woman following with the cap and the overcoat. The young soldiers quickly unfastened the braces from the prisoner's legs, and they hopped indoors. They were in their stocking-feet, and outside the stars flashed cold. They stood in the doorway watching. The man lay quite still on the cold ground.

"Now," said the sergeant, in a subdued voice, "I'll loosen the knot, and he can work himself free, if you go in, Missis."

She gave a last look at the dishevelled, bound man, as he sat on the ground. Then she went indoors, followed quickly by the sergeant. Then they were heard locking and barring the door.

The man seated on the ground outside worked and strained at the rope. But it was not so easy to undo himself even now. So, with hands bound, making an effort, he got on his feet, and went and worked the cord against the rough edge of an old wall. The rope, being of a kind of plaited grass, soon frayed and broke, and he freed himself. He had various contusions. His arms were hurt and bruised from the bonds. He rubbed them slowly. Then he pulled his clothes straight, stooped, put on his cap, struggled into his overcoat, and walked away.

The stars were very brilliant. Clear as crystal, the beam from the lighthouse under the cliffs struck rhythmically on the night. Dazed, the man walked along the road past the churchyard. Then he stood leaning up against a wall, for a long time.

He was roused because his feet were so cold. So he pulled himself together, and turned again in the silent night, back towards the inn.

The bar was in darkness. But there was a light in the kitchen. He hesitated. Then very quietly he tried the door.

He was surprised to find it open. He entered, and quietly closed it behind him. Then he went down the step past the bar-counter, and through to the lighted doorway of the kitchen. There sat his wife, planted in front of the range, where a furze fire was burning. She sat in a chair full in front of the range, her knees wide apart on the fender. She looked over her shoulder at him as he entered, but she did not speak. Then she stared in the fire again.

It was a small, narrow kitchen. He dropped his cap on the table that was covered with yellowish American cloth, and took a seat with his back to the wall, near the oven. His wife still sat with her knees apart, her feet on the steel fender and stared into the fire, motionless. Her skin was smooth and rosy in the firelight. Everything in the house was very clean and bright. The man sat silent, too, his head dropped. And thus they remained.

It was a question who would speak first. The woman leaned forward and poked the ends of the sticks in between the bars of the range. He lifted his head and looked at her.

"Others gone to bed, have they?" he asked.

But she remained closed in silence.

" 'S a cold night, out," he said, as if to himself.

And he laid his large, yet well-shapen workman's hand on the top of the stove, that was polished black and smooth as velvet. She would not look at him, yet she glanced out of the corners of her eyes.

His eyes were fixed brightly on her, the pupils large and electric like those of a cat.

"I should have picked you out among thousands," he said. "Though you're bigger than I'd have believed. Fine flesh you've made."

She was silent for some time. Then she turned in her chair upon him.

"What do you think of yourself," she said, "coming back on me like this after over fifteen year? You don't think I've not heard of you, neither, in Butte City and elsewhere?"

He was watching her with his clear, translucent, unchallenged eyes.

"Yes," he said. "Chaps comes an' goes—I've heard tell of you from time to time."

She drew herself up.

"And what lies have you heard about *me*?" she demanded superbly.

"I dunno as I've heard any lies at all—'cept as you was getting on very well, like."

His voice ran warily and detached. Her anger stirred again in her violently. But she subdued it, because of the danger there was in him, and more, perhaps, because of the beauty of his head and his level drawn brows, which she could not bear to forfeit.

"That's more than I can say of *you*," she said. "I've heard more harm than good about *you*."

"Ay, I dessay," he said looking in the fire. It was a long time since he had seen the furze burning, he said to himself. There was a silence, during which she watched his face.

"Do you call yourself a *man*?" she said, more in contemptuous reproach than in anger. "Leave a woman as you've left me, you don't care to what!—and then to turn up in *this* fashion, without a word to say for yourself."

He stirred in his chair, planted his feet apart, and resting his arms on his knees, looked steadily into the fire without answering. So near to her was his head, and the close black hair, she could scarcely refrain from starting away, as if it would bite her.

"Do you call that the action of a *man*?" she repeated.

"No," he said, reaching and poking the bits of wood into the fire with his fingers. "I didn't call it anything, as I know of.

It's no good calling things by any names whatsoever, as I know of.

She watched him in his actions. There was a longer and longer pause between each speech, though neither knew it.

"I *wonder* what you think of yourself!" she exclaimed, with vexed emphasis. "I *wonder* what sort of a fellow you take yourself to be!" She was really perplexed as well as angry.

"Well," he said, lifting his head to look at her, "I guess I'll answer for my own faults, if everybody else'll answer for theirs."

Her heart beat fiery hot as he lifted his face to her. She breathed heavily, averting her face, almost losing her self-control.

"And what do you take *me* to be?" she cried, in real helplessness.

His face was lifted, watching her soft, averted face. And the softly heaving mass of her breasts.

"I take you," he said, with that laconic truthfulness which exercised such power over her, "to be the deuce of a fine woman—darn me if you're not as fine a built woman as I've seen, handsome with it as well. I shouldn't have expected you to put on such handsome flesh: 'struth I shouldn't."

Her heart beat fiery hot, as he watched her with those bright agate eyes, fixedly.

"Been very handsome to *you*, for fifteen years, my sakes!" she replied.

He made no answer to this, but sat with his bright, quick eyes upon her.

Then he rose. She started involuntarily. But he only said, in his laconic, measured way:

"It's warm in here now."

And he pulled off his overcoat, throwing it on the table. She sat as if slightly cowed, whilst he did so.

"Them ropes has given my arms something, by Ga—ard," he drawled, feeling his arms with his hands.

Still she sat in her chair before him, slightly cowed.

"You was sharp, wasn't you, to catch me like that, eh?" he smiled slowly. "By Ga—ard, you had me fixed proper, proper you had. Darn me, you fixed me up proper—proper, you did."

He leaned forwards in his chair towards her.

"I don't think no worse of you for it, no, darned if I do. Fine pluck in a woman's what I admire. That I do, indeed."

She only gazed into the fire.

"We fet from the start, we did. And, my word, you begin again quick the minute you see me, you did. Darn me, you was too sharp for me. A darn fine woman, puts up a darn good fight. Darn me if I could find a woman in all the darn States as could get me down like that. Wonderful fine woman you be, truth to say, at this minute."

She only sat glowering into the fire.

"As grand a pluck as a man could wish to find in a woman, true as I'm here," he said, reaching forward his hand and tentatively touching her between her full, warm breasts, quietly.

She started, and seemed to shudder. But his hand insinuated itself between her breasts, as she continued to gaze in the fire.

"And don't you think I've come back here a-begging," he said. "I've more than *one* thousand pounds to my name, I have. And a bit of a fight for a how-de-do pleases me, that it do. But that doesn't mean as you're going to deny as you're my Missis . . ."

THE PRIMROSE PATH

A YOUNG man came out of the Victoria station, looking un-
decidedly at the taxi-cabs, dark red and black, pressing against
the kerb under the glass roof. Several men in greatcoats and
brass buttons jerked themselves erect to catch his attention, at
the same time keeping an eye on the other people as they
filtered through the open doorways of the station. Berry, however, was occupied by one of the men, a big, burly fellow
whose blue eyes glared back and whose red-brown moustache
bristled in defiance.

"Do you *want* a cab, sir?" the man asked, in a half-mocking,
challenging voice.

Berry hesitated still.

"Are you Daniel Sutton?" he asked.

"Yes," replied the other defiantly, with uneasy conscience.

"Then you are my uncle," said Berry.

They were alike in colouring, and somewhat in features, but
the taxi driver was a powerful, well-fleshed man who glared at
the world aggressively, being really on the defensive against
his own heart. His nephew, of the same height, was thin, well-
dressed, quiet and indifferent in his manner. And yet they
were obviously kin.

"And who the devil are you?" asked the taxi driver.

"I'm Daniel Berry," replied the nephew.

"Well, I'm damned—never saw you since you were a kid."
Rather awkwardly at this late hour the two shook hands.
"How are you, lad?"

"All right. I thought you were in Australia."

"Been back three months—bought a couple of these damned
things"—he kicked the tyre of his taxi-cab in affectionate
disgust. There was a moment's silence.

"Oh, but I'm going back out there. I can't stand this canker-
ing, rotten-hearted hell of a country any more; you want to
come out to Sydney with me, lad. That's the place for you—
beautiful place, oh, you could wish for nothing better. And
money in it, too. How's your mother?"

"She died at Christmas," said the young man.

"Dead! What!—our Anna!" The big man's eyes stared, and

427

he recoiled in fear. "God, lad," he said, "that's three of 'em gone!"

The two men looked away at the people passing along the pale grey pavements, under the wall of Trinity Church.

"Well, strike me lucky!" said the taxi driver at last, out of breath. "She wor th' best o' th' bunch of 'em. I see nowt nor hear nowt from any of 'em—they're not worth it, I'll be damned if they are—our sermon-lapping Adela and Maud," he looked scornfully at his nephew. "But she was the best of 'em, our Anna was, that's a fact."

He was talking because he was afraid.

"An' after a hard life like she'd had. How old was she, lad?"

"Fifty-five."

"Fifty-five . . ." He hesitated. Then, in a rather hushed voice, he asked the question that frightened him: "And what was it, then?"

"Cancer."

"Cancer again, like Julia! I never knew there was cancer in our family. Oh, my good God, our poor Anna, after the life she'd had! What, lad, do you see any God at the back of that? I'm damned if I do."

He was glaring, very blue-eyed and fierce, at his nephew. Berry lifted his shoulders slightly.

"God?" went on the taxi driver, in a curious intense tone. "You've only to look at the folk in the street to know there's nothing keeps it going but gravitation. Look at 'em. Look at him!" A mongrel-looking man was nosing past. "Wouldn't *he* murder you for your watch-chain, but that he's afraid of society? He's got it *in* him. . . . Look at 'em."

Berry watched the townspeople go by, and, sensitively feeling his uncle's antipathy, it seemed he was watching a sort of *danse macabre* of ugly criminals.

"Did you ever see such a God-forsaken crew creeping about! It gives you the very horrors to look at 'em. I sit in this damned car and watch 'em till, I can tell you, I feel like running the cab amuck among 'em, and running myself to kingdom come——"

Berry wondered at this outburst. He knew his uncle was the black sheep, the youngest, the darling of his mother's family. He knew him to be at outs with respectability, mixing with the looser, sporting type, all betting and drinking and showing dogs and birds, and racing. As a critic of life, however, he did not know him. But the young man felt curiously understanding. "He uses words like I do, he talks nearly as I talk, except that I shouldn't say those things. But I might feel like that, in myself, if I went a certain road."

"I've got to go to Watmore," he said. "Can you take me?"

"When d'you want to go?" asked the uncle fiercely.

"Now."

"Come on, then. What d'yer stand gassin' on th' causeway for?"

The nephew took his seat beside the driver. The cab began to quiver, then it started forward with a whirr. The uncle, his hands and feet acting mechanically, kept his blue eyes fixed on the high road into whose traffic the car was insinuating its way. Berry felt curiously as if he were sitting beside an older development of himself. His mind went back to his mother. She had been twenty years older than this brother of hers, whom she had loved so dearly. "He was one of the most affectionate little lads, and such a curly head! I could never have believed he would grow into the great, coarse bully he is—for he's nothing else. My father made a god of him—well, it's a good thing his father is dead. He got in with that sporting gang, that's what did it. Things were made too easy for him, and so he thought of no one but himself, and this is the result."

Not that "Joky" Sutton was so very black a sheep. He had lived idly till he was eighteen, then had suddenly married a young, beautiful girl with clear brows and dark-grey eyes, a factory girl. Having taken her to live with his parents he, lover of dogs and pigeons, went on to the staff of a sporting paper. But his wife was without uplift or warmth. Though they made money enough, their house was dark and cold and uninviting. He had two or three dogs, and the whole attic was turned into a great pigeon-house. He and his wife lived together roughly, with no warmth, no refinement, no touch of beauty anywhere, except that she was beautiful. He was a blustering, impetuous man, she was rather cold in her soul, did not care about anything very much, was rather capable and close with money. And she had a common accent in her speech. He outdid her a thousand times in coarse language, and yet that cold twang in her voice tortured him with shame that he stamped down in bullying and in becoming more violent in his own speech.

Only his dogs adored him, and to them, and to his pigeons, he talked with rough, yet curiously tender caresses while they leaped and fluttered for joy.

After he and his wife had been married for seven years a little girl was born to them, then later, another. But the husband and wife drew no nearer together. She had an affection for her children almost like a cool governess. He had an emotional man's fear of sentiment, which helped to nip his wife from putting out any shoots. He treated his children roughly, and pretended to think it a good job when one was adopted by a well-to-do maternal aunt. But in his soul he hated his wife that she could give away one of his children. For after her cool fashion, she loved him. With a chaos of a man such as he, she had no chance of being anything but cold and hard, poor thing. For she did love him.

In the end he fell absurdly and violently in love with a rather sentimental young woman who read Browning. He made his wife an allowance and established a new *ménage* with the young lady, shortly after emigrating with her to Australia. Meanwhile his wife had gone to live with a publican, a widower, with whom she had had one of those curious, tacit understandings of which quiet women are capable, something like an arrangement for provision in the future.

This was as much as the nephew knew. He sat beside his uncle, wondering how things stood at the present. They raced lightly out past the cemetery and along the boulevard, then turned into the rather grimy country. The mud flew out on either side, there was a fine mist of rain which blew in their faces. Berry covered himself up.

In the lanes the high hedges shone black with rain. The silvery-grey sky, faintly dappled, spread wide over the low, green land. The elder man glanced fiercely up the road, then turned his red face to his nephew.

"And how're you going on, lad?" he said loudly. Berry noticed that his uncle was slightly uneasy of him. It made him also uncomfortable. The elder man had evidently something pressing on his soul.

"Who are you living with in town?" asked the nephew. "Have you gone back to Aunt Maud?"

"No," barked the uncle. "She wouldn't have me. I offered to—I wanted to—but she wouldn't."

"You're alone, then?"

"No, I'm not alone."

He turned and glared with his fierce blue eyes at his nephew, but said no more for some time. The car ran on through the mud, under the wet wall of the park.

"That other devil tried to poison me," suddenly shouted the elder man. "The one I went to Australia with." At which, in spite of himself, the younger smiled in secret.

"How was that?" he asked.

"Wanted to get rid of me. She got in with another fellow on the ship. . . . By Jove, I was bad."

"Where—on the ship?"

"No," bellowed the other. "No. That was in Wellington, New Zealand. I was bad, and got lower an' lower—couldn't think what was up. I could hardly crawl about. As certain as I'm here, she was poisoning me, to get to th' other chap—I'm certain of it."

"And what did you do?"

"I cleared out—went to Sydney——"

"And left her?"

"Yes, I thought begod I'd better clear out if I wanted to live."

"And you were all right in Sydney?"

"Better in no time—I *know* she was putting poison in my coffee."

"Hm!"

There was a glum silence. The driver stared at the road ahead, fixedly, managing the car as if it were a live thing. The nephew felt that his uncle was afraid, quite stupefied with fear, fear of life, of death, of himself.

"You're in rooms, then?" asked the nephew.

"No, I'm in a house of my own," said the uncle defiantly, "wi' th' best little woman in th' Midlands. She's a marvel. Why don't you come an see us?"

"I will. Who is she?"

"Oh, she's a good girl—a beautiful little thing. I was clean gone on her first time I saw her. An' she was on me. Her mother lives with us—respectable girl, none o' your . . ."

"And how old is she?"

"How old is she? She's twenty-one."

"Poor thing."

"*She's* right enough."

"You'd marry her—getting a divorce——?"

"I shall marry her."

There was a little antagonism between the two men.

"Where's Aunt Maud?" asked the younger.

"She's at the 'Railway Arms'—we passed it, just against Rollin's Mill Crossing. . . . They sent me a note this morning to go an' see her when I can spare time. She's got consumption."

"Good Lord! Are you going?"

"Yes——"

But again Berry felt that his uncle was afraid.

The young man got through his commission in the village, had a drink with his uncle at the inn, and the two were returning home. The elder man's subject of conversation was Australia. As they drew near the town they grew silent, thinking both of the public-house. At last they saw the gates of the railway crossing were closed before them.

"Shan't you call?" asked Berry, jerking his head in the direction of the inn, which stood at the corner between two roads, its sign hanging under a bare horse-chestnut tree in front.

"I might as well. Come in an' have a drink," said the uncle.

It had been raining all the morning, so shallow pools of water lay about. A brewer's wagon, with wet barrels and warm-smelling horses, stood near the door of the inn. Everywhere seemed silent, but for the rattle of trains at the crossing. The two men went uneasily up the steps and into the bar. The place was paddled with wet feet, empty. As the barman was heard approaching, the uncle asked, his usual bluster slightly hushed by fear:

"What yer goin' ta have, lad? Same as last time?"

A man entered, evidently the proprietor. He was good-looking, with a long, heavy face and quick, dark eyes. His glance at Sutton was swift, a start, a recognition, and a withdrawal, into heavy neutrality.

"How are yer, Dan?" he said, scarcely troubling to speak.

"Are yer, George?" replied Sutton, hanging back. "My nephew, Dan Berry. Give us Red Seal, George."

The publican nodded to the younger man, and set the glasses on the bar. He pushed forward the two glasses, then leaned back in the dark corner behind the door, his arms folded, evidently preferring to get back from the watchful eyes of the nephew.

"——'s luck," said Sutton.

The publican nodded in acknowledgment. Sutton and his nephew drank.

"Why the hell don't you get that road mended in Cinder Hill——" said Sutton fiercely, pushing back his driver's cap and showing his short-cut, bristling hair.

"They can't find it in their hearts to pull it up," replied the publican, laconically.

"Find in their hearts! They want settin' in barrows an' runnin' up an' down it till they cried for mercy."

Sutton put down his glass. The publican renewed it with a sure hand, at ease in whatsoever he did. Then he leaned back against the bar. He wore no coat. He stood with arms folded, his chin on his chest, his long moustache hanging. His back was round and slack, so that the lower part of his abdomen stuck forward, though he was not stout. His cheek was healthy, brown-red, and he was muscular. Yet there was about him this physical slackness, a reluctance in his slow, sure movements. His eyes were keen under his dark brows, but reluctant also, as if he were gloomily apathetic.

There was a halt. The publican evidently would say nothing. Berry looked at the mahogany bar-counter, slopped with beer, at the whisky-bottles on the shelves. Sutton, his cap pushed back, showing a white brow above a weather-reddened face, rubbed his cropped hair uneasily.

The publican glanced round suddenly. It seemed that only his dark eyes moved.

"Going up?" he asked.

And something, perhaps his eyes, indicated the unseen bedchamber.

"Ay—that's what I came for," replied Sutton, shifting nervously from one foot to the other. "She's been asking for me?"

"This morning," replied the publican, neutral.

Then he put up a flap of the bar, and turned away through the dark doorway behind. Sutton, pulling off his cap, showing a round, short-cropped head which now was ducked forward, followed after him, the buttons holding the strap of his greatcoat behind glittering for a moment.

They climbed the dark stairs, the husband placing his feet carefully, because of his big boots. Then he followed down the passage, trying vaguely to keep a grip on his bowels, which seemed to be melting away, and definitely wishing for a neat brandy. The publican opened a door. Sutton, big and burly in his greatcoat, went past him.

The bedroom seemed light and warm after the passage. There was a red eiderdown on the bed. Then, making an effort, Sutton turned his eyes to see the sick woman. He met her eyes direct, dark, dilated. It was such a shock he almost started away. For a second he remained in torture, as if some invisible flame were playing on him to reduce his bones and fuse him down. Then he saw the sharp white edge of her jaw, and the black hair beside the hollow cheek. With a start he went towards the bed.

"Hello, Maud!" he said. "Why, what ye been doin'?"

The publican stood at the window with his back to the bed. The husband, like one condemned but on the point of starting away, stood by the bedside staring in horror at his wife, whose dilated grey eyes, nearly all black now, watched him wearily, as if she were looking at something a long way off.

Going exceedingly pale, he jerked up his head and stared at the wall over the pillows. There was a little coloured picture of a bird perched on a bell, and a nest among ivy leaves beneath. It appealed to him, made him wonder, roused a feeling of childish magic in him. They were wonderfully fresh, green ivy leaves, and nobody had seen the nest among them save him.

Then suddenly he looked down again at the face on the bed, to try and recognise it. He knew the white brow and the beautiful clear eyebrows. That was his wife, with whom he had passed his youth, flesh of his flesh, his, himself. Then those tired eyes, which met his again from a long way off, disturbed him until he did not know where he was. Only the sunken cheeks and the mouth that seemed to protrude now were foreign to him, and filled him with horror. It seemed he lost his identity. He was the young husband of the woman with the clear brows; he was the married man fighting with her whose eyes watched him, a little indifferently, from a long way off; and he was a child in horror of that protruding mouth.

There came a crackling sound of her voice. He knew she had consumption of the throat, and braced himself hard to bear the noise.

"What was it, Maud?" he asked in panic.

Then the broken, crackling voice came again. He was too

terrified of the sound of it to hear what was said. There was a pause.

"You'll take Winnie?" the publican's voice interpreted from the window.

"Don't you bother, Maud, I'll take her," he said, stupefying his mind so as not to understand.

He looked curiously round the room. It was not a bad bed-room, light and warm. There were many medicine bottles aggregated in a corner of the washstand—and a bottle of Three Star brandy, half full. And there were also photographs of strange people on the chest of drawers. It was not a bad room.

Again he started as if he were shot. She was speaking. He bent down, but did not look at her.

"Be good to her," she whispered.

When he realised her meaning, that he should be good to their child when the mother was gone, a blade went through his flesh.

"I'll be good to her, Maud, don't you bother," he said, beginning to feel shaky.

He looked again at the picture of the bird. It perched cheerfully under a blue sky, with robust, jolly ivy leaves near. He was gathering his courage to depart. He looked down, but struggled hard not to take in the sight of his wife's face.

"I s'll come again, Maud," he said. "I hope you'll go on all right. Is there anything as you want?"

There was an almost imperceptible shake of the head from the sick woman, making his heart melt swiftly again. Then, dragging his limbs, he got out of the room and down the stairs.

The landlord came after him.

"I'll let you know if anything happens," the publican said, still laconic, but with his eyes dark and swift.

"Ay, a' right," said Sutton blindly. He looked round for his cap, which he had all the time in his hand. Then he got out of doors.

In a moment the uncle and nephew were in the car jolting on the level crossing. The elder man seemed as if something tight in his brain made him open his eyes wide, and stare. He held the steering-wheel firmly. He knew he could steer accurately, to a hair's breadth. Glaring fixedly ahead, he let the car go, till it bounded over the uneven road. There were three coal-carts in a string. In an instant the car grazed past them, almost biting the kerb on the other side. Sutton aimed his car like a projectile, staring ahead. He did not want to know, to think, to realise, he wanted to be only the driver of that quick taxi.

The town drew near suddenly. There were allotment-gardens, with dark-purple twiggy fruit trees and wet alleys between the hedges. Then suddenly the streets of dwelling-houses whirled close, and the car was climbing the hill, with an angry whirr—up—up—till they rode out on to the crest and could see the tramcars, dark red and yellow, threading their way round the corner below, and all the traffic roaring between the shops.

"Got anywhere to go?" asked Sutton of his nephew.

"I was going to see one or two people."

"Come an' have a bit o' dinner with us," said the other.

Berry knew that his uncle wanted to be distracted, so that he should not think nor realise. The big man was running hard away from the horror of realisation.

"All right," Berry agreed.

The car went quickly through the town. It ran up a long street nearly into the country again. Then it pulled up at a house that stood alone, below the road.

"I s'll be back in ten minutes," said the uncle.

The car went on to the garage. Berry stood curiously at the top of the stone stairs that led from the high-road down to the level of the house, an old stone place. The garden was dilapidated. Broken fruit trees leaned at a sharp angle down the steep bank. Right across the dim grey atmosphere, in a kind of valley on the edge of the town, new suburb-patches showed pinkish on the dark earth. It was a kind of unresolved border-land.

Berry went down the steps. Through the broken black fence of the orchard, long grass showed yellow. The place seemed deserted. He knocked, then knocked again. An elderly woman appeared. She looked like a housekeeper. At first she said suspiciously that Mr. Sutton was not in.

"My uncle just put me down. He'll be in in ten minutes," replied the visitor.

"Oh, are you the Mr. Berry who is related to him?" exclaimed the elderly woman. "Come in—come in."

She was at once kindly and a little bit servile. The young man entered. It was an old house, rather dark, and sparsely furnished. The elderly woman sat nervously on the edge of one of the chairs in a drawing-room that looked as if it were furnished from dismal relics of dismal homes, and there was a little straggling attempt at conversation. Mrs. Greenwell was evidently a working-class woman unused to service or to any formality.

Presently she gathered up courage to invite her visitor into the dining-room. There from the table under the window rose a tall, slim girl with a cat in her arms. She was evidently a little more lady-like than was habitual to her, but she had a gentle, delicate, small nature. Her brown hair almost covered her ears, her dark lashes came down in shy awkwardness over her beautiful blue eyes. She shook hands in a frank way, yet she was shrinking. Evidently she was not sure how her position would affect her visitor. And yet she was assured in herself, shrinking and timid as she was.

"She must be a good deal in love with him," thought Berry.

Both women glanced shamefacedly at the roughly laid table. Evidently they ate in a rather rough and ready fashion.

Elaine—she had this poetic name—fingered her cat timidly, not knowing what to say or to do, unable even to ask her visitor to sit down. He noticed how her skirt hung almost flat on her hips. She was young, scarce developed, a long, slender thing. Her clothing was warm and exquisite.

The elder woman bustled out to the kitchen. Berry fondled the terrier dogs that had come curiously to his heels, and glanced out of the window at the wet, deserted orchard.

This room, too, was not well furnished, and rather dark. But there was a big red fire.

"He always has fox-terriers," he said.

"Yes," she answered, showing her teeth in a smile.

"Do you like them, too?"

"Yes"—she glanced down at the dogs. "I like Tam better than Sally——"

Her speech always tailed off into an awkward silence.

"We've been to see Aunt Maud," said the nephew.

Her eyes, blue and scared and shrinking, met his.

"Dan had a letter," he explained. "She's very bad."

"Isn't it horrible!" she exclaimed, her face crumbling up with fear.

The old woman, evidently a hard-used, rather down-trodden workman's wife, came in with two soup-plates. She glanced anxiously to see how her daughter was progressing with the visitor.

"Mother, Dan's been to see Maud," said Elaine, in a quiet voice full of fear and trouble.

The old woman looked up anxiously, in question.

"I think she wanted him to take the child. She's very bad, I believe," explained Berry.

"Oh, we should take Winnie!" cried Elaine. But both women seemed uncertain, wavering in their position. Already Berry could see that his uncle had bullied them, as he bullied everybody. But they were used to unpleasant men, and seemed to keep at a distance.

"Will you have some soup?" asked the mother humbly.

She evidently did the work. The daughter was to be a lady, more or less, always dressed and nice for when Sutton came in.

They heard him heavily running down the steps outside. The dogs got up. Elaine seemed to forget the visitor. It was as if she came into life. Yet she was nervous and afraid. The mother stood as if ready to exculpate herself.

Sutton burst open the door. Big, blustering, wet in his immense grey coat, he came into the dining-room.

"Hello!" he said to his nephew, "making yourself at home?"

"Oh yes," replied Berry.

"Hello, Jack," he said to the girl. "Got owt to grizzle about?"

"What for?" she asked, in a clear, half-challenging voice, that had that peculiar twang, almost petulant, so female and so attractive. Yet she was defiant like a boy.

"It's a wonder if you haven't," growled Sutton. And, with a really intimate movement, he stooped down and fondled his dogs, though paying no attention to them. Then he stood up, and remained with feet apart on the hearth-rug, his head ducked forward, watching the girl. He seemed abstracted, as if he could only watch her. His greatcoat hung open, so that she could see his figure, simple and human in the great husk of cloth. She stood nervously with her hands behind her, glancing at him, unable to see anything else. And he was scarcely conscious but of her. His eyes were still strained and staring, and as they followed the girl, when, long-limbed and languid, she moved away, it was as if he saw in her something impersonal, the female, not the woman.

"Had your dinner?' he asked.

"We were just going to have it," she replied, with the same

curious little vibration in her voice, like the twang of a string.

The mother entered, bringing a saucepan from which she ladled soup into three plates.

"Sit down, lad," said Sutton. "You sit down, Jack, an' give me mine here."

"Oh, aren't you coming to table?" she complained .

"No, I tell you," he snarled, almost pretending to be disagreeable. But she was slightly afraid even of the pretence, which pleased and relieved him. He stood on the hearth-rug eating his soup noisily.

"Aren't you going to take your coat off?" she said. "It's filling the place full of steam."

He did not answer, but, with his head bent forward over the plate, he ate his soup hastily, to get it done with. When he put down his empty plate, she rose and went to him.

"Do take your coat off, Dan," she said, and she took hold of the breast of his coat, trying to push it back over his shoulder. But she could not. Only the stare in his eyes changed to a glare as her hand moved over his shoulder. He looked down into her eyes. She became pale, rather frightened-looking, and she turned her face away, and it was drawn slightly with love and fear and misery. She tried again to put off his coat, her thin wrists pulling at it. He stood solidly planted, and did not look at her, but stared straight in front. She was playing with passion, afraid of it, and really wretched because it left her, the person, out of count. Yet she continued. And there came into his bearing, into his eyes, the curious smile of passion, pushing away even the death-horror. It was life stronger than death in him. She stood close to his breast. Their eyes met, and she was carried away.

"Take your coat off, Dan," she said coaxingly, in a low tone meant for no one but him. And she slid her hands on his shoulder, and he yielded, so that the coat was pushed back. She had flushed, and her eyes had grown very bright. She got hold of the cuff of his coat. Gently, he eased himself, so that she drew it off. Then he stood in a thin suit, which revealed his vigorous, almost mature form.

"What a weight!" she exclaimed, in a peculiar penetrating voice, as she went out hugging the overcoat. In a moment she came back.

He stood still in the same position, a frown over his fiercely staring eyes. The pain, the fear, the horror in his breast were all burning away in the new, fiercest flame of passion.

"Get your dinner," he said roughly to her.

"I've had all I want," she said. "You come an' have yours."

He looked at the table as if he found it difficult to see things.

"I want no more," he said.

She stood close to his chest. She wanted to touch him and to comfort him. There was something about him now that fascinated her. Berry felt slightly ashamed that she seemed to ignore the presence of others in the room.

The mother came in. She glanced at Sutton, standing planted on the hearth-rug, his head ducked, the heavy frown hiding his face. There was a peculiar braced intensity about him that made the elder woman afraid. Suddenly he jerked his head round to his nephew.

"Get on wi' your dinner, lad," he said, and he went to the door. The dogs, which had continually lain down and got up again, uneasy, now rose and watched. The girl went after him, saying, clearly:

"What did you want, Dan?"

Her slim, quick figure was gone, the door was closed behind her.

There was silence. The mother, still more slave-like in her movement, sat down in a low chair. Berry drank some beer.

"That girl will leave him," he said to himself. "She'll hate him like poison. And serve him right. Then she'll go off with somebody else."

And she did.

THE HORSE DEALER'S DAUGHTER

"WELL, Mabel, and what are you going to do with yourself?" asked Joe, with foolish flippancy. He felt quite safe himself. Without listening for an answer, he turned aside, worked a grain of tobacco to the tip of his tongue, and spat it out. He did not care about anything, since he felt safe himself.

The three brothers and the sister sat round the desolate breakfast-table, attempting some sort of desultory consultation. The morning's post had given the final tap to the family fortunes, and all was over. The dreary dining-room itself, with its heavy mahogany furniture, looked as if it were waiting to be done away with.

But the consultation amounted to nothing. There was a strange air of ineffectuality about the three men, as they sprawled at table, smoking and reflecting vaguely on their own condition. The girl was alone, a rather short, sullen-looking young woman of twenty-seven. She did not share the same life as her brothers. She would have been good-looking, save for the impressive fixity of her face, 'bull-dog', as her brothers called it.

There was a confused tramping of horses' feet outside. The three men all sprawled round in their chairs to watch. Beyond the dark holly bushes that separated the strip of lawn from the high-road, they could see a cavalcade of shire horses swinging out of their own yard, being taken for exercise. This was the last time. These were the last horses that would go through their hands. The young men watched with critical, callous look. They were all frightened at the collapse of their lives, and the sense of disaster in which they were involved left them no inner freedom.

Yet they were three fine, well-set fellows enough. Joe, the eldest, was a man of thirty-three, broad and handsome in a hot, flushed way. His face was red, he twisted his black moustache over a thick finger, his eyes were shallow and restless. He had a sensual way of uncovering his teeth when he laughed, and his bearing was stupid. Now he watched the horses with a glazed look of helplessness in his eyes, a certain stupor of downfall.

The great draught-horses swung past. They were tied head

to tail, four of them, and they heaved along to where a lane branched off from the high-road, planting their great hoofs floutingly in the fine black mud, swinging their great rounded haunches sumptuously, and trotting a few sudden steps as they were led into the lane, round the corner. Every movement showed a massive, slumbrous strength, and a stupidity which held them in subjection. The groom at the head looked back, jerking the leading rope. And the cavalcade moved out of sight up the lane, the tail of the last horse, bobbed up tight and stiff, held out taut from the swinging great haunches as they rocked behind the hedges in a motion-like sleep.

Joe watched with glazed hopeless eyes. The horses were almost like his own body to him. He felt he was done for now. Luckily he was engaged to a woman as old as himself, and therefore her father, who was steward of a neighbouring estate, would provide him with a job. He would marry and go into harness. His life was over, he would be a subject animal now.

He turned uneasily aside, the retreating steps of the horses echoing in his ears. Then, with foolish restlessness, he reached for the scraps of bacon-rind from the plates, and making a faint whistling sound, flung them to the terrier that lay against the fender. He watched the dog swallow them, and waited till the creature looked into his eyes. Then a faint grin came on his face, and in a high, foolish voice he said:

"You won't get much more bacon, shall you, you little b—?"

The dog faintly and dismally wagged its tail, then lowered its haunches, circled round, and lay down again.

There was another helpless silence at the table. Joe sprawled uneasily in his seat, not willing to go till the family conclave was dissolved. Fred Henry, the second brother, was erect, clean-limbed, alert. He had watched the passing of the horses with more *sang-froid*. If he was an animal, like Joe, he was an animal which controls, not one which is controlled. He was master of any horse, and he carried himself with a well-tempered air of mastery. But he was not master of the situations of life. He pushed his coarse brown moustache upwards, off his lip, and glanced irritably at his sister, who sat impassive and inscrutable.

"You'll go and stop with Lucy for a bit, shan't you?" he asked. The girl did not answer.

"I don't see what else you can do," persisted Fred Henry.

"Go as a skivvy," Joe interpolated laconically.

The girl did not move a muscle.

"If I was her, I should go in for training for a nurse," said Malcolm, the youngest of them all. He was the baby of the family, a young man of twenty-two, with a fresh, jaunty *museau*.

But Mabel did not take any notice of him. They had talked at her and round her for so many years, that she hardly heard them at all.

The marble clock on the mantelpiece softly chimed the half-hour, the dog rose uneasily from the hearth-rug and looked at the party at the breakfast-table. But still they sat on in ineffectual conclave.

"Oh, all right," said Joe suddenly, apropos of nothing. "I'll get a move on."

He pushed back his chair, straddled his knees with a downward jerk, to get them free, in horsey fashion, and went to the fire. Still he did not go out of the room; he was curious to know what the others would do or say. He began to charge his pipe, looking down at the dog and saying in a high, affected voice:

"Going wi' me? Going wi' me are ter? Tha'rt goin' further than tha counts on just now, dost hear?"

The dog faintly wagged its tail, the man stuck out his jaw and covered his pipe with his hands, and puffed intently, losing himself in the tobacco, looking down all the while at the dog with an absent brown eye. The dog looked up at him in mournful distrust. Joe stood with his knees stuck out, in real horsey fashion.

"Have you had a letter from Lucy?" Fred Henry asked of his sister.

"Last week," came the neutral reply.

"And what does she say?"

There was no answer.

"Does she *ask* you to go and stop there?" persisted Fred Henry.

"She says I can if I like."

"Well, then, you'd better. Tell her you'll come on Monday." This was received in silence.

"That's what you'll do then, is it?" said Fred Henry, in some exasperation.

But she made no answer. There was a silence of futility and

irritation in the room. Malcolm grinned fatuously.

"You'll have to make up your mind between now and next Wednesday," said Joe loudly, "or else find yourself lodgings on the kerbstone."

The face of the young woman darkened, but she sat on immutable.

"Here's Jack Ferguson!" exclaimed Malcolm, who was looking aimlessly out of the window.

"Where?" exclaimed Joe loudly.

"Just gone past."

"Coming in?"

Malcolm craned his neck to see the gate.

"Yes," he said.

There was a silence. Mabel sat on like one condemned, at the head of the table. Then a whistle was heard from the kitchen. The dog got up and barked sharply. Joe opened the door and shouted:

"Come on."

After a moment a young man entered. He was muffled up in overcoat and a purple woollen scarf, and his tweed cap, which he did not remove, was pulled down on his head. He was of medium height, his face was rather long and pale, his eyes looked tired.

"Hello, Jack! Well, Jack!" exclaimed Malcolm and Joe. Fred Henry merely said: "Jack."

"What's doing?" asked the newcomer, evidently addressing Fred Henry.

"Same. We've got to be out by Wednesday. Got a cold?"

"I have—got it bad, too."

"Why don't you stop in?"

"*Me* stop in? When I can't stand on my legs, perhaps I shall have a chance." The young man spoke huskily. He had a slight Scotch accent.

"It's a knock-out, isn't it," said Joe, boisterously, "if a doctor goes round croaking with a cold. Looks bad for the patients, doesn't it?"

The young doctor looked at him slowly.

"Anything the matter with *you*, then?" he asked sarcastically.

"Not as I know of. Damn your eyes, I hope not. Why?"

"I thought you were very concerned about the patients, wondered if you might be one yourself."

"Damn it, no, I've never been patient to no flaming doctor, and hope I never shall be," returned Joe.

At this point Mabel rose from the table, and they all seemed to become aware of her existence. She began putting the dishes together. The young doctor looked at her, but did not address her. He had not greeted her. She went out of the room with the tray, her face impassive and unchanged.

"When are you off then, all of you?" asked the doctor.

"I'm catching the eleven-forty," replied Malcolm. "Are you goin' down wi' th' trap, Joe?"

"Yes, I've told you I'm going down wi' th' trap, haven't I?"

"We'd better be getting her in then. So long, Jack, if I don't see you before I go," said Malcolm, shaking hands.

He went out, followed by Joe, who seemed to have his tail between his legs.

"Well, this is the devil's own," exclaimed the doctor, when he was left alone with Fred Henry. "Going before Wednesday, are you?"

"That's the orders," replied the other.

"Where, to Northampton?"

"That's it."

"The devil!" exclaimed Ferguson, with quiet chagrin.

And there was silence between the two.

"All settled up, are you?" asked Ferguson.

"About."

There was another pause.

"Well, I shall miss yer, Freddy, boy," said the young doctor.

"And I shall miss thee, Jack," returned the other.

"Miss you like hell," mused the doctor.

Fred Henry turned aside. There was nothing to say. Mabel came in again, to finish clearing the table.

"What are *you* going to do, then, Miss Pervin?" asked Fergusson. "Going to your sister's, are you?"

Mabel looked at him with her steady, dangerous eyes, that always made him uncomfortable, unsettling his superficial ease.

"No," she said.

"Well, what in the name of fortune *are* you going to do? Say what you mean to do," cried Fred Henry, with futile intensity.

But she only averted her head, and continued her work. She folded the white table-cloth, and put on the chenille cloth.

"The sulkiest bitch that ever trod!" muttered her brother.

But she finished her task with perfectly impassive face, the young doctor watching her interestedly all the while. Then she went out.

Fred Henry stared after her, clenching his lips, his blue eyes fixing in sharp antagonism, as he made a grimace of sour exasperation.

"You could bray her into bits, and that's all you'd get out of her," he said, in a small, narrowed tone.

The doctor smiled faintly.

"What's she *going* to do, then?" he asked.

"Strike me if *I* know!" returned the other.

There was a pause. Then the doctor stirred.

"I'll be seeing you to-night, shall I?" he said to his friend.

"Ay—where's it to be? Are we going over to Jessdale?"

"I don't know. I've got such a cold on me. I'll come round to the 'Moon and Stars', anyway."

"Let Lizzie and May miss their night for once, eh?"

"That's it—if I feel as I do now."

"All's one——"

The two young men went through the passage and down to the back door together. The house was large, but it was servant-less now, and desolate. At the back was a small bricked house-yard and beyond that a big square, gravelled fine and red, and having stables on two sides. Sloping, dank, winter-dark fields stretched away on the open sides.

But the stables were empty. Joseph Pervin, the father of the family, had been a man of no education, who had become a fairly large horse dealer. The stables had been full of horses, there was a great turmoil and come-and-go of horses and of dealers and grooms. Then the kitchen was full of servants. But of late things had declined. The old man had married a second time, to retrieve his fortunes. Now he was dead and everything was gone to the dogs, there was nothing but debt and threatening.

For months, Mabel had been servantless in the big house, keeping the home together in penury for her ineffectual brothers. She had kept house for ten years. But previously it was with unstinted means. Then, however brutal and coarse everything was, the sense of money had kept her proud, confident. The men might be foul-mouthed, the women in the kitchen might have bad reputations, her brothers might have illegitimate children. But so long as there was money, the girl felt herself established, and brutally proud, reserved.

No company came to the house, save dealers and coarse men. Mabel had no associates of her own sex, after her sister went away. But she did not mind. She went regularly to church, she attended to her father. And she lived in the memory of her mother, who had died when she was fourteen, and whom she had loved. She had loved her father, too, in a different way, depending upon him, and feeling secure in him, until at the age of fifty-four he married again. And then she had set hard against him. Now he had died and left them all hopelessly in debt.

She had suffered badly during the period of poverty. Nothing, however, could shake the curious, sullen, animal pride that dominated each member of the family. Now, for Mabel, the end had come. Still she would not cast about her. She would follow her own way just the same. She would always hold the keys of her own situation. Mindless and persistent, she endured from day to day. Why should she think? Why should she answer anybody? It was enough that this was the end, and there was no way out. She need not pass any more darkly along the main street of the small town, avoiding every eye. She need not demean herself any more, going into the shops and buying the cheapest food. This was at an end. She thought of nobody, not even of herself. Mindless and persistent, she seemed in a sort of ecstasy to be coming nearer to her fulfilment, her own glorification, approaching her dead mother, who was glorified.

In the afternoon she took a little bag, with shears and sponge and a small scrubbing-brush, and went out. It was a grey, wintry day, with saddened, dark green fields and an atmosphere blackened by the smoke of foundries not far off. She went quickly, darkly along the causeway, heeding nobody, through the town to the churchyard.

There she always felt secure, as if no one could see her, although as a matter of fact she was exposed to the stare of everyone who passed along under the churchyard wall. Nevertheless, once under the shadow of the great looming church, among the graves, she felt immune from the world, reserved within the thick churchyard wall as in another country.

Carefully she clipped the grass from the grave, and arranged the pinky white, small chrysanthemums in the tin cross. When this was done, she took an empty jar from a neighbouring grave, brought water, and carefully, most scrupulously sponged the marble headstone and the coping-stone.

It gave her sincere satisfaction to do this. She felt in immediate contact with the world of her mother. She took minute pains, went through the park in a state bordering on pure happiness, as if in performing this task she came into a subtle, intimate connection with her mother. For the life she followed here in the world was far less real than the world of death she inherited from her mother.

The doctor's house was just by the church. Fergusson, being a mere hired assistant, was slave to the country-side. As he hurried now to attend to the out-patients in the surgery, glancing across the graveyard with his quick eye, he saw the girl at her task at the grave. She seemed so intent and remote, it was like looking into another world. Some mystical element was touched in him. He slowed down as he walked, watching her as if spellbound.

She lifted her eyes, feeling him looking. Their eyes met. And each looked again at once, each feeling, in some way, found out by the other. He lifted his cap and passed on down the road. There remained distinct in his consciousness, like a vision, the memory of her face, lifted from the tombstone in the churchyard, and looking at him with slow, large, portentous eyes. It *was* portentous, her face. It seemed to mesmerise him. There was a heavy power in her eyes which laid hold of his whole being, as if he had drunk some powerful drug. He had been feeling weak and done before. Now the life came back into him, he felt delivered from his own fretted, daily self.

He finished his duties at the surgery as quickly as might be, hastily filling up the bottles of the waiting people with cheap drugs. Then, in perpetual haste, he set off again to visit several cases in another part of his round, before tea-time. At all times he preferred to walk if he could, but particularly when he was not well. He fancied the motion restored him.

The afternoon was falling. It was grey, deadened, and wintry, with a slow, moist, heavy coldness sinking in and deadening all the faculties. But why should he think or notice? He hastily climbed the hill and turned across the dark green fields, following the black cinder-track. In the distance, across a shallow dip in the country, the small town was clustered like smouldering ash, a tower, a spire, a heap of low, raw, extinct houses. And on the nearest fringe of the town, sloping into the dip, was Oldmeadow, the Pervins' house. He could see the stables and the outbuildings distinctly, as they lay towards him on the slope. Well, he would not go there many more times! Another resource would be lost to him, another place gone: the only company he cared for in the alien, ugly little town he was losing. Nothing but work, drudgery, constant hastening from dwelling to dwelling among the colliers and the iron-workers. It wore him out, but at the same time he had a craving for it. It was a stimulant to him to be in the homes of the working people, moving, as it were, through the innermost body of their life. His nerves were excited and gratified. He could come so near, into the very lives of the rough, inarticulate, powerfully emotional men and women. He grumbled, he said he hated the hellish hole. But as a matter of fact it excited him, the contact with the rough, strongly-feeling people was a stimulant applied direct to his nerves.

Below Oldmeadow, in the green, shallow, soddened hollow of fields, lay a square, deep pond. Roving across the landscape, the doctor's quick eye detected a figure in black passing through the gate of the field, down towards the pond. He looked again. It would be Mabel Pervin. His mind suddenly became alive and attentive.

Why was she going down there? He pulled up on the path on the slope above, and stood staring. He could just make sure of the small black figure moving in the hollow of the failing day. He seemed to see her in the midst of such obscurity, that he was like a clairvoyant, seeing rather with the mind's eye than with ordinary sight. Yet he could see her positively enough, whilst he kept his eye attentive. He felt, if he looked away from her, in the thick, ugly falling dusk, he would lose her altogether.

He followed her minutely as she moved, direct and intent, like something transmitted rather than stirring in voluntary activity, straight down the field towards the pond. There she stood on the bank for a moment. She never raised her head. Then she waded slowly into the water.

He stood motionless as the small black figure walked slowly and deliberately towards the centre of the pond, very slowly, gradually moving deeper into the motionless water, and still moving forward as the water got up to her breast. Then he could see her no more in the dusk of the dead afternoon.

"There!" he exclaimed. "Would you believe it?"

And he hastened straight down, running over the wet, soddened fields, pushing through the hedges, down into the depression of callous wintry obscurity. It took him several minutes to come to the pond. He stood on the bank, breathing heavily. He could see nothing. His eyes seemed to penetrate the dead water. Yes, perhaps that was the dark shadow of her black clothing beneath the surface of the water.

He slowly ventured into the pond. The bottom was deep, soft clay, he sank in, and the water clasped dead cold round his legs. As he stirred he could smell the cold, rotten clay that fouled up into the water. It was objectionable in his lungs. Still, repelled and yet not heeding, he moved deeper into the pond. The cold water rose over his thighs, over his loins, upon his abdomen. The lower part of his body was all sunk in the hideous cold element. And the bottom was so deeply soft and uncertain, he was afraid of pitching with his mouth underneath. He could not swim, and was afraid.

He crouched a little, spreading his hands under the water and moving them round, trying to feel for her. The dead cold pond swayed upon his chest. He moved again, a little deeper, and again, with his hands underneath, he felt all around under the water. And he touched her clothing. But it evaded his fingers. He made a desperate effort to grasp it.

And so doing he lost his balance and went under, horribly, suffocating in the foul earthy water, struggling madly for a few moments. At last, after what seemed an eternity, he got his footing, rose again into the air and looked around. He gasped, and knew he was in the world. Then he looked at the water. She had risen near him. He grasped her clothing, and drawing her nearer, turned to take his way to land again.

He went very slowly, carefully, absorbed in the slow progress. He rose higher, climbing out of the pond. The water was now only about his legs; he was thankful, full of relief to be out of the clutches of the pond. He lifted her and staggered on to the bank, out of the horror of wet, grey clay.

He laid her down on the bank. She was quite unconscious and running with water. He made the water come from her mouth, he worked to restore her. He did not have to work very long before he could feel the breathing begin again in her;

she was breathing naturally. He worked a little longer. He could feel her live beneath his hands; she was coming back. He wiped her face, wrapped her in his overcoat, looked round into the dim, dark grey world, then lifted her and staggered down the bank and across the fields.

It seemed an unthinkably long way, and his burden so heavy he felt he would never get to the house. But at last he was in the stable-yard, and then in the house-yard. He opened the door and went into the house. In the kitchen he laid her down on the hearth-rug and called. The house was empty. But the fire was burning in the grate.

Then again he kneeled to attend to her. She was breathing regularly, her eyes were wide open and as if conscious, but there seemed something missing in her look. She was conscious in herself, but unconscious of her surroundings.

He ran upstairs, took blankets from a bed, and put them before the fire to warm. Then he removed her saturated, earthy-smelling clothing, rubbed her dry with a towel, and wrapped her naked in the blankets. Then he went into the dining-room, to look for spirits. There was a little whisky. He drank a gulp himself, and put some into her mouth.

The effect was instantaneous. She looked full into his face, as if she had been seeing him for some time, and yet had only just become conscious of him.

"Dr. Fergusson?" she said.

"What?" he answered.

He was divesting himself of his coat, intending to find some dry clothing upstairs. He could not bear the smell of the dead, clayey water, and he was mortally afraid for his own health.

"What did I do?" she asked.

"Walked into the pond," he replied. He had begun to shudder like one sick, and could hardly attend to her. Her eyes remained full on him, he seemed to be going dark in his mind, looking back at her helplessly. The shuddering became quieter in him, his life came back to him, dark and unknowing, but strong again.

"Was I out of my mind?" she asked, while her eyes were fixed on him all the time.

"Maybe, for the moment," he replied. He felt quiet, because his strength had come back. The strange fretful strain had left him.

"Am I out of my mind now?" she asked.

"Are you?" he reflected a moment. "No," he answered truthfully, "I don't see that you are." He turned his face aside. He was afraid now, because he felt dazed, and felt dimly that her power was stronger than his, in this issue. And she continued to look at him fixedly all the time. "Can you tell me where I shall find some dry things to put on?" he asked.

"Did you dive into the pond for me?" she asked.

"No," he answered. "I walked in. But I went in overhead as well."

There was silence for a moment. He hesitated. He very much wanted to go upstairs to get into dry clothing. But there was another desire in him. And she seemed to hold him. His will seemed to have gone to sleep, and left him, standing there slack before her. But he felt warm inside himself. He did not shudder at all, though his clothes were sodden on him.

"Why did you?" she asked.

"Because I didn't want you to do such a foolish thing," he said.

"It wasn't foolish," she said, still gazing at him as she lay on the floor, with a sofa cushion under her head. "It was the right thing to do. *I* knew best, then."

"I'll go and shift these wet things," he said. But still he had not the power to move out of her presence, until she sent him. It was as if she had the life of his body in her hands, and he could not extricate himself. Or perhaps he did not want to.

Suddenly she sat up. Then she became aware of her own immediate condition. She felt the blankets about her, she knew her own limbs. For a moment it seemed as if her reason were going. She looked round, with wild eye, as if seeking something. He stood still with fear. She saw her clothing lying scattered.

"Who undressed me?" she asked, her eyes resting full and inevitable on his face.

"I did," he replied, "to bring you round."

For some moments she sat and gazed at him awfully, her lips parted.

"Do you love me, then?" she asked.

He only stood and stared at her, fascinated. His soul seemed to melt.

She shuffled forward on her knees, and put her arms round him, round his legs, as he stood there, pressing her breasts against his knees and thighs, clutching him with strange, con-

vulsive certainty, pressing his thighs against her, drawing him
to her face, her throat, as she looked up at him with flaring,
humble eyes of transfiguration, triumphant in first possession.

"You love me," she murmured, in strange transport, yearning and triumphant and confident. "You love me. I know you
love me, I know."

And she was passionately kissing his knees, through the wet
clothing, passionately and indiscriminately kissing his knees,
his legs, as if unaware of everything.

He looked down at the tangled wet hair, the wild, bare,
animal shoulders. He was amazed, bewildered, and afraid. He
had never thought of loving her. He had never wanted to love
her. When he rescued her and restored her, he was a doctor,
and she was a patient. He had had no single personal thought
of her. Nay, this introduction of the personal element was
very distasteful to him, a violation of his professional honour.
It was horrible to have her there embracing his knees. It was
horrible. He revolted from it, violently. And yet—and yet—
he had not the power to break away.

She looked at him again, with the same supplication of
powerful love, and that same transcendent, frightening light
of triumph. In view of the delicate flame which seemed to
come from her face like a light, he was powerless. And yet
he had never intended to love her. He had never intended.
And something stubborn in him could not give way.

"You love me," she repeated, in a murmur of deep,
rhapsodic assurance. "You love me."

Her hands were drawing him, drawing him down to her. He
was afraid, even a little horrified. For he had, really, no intention of loving her. Yet her hands were drawing him towards
her. He put out his hand quickly to steady himself, and
grasped her bare shoulder. A flame seemed to burn the hand
that grasped her soft shoulder. He had no intention of loving
her: his whole will was against his yielding. It was horrible.
And yet wonderful was the touch of her shoulders, beautiful
the shining of her face. Was she perhaps mad? He had a
horror of yielding to her. Yet something in him ached also.

He had been staring away at the door, away from her. But
his hand remained on her shoulder. She had gone suddenly
very still. He looked down at her. Her eyes were now wide
with fear, with doubt, the light was dying from her face, a
shadow of terrible greyness was returning. He could not bear

the touch of her eyes' question upon him, and the look of death behind the question.

With an inward groan he gave way, and let his heart yield towards her. A sudden gentle smile came on his face. And her eyes, which never left his face, slowly, slowly filled with tears. He watched the strange water rise in her eyes, like some slow fountain coming up. And his heart seemed to burn and melt away in his breast.

He could not bear to look at her any more. He dropped on his knees and caught her head with his arms and pressed her face against his throat. She was very still. His heart, which seemed to have broken, was burning with a kind of agony in his breast. And he felt her slow, hot tears wetting his throat. But he could not move.

He felt the hot tears wet his neck and the hollows of his neck, and he remained motionless, suspended through one of man's eternities. Only now it had become indispensable to him to have her face pressed close to him; he could never let her go again. He could never let her head go away from the close clutch of his arm. He wanted to remain like that for ever, with his heart hurting him in a pain that was also life to him. Without knowing, he was looking down on her damp, soft brown hair.

Then, as it were suddenly, he smelt the horrid stagnant smell of that water. And at the same moment she drew away from him and looked at him. Her eyes were wistful and unfathomable. He was afraid of them, and he fell to kissing her, not knowing what he was doing. He wanted her eyes not to have that terrible, wistful, unfathomable look.

When she turned her face to him again, a faint delicate flush was glowing, and there was again dawning that terrible shining of joy in her eyes, which really terrified him, and yet which he now wanted to see, because he feared the look of doubt still more.

"You love me?" she said, rather faltering.

"Yes." The word cost him a painful effort. Not because it wasn't true. But because it was too newly true, the *saying* seemed to tear open again his newly-torn heart. And he hardly wanted it to be true, even now.

She lifted her face to him, and he bent forward and kissed her on the mouth, gently, with the one kiss that is an eternal pledge. And as he kissed her his heart strained again in his breast. He never intended to love her. But now it was over. He had crossed over the gulf to her, and all that he had left behind had shrivelled and become void.

After the kiss, her eyes again slowly filled with tears. She sat still, away from him, with her face drooped aside, and her hands folded in her lap. The tears fell very slowly. There was complete silence. He too sat there motionless and silent on the hearth-rug. The strange pain of his heart that was broken seemed to consume him. That he should love her? That this was love! That he should be ripped open in this way! Him, a doctor! How they would all jeer if they knew! It was agony to him to think they might know.

In the curious naked pain of the thought he looked again to her. She was sitting there drooped into a muse. He saw a tear fall, and his heart flared hot. He saw for the first time that one of her shoulders was quite uncovered, one arm bare, he could see one of her small breasts; dimly, because it had become almost dark in the room.

"Why are you crying?" he asked, in an altered voice.

She looked up at him, and behind her tears the consciousness of her situation for the first time brought a dark look of shame to her eyes.

"I'm not crying, really," she said, watching him, half frightened.

He reached his hand, and softly closed it on her bare arm.

"I love you! I love you!" he said in a soft, low vibrating voice, unlike himself.

She shrank, and dropped her head. The soft, penetrating grip of his hand on her arm distressed her. She looked up at him.

"I want to go," she said. "I want to go and get you some dry things."

"Why?" he said. "I'm all right."

"But I want to go," she said. "And I want you to change your things."

He released her arm, and she wrapped herself in the blanket, looking at him rather frightened. And still she did not rise.

"Kiss me," she said wistfully.

He kissed her, but briefly, half in anger.

Then, after a second, she rose nervously, all mixed up in the blanket. He watched her in her confusion as she tried to extricate herself and wrap herself up so that she could walk.

He watched her relentlessly, as she knew. And as she went, the blanket trailing, and as he saw a glimpse of her feet and her white leg, he tried to remember her as she was when he had wrapped her in the blanket. But then he didn't want to remember, because she had been nothing to him then, and his nature revolted from remembering her as she was when she was nothing to him.

A tumbling, muffled noise from within the dark house startled him. Then he heard her voice: "There are clothes." He rose and went to the foot of the stairs, and gathered up the garments she had thrown down. Then he came back to the fire, to rub himself down and dress. He grinned at his own appearance when he had finished.

The fire was sinking, so he put on coal. The house was now quite dark, save for the light of a street-lamp that shone in faintly from beyond the holly trees. He lit the gas with matches he found on the mantelpiece. Then he emptied the pockets of his own clothes, and threw all his wet things in a heap into the scullery. After which he gathered up her sodden clothes, gently, and put them in a separate heap on the copper-top in the scullery.

It was six o'clock on the clock. His own watch had stopped. He ought to go back to the surgery. He waited, and still she did not come down. So he went to the foot of the stairs and called:

"I shall have to go."

Almost immediately he heard her coming down. She had on her best dress of black voile, and her hair was tidy, but still damp. She looked at him—and in spite of herself, smiled.

"I don't like you in those clothes," she said.

"Do I look a sight?" he answered.

They were shy of one another.

"I'll make you some tea," she said.

"No, I must go."

"Must you?" And she looked at him again with the wide, strained, doubtful eyes. And again, from the pain of his breast, he knew how he loved her. He went and bent to kiss her, gently, passionately, with his heart's painful kiss.

"And my hair smells so horrible," she murmured in distraction. "And I'm so awful, I'm so awful! Oh no, I'm too awful." And she broke into bitter, heart-broken sobbing. "You can't want to love me, I'm horrible."

"Don't be silly, don't be silly," he said, trying to comfort her, kissing her, holding her in his arms. "I want you, I want to marry you, we're going to be married, quickly, quickly—to-morrow if I can."

But she only sobbed terribly, and cried:

"I feel awful. I feel awful. I feel I'm horrible to you."

"No, I want you, I want you," was all he answered, blindly, with that terrible intonation which frightened her almost more than her horror lest he should *not* want her.

FANNY AND ANNIE

FLAME-LURID his face as he turned among the throng of flame-lit and dark faces upon the platform. In the light of the furnace she caught sight of his drifting countenance, like a piece of floating fire. And the nostalgia, the doom of home-coming went through her veins like a drug. His eternal face, flame-lit now! The pulse and darkness of red fire from the furnace towers in the sky, lighting the desultory, industrial crowd on the wayside station, lit him and went out.

Of course he did not see her. Flame-lit and unseeing! Always the same, with his meeting eyebrows, his common cap, and his red-and-black scarf knotted round his throat. Not even a collar to meet her! The flames had sunk, there was shadow.

She opened the door of her grimy, branch-line carriage, and began to get down her bags. The porter was nowhere, of course, but there was Harry, obscure, on the outer edge of the little crowd, missing her, of course.

"Here! Harry!" she called, waving her umbrella in the twilight. He hurried forward.

"Tha's come, has ter?" he said, in a sort of cheerful welcome. She got down, rather flustered, and gave him a peck of a kiss.

"Two suit-cases!" she said.

Her soul groaned within her, as he clambered into the carriage after her bags. Up shot the fire in the twilight sky, from the great furnace behind the station. She felt the red flame go across her face. She had come back, she had come back for good. And her spirit groaned dismally. She doubted if she could bear it.

There, on the sordid little station under the furnaces, she stood, tall and distinguished, in her well-made coat and skirt and her broad grey velour hat. She held her umbrella, her bead chatelaine, and a little leather case in her grey-gloved hands, while Harry staggered out of the ugly little train with her bags.

"There's a trunk at the back," she said in her bright voice.

But she was not feeling bright. The twin black cones of the iron foundry blasted their sky-high fires into the night. The whole scene was lurid. The train waited cheerfully. It would wait another ten minutes. She knew it. It was all so deadly familiar.

Let us confess it at once. She was a lady's maid, thirty years old, come back to marry her first-love, a foundry worker: after having kept him dangling, off and on, for a dozen years. Why had she come back? Did she love him? No. She didn't pretend to. She had loved her brilliant and ambitious cousin, who had jilted her, and who had died. She had had other affairs which had come to nothing. So here she was, come back suddenly to marry her first-love, who had waited—or remained single—all these years.

"Won't a porter carry those?" she said, as Harry strode with his workman's stride down the platform towards the guard's van.

"I can manage," he said.

And with her umbrella, her chatelaine, and her little leather case, she followed him.

The trunk was there.

"We'll get Heather's greengrocer's cart to fetch it up," he said.

"Isn't there a cab?" said Fanny, knowing dismally enough that there wasn't.

"I'll just put it aside o' the penny-in-the-slot, and Heather's greengrocers'll fetch it about half-past eight," he said.

He seized the box by its two handles and staggered with it across the level-crossing, bumping his legs against it as he waddled. Then he dropped it by the red sweetmeats machine.

"Will it be safe there?" she said.

"Ay—safe as houses," he answered. He returned for the two bags. Thus laden, they started to plod up the hill, under the great long black building of the foundry. She walked beside him—workman of workmen he was, trudging with that luggage. The red lights flared over the deepening darkness. From the foundry came the horrible, slow clang clang, clang of iron, a great noise, with an interval just long enough to make it unendurable.

Compare this with the arrival at Gloucester: the carriage for her mistress, the dog-cart for herself with the luggage; the drive out past the river, the pleasant trees of the carriage-approach; and herself sitting beside Arthur, everybody so polite to her.

She had come home—for good! Her heart nearly stopped beating as she trudged up that hideous and interminable hill, beside the laden figure. What a come-down! What a come-down! She could not take it with her usual bright cheerfulness. She knew it all too well. It is easy to bear up against the unusual, but the deadly familiarity of an old stale past!

He dumped the bags down under a lamp-post, for a rest. There they stood, the two of them, in the lamp-light. Passers-by stared at her, and gave good night to Harry. Her they hardly knew, she had become a stranger.

"They're too heavy for you, let me carry one," she said.

"They begin to weigh a bit by the time you've gone a mile," he answered.

"Let me carry the little one," she insisted.

"Tha can ha'e it for a minute, if ter's a mind," he said, handing over the valise.

And thus they arrived in the streets of shops of the little ugly town on top of the hill. How everybody stared at her; my word, how they stared! And the cinema was just going in, and the queues were tailing down the road to the corner. And everybody took full stock of her. "Night, Harry!" shouted the fellows, in an interested voice.

However, they arrived at her aunt's—a little sweet-shop in a side street. They 'pinged' the door-bell, and her aunt came running forward out of the kitchen.

"There you are, child! Dying for a cup of tea, I'm sure. How are you?"

Fanny's aunt kissed her, and it was all Fanny could do to refrain from bursting into tears, she felt so low. Perhaps it was her tea she wanted.

"You've had a drag with that luggage," said Fanny's aunt to Harry.

"Ay—I'm not sorry to put it down," he said, looking at his hand which was crushed and cramped by the bag handle.

Then he departed to see about Heather's greengrocery cart.

When Fanny sat at tea, her aunt, a grey-haired, fair-faced little woman, looked at her with an admiring heart, feeling bitterly sore for her. For Fanny was beautiful: tall, erect, finely coloured, with her delicately arched nose, her rich brown hair, her large lustrous-grey eyes. A passionate woman

—a woman to be afraid of. So proud, so inwardly violent!
She came of a violent race.

It needed a woman to sympathise with her. Men had not
the courage. Poor Fanny! She was such a lady, and so straight
and magnificent. And yet everything seemed to do her down.
Every time she seemed to be doomed to humiliation and disappointment, this handsome, brilliantly sensitive woman, with
her nervous, over-wrought laugh.

"So you've really come back, child?" said her aunt.

"I really have, Aunt," said Fanny.

"Poor Harry! I'm not sure, you know, Fanny, that you're
not taking a bit of an advantage of him."

"Oh, Aunt, he's waited so long, he may as well have what
he's waited for." Fanny laughed grimly.

"Yes, child, he's waited so long, that I'm not sure it isn't a
bit hard on him. You know, I *like* him, Fanny—though as
you know quite well, I don't think he's good enough for you.
And I think he thinks so himself, poor fellow."

"Don't you be so sure of that, Aunt. Harry is common, but
he's not humble. He wouldn't think the Queen was any too
good for him, if he's a mind to her."

"Well—it's as well if he has a proper opinion of himself."

"It depends what you call proper," said Fanny. "But he's
got his good points——"

"Oh, he's a nice fellow, and I like him, I do like him. Only,
as I tell you, he's not good enough for you."

"I've made up my mind, Aunt," said Fanny, grimly.

"Yes," mused the aunt. "They say all things come to him
who waits——"

"More than he's bargained, for, eh, Aunt?" laughed Fanny
rather bitterly.

The poor aunt, this bitterness grieved her for her niece.

They were interrupted by the ping of the shop-bell, and
Harry's call of "Right!" But as he did not come in at once,
Fanny, feeling solicitous for him presumably at the moment,
rose and went into the shop. She saw a cart outside, and went
to the door.

And the moment she stood in the doorway, she heard a
woman's common vituperative voice crying from the darkness
of the opposite side of the road:

"Tha'rt theer, are ter? I'll shame thee, Mester. I'll shame
thee. see if I dunna."

Startled, Fanny started across the darkness, and saw a woman in a black bonnet go under one of the lamps up the side street.

Harry and Bill Heather had dragged the trunk off the little dray, and she retreated before them as they came up the shop step with it.

"Wheer shal ha'e it?" asked Harry.

"Best take it upstairs," said Fanny.

She went up first to light the gas.

When Heather had gone, and Harry was sitting down having tea and pork-pie, Fanny asked:

"Who was that woman shouting?"

"Nay, I canna tell thee. To somebody, I s'd think," replied Harry. Fanny looked at him, but asked no more.

He was a fair-haired fellow of thirty-two, with a fair moustache. He was broad in his speech, and looked like a foundry-hand, which he was. But women always liked him. There was something of a mother's lad about him—something warm and playful and really sensitive.

He had his attractions even for Fanny. What she rebelled against so bitterly was that he had no sort of ambition. He was a moulder, but of very commonplace skill. He was thirty-two years old, and hadn't saved twenty pounds. She would have to provide the money for the home. He didn't care. He just didn't care. He had no initiative at all. He had no vices—no obvious ones. But he was just indifferent, spending as he went, and not caring. Yet he did not look happy. She remembered his face in the fire-glow: something haunted, abstracted about it. As he sat there eating his pork-pie, bulging his cheek out, she felt he was like a doom to her. And she raged against the doom of him. It wasn't that he was gross. His *way* was common, almost on purpose. But he himself wasn't really common. For instance, his food was not particularly important to him, he was not greedy. He had a charm, too, particularly for women, with his blondness and his sensitiveness and his way of making a woman feel that she was a higher being. But Fanny knew him, knew the peculiar obstinate limitedness of him, that would nearly send her mad.

He stayed till about half-past nine. She went to the door with him.

"When are you coming up?" he said, jerking his head in the direction, presumably, of his own home.

"I'll come to-morrow afternoon," she said brightly. Between Fanny and Mrs. Goodall, his mother, there was naturally no love lost.

Again she gave him an awkward little kiss, and said good night.

"You can't wonder, you know, child, if he doesn't seem so very keen," said her aunt. "It's your own fault."

"Oh, Aunt, I couldn't stand him when he was keen. I can do with him a lot better as he is."

The two women sat and talked far into the night. They understood each other. The aunt, too, had married as Fanny was marrying: a man who was no companion to her, a violent man, brother of Fanny's father. He was dead, Fanny's father was dead.

Poor Aunt Lizzie, she cried woefully over her bright niece, when she had gone to bed.

Fanny paid the promised visit to his people the next afternoon. Mrs. Goodall was a large woman with smooth-parted hair, a common, obstinate woman, who had spoiled her four lads and her one vixen of a married daughter. She was one of those old-fashioned powerful natures that couldn't do with looks or education or any form of showing-off. She fairly hated the sound of correct English. She *thee'd* and *tha'd* her prospective daughter-in-law, and said:

"I'm none as ormin' as I look, seest ta."

Fanny did not think her prospective mother-in-law looked at all orming, so the speech was unnecessary.

"I towd him mysen," said Mrs. Goodall, " 'Er's held back all this long, let 'er stop as 'er is. 'E'd none ha' had thee for *my* tellin'—tha hears. No, 'e's a fool, an' I know it. I says to him: 'Tha looks a man, doesn't ter, at thy age, goin' an' openin' to her when ter hears her scrat' at th' gate, after she's done galli-vantin' round wherever she's a mind. That looks rare an' soft.' But it's no use o' any talking: he answered that letter o' thine and made his own bad bargain."

But in spite of the old woman's anger, she was also flattered at Fanny's coming back to Harry. For Mrs. Goodall was impressed by Fanny—a woman of her own match. And more than this, everybody knew that Fanny's Aunt Kate had left her two hundred pounds: this apart from the girl's savings.

So there was high tea in Princes Street when Harry came home black from work, and a rather acrid odour of cordiality,

the vixen Jinny darting in to say vulgar things. Of course
Jinny lived in a house whose garden end joined the paternal
garden. They were a clan who stuck together, these Goodalls.

It was arranged that Fanny should come to tea again on the
Sunday, and the wedding was discussed. It should take place
in a fortnight's time at Morley Chapel. Morley was a hamlet
on the edge of the real country, and in its little Congregational
Chapel Fanny and Harry had first met.

What a creature of habit he was! He was still in the choir
of Morley Chapel—not very regular. He belonged just because
he had a tenor voice, and enjoyed singing. Indeed, his solos
were only spoilt to local fame because when he sang he
handled his aitches so hopelessly.

> "And I saw 'eaven hopened
> And be'old, a wite 'orse——"

This was one of Harry's classics, only surpassed by the fine
outburst of his heaving:

> "Hangels—hever bright an' fair——"

It was a pity, but it was unalterable. He had a good voice,
and he sang with a certain lacerating fire, but his pronuncia-
tion made it all funny. And *nothing* could alter him.

So he was never heard save at cheap concerts and in the
little, poorer chapels. The other scoffed.

Now the month was September, and Sunday was Harvest
Festival at Morley Chapel, and Harry was singing solos. So
that Fanny was to go to service, and come home to a grand
spread of Sunday tea with him. Poor Fanny! One of the most
wonderful afternoons had been a Sunday afternoon service,
with her cousin Luther at her side, Harvest Festival in Morley
Chapel. Harry had sung solos then—ten years ago. She
remembered his pale-blue tie, and the purple asters and the
great vegetable marrows in which he was famed, and her
cousin Luther at her side, young, clever, come down from
London, where he was getting on well, learning his Latin and
his French and German so brilliantly.

However, once again it was Harvest Festival at Morley
Chapel, and once again, as ten years before, a soft, exquisite
September day, with the last roses pink in the cottage gardens,
the last dahlias crimson, the last sunflowers yellow. And again
the little old chapel was a bower, with its famous sheaves of

corn and corn-plaited pillars, its great bunches of grapes, dangling like tassels from the pulpit corners, its marrows and potatoes and pears and apples and damsons, its purple asters and yellow Japanese sunflowers. Just as before, the red dahlias round the pillars were dropping, weak-headed among the oats. The place was crowded and hot, the plates of tomatoes seemed balanced perilous on the gallery front, the Rev. Enderby was weirder than ever to look at, so long and emaciated and hairless.

The Rev. Enderby, probably forewarned, came and shook hands with her and welcomed her, in his broad northern, melancholy sing-song before he mounted the pulpit. Fanny was handsome in a gauzy dress and a beautiful lace hat. Being a little late, she sat in a chair in the side-aisle wedged in, right in front of the chapel. Harry was in the gallery above, and she could only see him from the eyes upwards. She noticed again how his eyebrows met, blond and not very marked, over his nose. He was attractive, too: physically lovable, very. If only—if only her *pride* had not suffered! she felt he dragged her down.

> "Come, ye thankful people, come,
> Raise the song of harvest-home.
> All is safely gathered in
> Ere the winter storms begin——"

Even the hymn was a falsehood, as the season had been wet, and half the crops were still out, and in a poor way.

Poor Fanny! She sang little, and looked beautiful through that inappropiate hymn. Above her stood Harry—mercifully in a dark suit and a dark tie, looking almost handsome. And his lacerating, pure tenor sounded well, when the words were drowned in the general commotion. Brilliant she looked, and brilliant she felt, for she was hot and angrily miserable and inflamed with a sort of fatal despair. Because there was about him a physical attraction which she really hated, but which she could not escape from. He was the first man who had ever kissed her. And his kisses, even while she rebelled from them, had lived in her blood and sent roots down into her soul. After all this time she had come back to them. And her soul groaned, for she felt dragged down, dragged down to earth, as a bird which some dog has got down in the dust. She knew her life

would be unhappy. She knew that what she was doing was
fatal. Yet it was her doom. She had to come back to him.

He had to sing two solos this afternoon: one before the
"address" from the pulpit and one after. Fanny looked in
him, and wondered he was not too shy to stand up there in
front of all the people. But no, he was not shy. He had even
a kind of assurance on his face as he looked down from the
choir gallery at her: the assurance of a common man
deliberately entrenched in his commonness. Oh, such a rage
went through her veins as she saw the air of triumph, laconic,
indifferent triumph which sat so obstinately and recklessly on
his eyelids as he looked down at her. Ah, she despised him!
But there he stood up in that choir gallery like Balaam's ass in
front of her, and she could not get beyond him. A certain winsomeness also about him. A certain physical winsomeness, and
as if his flesh were new and lovely to touch. The thorn of
desire rankled bitterly in her heart.

He, it goes without saying, sang like a canary, this particular
afternoon, with a certain defiant passion which pleasantly
crisped the blood of the congregation. Fanny felt the crisp
flames go through her veins as she listened. Even the curious
loud-mouthed vernacular had a certain fascination. But, oh,
also, it was so repugnant. He would triumph over her,
obstinately he would drag her right back into the common
people: a doom, a vulgar doom.

The second performance was an anthem, in which Harry
sang the solo parts. It was clumsy, but beautiful, with lovely
words.

"They that sow in tears shall reap in joy,
    He that goeth forth and weepeth, bearing precious seed
    Shall doubtless come again with rejoicing, bringing his
        sheaves with him——"

"Shall doubtless come, Shall doubtless come——" softly intoned the altos—"Bringing his she-e-eaves with him," the
trebles flourished brightly, and then again began the half-
wistful solo:

"They that sow in tears shall reap in joy——"

Yes, it was effective and moving.
But at the moment when Harry's voice sank carelessly down

to his close, and the choir, standing behind him, were opening their mouths for the final triumphant outburst, a shouting female voice rose up from the body of the congregation. The organ gave one startled trump, and went silent; the choir stood transfixed.

"You look well standing there, singing in God's holy house," came the loud, angry female shout. Everybody turned electrified. A stoutish, red-faced woman in a black bonnet was standing up denouncing the soloist. Almost fainting with shock, the congregation realised it. "You look well, don't you, standing there singing solos in God's holy house, you, Goodall. But I said I'd shame on you. You look well, bringing your young woman here with you, don't you? I'll let her know who she's dealing with. A scamp as won't take the consequences of what he's done." The hard-faced, frenzied woman turned in the direction of Fanny. "*That's* what Harry Goodall is, if you want to know."

And she sat down again in her seat. Fanny, startled like all the rest, had turned to look. She had gone white, and then a burning red, under the attack. She knew the woman: a Mrs. Nixon, a devil of a woman, who beat her pathetic, drunken, red-nosed second husband, Bob, and her two lanky daughters, grown-up as they were. A notorious character. Fanny turned round again, and sat motionless as eternity in her seat.

There was a minute of perfect silence and suspense. The audience was open-mouthed and dumb; the choir stood like Lot's wife; and Harry, with his music-sheet, stood there uplifted, looking down with a dumb sort of indifference on Mrs. Nixon, his face naïve and faintly mocking. Mrs. Nixon sat defiant in her seat, braving them all.

Then a rustle, like a wood when the wind suddenly catches the leaves. And then the tall, weird minister got to his feet, and in his strong, bell-like, beautiful voice—the only beautiful thing about him—he said with infinite mournful pathos:

"Let us unite in singing the last hymn on the hymn-sheet; the last hymn on the hymn-sheet, number eleven.

> 'Fair waved the golden corn
> In Canaan's pleasant land.' "

The organ tuned up promptly. During the hymn the offertory was taken. And after the hymn, the prayer.

Mr. Enderby came from Northumberland. Like Harry, he had never been able to conquer his accent, which was very broad. He was a little simple, one of God's fools, perhaps, an odd bachelor soul, emotional, ugly, but very gentle.

"And if, O our dear Lord, beloved Jesus, there should fall a shadow of sin upon our harvest, we leave it to Thee to judge, for Thou art judge. We lift our spirits and our sorrow, Jesus, to Thee, and our mouths are dumb. O Lord, keep us from froward speech, restrain us from foolish words and thoughts, we pray Thee, Lord Jesus, who knowest all and judgest all."

Thus the minister said in his sad, resonant voice, washed his hands before the Lord. Fanny bent forward open-eyed during the prayer. She could see the roundish head of Harry, also bent forward. His face was inscrutable and expressionless. The shock left her bewildered. Anger perhaps was her dominating emotion.

The audience began to rustle to its feet, to ooze slowly and excitedly out of the chapel, looking with wildly interested eyes at Fanny, at Mrs. Nixon, and at Harry. Mrs. Nixon, shortish, stood defiant in her pew, facing the aisle, as if announcing that, without rolling her sleeves up, she was ready for anybody. Fanny sat quite still. Luckily the people did not have to pass her. And Harry, with red ears, was making his way sheepishly out of the gallery. The loud noise of the organ covered all the downstairs commotion of exit.

The minister sat silent and inscrutable in his pulpit, rather like a death's-head, while the congregation filed out. When the last lingerers had unwillingly departed, craning their necks to stare at the still seated Fanny, he rose, stalked in his hooked fashion down the little country chapel and fastened the door. Then he returned and sat down by the silent young woman.

"This is most unfortunate, most unfortunate!" he moaned. "I am so sorry, I am so sorry, indeed, indeed, ah, indeed!" he sighed himself to a close.

"It's a sudden surprise, that's one thing," said Fanny brightly.

"Yes—yes—indeed. Yes, a surprise, yes. I don't know the woman, I don't know her."

"I know her," said Fanny. "She's a bad one."

"Well! Well!" said the minister. "I don't know her. I don't understand. I don't understand at all. But it is to be regretted, it is very much to be regretted. I am very sorry."

Fanny was watching the vestry door. The gallery stairs

communicated with the vestry, not with the body of the
chapel. She knew the choir members had been peeping for
information.

At last Harry came—rather sheepishly—with his hat in his
hand.

"Well!" said Fanny, rising to her feet.

"We've had a bit of an extra," said Harry.

"I should think so," said Fanny.

"A most unfortunate circumstance—a most *unfortunate*
circumstance. Do you understand it, Harry? I don't understand it at all."

"Ay, I understand it. The daughter's goin' to have a childt,
an' 'er lays it to me."

"And has she no occasion to?" asked Fanny, rather
censorious.

"It's no more mine than it is some other chap's," said Harry,
looking aside.

There was a moment of pause.

"Which girl is it?" asked Fanny.

"Annie—the young one——"

There followed another silence.

"I don't think I know them, do I?" asked the minister.

"I shouldn't think so. Their name's Nixon—mother married
old Bob for her second husband. She's a tanger, she's driven
the gel to what she is. They live in Manners Road."

"Why, what's amiss with the girl?" asked Fanny sharply.
"She was all right when I knew her."

"Ay—she's all right. But she's always in an' out o' th' pubs,
wi' th' fellows," said Harry.

"A nice thing!" said Fanny.

Harry glanced towards the door. He wanted to get out.

"Most distressing, indeed!" the minister slowly shook his
head.

"What about to-night, Mr. Enderby?" asked Harry, in rather
a small voice. "Shall you want me?"

Mr. Enderby looked up painedly, and put his hand to his
brow. He studied Harry for some time, vacantly. There was
the faintest sort of a resemblance between the two men.

"Yes," he said. "Yes, I think. I think we must take no
notice and cause as little remark as possible."

Fanny hesitated. Then she said to Harry:

"But *will* you come?"

He looked at her.

"Ay, I s'll come," he said.

Then he turned to Mr. Enderby.

"Well, good afternoon, Mr. Enderby," he said.

"Good afternoon, Harry, good afternoon," replied the mournful minister. Fanny followed Harry to the door, and for some time they walked in silence through the late afternoon.

"And it's yours as much as anybody else's?" she said.

"Ay," he answered shortly.

And they went without another word, for the long mile or so, till they came to the corner of the street where Harry lived. Fanny hesitated. Should she go on to her aunt's? Should she? It would mean leaving all this, for ever. Harry stood silent.

Some obstinacy made her turn with him along the road to his own home. When they entered the house-place, the whole family was there, mother and father and Jinny, with Jinny's husband and children and Harry's two brothers.

"You've been having your ears warmed, they tell me," said Mrs. Goodall grimly.

"Who told thee?" asked Harry shortly.

"Maggie and Luke's both been in."

"You look well, don't you!" said interfering Jinny.

Harry went and hung his hat up, without replying.

"Come upstairs and take your hat off," said Mrs. Goodall to Fanny, almost kindly. It would have annoyed her very much if Fanny had dropped her son at this moment.

"What's 'er say, then?" asked the father secretly of Harry, jerking his head in the direction of the stairs whence Fanny had disappeared.

"Nowt yet," said Harry.

"Serve you right if she chucks you now," said Jinny. "I'll bet it's right about Annie Nixon an' you."

"Tha bets so much," said Harry.

"Yi—but you can't deny it," said Jinny.

"I can if I've a mind."

His father looked at him enquiringly.

"It's no more mine than it is Bill Bower's, or Ted Slaney's, or six or seven on 'em," said Harry to his father.

And the father nodded silently.

"That'll not get you out of it, in court," said Jinny.

Upstairs Fanny evaded all the thrusts made by his mother, and did not declare her hand. She tidied her hair, washed her

hands, and put the tiniest bit of powder on her face, for cool-
ness, there in front of Mrs. Goodall's indignant gaze. It was
like a declaration of independence. But the old woman said
nothing.

They came down to Sunday tea, with sardines and tinned
salmon and tinned peaches, besides tarts and cakes. The
chatter was general. It concerned the Nixon family and the
scandal.

"Oh, she's a foul-mouthed woman," said Jinny of Mrs.
Nixon. "She may well talk about God's holy house, *she* had.
It's first time she's set foot in it, ever since she dropped off
from being converted. She's a devil and she always was one.
Can't you remember how she treated Bob's children, mother,
when we lived down in the Buildings? I can remember when
I was a little girl she used to bathe them in the yard, in the
cold, so that they shouldn't splash the house. She'd half kill
them if they made a mark on the floor, and the language she'd
use! And one Saturday I can remember Garry, that was Bob's
own girl, she ran off when her stepmother was going to bathe
her—ran off without a rag of clothes on—can you remember,
mother? And she hid in Smedley's closes—it was the time of
mowing-grass—and nobody could find her. She hid out there
all night, didn't she, mother? Nobody could find her. My word,
there was a talk. They found her on Sunday morning——"

"Fred Coutts threatened to break every bone in the woman's
body, if she touched the children again," put in the father.

"Anyhow, they frightened her," said Jinny. "But she was
nearly as bad with her own two. And anybody can see that
she'd driven old Bob till he's gone soft."

"Ah, soft as mush," said Jack Goodall. " 'E'd never addle a
week's wages, nor yet a day's, if th' chaps didn't make it up
to him."

"My word, if he didn't bring her a week's wage, she'd pull
his head off," said Jinny.

"But a clean woman, and respectable, except for her foul
mouth," said Mr. Goodall. "Keeps to herself like a bulldog.
Never lets anybody come near the house, and neighbours with
nobody."

"Wanted it thrashed out of her," said Mr. Goodall, a silent,
evasive sort of man.

"Where Bob gets the money for his drink from is a
mystery," said Jinny.

"Chaps treats him," said Harry.

"Well, he's got the pair of frightenedest rabbit-eyes you'd wish to see," said Jinny.

"Ay, with a drunken man's murder in them, *I* think," said Mrs. Goodall.

So the talk went on after tea, till it was practically time to start off to the chapel again.

"You'll have to be getting ready, Fanny," said Mrs. Goodall.

"I'm not going to-night," said Fanny abruptly. And there was a sudden halt in the family. "I'll stop with *you* to-night, mother," she added.

"Best you had, my gel," said Mrs. Goodall, flattered and assured.

THE PRINCESS

To her father, she was The Princess. To her Boston aunts and uncles she was just *Dollie Urquhart, poor little thing.*

Colin Urquhart was just a bit mad. He was of an old Scottish family, and he claimed royal blood. The blood of Scottish kings flowed in his veins. On this point, his American relatives said, he was just a bit "off". They could not bear any more to be told *which* royal blood of Scotland blued his veins. The whole thing was rather ridiculous, and a sore point. The only fact they remembered was that it was not Stuart.

He was a handsome man, with a wide-open blue eye that seemed sometimes to be looking at nothing, soft black hair brushed rather low on his low, broad brow, and a very attractive body. Add to this a most beautiful speaking voice, usually rather hushed and diffident, but sometimes resonant and powerful like bronze, and you have the sum of his charms. He looked like some old Celtic hero. He looked as if he should have worn a greyish kilt and a sporran, and shown his knees. His voice came direct out of the hushed Ossianic past.

For the rest, he was one of those gentlemen of sufficient but not excessive means who fifty years ago wandered vaguely about, never arriving anywhere, never doing anything, and never definitely being anything, yet well received in the good society of more than one country.

He did not marry till he was nearly forty, and then it was a wealthy Miss Prescott, from New England. Hannah Prescott at twenty-two was fascinated by the man with the soft black hair not yet touched by grey, and the wide, rather vague blue eyes. Many women had been fascinated before her. But Colin Urquhart, by his very vagueness, had avoided any decisive connection.

Mrs. Urquhart lived three years in the mist and glamour of her husband's presence. And then it broke her. It was like living with a fascinating spectre. About most things he was completely, even ghostly oblivious. He was always charming, courteous, perfectly gracious in that hushed, musical voice of his. But absent. When all came to all, he just wasn't there. "Not all there," as the vulgar say.

He was the father of the little girl she bore at the end of the first year. But this did not substantiate him the more. His very beauty and his haunting musical quality became dreadful to her after the first few months. The strange echo: he was like a living echo! His very flesh, when you touched it, did not seem quite the flesh of a real man.

Perhaps it was that he was a little bit mad. She thought it definitely the night her baby was born.

"Ah, so my little princess has come at last!" he said, in his throaty, singing Celtic voice, like a glad chant, swaying absorbed.

It was a tiny, frail baby, with wide, amazed blue eyes. They christened it Mary Henrietta. She called the little thing *My Dollie*. He called it always *My Princess*.

It was useless to fly at him. He just opened his wide blue eyes wider, and took a child-like, silent dignity there was no getting past.

Hannah Prescott had never been robust. She had no great desire to live. So when the baby was two years old she suddenly died.

The Prescotts felt a deep but unadmitted resentment against Colin Urquhart. They said he was selfish. Therefore they discontinued Hannah's income, a month after her burial in Florence, after they had urged the father to give the child over to them, and he had courteously, musically, but quite finally refused. He treated the Prescotts as if they were not of his world, not realities to him: just casual phenomena, or gramophones, talking-machines that had to be answered. He answered them. But of their actual existence he was never once aware.

They debated having him certified unsuitable to be guardian of his own child. But that would have created a scandal. So they did the simplest thing, after all—washed their hands of him. But they wrote scrupulously to the child, and sent her modest presents of money at Christmas, and on the anniversary of the death of her mother.

To The Princess her Boston relatives were for many years just a nominal reality. She lived with her father, and he travelled continually, though in a modest way, living on his moderate income. And never going to America. The child changed nurses all the time. In Italy it was a contadina; in India she had an ayah; in Germany she had a yellow-haired peasant girl.

Father and child were inseparable. He was not a recluse. Wherever he went he was to be seen paying formal calls going out to luncheon or to tea, rarely to dinner. And always with the child. People called her Princess Urquhart, as if that were her christened name.

She was a quick, dainty little thing with dark gold hair that went a soft brown, and wide, slightly prominent blue eyes that were at once so candid and so knowing. She was always grown up; she never really grew up. Always strangely wise, and always childish.

It was her father's fault.

"My little Princess must never take too much notice of people and the things they say and do," he repeated to her. "People don't know what they are doing and saying. They chatter-chatter, and they hurt one another, and they hurt themselves very often, till they cry. But don't take any notice, my little Princess. Because it is all nothing. Inside everybody there is another creature, a demon which doesn't care at all. You peel away all the things they say and do and feel, as cook peels away the outside of the onions. And in the middle of everybody there is a green demon which you can't peel away. And this green demon never changes, and it doesn't care at all about all the things that happen to the outside leaves of the person, all the chatter-chatter, and all the husbands and wives and children, and troubles and fusses. You peel everything away from people, and there is a green, upright demon in every man and woman; and this demon is a man's real self, and a woman's real self. It doesn't really care about anybody, it belongs to the demons and the primitive fairies, who never care. But, even so, there are big demons and mean demons, and splendid demonish fairies, and vulgar ones. But there are no royal fairy women left. Only you, my little Princess. You are the last of the royal race of the old people; the last, my Princess. There are no others. You and I are the last. When I am dead there will be only you. And that is why, darling, you will never care for any of the people in the world very much. Because their demons are all dwindled and vulgar. They are not royal. Only you are royal, after me. Always remember that. And always remember, it is a *great secret*. If you tell people, they will try to kill you, because they will envy you for being a Princess. It is our great secret, darling. I am a prince, and you a princess, of the old, old blood. And we keep our secret between us, all alone. And so, darling, you must treat all people very politely, because *noblesse oblige*. But you must never forget that you alone are the last of Princesses, and that all other are less than you are, less noble, more vulgar. Treat them politely and gently and kindly, darling. But you are the Princess, and they are commoners. Never try to think of them as if they were like you. They are not. You will find, always, that they are lacking, lacking in the royal touch, which only you have——"

The Princess learned her lesson early—the first lesson, of absolute reticence, the impossibility of intimacy with any other than her father; the second lesson, of naïve, slightly benevolent politeness. As a small child, something crystallised in her character, making her clear and finished, and as impervious as crystal.

"Dear child!" her hostesses said of her. "She is so quaint and old-fashioned; such a lady, poor little mite!"

She was erect, and very dainty. Always small, nearly tiny in physique, she seemed like a changeling beside her big, handsome, slightly mad father. She dressed very simply, usually in blue or delicate greys, with little collars of old Milan point, or very finely-worked linen. She had exquisite little hands, that made the piano sound like a spinet when she played. She was rather given to wearing cloaks and capes, instead of coats, out of doors, and little eighteenth-century sort of hats. Her complexion was pure apple-blossom.

She looked as if she had stepped out of a picture. But no one, to her dying day, ever knew exactly the strange picture her father had framed her in and from which she never stepped.

Her grandfather and grandmother and her Aunt Maud demanded twice to see her, once in Rome and once in Paris. Each time they were charmed, piqued, and annoyed. She was so exquisite and such a little virgin. At the same time so knowing and so oddly assured. That odd, assured touch of condescension, and the inward coldness, infuriated her American relations.

Only she really fascinated her grandfather. He was spellbound; in a way, in love with the little faultless thing. His wife would catch him brooding, musing over his grandchild,

long months after the meeting, and craving to see her again.
He cherished to the end the fond hope that she might come
to live with him and her grandmother.

"Thank you so much, grandfather. You are so very kind.
But Papa and I are such an old couple, you see, such a crochety
old couple, living in a world of our own."

Her father let her see the world—from the outside. And he
let her read. When she was in her teens she read Zola and
Maupassant, and with the eyes of Zola and Maupassant she
looked on Paris. A little later she read Tolstoi and Dostoevsky.
The latter confused her. The others, she seemed to understand
with a very shrewd, canny understanding, just as she understood the Decameron stories as she read them in their old
Italian, or the Nibelung poems. Strange and *uncanny*, she
seemed to understand things in a cold light perfectly, with all
the flush of fire absent. She was something like a changeling,
not quite human.

This earned her, also, strange antipathies. Cabmen and railway porters, especially in Paris and Rome, would suddenly
treat her with brutal rudeness, when she was alone. They
seemed to look on her with sudden violent antipathy. They
sensed in her curious impertinence, an easy, sterile impertinence towards the things *they* felt most. She was so assured,
and her flower of maidenhood was so scentless. She could look
at a lusty, sensual Roman cabman as if he were a sort of
grotesque, to make her smile. She knew all about him, in
Zola. And the peculiar condescension with which she would
give him her order, as if she, frail, beautiful thing, were the
only reality, and he, coarse monster, was a sort of Caliban
floundering in the mud on the margin of the pool of the
perfect lotus, would suddenly enrage the fellow, the real
Mediterranean who prided himself on his *beauté male*, and to
whom the phallic mystery was still the only mystery. And
he would turn a terrible face on her, bully her in a brutal,
coarse fashion—hideous. For to him she had only the
blasphemous impertinence of her own sterility.

Encounters like these made her tremble, and made her know
she must have support from the outside. The power of her
spirit did not extend to these low people, and they had all the
physical power. She realised an implacability of hatred in
their turning on her. But she did not lose her head. She
quietly paid out money and turned away.

Those were dangerous moments, though, and she learned to be prepared for them. The Princess she was, and the fairy from the North, and could never understand the volcanic phallic rage with which coarse people could turn on her in a paroxysm of hatred. They never turned on her father like that. And quite early she decided it was the New England mother in her whom they hated. Never for one minute could she see with the old Roman eyes, see herself as sterility, the barren flower taking on airs and an intolerable impertinence. This was what the Roman cabman saw in her. And he longed to crush the barren blossom. Its sexless beauty and its authority put him in a passion of brutal revolt.

When she was nineteen her grandfather died, leaving her a considerable fortune in the safe hands of responsible trustees. They would deliver her her income, but only on condition that she resided for six months in the year in the United States.

"Why should they make me conditions?" she said to her father. "I refuse to be imprisoned six months in the year in the United States. We will tell them to keep their money."

"Let us be wise, my little Princess, let us be wise. No, we are almost poor, and we are never safe from rudeness. I cannot allow anybody to be rude to me. I hate it, I hate it!" His eyes flamed as he said it. "I could kill any man or woman who is rude to me. But we are in exile in the world. We are powerless. If we were really poor, we should be quite powerless, and then I should die. No, my Princess. Let us take their money, then they will not dare to be rude to us. Let us take it, as we put on clothes, to cover ourselves from their aggressions."

There began a new phase, when the father and daughter spent their summers on the Great Lakes or in California, or in the South-West. The father was something of a poet, the daughter something of a painter. He wrote poems about the lakes or the redwood trees, and she made dainty drawings. He was physically a strong man, and he loved the out-of-doors. He would go off with her for days, paddling in a canoe and sleeping by a camp-fire. Frail little Princess, she was always undaunted, always undaunted. She would ride with him on horseback over the mountain trails till she was so tired she was nothing but a bodiless consciousness sitting astride her pony. But she never gave in. And at night he folded her in her blanket on a bed of balsam pine twigs, and she lay and looked at the stars unmurmuring. She was fulfilling her rôle.

People said to her as the years passed, and she was a woman of twenty-five, then a woman of thirty, and always the same virgin dainty Princess, 'knowing' in a dispassionate way, like an old woman, and utterly intact:

"Don't you ever think what you will do when your father is no longer with you?"

She looked at her interlocutor with that cold, elfin detachment of hers:

"No, I never think of it," she said.

She had a tiny, but exquisite little house in London, and another small, perfect house in Connecticut, each with a faithful housekeeper. Two homes, if she chose. And she knew many interesting literary and artistic people. What more?

So the years passed imperceptibly. And she had that quality of the sexless fairies, she did not change. At thirty-three she looked twenty-three.

Her father, however, was ageing, and becoming more and more queer. It was now her task to be his guardian in his private madness. He spent the last three years of life in the house in Connecticut. He was very much estranged, sometimes had fits of violence which almost killed the little Princess. Physical violence was horrible to her; it seemed to shatter her heart. But she found a woman a few years younger than herself, well-educated and sensitive, to be a sort of nurse-companion to the mad old man. So the fact of madness was never openly admitted. Miss Cummins, the companion, had a passionate loyalty to the Princess, and a curious affection, tinged with love, for the handsome, white-haired, courteous old man, who was never at all aware of his fits of violence once they had passed.

The Princess was thirty-eight years old when her father died. And quite unchanged. She was still tiny, and like a dignified, scentless flower. Her soft brownish hair, almost the colour of beaver fur, was bobbed, and fluffed softly round her apple-blossom face, that was modelled with an arched nose like a proud old Florentine portrait. In her voice, manner and bearing she was exceedingly still, like a flower that has blossomed in a shadowy place. And from her blue eyes looked out the Princess's eternal laconic challenge, that grew almost sardonic as the years passed. She was the Princess, and sardonically she looked out on a princeless world.

She was relieved when her father died, and at the same time, it was as if everything had evaporated around her. She had lived in a sort of hot-house, in the aura of her father's madness. Suddenly the hot-house had been removed from around her, and she was in the raw, vast, vulgar open air.

Quoi faire? What was she to do? She seemed faced with absolute nothingness. Only she had Miss Cummins, who shared with her the secret, and almost the passion for her father. In fact, the Princess felt that her passion for her mad father had in some curious way transferred itself largely to Charlotte Cummins during the last years. And now Miss Cummins was the vessel that held the passion for the dead man. She herself, the Princess, was an empty vessel.

An empty vessel in the enormous warehouse of the world.

Quoi faire? What was she to do? She felt that, since she could not evaporate into nothingness, like alcohol from an un-stoppered bottle, she must *do* something. Never before in her life had she felt the incumbency. Never, never had she felt she must *do* anything. That was left to the vulgar.

Now her father was dead, she found herself on the *fringe* of the vulgar crowd, sharing their necessity to *do* something. It was a little humiliating. She felt herself becoming vulgarised. At the same time she found herself looking at men with a shrewder eye: an eye to marriage. Not that she felt any sudden interest in men, or attraction towards them. No. She was still neither interested nor attracted towards men vitally. But *marriage*, that peculiar abstraction, had imposed a sort of spell on her. She thought that *marriage*, in the blank abstract, was the thing she ought to *do*. That *marriage* implied a man she also knew. She knew all the facts. But the man seemed a property of her own mind rather than a thing in himself, another thing.

His father died in the summer, the month after her thirty-eighth birthday. When all was over, the obvious thing to do, of course, was to travel. With Miss Cummins. The two women knew each other intimately, but they were always Miss Urquhart and Miss Cummins to one another, and a certain distance was instinctively maintained. Miss Cummins, from Philadelphia, of scholastic stock, and intelligent but un-travelled, four years younger than the Princess, felt herself immensely the junior of her 'lady'. She had a sort of passionate veneration for the Princess, who seemed to her ageless, timeless. She could not see the rows of tiny, dainty, exquisite shoes in the Princess's cupboard without feeling a stab at the heart, a stab of tenderness and reverence, almost of awe.

Miss Cummins also was virginal, but with a look of puzzled surprise in her brown eyes. Her skin was pale and clear, her features well modelled, but there was a certain blankness in her expression, where the Princess had an odd touch of Renaissance grandeur. Miss Cummins's voice was also hushed almost to a whisper; it was the inevitable effect of Colin Urquhart's room. But the hushedness had a hoarse quality.

The Princess did not want to go to Europe. Her face seemed turned west. Now her father was gone, she felt she would go west, westwards, as if for ever. Following, no doubt, the March of Empire, which is brought up rather short on the Pacific coast, among swarms of wallowing bathers.

No, not the Pacific coast. She would stop short of that. The South-West was less vulgar. She would go to New Mexico.

She and Miss Cummins arrived at the Rancho del Cerro Gordo towards the end of August, when the crowd was beginning to drift back east. The ranch lay by a stream on the desert some four miles from the foot of the mountains, a mile away from the Indian pueblo of San Cristobal. It was a ranch for the rich; the Princess paid thirty dollars a day for herself and Miss Cummins. But then she had a little cottage to herself, among the apple trees of the orchard, with an excellent cook. She and Miss Cummins, however, took dinner at evening in the large guest-house. For the Princess still entertained the idea of *marriage*.

The guests at the Rancho del Cerro Gordo were of all sorts, except the poor sort. They were practically all rich, and many were romantic. Some were charming, others were vulgar, some were movie people, quite quaint and not unattractive in their vulgarity, and many were Jews. The Princess did not care for Jews, though they were usually the most interesting to *talk* to. So she talked a good deal with the Jews, and painted with the artists, and rode with the young men from college, and had altogether quite a good time. And yet she felt something of a fish out of water, or a bird in the wrong forest. And *marriage* remained still completely in the abstract. No connecting it with any of these young men, even the nice ones.

The Princess looked just twenty-five. The freshness of her mouth, the hushed, delicate-complexioned virginity of her face gave her not a day more. Only a certain laconic look in her eyes was disconcerting. When she was *forced* to write her age, she put twenty-eight, making the figure *two* rather badly, so that it just avoided being a three.

Men hinted marriage at her. Especially boys from college suggested it from a distance. But they all failed before the look of sardonic ridicule in the Princess's eyes. It always seemed to her rather preposterous, quite ridiculous, and a tiny bit impertinent on their part.

The only man that intrigued her at all was one of the guides, a man called Romero—Domingo Romero. It was he who had sold the ranch itself to the Wilkiesons, ten years before, for two thousand dollars. He had gone away, then reappeared at the old place. For he was the son of the old Romero, the last of the Spanish family that had owned miles of land around San Cristobal. But the coming of the white man and the failure of the vast flocks of sheep, and the fatal inertia which overcomes all men, at last, on the desert near the mountains, had finished the Romero family. The last descendants were just Mexican peasants.

Domingo, the heir, had spent his two thousand dollars, and was working for white people. He was now about thirty years old, a tall, silent fellow, with a heavy closed mouth and black eyes that looked across at one almost sullenly. From behind he was handsome, with a strong, natural body, and the back of his neck very dark and well-shapen, strong with life. But his dark face was long and heavy, almost sinister, with that peculiar heavy meaningless in it, characteristic of the Mexicans of his own locality. They are strong, they seem healthy. They laugh and joke with one another. But their physique and their natures seem static, as if there were nowhere, nowhere at all for their energies to go, and their faces, degenerating to misshapen heaviness, seem to have no *raison d'être*, no radical meaning. Waiting either to die or to be aroused into passion and hope. In some of the black eyes a queer, haunting mystic quality, sombre and a bit gruesome, the skull-and-cross-bones look of the Penitentes. They had found their *raison d'être* in self-torture and death-worship. Unable to wrest a *positive* significance for themselves from the vast, beautiful, but vindictive landscape they were born into, they turned on their own selves, and worshipped death through self-torture. The mystic gloom of this showed in their eyes.

But as a rule the dark eyes of the Mexicans were heavy and half alive, sometimes hostile, sometimes kindly, often with the fatal Indian glaze on them, or the fatal Indian glint.

Domingo Romero was *almost* a typical Mexican to look at, with the typical heavy, dark, long face, clean-shaven, with an almost brutally heavy mouth. His eyes were black and Indian-looking. Only, at the centre of their hopelessness was a spark of pride, or self-confidence, or dauntlessness. Just a spark in the midst of the blackness of static despair.

But this spark was the difference between him and the mass of men. It gave a certain alert sensitiveness to his bearing and a certain beauty to his appearance. He wore a low-crowned black hat, instead of the ponderous headgear of the usual Mexican, and his clothes were thinnish and graceful. Silent, aloof, almost imperceptible in the landscape, he was an admirable guide, with a startling quick intelligence that anticipated difficulties about to rise. He could cook, too, crouching over the camp-fire and moving his lean deft brown hands. The only fault he had was that he was not forthcoming, he wasn't chatty and cosy.

"Oh, don't send Romero with us," the Jews would say. "One can't get any response from him."

Tourists come and go, but they rarely *see* anything, inwardly. None of them ever saw the spark at the middle of Romero's eye; they were not alive enough to see it.

The Princess caught it one day, when she had him for a guide. She was fishing for trout in the canyon, Miss Cummins was reading a book, the horses were tied under the trees, Romero was fixing a proper fly on her line. He fixed the fly and handed her the line, looking up at her. And at that moment she caught the spark in his eye. And instantly she knew that he was a gentleman, that his 'demon', as her father would have said, was a fine demon. And instantly her manner towards him changed.

He had perched her on a rock over a quiet pool, beyond the cotton-wood trees. It was early September, and the canyon already cool, but the leaves of the cottonwoods were still green. The Princess stood on her rock, a small but perfectly-formed figure, wearing a soft, close grey sweater and neatly-cut grey riding-breeches, with tall black boots, her fluffy

H

brown hair straggling from under a little grey felt hat. A
woman? Not quite. A changeling of some sort, perched in
outline there on the rock, in the bristling wild canyon. She
knew perfectly well how to handle a line. Her father had
made a fisherman of her.

Romero, in a black shirt and with loose black trousers
pushed into wide black riding-boots, was fishing a little farther
down. He had put his hat on a rock behind him; his dark head
was bent a little forward, watching the water. He had caught
three trout. From time to time he glanced up-stream at the
Princess, perched there so daintily. He saw she had caught
nothing.

Soon he quietly drew in his line and came up to her. His
keen eye watched her line, watched her position. Then,
quietly, he suggested certain changes to her, putting his sensitive brown hand before her. And he withdrew a little, and
stood in silence, leaning against a tree, watching her. He was
helping her across the distance. She knew it, and thrilled. And
in a moment she had a bite. In two minutes she landed a good
trout. She looked round at him quickly, her eyes sparkling,
the colour heightened in her cheeks. And as she met his eyes
a smile of greeting went over his dark face, very sudden, with
an odd sweetness.

She knew he was helping her. And she felt in his presence
a subtle, insidious male *kindliness* she had never known before
waiting upon her. Her cheek flushed, and her blue eyes
darkened.

After this, she always looked for him, and for that curious
dark beam of a man's kindliness which he could give her, as it
were, from his chest, from his heart. It was something she had
never known before.

A vague, unspoken intimacy grew up between them. She
liked his voice, his appearance, his presence. His natural
language was Spanish; he spoke English like a foreign language,
rather slow, with a slight hesitation, but with a sad, plangent
sonority lingering over from his Spanish. There was a certain
subtle correctness in his appearance; he was always perfectly
shaved; his hair was thick and rather long on top, but always
carefully groomed behind. And his fine black cashmere shirt,
his wide leather belt, his well-cut, wide black trousers going
into the embroidered cowboy boots had a certain inextinguish-
able elegance. He wore no silver rings or buckles. Only his

boots were embroidered and decorated at the top with an in-
lay of white *suède*. He seemed elegant, slender, yet he was
very strong.

And at the same time, curiously, he gave her the feeling
that death was not far from him. Perhaps he too was half in
love with death. However that may be, the sense she had that
death was not far from him made him 'possible' to her.

Small as she was, she was quite a good horsewoman. They
gave her at the ranch a sorrel mare, very lovely in colour, and
well-made, with a powerful broad neck and the hollow back
that betokens a swift runner. Tansy, she was called. Her only
fault was the usual mare's failing, she was inclined to be
hysterical.

So that every day the Princess set off with Miss Cummins
and Romero, on horseback, riding into the mountains. Once
they went camping for several days, with two more friends in
the party.

"I think I like it better," the Princess said to Romero, "when
we three go alone."

And he gave her one of his quick, transfiguring smiles.

It was curious no white man had ever showed her this
capacity for subtle gentleness, this power to *help* her in
silence across a distance, if she were fishing without success,
or tired of her horse, or if Tansy suddenly got scared. It was
as if Romero could send her *from his heart* a dark beam of
succour and sustaining. She had never known this before, and
it was very thrilling.

Then the smile that suddenly creased his dark face, showing the strong white teeth. It creased his face almost into a
savage grotesque. And at the same time there was in it something so warm, such a dark flame of kindliness for her, she
was elated into her true Princess self.

Then that vivid, latent spark in his eye, which she had seen,
and which she knew he was aware she had seen. It made an
inter-recognition between them, silent and delicate. Here he
was delicate as a woman in this subtle inter-recognition.

And yet his presence only put to flight in her the *idée fixe*
of 'marriage'. For some reason, in her strange little brain, the
idea of *marrying* him could not enter. Not for any definite
reason. He was in himself a gentleman, and she had plenty
of money for two. There was no actual obstacle. Nor was she
conventional.

No, now she came down to it, it was as if their two
'dæmons' could marry, were perhaps married. Only their
two *selves*, Miss Urquhart and Señor Domingo Romero, were
for some reason incompatible. There was a peculiar subtle
intimacy of inter-recognition between them. But she did not
see in the least how it would lead to marriage. Almost she
could more easily marry one of the nice boys from Harvard
or Yale.

The time passed, and she let it pass. The end of September
came, with aspens going yellow on the mountain heights, and
oak-scrub going red. But as yet the cottonwoods in the valley
and canyons had not changed.

"When will you go away?" Romero asked her, looking at
her fixedly, with a blank black eye.

"By the end of October," she said. "I have promised to be
in Santa Barbara at the beginning of November."

He was hiding the spark in his eye from her. But she saw
the peculiar sullen thickening of his heavy mouth.

She had complained to him many times that one never saw
any wild animals, except chipmunks and squirrels, and perhaps a skunk and a porcupine. Never a deer, or a bear, or a
mountain lion.

"Are these no bigger animals in these mountains?" she
asked, dissatisfied.

"Yes," he said. "There are deer—I see their tracks. And I
saw the tracks of a bear."

"But why can one never see the animals themselves?" She
looked dissatisfied and wistful like a child.

"Why, it's pretty hard for you to see them. They won't let
you come close. You have to keep still, in a place where they
come. Or else you have to follow their tracks a long way."

"I can't bear to go away till I've seen them: a bear, or a
deer——"

The smile came suddenly on his face, indulgent.

"Well, what do you want? Do you want to go up into the
mountains to some place, to wait till they come?"

"Yes," she said, looking up at him with a sudden naïve
impulse of recklessness.

And immediately his face became sombre again, responsible.

"Well," he said, with slight irony, a touch of mockery of
her. "You will have to find a house. It's very cold at night
now. You would have to stay all night in a house."

"And there are no houses up there?" she said.

"Yes," he replied. "There is a little shack that belongs to me, that a miner built a long time ago, looking for gold. You can go there and stay one night, and maybe you see something. Maybe! I don't know. Maybe nothing come."

"How much chance is there?"

"Well, I don't know. Last time when I was there I see three deer come down to drink at the water, and I shot two raccoons. But maybe this time we don't see anything."

"Is there water there?" she asked.

"Yes, there is a little round pond, you know, below the spruce trees. And the water from the snow runs into it."

"Is it far away?" she asked.

"Yes, pretty far. You see that ridge there"—and turning to the mountains he lifted his arm in the gesture which is somehow so moving, out in the West, pointing to the distance— "that ridge where there are no trees, only rock"—his black eyes were focussed on the distance, his face impassive, but as if in pain—"you go round that ridge, and along, then you come down through the spruce trees to where that cabin is. My father bought that placer claim from a miner who was broke, but nobody ever found any gold or anything, and nobody ever goes there. Too lonesome!"

The Princess watched the massive, heavy-sitting, beautiful bulk of the Rocky Mountains. It was early in October, and the aspens were already losing their gold leaves; high up, the spruce and pine seemed to be growing darker; the great flat patches of oak scrub on the heights were red like gore.

"Can I go over there?" she asked, turning to him and meeting the spark in his eye.

His face was heavy with responsibility.

"Yes," he said, "you can go. But there'll be snow over the ridge, and it's awful cold, and awful lonesome."

"I should like to go," she said, persistent.

"All right," he said. "You can go if you want to."

She doubted, though, if the Wilkiesons would let her go; at least alone with Romero and Miss Cummins.

Yet an obstinacy characteristic of her nature, an obstinacy tinged perhaps with madness, had taken hold of her. She wanted to look over the mountains into their secret heart. She wanted to descend to the cabin below the spruce trees, near the tarn of bright green water. She wanted to see the wild animals move about in their wild unconsciousness.

"Let us say to the Wilkiesons that we want to make the trip round the Frijoles canyon," she said.

The trip round the Frijoles canyon was a usual thing. It would not be strenuous, nor cold, nor lonely: they could sleep in the log house that was called an hotel.

Romero looked at her quickly.

"If you want to say that," he replied, "you can tell Mrs. Wilkieson. Only I know she'll be mad with me if I take you up in the mountains to that place. And I've got to go there first with a pack-horse, to take lots of blankets and some bread. Maybe Miss Cummins can't stand it. Maybe not. It's a hard trip."

He was speaking, and thinking, in the heavy, disconnected Mexican fashion.

"Never mind!" The Princess was suddenly very decisive and stiff with authority. "I want to do it. I will arange with Mrs. Wilkieson. And we'll go on Saturday."

He shook his head slowly.

"I've got to go up on Sunday with a pack-horse and blankets," he said. "Can't do it before."

"Very well!" she said, rather piqued. "Then we'll start on Monday."

She hated being thwarted even the tiniest bit.

He knew that if he started with the pack on Sunday at dawn he would not be back until late at night. But he consented that they should start on Monday morning at seven. The obedient Miss Cummins was told to prepare for the Frijoles trip. On Sunday Romero had his day off. He had not put in an appearance when the Princess retired on Sunday night, but on Monday morning, as she was dressing, she saw him bringing in the three horses from the corral. She was in high spirits.

The night had been cold. There was ice at the edges of the irrigation ditch, and the chipmunks crawled into the sun and lay with wide, dumb, anxious eyes, almost too numb to run.

"We may be away two or three days," said the Princess.

"Very well. We won't begin to be anxious about you before Thursday, then," said Mrs. Wilkieson, who was young and capable: from Chicago. "Anyway," she added, "Romero will see you through. He's so trustworthy."

The sun was already on the desert as they set off towards the mountains, making the greasewood and the sage pale as pale-grey sands, luminous the great level around them. To the right glinted the shadows of the adobe pueblo, flat and almost invisible on the plain, earth of its earth. Behind lay the ranch and the tufts of tall, plumy cottonwoods, whose summits were yellowing under the perfect blue sky.

Autumn breaking into colour in the great spaces of the South-West.

But the three trotted gently along the trail, towards the sun that sparkled yellow just above the dark bulk of the ponderous mountains. Side-slopes were already gleaming yellow, flaming with a second light, under coldish blue of the pale sky. The front slopes were in shadow, with submerged lustre of red oak scrub and dull-gold aspens, blue-black pines and grey-blue rock. While the canyon was full of a deep blueness.

They rode single file, Romero first, on a black horse. Himself in black, made a flickering black spot in the delicate pallor of the great landscape, where even pine trees at a distance take a film of blue paler than their green. Romero rode on in silence past the tufts of furry greasewood. The Princess came next, on her sorrel mare. And Miss Cummins, who was not quite happy on horseback, came last, in the pale dust that the others kicked up. Sometimes her horse sneezed, and she started.

But on they went at a gentle trot. Romero never looked round. He could hear the sound of the hoofs following, and that was all he wanted.

For the rest, he held ahead. And the Princess, with that black, unheeding figure always travelling away from her, felt strangely helpless, withal elated.

They neared the pale, round foot-hills, dotted with the round dark piñon and cedar shrubs. The horses clinked and trotted among the stones. Occasionally a big round greasewood held out fleecy tufts of flowers, pure gold. They wound into blue shadow, then up a steep stony slope, with the world lying pallid away behind and below. Then they dropped into the shadow of the San Cristobal canyon.

The stream was running full and swift. Occasionally the horses snatched at a tuft of grass. The trail narrowed and became rocky; the rocks closed in; it was dark and cool as the horses climbed and climbed upwards, and the tree trunks crowded in the shadowy, silent tightness of the canyon. They were among cottonwood trees that ran straight up and smooth and round to an extraordinary height. Above, the tips were gold, and it was sun. But away below, where the horses struggled up the rocks and wound among the trunks, there was still blue shadow by the sound of waters and an occasional grey festoon of old man's beard, and here and there a pale, dripping crane's-bill flower among the tangle and the débris of the virgin place. And again the chill entered the Princess's heart as she realised what a tangle of decay and despair lay in the virgin forests.

They scrambled downwards, splashed across stream, up rocks and along the trail of the other side. Romero's black horse stopped, looked down quizzically at the fallen trees, then stepped over lightly. The Princess's sorrel followed, carefully. But Misss Cummins's buckskin made a fuss, and had to be got round.

In the same silence, save for the clinking of the horses and the splashing as the trail crossed stream, they worked their way upwards in the tight, tangled shadow of the canyon. Sometimes, crossing stream, the Princess would glance upwards, and then always her heart caught in her breast. For high up, away in heaven, the mountain heights shone yellow, dappled with dark spruce firs, clear almost as speckled daffodils against the pale turquoise blue lying high and serene above the dark-blue shadow where the Princess was. And she would snatch at the blood-red leaves of the oak as her horse crossed a more open slope, not knowing what she felt.

They were getting fairly high, occasionally lifted above the canyon itself, in the low groove below the speckled, gold-sparkling heights which towered beyond. Then again they dipped and crossed stream, the horses stepping gingerly across a tangle of fallen, frail aspen stems, then suddenly floundering in a mass of rocks. The black emerged ahead, his black tail waving. The Princess let her mare find her own footing; then she too emerged from the clatter. She rode on after the black. Then came a great frantic rattle of the buckskin behind. The Princess was aware of Romero's dark face looking round, with a strange, demon-like watchfulness, before she herself looked round, to see the buckskin scrambling rather lamely beyond the rocks, with one of his pale buff knees already red with blood.

"He almost went down!" called Miss Cummins.

But Romero was already out of the saddle and hastening down the path. He made quiet little noises to the buckskin, and began examining the cut knee.

"Is he hurt?" cried Miss Cummins anxiously, and she climbed hastily down.

"Oh, my goodness!" she cried, as she saw the blood running down the slender buff leg of the horse in a thin trickle. "Isn't that *awful?*" She spoke in a stricken voice, and her face was white.

Romero was still carefully feeling the knee of the buckskin. Then he made him walk a few paces. And at last he stood up straight and shook his head.

"Not very bad!" he said. "Nothing broken."

Again he bent and worked at the knees. Then he looked up at the Princess.

"He can go on," he said. "It's not bad."

The Princess looked down at the dark face in silence.

"What, go on right up here?" cried Miss Cummins. "How many hours?"

"About five!" said Romero simply.

"Five hours!" cried Miss Cummins. "A horse with a lame knee! And a steep mountain! Why-y!"

"Yes, it's pretty steep up there," said Romero, pushing back his hat and staring fixedly at the bleeding knee. The buckskin stood in a stricken sort of dejection. "But I think he'll make it all right," the man added.

"Oh!" cried Miss Cummins, her eyes bright with sudden passion of unshed tears. "I wouldn't think of it. I wouldn't ride him up there, not for any money."

"Why wouldn't you?" asked Romero.

"It *hurts* him."

Romero bent down again to the horse's knee.

"Maybe it hurts him a little," he said. "But he can make it all right, and his leg won't get stiff."

"What! Ride him five hours up the steep mountains?" cried Miss Cummins. "I couldn't. I just couldn't do it. I'll lead him a little way and see if he can go. But I *couldn't* ride him again. I couldn't. Let me walk."

"But Miss Cummins, dear, if Romero says he'll be all right?" said the Princess.

"I know it hurts him. Oh, I just couldn't bear it."

There was no doing anything with Miss Cummins. The thought of a hurt animal always put her into a sort of hysterics.

They walked forward a little, leading the buckskin. He limped rather badly. Miss Cummins sat on a rock.

"Why, it's agony to see him!" she cried. "It's *cruel*!"

"He won't limp after a bit, if you take no notice of him," said Romero. "Now he plays up, and limps very much, because he wants to make you see."

"I don't think there can be much playing up," said Miss Cummins bitterly. "We can *see* how it must hurt him."

"It don't hurt much," said Romero.

But now Miss Cummins was silent with antipathy.

It was a deadlock. The party remained motionless on the trail, the Princess in the saddle, Miss Cummins seated on a rock, Romero standing black and remote near the drooping buckskin.

"Well!" said the man suddenly at last. "I guess we go back, then."

And he looked up swiftly at his horse, which was cropping at the mountain herbage and treading on the trailing reins.

"No!" cried the Princess. "Oh no!" Her voice rang with a great wail of disappointment and anger. Then she checked herself.

Miss Cummins rose with energy.

"Let me lead the buckskin home," she said, with cold dignity, "and you two go on."

This was received in silence. The Princess was looking down at her with a sardonic, almost cruel gaze.

"We've only come about two hours," said Miss Cummins. "I don't mind a bit leading him home. But I *couldn't* ride him. I *couldn't* have him ridden with that knee."

This again was received in dead silence. Romero remained impassive, almost inert.

"Very well, then," said the Princess. "You lead him home. You'll be quite all right. Nothing can happen to you, possibly. And say to them that we have gone on and shall be home to-morrow—or the day after."

She spoke coldly and distinctly. For she could not bear to be thwarted.

"Better all go back, and come again another day," said Romero—non-committal.

"There will never *be* another day," cried the Princess. "I want to go on."

She looked at him square in the eyes, and met the spark in his eye.

He raised his shoulders slightly.

"If you want it," he said. "I'll go on with you. But Miss Cummins can ride my horse to the end of the canyon, and I lead the buckskin. Then I come back to you."

It was arranged so. Miss Cummins had her saddle put on Romero's black horse, Romero took the buckskin's bridle, and they started back. The Princess rode very slowly on, upwards, alone. She was at first so angry with Miss Cummins that she was blind to everything else. She just let her mare follow her own inclinations.

The peculiar spell of anger carried the Princess on, almost unconscious, for an hour or so. And by this time she was beginning to climb pretty high. Her horse walked steadily all the time. They emerged on a bare slope, and the trail wound through frail aspen stems. Here a wind swept, and some of the aspens were already bare. Others were fluttering their discs of pure, solid yellow leaves, so *nearly* like petals, while the slope ahead was one soft, glowing fleece of daffodil yellow; fleecy like a golden foxskin, and yellow as daffodils alive in the wind and the high mountain sun.

She paused and looked back. The near great slopes were mottled with gold and the dark hue of spruce, like some un-singed eagle, and the light lay gleaming upon them. Away through the gap of the canyon she could see the pale blue of the egg-like desert, with the crumpled dark crack of the Rio Grande Canyon. And far, far off, the blue mountains like a fence of angels on the horizon.

And she thought of her adventure. She was going on alone with Romero. But then she was very sure of herself, and Romero was not the kind of man to do anything to her against her will. This was her first thought. And she just had a fixed desire to go over the brim of the mountains, to look into the inner chaos of the Rockies. And she wanted to go with Romero, because he had some peculiar kinship with her; there was some peculiar link between the two of them. Miss Cummins anyhow would have been only a discordant note.

She rode on, and emerged at length in the lap of the summit. Beyond her was a great concave of stone and stark, dead-grey trees, where the mountain ended against the sky. But nearer was the dense black, bristling spruce, and at her feet was the lap of the summit, a flat little vallay of sere grass and quiet-standing yellow aspens, the stream trickling like a thread across.

It was a little valley or shell from which the stream was gently poured into the lower rocks and trees of the canyon. Around her was a fairly-like gentleness, the delicate sere grass, the groves of delicate-stemmed aspens dropping their flakes of bright yellow. And the delicate, quick little stream threading through the wild, sere grass.

Here one might expect deer and fawns and wild things, as in a little paradise. Here she was to wait for Romero, and they were to have lunch.

She unfastened her saddle and pulled it to the ground with a crash, letting her horse wander with a long rope. How beautiful Tansy looked, sorrel, among the yellow leaves that lay like a patina on the sere ground. The Princess herself wore a fleecy sweater of a pale, sere buff, like the grass, and riding-breeches of a pure orange-tawny colour. She felt quite in the picture.

From her saddle-pouches she took the packages of lunch, spread a little cloth, and sat to wait for Romero. Then she made a little fire. Then she ate a devilled egg. Then she ran after Tansy, who was straying across-stream. Then she sat in the sun, in the stillness near the aspens, and waited.

The sky was blue. Her little alp was soft and delicate as fairy-land. But beyond and up jutted the great slopes, dark with the pointed feathers of spruce, bristling with grey dead trees among grey rock, or dappled with dark and gold. The beautiful, but fierce, heavy cruel mountains, with their moments of tenderness.

She saw Tansy start, and begin to run. Two ghost-like figures on horseback emerged from the black of the spruce across the stream. It was two Indians on horseback, swathed like seated mummies in their pale-grey cotton blankets. Their guns jutted beyond the saddles. They rode straight towards her, to her thread of smoke.

As they came near, they unswathed themselves and greeted her, looking at her curiously from their dark eyes. Their black hair was somewhat untidy, the long rolled plaits on their shoulders were soiled. They looked tired.

They got down from their horses near her little fire—a

camp was a camp—swathed their blankets round their hips, pulled the saddles from their ponies and turned them loose, then sat down. One was a young Indian whom she had met before, the other was an older man.

"You all alone?" said the younger man.

"Romero will be here in a minute," she said, glancing back along the trail.

"Ah, Romero! You with him? Where are you going?"

"Round the ridge," she said. "Where are you going?"

"We going down to Pueblo."

"Been out hunting? How long have you been out?"

"Yes. Been out five days." The young Indian gave a little meaningless laugh.

"Got anything?"

"No. We see tracks of two deer—but not got nothing."

The Princess noticed a suspicious-looking bulk under one of the saddles—surely a folded-up deer. But she said nothing.

"You must have been cold," she said.

"Yes, very cold in the night. And hungry. Got nothing to eat since yesterday. Eat it all up." And again he laughed his little meaningless laugh. Under their dark skins, the two men looked peaked and hungry. The Princess rummaged for food among the saddle-bags. There was a lump of bacon—the regular stand-back—and some bread. She gave them this, and they began toasting slices of it on long sticks at the fire. Such was the little camp Romero saw as he rode down the slope: the Princess in her orange breeches, her head tied in a blue-and-brown silk kerchief, sitting opposite the two dark-headed Indians across the camp-fire, while one of the Indians was leaning forward toasting bacon, his two plaits of braid-hair dangling as if wearily.

Romero rode up, his face expressionless. The Indians greeted him in Spanish. He unsaddled his horse, took food from the bags, and sat down at the camp to eat. The Princess went to the stream for water, and to wash her hands.

"Got coffee?" asked the Indians.

"No coffee this outfit," said Romero.

They lingered an hour or more in the warm midday sun. Then Romero saddled the horses. The Indians still squatted by the fire. Romero and the Princess rode away, calling *Adios!* to the Indians over the stream and into the dense spruce whence two strange figures had emerged.

When they were alone, Romero turned and looked at her curiously, in a way she could not understand, with such a hard glint in his eyes. And for the first time she wondered if she was rash.

"I hope you don't mind going alone with me," she said.

"If you want it," he replied.

They emerged at the foot of the great bare slope of rocky summit, where dead spruce trees stood sparse and bristling like bristles on a grey dead hog. Romero said the Mexicans, twenty years back, had fired the mountains, to drive out the whites. This grey concave slope of summit was corpse-like.

The trail was almost invisible. Romero watched for the trees which the Forest Service had blazed. And they climbed the stark corpse slope, among dead spruce, fallen and ash-grey, into the wind. The wind came rushing from the west, up the funnel of the canyon, from the desert. And there was the desert, like a vast mirage tilting slowly upwards towards the west, immense and pallid, away beyond the funnel of the canyon. The Princess could hardly look.

For an hour their horses rushed the slope, hastening with a great working of the haunches upwards, and halting to breathe, scrambling again, and rowing their way up length by length, on the livid, slanting wall. While the wind blew like some vast machine.

After an hour they were working their way on the incline, no longer forcing straight up. All was grey and dead around them; the horses picked their way over the silver-grey corpses of the spruce. But they were near the top, near the ridge.

Even the horses made a rush for the last bit. They had worked round to a scrap of spruce forest near the very top. They hurried in, out of the huge, monstrous, mechanical wind, that whistled inhumanly and was palely cold. So, stepping through the dark screen of trees, they emerged over the crest.

In front now was nothing but mountains, ponderous, massive, down-sitting mountains, in a huge and intricate knot, empty of life or soul. Under the bristling black feathers of spruce near-by lay patches of white snow. The lifeless valleys were concaves of rock and spruce, the rounded summits and the hog-backed summits of grey rock crowded one behind the other like some monstrous herd in arrest.

It frightened the Princess, it was so inhuman. She had not thought it could be so inhuman, so, as it were, anti-life. And yet now one of her desires was fulfilled. She had seen it, the massive, gruesome, repellent core of the Rockies. She saw it there beneath her eyes, in its gigantic, heavy gruesomeness.

And she wanted to go back. At this moment she wanted to turn back. She had looked down into the intestinal knot of these mountains. She was frightened. She wanted to go back.

But Romero was riding on, on the lee side of the spruce forest, above the concaves of the inner mountains. He turned round to her and pointed at the slope with a dark hand.

"Here a miner has been trying for gold," he said. It was a grey scratched-out heap near a hole—like a great badger hole. And it looked quite fresh.

"Quite lately?" said the Princess.

"No, long ago—twenty, thirty years." He had reined in his horse and was looking at the mountains. "Look!" he said. "There goes the Forest Service trail—along those ridges, on the top, way over there till it comes to Lucytown, where is the Goverment road. We go down there—no trail—see behind that mountain—you see the top, no trees, and some grass?"

His arm was lifted, his brown hand pointing, his dark eyes piercing into the distance, as he sat on his black horse twisting round to her. Strange and ominous, only the demon of himself, he seemed to her. She was dazed and a little sick, at that height, and she could not see any more. Only she saw an eagle turning in the air beyond, and the light from the west showed the pattern on him underneath.

"Shall I ever be able to go so far?" asked the Princess faintly, petulantly.

"Oh yes! All easy now. No more hard places."

They worked along the ridge, up and down, keeping on the lee side, the inner side, in the dark shadow. It was cold. Then the trail laddered up again, and they emerged on a narrow ridge-track, with the mountain slipping away enormously on either side. The Princess was afraid. For one moment she looked out, and saw the desert, the desert ridges, more desert, more blue ridges, shining pale and very vast, far below, vastly palely tilting to the western horizon. It was ethereal and terrifying in its gleaming, pale, half-burnished immensity, tilted at the west. She could not bear it. To the left was the ponderous, involved mass of mountains all kneeling heavily.

She closed her eyes and let her consciousness evaporate

away. The mare followed the trail. So on and on, in the wind again.

They turned their backs to the wind, facing inwards to the mountains. She thought they had left the trail; it was quite invisible.

"No," he said, lifting his hand and pointing. "Don't you see the blazed trees?"

And making an effort of consciousness, she was able to perceive on a pale-grey dead spruce stem the old marks where an axe had chipped a piece away. But with the height, the cold, the wind, her brain was numb.

They turned again and began to descend; he told her they had left the trail. The horses slithered in the loose stones, picking their way downward. It was afternoon, the sun stood obtrusive and gleaming in the lower heavens—about four o'clock. The horses went steadily, slowly, but obstinately onwards. The air was getting colder. They were in among the lumpish peaks and steep concave valleys. She was barely conscious at all of Romero.

He dismounted and came to help her from her saddle. She tottered, but would not betray her feebleness.

"We must slide down here," he said. "I can lead the horses."

They were on a ridge, and facing a steep bare slope of pallid, tawny mountain grass on which the western sun shone full. It was steep and concave. The Princess felt she might start slipping, and go down like a toboggan into the great hollow.

But she pulled herself together. Her eye blazed up again with excitement and determination. A wind rushed past her; she could hear the shriek of spruce trees far below. Bright spots came on her cheeks as her hair blew across. She looked a wild, fairy-like little thing.

"No," she said. "I will take my horse."

"Then mind she doesn't slip down on top of you," said Romero. And away he went, nimbly dropping down the pale, steep incline, making from rock to rock, down the grass, and following any little slanting groove. His horse hopped and slithered after him, and sometimes stopped dead, with forefeet pressed back, refusing to go farther. He, below his horse, looked up and pulled the reins gently, and encouraged the creature. Then the horse once more dropped his forefeet with a jerk, and the descent continued.

The Princess set off in blind, reckless pursuit, tottering and yet nimble. And Romero, looking constantly back to see how she was faring, saw her fluttering down like some queer little bird, her orange breeches twinkling like the legs of some duck, and her head, tied in the blue and buff kerchief, bound round and round like the head of some blue-topped bird. The sorrel mare rocked and slipped behind her. But down came the Princess in a reckless intensity, a tiny, vivid spot on the great hollow flank of the tawny mountain. So tiny! Tiny as a frail bird's egg. It made Romero's mind go blank with wonder.

But they had to get down, out of that cold and dragging wind. The spruce trees stood below, where a tiny stream emerged in stones. Away plunged Romero, zigzagging down. And away behind, up the slope, fluttered the tiny, bright-coloured Princess, holding the end of the long reins, and leading the lumbering, four-footed, sliding mare.

At last they were down. Romero sat in the sun, below the wind, beside some squaw-berry bushes. The Princess came near, the colour flaming in her cheeks, her eyes dark blue, much darker than the kerchief on her head, and glowing unnaturally.

"We make it," said Romero.

"Yes," said the Princess, dropping the reins and subsiding on to the grass, unable to speak, unable to think.

But, thank heaven, they were out of the wind and in the sun.

In a few minutes her consciousness and her control began to come back. She drank a little water. Romero was attending to the saddles. Then they set off again, leading the horses still a little farther down the tiny stream-bed. Then they could mount.

They rode down a bank and into a valley grove dense with aspens. Winding through the thin, crowding, pale-smooth stems, the sun shone flickering beyond them, and the disc-like aspen leaves, waving queer mechanical signals, seemed to be splashing the gold light before her eyes. She rode on in a splashing dazzle of gold.

Then they entered shadow and the dark, resinous spruce trees. The fierce boughs always wanted to sweep her off her horse. She had to twist and squirm past.

But there was a semblance of an old trail. And all at once they emerged in the sun on the edge of the spruce grove, and there was a little cabin, and the bottom of a small, naked valley with grey rock and heaps of stones, and a round pool of intense green water, dark green. The sun was just about to leave it.

Indeed, as she stood, the shadow came over the cabin and over herself; they were in the lower gloom, a twilight. Above, the heights still blazed.

It was a little hole of a cabin, near the spruce trees, with an earthen floor and an unhinged door. There was a wooden bed-bunk, three old sawn-off log-lengths to sit on as stools, and a sort of fireplace; no room for anything else. The little hole would hardly contain two people. The roof had gone—but Romero had laid on thick spruce boughs.

The strange squalor of the primitive forest pervaded the place, the squalor of animals and their droppings, the squalor of the wild. The Princess knew the peculiar repulsiveness of it. She was tired and faint.

Romero hastily got a handful of twigs, set a little fire going in the stove grate, and went out to attend to the horses. The Princess vaguely, mechanically, put sticks on the fire, in a sort of stupor, watching the blaze, stupefied and fascinated. She could not make much fire—it would set the whole cabin alight. And smoke oozed out of the dilapidated mud-and-stone chimney.

When Romero came in with the saddle-pouches and saddles, hanging the saddles on the wall, there sat the little Princess on her stump of wood in front of the dilapidated fire-grate, warming her tiny hands at the blaze, while her oranges breeches glowed almost like another fire. She was in a sort of stupor.

"You have some whisky now, or some tea? Or wait for some soup?" he asked

She rose and looked at him with bright, dazed eyes, half comprehending; the colour glowing hectic in her cheeks.

"Some tea," she said, "with a little whisky in it. Where's the kettle?"

"Wait," he said. "I'll bring the things."

She took her cloak from the back of her saddle, and followed him into the open. It was a deep cup of shadow. But above the sky was still shining, and the heights of the mountains were blazing with aspen like fire blazing.

Their horses were cropping the grass among the stones. Romero clambered up a heap of grey stones and began lifting away logs and rocks, till he had opened the mouth of one of

the miner's little old workings. This was his cache. He brought
out bundles of blankets, pans for cooking, a little petrol
camp-stove, an axe, the regular camp outfit. He seemed so
quick and energetic and full of force. This quick force dis-
mayed the Princess a little.

She took a saucepan and went down the stones to the water.
It was very still and mysterious, and of a deep green colour,
yet pure, transparent as glass. How cold the place was! How
mysterious and fearful.

She crouched in her dark cloak by the water, rinsing the
saucepan, feeling the cold heavy above her, the shadow like
a vast weight upon her, bowing her down. The sun was
leaving the mountain-tops, departing, leaving her under profound shadow. Soon it would crush her down completely.

Sparks? Or eyes looking at her across the water? She gazed,
hypnotised. And with her sharp eyes she made out in the
dusk the pale form of a bob-cat crouching by the water's edge,
pale as the stones amongs which it crouched, opposite. And
it was watching her with cold, electric eyes of strange intentness, a sort of cold, icy wonder and fearlessness. She saw its
museau pushed forward, its tufted ears pricking intensely up.
It was watching her with cold, animal curiosity, something
demonish and conscienceless.

She made a swift movement, spilling her water. And in a
flash the creature was gone, leaping like a cat that is escaping;
but strange and soft in its motion, with its little bob-tail.
Rather fascinating. Yet that cold, intent, demonish watching!
She shivered with cold and fear. She knew well enough the
dread and repulsiveness of the wild.

Romero carried in the bundles of bedding and the camp
outfit. The windowless cabin was already dark inside. He lit
a lantern, and then went out again with the axe. She heard
him chopping wood as she fed sticks to the fire under her
water. When he came in with an armful of oak-scrub faggots,
she had just thrown the tea into the water.

"Sit down," she said, "and drink tea."

He poured a little bootleg whisky into the enamel cups, and
in the silence the two sat on the log-ends, sipping the hot
liquid and coughing occasionally from the smoke.

"We burn these oak sticks," he said. "They don't make
hardly any smoke."

Curious and remote he was, saying nothing except what had

to be said. And she, for her part, was as remote from him. They seemed far, far apart, worlds apart, now they were so near.

He unwrapped one bundle of bedding, and spread the blankets and the sheepskin in the wooden bunk.

"You lie down and rest," he said, "and I make the supper."

She decided to do so. Wrapping her cloak round her, she lay down in the bunk, turning her face to the wall. She could hear him preparing supper over the little petrol stove. Soon she could smell the soup he was heating; and soon she heard the hissing of fried chicken in a pan.

"You eat your supper now?" he said.

With a jerky, despairing movement, she sat up in the bunk, tossing back her hair. She felt cornered.

"Give it me here," she said.

He handed her first the cupful of soup. She sat among the blankets, eating it slowly. She was hungry. Then he gave her an enamel plate with pieces of fried chicken and currant jelly, butter and bread. It was very good. As they ate the chicken he made the coffee. She said never a word. A certain resentment filled her. She was cornered.

When supper was over he washed the dishes, dried them, and put everything away carefully, else there would have been no room to move in the hole of a cabin. The oak-wood gave out a good bright heat.

He stood for a few moments at a loss. Then he asked her: "You want to go to bed soon?"

"Soon," she said. "Where are you going to sleep?"

"I make my bed here——" he pointed to the floor along the wall. "Too cold out of doors."

"Yes," she said. "I suppose it is."

She sat immobile, her cheeks hot, full of conflicting thoughts. And she watched him while he folded the blankets on the floor, a sheepskin underneath. Then she went out into night.

The stars were big. Mars sat on the edge of a mountain, for all the world like the blazing eye of a crouching mountain lion. But she herself was deep, deep below in a pit of shadow. In the intense silence she seemed to hear the spruce forest crackling with electricity and cold. Strange, foreign stars floated on that unmoving water. The night was going to freeze. Over the hills came the far sobbing-singing howling of the coyotes. She wondered how the horses would be.

Shuddering a little, she turned to the cabin. Warm light showed through its chinks. She pushed at the rickety, half-opened door.

"What about the horses?" she said.

"My black, he won't go away. And your mare will stay with him. You want to go to bed now?"

"I think I do."

"All right. I feed the horses some oats."

And he went out into the night.

He did not come back for some time. She was lying wrapped up tight in the bunk.

He blew out the lantern, and sat down on his bedding to take off his clothes. She lay with her back turned. And soon, in the silence, she was asleep.

She dreamed it was snowing, and the snow was falling on her through the roof, softly, softly, helplessly, and she was going to be buried alive. She was growing colder and colder, the snow was weighing down on her. The snow was going to absorb her.

She awoke with a sudden convulsion, like pain. She was really very cold; perhaps the heavy blankets had numbed her. Her heart seemed unable to beat, she felt she could not move.

With another convulsion she sat up. It was intensely dark. There was not even a spark of fire, the light wood had burned right away. She sat in thick oblivious darkness. Only through a chink she could see a star.

What did she want? Oh, what did she want? She sat in bed and rocked herself woefully. She could hear the steady breathing of the sleeping man. She was shivering with cold; her heart seemed as if it could not beat. She wanted warmth, protection, she wanted to be taken away from herself. And at the same time, perhaps more deeply than anything, she wanted to keep herself intact, intact, untouched, that no one should have any power over her, or rights to her. It was a wild necessity in her that no one, particularly no man, should have any rights or power over her, that no one and nothing should possess her.

Yet that other thing! And she was so cold, so shivering, and her heart could not beat. Oh, would not someone help her heart to beat?

She tried to speak, and could not. Then she cleared her throat.

"Romero," she said strangely, "it is so cold."

Where did her voice come from, and whose voice was it, in the dark?

She heard him at once sit up, and his voice, startled, with a resonance that seemed to vibrate against her, saying:

"You want me to make you warm?"

"Yes."

As soon as he had lifted her in his arms, she wanted to scream to him not to touch her. She stiffened herself. Yet she was dumb.

And he was warm, but with a terrible animal warmth that seemed to annihilate her. He panted like an animal with desire. And she was given over to this thing.

She had never, never wanted to be given over to this. But she had *willed* that it should happen to her. And according to her will, she lay and let it happen. But she never wanted it. She never wanted to be thus assailed and handled, and mauled. She wanted to keep herself to herself.

However, she had willed it to happen, and it had happened. She panted with relief when it was over.

Yet even now she had to lie within the hard, powerful clasp of this other creature, this man. She dreaded to struggle to go away. She dreaded almost too much the icy cold of that other bunk.

"Do you want to go away from me?" asked his strange voice. Oh, if it could only have been a thousand miles away from her! Yet she had willed to have it thus close.

"No," she said.

And she could feel a curious joy and pride surging up again in him: at her expense. Because he had got her. She felt like a victim there. And he was exulting in his power over her, his possession, his pleasure.

When dawn came, he was fast asleep. She sat up suddenly.

"I want a fire," she said.

He opened his brown eyes wide, and smiled with a curious tender luxuriousness.

"I want you to make a fire," she said.

He glanced at the chinks of light. His brown face hardened to the day.

"All right," he said. "I'll make it."

She did her face while he dressed. She could not bear to look at him. He was so suffused with pride and luxury. She hid her face almost in despair. But feeling the cold blast of air as he opened the door, she wriggled down into the warm place where he had been. How soon the warmth ebbed, when he had gone!

He made a fire and went out, returning after a while with water.

"You stay in bed till the sun comes," he said. "It very cold."

"Hand me my cloak."

She wrapped the cloak fast round her, and sat up among the blankets. The warmth was already spreading from the fire.

"I suppose we will start back as soon as we've had breakfast?"

He was crouching at his camp-stove making scrambled eggs. He looked up suddenly, transfixed, and his brown eyes, so soft and luxuriously widened, looked straight at her.

"You want to?" he said.

"We'd better get back as soon as possible," she said, turning aside from his eyes.

"You want to get away from me?" he asked, repeating the question of the night in a sort of dread.

"I want to get away from here," she said decisively. And it was true. She wanted supremely to get away, back to the world of people.

He rose slowly to his feet, holding the aluminium frying-pan.

"Don't you like last night?" he asked.

"Not really," she said. "Why? Do you?"

He put down the frying-pan and stood staring at the wall. She could see she had given him a cruel blow. But she did not relent. She was getting her own back. She wanted to re-gain possession of all herself, and in some mysterious way she felt that he possessed some part of her still.

He looked round at her slowly, his face greyish and heavy.

"You Americans," he said, "you always want to do a man down."

"I am not American," she said. "I am British. And I don't want to do any man down. I only want to go back now."

"And what will you say about me, down there?"

"That you were very kind to me, and very good."

He crouched down again, and went on turning the eggs. He gave her her plate, and her coffee, and sat down to his own food.

But again he seemed not to be able to swallow. He looked up at her.

"You don't like last night?" he asked.

"Not really," she said, though with some difficulty. "I don't care for that kind of thing."

A blank sort of wonder spread over his face at these words, followed immediately by a black look of anger, and then a stony, sinister despair.

"You don't?" he said, looking her in the eyes.

"Not really," she replied, looking back with steady hostility into his eyes.

Then a dark flame seemed to come from his face.

"I make you," he said, as if to himself.

He rose and reached her clothes, that hung on a peg: the fine linen underwear, the orange breeches, the fleecy jumper, the blue-and-bluff kerchief; then he took up her riding-boots and her bead moccasins. Crushing everything in his arms, he opened the door. Sitting up, she saw him stride down to the dark-green pool in the frozen shadow of that deep cup of a valley. He tossed the clothing and the boots out on the pool. Ice had formed. And on the pure, dark green mirror, in the slaty shadow, the Princess saw her things lying, the white linen, the orange breeches, the black boots, the blue moccasins, a tangled heap of colour. Romero picked up rocks and heaved them out at the ice, till the surface broke and the fluttering clothing disappeared in the rattling water, while the valley echoed and shouted again with the sound.

She sat in despair among the blankets, hugging tight her pale-blue cloak. Romero strode straight back to the cabin.

"Now you stay here with me," he said.

She was furious. Her blue eyes met his. They were like two demons watching one another. In his face, beyond a sort of unrelieved gloom, was a demonish desire for death.

He saw her looking round the cabin, scheming. He saw her eyes on his rifle. He took the gun and went out with it. Returning, he pulled out her saddle, carried it to the tarn, and threw it in. Then he fetched his own saddle, and did the same.

"Now will you go away?" he said, looking at her with a smile.

She debated within herself whether to coax him and wheedle him. But she knew he was already beyond it. She sat among her blankets in a frozen sort of despair, hard as hard ice with anger.

He did the chores, and disappeared with the gun. She got up in her blue pyjamas, huddled in her cloak, and stood in the doorway. The dark-green pool was motionless again, the stony slopes were pallid and frozen. Shadow still lay, like an after-death, deep in this valley. Always in the distance she saw the horses feeding. If she could catch one! The brilliant yellow sun was half-way down the mountain. It was nine o'clock.

All day she was alone, and she was frightened. What she was frightened of she didn't know. Perhaps the crackling in the dark spruce wood. Perhaps just the savage, heartless wildness of the mountains. But all day she sat in the sun in the doorway of the cabin, watching, watching for hope. And all the time her bowels were cramped with fear.

She saw a dark spot that probably was a bear, roving across the pale grassy slope in the far distance, in the sun.

When, in the afternoon, she saw Romero approaching, with silent suddenness, carrying his gun and a dead deer, the cramp in her bowels relaxed, then became colder. She dreaded him with a cold dread.

"There is deer-meat," he said, throwing the dead doe at her feet.

"You don't want to go away from here," he said. "This is a nice place."

She shrank into the cabin.

"Come into the sun," he said, following her. She looked up at him with hostile, frightened eyes.

"Come into the sun," he repeated, taking her gently by the arm, in a powerful grasp.

She knew it was useless to rebel. Quietly he led her out, and seated himself in the doorway, holding her still by the arm.

"In the sun it is warm," he said. "Look, this is a nice place. You are such a pretty white woman, why do you want to act mean to me? Isn't this a nice place? Come! Come here! It is sure warm here."

He drew her to him, and in spite of her stony resistance, he took her cloak from her, holding her in her thin blue pyjamas.

"You sure are a pretty little white woman, small and pretty," he said. "You sure won't act mean to me—you don't want to, I know you don't."

She, stony and powerless, had to submit to him. The sun shone on her white, delicate skin.

"I sure don't mind hell fire," he said. "After this."

A queer, luxurious good humour seemed to possess him again. But though outwardly she was powerless, inwardly she resisted him, absolutely and stonily.

When later he was leaving her again, she said to him suddenly:

"You think you can conquer me this way. But you can't. You can never conquer me."

He stood arrested, looking back at her, with many emotions conflicting in his face—wonder, surprise, a touch of horror, and an unconscious pain that crumpled his face till it was like a mask. Then he went out without saying a word, hung the dead deer on a bough, and started to flay it. While he was at this butcher's work, the sun sank and cold night came on again.

"You see," he said to her as he crouched, cooking the supper, "I ain't going to let you go. I reckon you called to me in the night, and I've some right. If you want to fix it up right now with me, and say you want to be with me, we'll fix it up now and go down to the ranch to-morrow and get married or whatever you want. But you've got to say you want to be with me. Else I shall stay right here, till something happens."

She waited a while before she answered:

"I don't want to be with anybody against my will. I don't dislike you; at least, I didn't, till you tried to put your will over mine. I won't have anybody's will put over me. You can't succeed. Nobody could. You can never get me under your will. And you won't have long to try, because soon they will send someone to look for me."

He pondered this last, and she regretted having said it. Then, sombre, he bent to the cooking again.

He could not conquer her, however much he violated her. Because her spirit was hard and flawless as a diamond. But he could shatter her. This she knew. Much more, and she would be shattered.

In a sombre, violent excess he tried to expend his desire for her. And she was racked with a agony, and felt each time she would die. Because, in some peculiar way, he had got hold of her, some unrealised part of her which she never wished to realise. Racked with a burning, tearing anguish, she felt that the thread of her being would break, and she would die. The burning heat that racked her inwardly.

If only, only she could be alone again, cool and intact! If only she could recover herself again, cool and intact! Would she ever, ever, ever be able to bear herself again?

Even now she did not hate him. It was beyond that. Like some racking, hot doom. Personally he hardly existed.

The next day he would not let her have any fire, because of attracting attention with the smoke. It was a grey day, and she was cold. He stayed round, and heated soup on the petrol stove. She lay motionless in the blankets.

And in the afternoon she pulled the clothes over her head and broke into tears. She had never really cried in her life. He dragged the blankets away and looked to see what was shaking her. She sobbed in helpless hysterics. He covered her over again and went outside, looking at the mountains, where clouds were dragging and leaving a little snow. It was a violent, windy, horrible day, the evil of winter rushing down.

She cried for hours. And after this a great silence came between them. They were two people who had died. He did not touch her any more. In the night she lay and shivered like a dying dog. She felt that her very shivering would rupture something in her body, and she would die.

At last she had to speak.

"Could you make a fire? I am so cold," she said, with chattering teeth.

"Want to come over here?" came his voice.

"I would rather you made me a fire," she said, her teeth knocking together and chopping the words in two.

He got up and kindled a fire. At last the warmth spread, and she could sleep.

The next day was still chilly, with some wind. But the sun shone. He went about in silence, with a dead-looking face. It was now so dreary and so like death she wished he would do anything rather than continue in this negation. If now he asked her to go down with him to the world and marry him, she would do it. What did it matter? Nothing mattered any more.

But he would not ask her. His desire was dead and heavy like ice within him. He kept watch around the house.

On the fourth day as she sat huddled in the doorway in the sun, hugged in a blanket, she saw two horsemen come over the crest of the grassy slope—small figures. She gave a cry. He looked up quickly and saw the figures. The men had dismounted. They were looking for the trail.

"They are looking for me," she said.

"*Muy bien*," he answered in Spanish.

He went and fetched his gun, and sat with it across his knees.

"Oh!" she said. "Don't shoot!"

He looked across at her.

"Why?" he said. "You like staying with me?"

"No," she said. "But don't shoot."

"I ain't going to Pen," he said.

"You won't have to go to Pen," she said. "Don't shoot!"

"I'm going to shoot," he muttered.

And straightaway he knelt and took very careful aim. The Princess sat on in an agony of helplessness and hopelessness.

The shot rang out. In an instant she saw one of the horses on the pale grassy slope rear and go rolling down. The man had dropped in the grass, and was invisible. The second man clambered on his horse, and on that precipitous place went at a gallop in a long swerve towards the nearest spruce tree cover. Bang! Bang! went Romero's shots. But each time he missed, and the running horse leaped like a kangaroo towards cover.

It was hidden. Romero now got behind a rock; tense silence, in the brilliant sunshine. The Princess sat on the bunk inside the cabin, crouching, paralysed. For hours, it seemed, Romero knelt behind this rock, in his black shirt, bare-headed, watching. He had a beautiful, alert figure. The Princess wondered why she did not feel sorry for him. But her spirit was hard and cold, her heart could not melt. Though now she would have called him to her, with love.

But no, she did not love him. She would never love any

man. Never! It was fixed and sealed in her, almost vindictively.

Suddenly she was so startled she almost fell from the bunk. A shot rang out quite close from behind the cabin. Romero leaped straight into the air, his arms fell outstretched, turning as he leaped. And even while he was in the air, a second shot rang out, and he fell with a crash, squirming, his hands clutching the earth towards the cabin door.

The Princess sat absolutely motionless, transfixed, staring at the prostrate figure. In a few moments the figure of a man in the Forest Service appeared close to the house; a young man in a broad-brimmed Stetson hat, dark flannel shirt, and riding-boots, carrying a gun. He strode over to the prostrate figure.

"Got you, Romero!" he said aloud. And he turned the dead man over. There was already a little pool of blood where Romero's breast had been.

"H'm!" said the Forest Service man. "Guess I got you nearer than I thought."

And he squatted there, staring at the dead man.

The distant calling of his comrade aroused him. He stood up.

"Hullo, Bill!" he shouted. "Yep! Got him! Yep! Done him in, apparently."

The second man rode out of the forest on a grey horse. He had a ruddy, kind face, and round brown eyes, dilated with dismay.

"He's not passed out?" he asked anxiously.

"Looks like it," said the first young man coolly.

The second dismounted and bent over the body. Then he stood up again, and nodded.

"Yea-a!" he said. "He's done in all right. It's him all right, boy! It's Domingo Romero."

"Yep! I know it!" replied the other.

Then in perplexity he turned and looked into the cabin, where the Princess squatted, staring with big owl eyes from her red blanket.

"Hello!" he said, coming towards the hut. And he took his hat off. Oh, the sense of ridicule she felt! Though he did not mean any.

But she could not speak, no matter what she felt.

"What'd this man start firing for?" he asked.

She fumbled for words, with numb lips.

"He had gone out of his mind!" she said, with solemn, stammering conviction.

"Good Lord! You mean to say he'd gone out of his mind? Whew! That's pretty awful! That explains it then. H'm!"

He accepted the explanation without more ado.

With some difficulty they succeeded in getting the Princess down to the ranch. But she, too, was not a little mad.

"I'm not quite sure where I am," she said to Mrs. Wilkieson, as she lay in bed. "Do you mind explaining?"

Mrs. Wilkieson explained tactfully.

"Oh yes!" said the Princess. "I remember. And I had an accident in the mountains, didn't I? Didn't we meet a man who'd gone mad, and who shot my horse from under me?"

"Yes, you met a man who had gone out of his mind."

The real affair was hushed up. The Princess departed east in a fortnight's time, in Miss Cummins's care. Apparently she had recovered herself entirely. She was the Princess, and a virgin intact.

But her bobbed hair was grey at the temples, and her eyes were a little mad. She was slightly crazy.

"Since my accident in the mountains, when a man went mad and shot my horse from under me, and my guide had to shoot him dead, I have never felt quite myself."

So she put it.

Later, she married an elderly man, and seemed pleased.

TWO BLUE BIRDS

THERE was a woman who loved her husband, but she could not live with him. The husband, on his side, was sincerely attached to his wife, yet he could not live with her. They were both under forty, both handsome and both attractive. They had the most sincere regard for one another, and felt, in some odd way, eternally married to one another. They knew one another more intimately than they knew anybody else, they felt more known to one another than to any other person.

Yet they could not live together. Usually, they kept a thousand miles apart, geographically. But when he sat in the greyness of England, at the back of his mind, with a certain grim fidelity, he was aware of his wife, her strange yearning to be loyal and faithful, having her gallant affairs away in the sun, in the south. And she, as she drank her cocktail on the terrace over the sea, and turned her grey, sardonic eyes on the heavy dark face of her admirer, whom she really liked quite a lot, she was actually preoccupied with the clear-cut features of her handsome young husband, thinking of how he would be asking his secretary to do something for him, asking in that good-natured, confident voice of a man who knows that his request will be only too gladly fulfilled.

The secretary, of course, adored him. She was *very* competent, quite young, and quite good-looking. She adored him. But then all his servants always did, particularly his women-servants. His men-servants were likely to swindle him.

When a man has an adoring secretary, and you are the man's wife, what are you to do? Not that there was anything 'wrong'—if you know what I mean!—between them. Nothing you could call adultery, to come down to brass tacks. No, no! They were just the young master and his secretary. He dictated to her, she slaved for him and adored him, and the whole thing went on wheels.

He didn't 'adore' her. A man doesn't need to adore his secretary. But he depended on her. "I simply rely on Miss Wrexall." Whereas he could never rely on his wife. The one thing he knew finally about *her* was that she didn't intend to be relied on.

So they remained friends, in the awful unspoken intimacy of the once-married. Usually each year they went away together for a holiday, and, if they had not been man and wife, they would have found a great deal of fun and stimulation in one another. The fact that they were married, had been married for the last dozen years, and couldn't live together for the last three or four, spoilt them for one another. Each had a private feeling of bitterness about the other.

However, they were awfully kind. He was the soul of generosity, and held her in real tender esteem, no matter how many gallant affairs she had. Her gallant affairs were part of her modern necessity. "After all, I've got to *live*. I can't turn into a pillar of salt in five minutes just because you and I can't live together! It takes years for a woman like me to turn into a pillar of salt. At least I hope so!"

"Quite!" he replied. "Quite! By all means put them in pickle, make pickled cucumbers of them, before you crystallise out. That's my advice."

He was like that: so awfully clever and enigmatic. She could more or less fathom the idea of the pickled cucumbers, but the 'crystallising out'—what did that signify?

And did he mean to suggest that he himself had been well pickled and that further immersion was for him unnecessary, would spoil his flavour? Was that what he meant? And herself, was she the brine and the vale of tears?

You never knew how catty a man was being, when he was really clever and enigmatic, withal a bit whimsical. He was adorably whimsical, with a twist of his flexible, vain mouth, that had a long upper lip, so fraught with vanity! But then a handsome, clear-cut, histrionic young man like that, how could he help being vain? The women made him so.

Ah, the women! How nice men would be if there were no other women!

And how nice the women would be if there were no other men! That's the best of a secretary. She may have a husband, but a husband is the mere shred of a man, compared to a boss, a chief, a man who dictates to you and whose words you faithfully write down and then transcribe. Imagine a wife writing down anything her husband said to her! But a secretary! Every *and* and *but* of his she preserves for ever. What are candied violets in comparison!

Now it is all very well having gallant affairs under the southern sun, when you know there is a husband whom you adore dictating to a secretary whom you are too scornful to hate yet whom you rather despise, though you allow she has her good points, away north in the place you ought to regard as home. A gallant affair isn't much good when you've got a bit of grit in your eye. Or something at the back of your mind.

What's to be done? The husband, of course, did not send his wife away.

"You've got your secretary and your work," she said. "There's no room for me."

"There's a bedroom and a sitting-room exclusively for you," he replied. "And a garden and half a motor-car. But please yourself entirely. Do what gives you most pleasure."

"In that case," she said, "I'll just go south for the winter."

"Yes, do!" he said. "You always enjoy it."

"I always do," she replied.

They parted with a certain relentlessness that had a touch of wistful sentiment behind it. Off she went to her gallant affairs, that were like the curate's egg, palatable in parts. And he settled down to work. He said he hated working, but he never did anything else. Ten or eleven hours a day. That's what it is to be your own master!

So the winter wore away, and it was spring, when the swallows homeward fly, or northward, in this case. This winter, one of a series similar, had been rather hard to get through. The bit of grit in the gallant lady's eye had worked deeper in the more she blinked. Dark faces might be dark, and icy cocktails might lend a glow; she blinked her hardest to blink that bit of grit away, without success. Under the spicy balls of the mimosa she thought of that husband of hers in his library, and of that neat, competent but *common* little secretary of his, for ever taking down what he said!

"How a man can *stand* it! How *she* can stand it, common little thing as she is, I don't know!" the wife cried to herself.

She meant this dictating business, this ten hours a day intercourse, *à deux*, with nothing but a pencil between them, and a flow of words.

What was to be done? Matters, instead of improving, had

grown worse. The little secretary had brought her mother and sister into the establishment. The mother was a sort of cook-housekeeper, the sister was a sort of upper maid—she did the fine laundry, and looked after 'his' clothes, and valeted him beautifully. It was really an excellent arrangement. The old mother was a splendid plain cook, the sister was all that could be desired as a valet de chambre, a fine laundress, an upper parlour-maid, and a table-waiter. And all economical to a degree. They knew his affairs by heart. His secretary flew to town when a creditor became dangerous, and she *always* smoothed over the financial crisis.

'He', of course, had debts, and he was working to pay them off. And if he had been a fairy prince who could call the ants to help him, he would not have been more wonderful than in securing this secretary and her family. They took hardly any wages. And they seemed to perform the miracle of loaves and fishes daily.

'She', of course, was the wife who loved her husband, but helped him into debt, and she still was an expensive item. Yet when she appeared at her 'home', the secretarial family received her with most elaborate attentions and deference. The knight returning from the Crusades didn't create a greater stir. She felt like Queen Elizabeth at Kenilworth, a sovereign paying a visit to her faithful subjects. But perhaps there lurked always this hair in her soup! Won't they be glad to be rid of me again!

But they protested No! No! They had been waiting and hoping and praying she would come. They had been pining for her to be there, in charge: the mistress, 'his' wife. Ah, 'his' wife!

'His' wife! His halo was like a bucket over her head.

The cook-mother was 'of the people', so it was the upper-maid daughter who came for orders.

"What will you order for to-morrow's lunch and dinner, Mrs. Gee?"

"Well, what do you usually have?"

"Oh, we want *you* to say."

"No, what do you *usually* have?"

"We don't have anything fixed. Mother goes out and chooses the best she can find, that is nice and fresh. But she thought you would tell her now what to get."

"Oh, I don't know! I'm not very good at that sort of

thing. Ask her to go on just the same; I'm quite sure she knows best."

"Perhaps you'd like to suggest a sweet?"

"No, I don't care for sweets—and you know Mr. Gee doesn't. So don't make one for me."

Could anything be more impossible! They had the house spotless and running like a dream; how could an incompetent and extravagant wife dare to interfere, when she saw their amazing and almost inspired economy! But they ran the place on simply nothing!

Simply marvellous people! And the way they strewed palm branches under her feet!

But that only made her feel ridiculous.

"Don't you think the family manage very well?" he asked her tentatively.

"Awfully well! Almost romantically well!" she replied. "But I suppose you're perfectly happy?"

"I'm perfectly comfortable," he replied.

"I can see you are," she replied. "Amazingly so! I never knew such comfort! Are you sure it isn't bad for you?"

She eyed him stealthily. He looked very well, and extremely handsome, in his histrionic way. He was shockingly well-dressed and valeted. And he had that air of easy aplomb and good humour which is so becoming to a man, and which he only acquires when he is cock of his own little walk, made much of by his own hens.

"No!" he said, taking his pipe from his mouth and smiling whimsically round at her. "Do I look as if it were bad for me?"

"No, you don't," she replied promptly: thinking, naturally, as a woman is supposed to think nowadays, of his health and comfort, the foundation, apparently, of all happiness.

Then, of course, away she went on the back-wash.

"Perhaps for your work, though, it's not so good as it is for *you*," she said in a rather small voice. She knew he couldn't bear it if she mocked at his work for one moment. And he knew that rather small voice of hers.

"In what way?" he said, bristles rising.

"Oh, I don't know," she answered indifferently. "Perhaps it's not good for a man's work if he is too comfortable."

"I don't know about *that*!" he said, taking a dramatic turn round the library and drawing at his pipe. "Considering I work, actually, by the clock, for twelve hours a day, and for ten hours when it's a short day, I don't think you can say I am deteriorating from easy comfort."

"No, I suppose not," she admitted.

Yet she did think it, nevertheless. His comfortableness didn't consist so much in good food and a soft bed, as in having nobody, absolutely nobody and nothing to contradict him. "I do like to think he's got nothing to aggravate him," the secretary had said to the wife.

"Nothing to aggravate him!" What a position for a man! Fostered by women who would let nothing 'aggravate' him. If anything would aggravate his wounded vanity, this would!

So thought the wife. But what was to be done about it? In the silence of midnight she heard his voice in the distance, dictating away, like the voice of God to Samuel, alone and monotonous, and she imagined the little figure of the secretary busily scribbling shorthand. Then in the sunny hours of morning, while he was still in bed—he never rose till noon —from another distance came that sharp insect noise of the typewriter, like some immense grasshopper chirping and rattling. It was the secretary, poor thing, typing out his notes.

That girl—she was only twenty-eight—really slaved herself to skin and bone. She was small and neat, but she was actually worn out. She did far more work than he did, for she had not only to take down all those words he uttered, she had to type them out, make three copies, while he was still resting.

"What on earth she gets out of it," thought the wife, "I don't know. She's simply worn to the bone, for a very poor salary, and he's never kissed her, and never will, if I know anything about him."

Whether his never kissing her—the secretary, that is— made it worse or better, the wife did not decide. He never kissed anybody. Whether she herself—the wife, that is— wanted to be kissed by him, even that she was not clear about. She rather thought she didn't.

What on earth did she want then? She was his wife. What on earth did she want of him?

She certainly didn't want to take him down in shorthand,

and type out again all those words. And she didn't really want him to kiss her; she knew him too well. Yes, she knew him too well. If you know a man too well, you don't want him to kiss you.

What then? What did she want? Why had she such an extraordinary hang-over about him? Just because she was his wife? Why did she rather 'enjoy' other men—and she was relentless about enjoyment—without ever taking them seriously? And why must she take him so damn seriously, when she never really 'enjoyed' him?

Of course she *had* had good times with him, in the past, before—ah! before a thousand things, all amounting really to nothing. But she enjoyed him no more. She never even enjoyed being with him. There was a silent, ceaseless tension between them, that never broke, even when they were a thousand miles apart.

Awful! That's what you call being married! What's to be done about it? Ridiculous, to know it all and not do anything about it!

She came back once more, and there she was, in her own house, a sort of super-guest, even to him. And the secretarial family devoting their lives to him.

Devoting their lives to him! But actually! Three women pouring out their lives for him day and night! And what did they get in return? Not one kiss! Very little money, because they knew all about his debts, and had made it their life business to get them paid off! No expectations! Twelve hours' work a day! Comparative isolation, for he saw nobody!

And beyond that? Nothing! Perhaps a sense of uplift and importance because they saw his name and photograph in the newspaper sometimes. But would anybody believe that it was good enough?

Yet they adored it! They seemed to get a deep satisfaction out of it, like people with a mission. Extraordinary!

Well, if they did, let them. They were, of course, rather common, 'of the people'; there might be a sort of glamour in it for them.

But it was bad for him. No doubt about it. His work was getting diffuse and poor in quality—and what wonder! His whole tone was going down—becoming commoner. Of course it was bad for him.

Being his wife, she felt she ought to do something to save him. But how could she? That perfectly devoted, marvellous secretarial family, how could she make an attack on them? Yet she'd love to sweep them into oblivion. Of course they were bad for him: ruining his work, ruining his reputation as a writer, ruining his life. Ruining him with their slavish service.

Of course she ought to make an onslaught on them! But how *could* she? Such devotion! And what had she herself to offer in their place? Certainly not slavish devotion to him, nor to his flow of words! Certainly not!

She imagined him stripped once more naked of secretary and secretarial family, and she shuddered. It was like throwing the naked baby in the dust-bin. Couldn't do that!

Yet something must be done. She felt it. She was almost tempted to get into debt for another thousand pounds, and send in the bill, or have it sent in to him, as usual.

But no! Something more drastic!

Something more drastic, or perhaps more gentle. She wavered between the two. And wavering, she first did nothing, came to no decision, dragged vacantly on from day to day, waiting for sufficient energy to take her departure once more.

It was spring! What a fool she had been to come up in spring! And she was forty! What an idiot of a woman to go and be forty!

She went down the garden in the warm afternoon, when birds were whistling loudly from the cover, the sky being low and warm, and she had nothing to do. The garden was full of flowers: he loved them for their theatrical display. Lilac and snowball bushes, and laburnum and red may, tulips and anemones and coloured daisies. Lots of flowers! Borders of forget-me-nots! Bachelor's buttons! What absurd names flowers had! She would have called them blue dots and yellow blobs and white frills. Not so much sentiment, after all!

There is a certain nonsense, something showy and stagey about spring, with its pushing leaves and chorus-girl flowers, unless you have something corresponding inside you. Which she hadn't.

Oh, heaven! Beyond the hedge she heard a voice, a steady rather theatrical voice. Oh, heaven! He was dictating to his secretary in the garden. Good God, was there nowhere to get away from it!

She looked around: there was indeed plenty of escape. But what was the good of escaping? He would go on and on. She went quietly towards the hedge, and listened.

He was dictating a magazine article about the modern novel. "What the modern novel lacks is architecture." Good God! Architecture! He might just as well say: What the modern novel lacks is whalebone, or a teaspoon, or a tooth stopped.

Yet the secretary took it down, took it down, took it down! No, this could not go on! It was more than flesh and blood could bear.

She went quietly along the hedge, somewhat wolf-like in her prowl, a broad, strong woman in an expensive mustard-coloured silk jersey and cream-coloured pleated skirt. Her legs were long and shapely, and her shoes were expensive.

With a curious wolf-like stealth she turned the hedge and looked across at the small, shaded lawn where the daisies grew impertinently. 'He' was reclining in a coloured hammock under the pink-ffowering horse-chestnut tree, dressed in white serge with a fine yellow-coloured linen shirt. His elegant hand dropped over the side of the hammock and beat a sort of vague rhythm to his words. At a little wicker table the little secretary, in a green knitted frock, bent her dark head over her note-book, and diligently made those awful shorthand marks. He was not difficult to take down, as he dictated slowly, and kept a sort of rhythm, beating time with his dangling hand.

"In every novel there must be one outstanding character with which we always sympathise—with *whom* we always sympathise—even though we recognise it—even when we are most aware of the human frailties——"

Every man his own hero, thought the wife grimly, forgetting that every woman is intensely her own heroine.

But what did startle her was a blue bird dashing about near the feet of the absorbed, shorthand-scribbling little secretary. At least it was a blue-tit, blue with grey and some yellow. But to the wife it seemed blue, that juicy spring day, in the translucent afternoon. The blue bird, fluttering round the pretty but rather *common* little feet of the little secretary.

The blue bird! The blue bird of happiness! Well, I'm blest,
—thought the wife. Well, I'm blest!

And as she was being blest, appeared another blue bird—
that is, another blue-tit—and began to wrestle with the first
blue-tit. A couple of blue birds of happiness, having a fight
over it! Well, I'm blest!

She was more or less out of sight of the human preoccupied
pair. But 'he' was disturbed by the fighting blue birds, whose
little feathers began to float loose.

"Get out!" he said to them mildly, waving a dark-yellow
handkerchief at them. "Fight your little fight, and settle your
private affairs elsewhere, my dear little gentlemen."

The little secretary looked up quickly, for she had already
begun to write it down. He smiled at her his twisted whimsical
smile.

"No, don't take that down," he said affectionately. "Did you
you see those two tits laying into one another?"

"No!" said the little secretary, gazing brightly round, her
eyes half-blinded with work.

But she saw the queer, powerful, elegant, wolf-like figure
of the wife, behind her, and terror came into her eyes.

"I did!" said the wife, stepping forward with those curious,
shapely, she-wolf legs of hers, under the very short skirt.

"Aren't they extraordinarily vicious little beasts?" said he.

"Extraordinarily!" she re-echoed, stooping and and picking
up a little breast-feather. "Extraordinarily! See how the
feathers fly!"

And she got the feather on the tip of her finger, and looked
at it. Then she looked at the secretary, then she looked at
him. She had a queer, were-wolf expression between her
brows.

"I think," he began, "these are the loveliest afternoons,
when there's no direct sun, but all the sounds and the colours
and the scents are sort of dissolved, don't you know, in the
air, and the whole thing is steeped, steeped in spring. It's like
being on the inside; you know how I mean, like being inside
the egg and just ready to chip the shell."

"Quite like that!" she assented, without conviction.

There was a little pause. The secretary said nothing. They
were waiting for the wife to depart again.

"I suppose," said the latter, "you're awfully busy, as
usual?"

"Just about the same," he said, pursing his mouth deprecatingly.

Again the blank pause, in which he waited for her to go away again.

"I know I'm interrupting you," she said.

"As a matter of fact," he said, "I was just watching those two blue-tits."

"Pair of little demons!" said the wife, blowing away the yellow feather from her finger-tip.

"Absolutely!" he said.

"Well, I'd better go, and let you get on with your work," she said.

"No hurry!" he said, with benevolent nonchalance. "As a matter of fact, I don't think it's a great success, working out of doors."

"What made you try it?" said the wife. "You know you never could do it."

"Miss Wrexall suggested it might make a change. But I don't think it altogether helps, do you, Miss Wrexall?"

"I'm sorry," said the little secretary.

"Why should *you* be sorry?" said the wife, looking down at her as a wolf might look down half-benignly at a little black-and-tan mongrel. "You only suggested it for his good, I'm sure!"

"I thought the air might be good for him," the secretary admitted. "Why do people like you never think about yourselves?" the wife asked.

The secretary looked her in the eye.

"I suppose we do, in a different way," she said.

"A *very* different way!" said the wife ironically. "Why don't you make *him* think about *you*?" she added, slowly, with a sort of drawl. "On a soft spring afternoon like this, you ought to have him dictating poems to you, about the blue birds of happiness fluttering round your dainty little feet. I know *I* would, if I were his secretary."

There was a dead pause. The wife stood immobile and statuesque, in an attitude characteristic of her, half turning back to the little secretary, half averted. She half turned her back on everything.

The secretary looked at him.

"As a matter of fact," he said, "I was doing an article on the Future of the Novel."

"I know that," said the wife. "That's what's so awful! Why not something lively in the life of the novelist?"

There was a prolonged silence, in which he looked pained, and somewhat remote, statuesque. The little secretary hung her head. The wife sauntered slowly away.

"Just where were we, Miss Wrexall?" came the sound of his voice.

The little secretary started. She was feeling profoundly indignant. Their beautiful relationship, his and hers, to be so insulted!

But soon she was veering down-stream on the flow of his words, too busy to have any feelings, except one of elation at being so busy.

Tea-time came; the sister brought out the tea-tray into the garden. And immediately, the wife appeared. She had changed, and was wearing a chicory-blue dress of fine cloth. The little secretary had gathered up her papers and was departing, on rather high heels.

"Don't go, Miss Wrexall," said the wife.

The little secretary stopped short, then hesitated.

"Mother will be expecting me," she said.

"Tell her you're not coming. And ask your sister to bring another cup. I want you to have tea with us."

Miss Wrexall looked at the man, who was reared on one elbow in the hammock, and was looking enigmatical, Hamletish.

He glanced at her quickly, then pursed his mouth in a boyish negligence.

"Yes, stay and have tea with us for once," he said. "I see strawberries, and I know you're the bird for them."

She glanced at him, smiled wanly, and hurried away to tell her mother. She even stayed long enough to slip on a silk dress.

"Why, how smart you are!" said the wife, when the little secretary reappeared on the lawn, in chicory-blue silk.

"Oh, don't look at my dress, compared to yours!" said Miss Wrexall. They were of the same colour, indeed!

"At least you earned yours, which is more than I did mine," said the wife, as she poured tea. "You like it strong?"

She looked with her heavy eyes at the smallish, birdy, blue-clad, overworked young woman, and her eyes seemed to speak many inexplicable dark volumes.

"Oh, as it comes, thank you," said Miss Wrexall, leaning nervously forward.

"It's coming pretty black, if you want to ruin your digestion," said the wife.

"Oh, I'll have some water in it, then."

"Better, I should say."

"How'd the work go—all right?" asked the wife, as they drank tea, and the two women looked at each other's blue dresses.

"Oh!" he said. "As well as you can expect. It was a piece of pure flummery. But it's what they want. Awful rot, wasn't it, Miss Wrexall?"

Miss Wrexall moved uneasily on her chair.

"It interested me," she said, "though not so much as the novel."

"The novel? Which novel?" said the wife. "Is there another new one?"

Miss Wrexall looked at him. Not for words would she give away any of his literary activities.

"Oh, I was just sketching out an idea to Miss Wrexall," he said.

"Tell us about it!" said the wife. "Miss Wrexall, you tell us what it's about."

She turned on her chair, and fixed the little secretary.

"I'm afraid"—Miss Wrexall squirmed—"I haven't got it very clearly myself, yet."

"Oh, go along! Tell us what you have got then!"

Miss Wrexall sat dumb and very vexed. She felt she was being baited. She looked at the blue pleatings of her skirt.

"I'm afraid I can't," she said.

"Why are you afraid you can't? You're so very competent. I'm sure you've got it all at your finger-ends. I expect you write a good deal of Mr. Gee's books for him, really. He gives you the hint, and you fill it all in. Isn't that how you do it?" She spoke ironically, and as if she were teasing a child. And then she glanced down at the fine pleatings of her own blue skirt, very fine and expensive.

"Of course you're not speaking seriously?" said Miss Wrexall, rising on her mettle.

"Of course I am! I've suspected for a long time—at least, for some time—that you write a good deal of Mr. Gee's books for him, from his hints."

It was said in a tone of raillery, but it was cruel.

"I should be terribly flattered," said Miss Wrexall, straightening herself, "if I didn't know you were only trying to make me feel a fool."

"Make you feel a fool? My dear child!—why, nothing could be farther from me! You're twice as clever, and a million times as competent as I am. Why, my dear child, I've the greatest admiration for you! I wouldn't do what you do, not for all the pearls in India. I *couldn't* anyhow——"

Miss Wrexall closed up and was silent.

"Do you mean to say my books read as if——" he began, rearing up and speaking in a harrowed voice.

"I do!" said the wife. "*Just* as if Miss Wrexall had written them from your hints. I *honestly* thought she did—when you were too busy——"

"How very clever of you!" he said.

"Very!" she said. "Especially if I was wrong!"

"Which you were," he said.

"How very extraordinary!" she cried. "Well, I am once more mistaken!"

There was a complete pause.

It was broken by Miss Wrexall, who was nervously twisting her fingers.

"You want to spoil what there is between me and him, I can see that," she said bitterly.

"My dear, but what *is* there between you and him?" asked the wife.

"I was *happy* working with him, working for him! I was *happy* working for him!" cried Miss Wrexall, tears of indignant anger and chagrin in her eyes.

"My dear child!" cried the wife, with simulated excitement, "go *on* being happy working with him, go on being happy while you can! If it makes you happy, why then, enjoy it! Of course! Do you think I'd be so cruel as to want to take it away from you?—working with him? *I* can't do shorthand and typewriting and double-entrance book-keeping, or whatever it's called. I tell you, I'm utterly incompetent. I never earn anything. I'm the parasite of the British oak, like the mistletoe. The blue bird doesn't flutter round my feet. Perhaps they're too big and trampling."

She looked down at her expensive shoes.

"If I *did* have a word of criticism to offer," she said turning to her husband, "it would be to you, Cameron, for taking so much from her and giving her nothing."

"But he gives me everything, everything!" cried Miss Wrexall. "He gives me everything!"

"What do you mean by everything?" said the wife, turning on her sternly.

Miss Wrexall pulled up short. There was a snap in the air, and a change of currents.

"I mean nothing that *you* need begrudge me," said the little secretary rather haughtily. "I've never made myself cheap."

There was a blank pause.

"My God!" said the wife. "You don't call that being cheap? Why, I should say you got nothing out of him at all, you only give! And if you don't call that making yourself cheap—my God!"

"You see, we see things different," said the secretary.

"I should say we do!—*thank God!*" rejoined the wife.

"On whose behalf are you thanking God?" he asked sarcastically.

"Everybody's, I suppose! Yours, because you get everything for nothing, and Miss Wrexall's, because she seems to like it, and mine because I'm well out of it all."

"You *needn't* be out of it all," cried Miss Wrexall magnanimously, "if you didn't *put* yourself out of it all."

"Thank you, my dear, for your offer," said the wife, rising. "but I'm afraid no man can expect *two* blue birds of happiness to flutter round his feet, tearing out their little feathers!"

With which she walked away.

After a tense and desperate interim, Miss Wrexall cried:

"And *really*, need any woman be jealous of *me?*"

"Quite!" he said.

And that was all he did say.

SUN

I

"TAKE her away, into the sun," the doctors said.

She herself was sceptical of the sun, but she permitted herself to be carried away, with her child, and a nurse, and her mother, over the sea.

The ship sailed at midnight. And for two hours her husband stayed with her, while the child was put to bed, and the passengers came on board. It was a black night, the Hudson swayed with heavy blackness, shaken over with spilled dribbles of light. She leaned on the rail, and looking down thought: This is the sea; it is deeper than one imagines, and fuller of memories. At that moment the sea seemed to heave like the serpent of chaos that has lived for ever.

"These partings are no good, you know," her husband was saying, at her side. "They're no good. I don't like them."

His tone was full of apprehension, misgiving, and there was a certain note of clinging to the last straw of hope.

"No, neither do I," she responded in a flat voice.

She remembered how bitterly they had wanted to get away from one another, he and she. The emotion of parting gave a slight tug at her emotions, but only caused the iron that had gone into her soul to gore deeper.

So, they looked at their sleeping son, and the father's eyes were wet. But it is not the wetting of the eyes which counts, it is the deep iron rhythm of habit, the year-long, life-long habits; the deep-set stroke of power.

And in their two lives the stroke of power was hostile, his and hers. Like two engines running at variance, they shattered one another.

"All ashore! All ashore!"

"Maurice, you must go!"

And she thought to herself: For him it is *All ashore!* For me it is *Out to sea!*

Well, he waved his hanky on the midnight dreariness of the pier as the boat inched away; one among a crowd. One among a crowd! *C'est ça!*

The ferry-boats, like great dishes piled with rows of lights,

528

were still slanting across the Hudson. That black mouth must be the Lackawanna Station.

The ship ebbed on, the Hudson seemed interminable. But at last they were round the bend, and there was the poor harvest of lights at the Battery. Liberty flung up her torch in a tantrum. There was the wash of the sea.

And though the Atlantic was grey as lava, she did come at last into the sun. Even she had a house above the bluest of seas, with a vast garden, or vineyard, all vines and olives steeply, terrace after terrace, to the strip of coast-plain; and the garden full of secret places, deep groves of lemon far down in the cleft of the earth, and hidden, pure green reservoirs of water; then a spring issuing out of a little cavern, where the old Sicules had drunk before the Greeks came; and a grey goat bleating, stabled in an ancient tomb, with all the niches empty. There was the scent of mimosa, and beyond, the snow of the volcano.

She saw it all, and in a measure it was soothing. But it was all external. She didn't really care about it. She was herself, just the same, with all her anger and frustration inside her, and her incapacity to feel anything real. The child irritated her, and preyed on her peace of mind. She felt so horribly, ghastly responsible for him: as if she must be responsible for every breath he drew. And that was torture to her, to the child, and to everybody else concerned.

"You know, Juliet, the doctor told you to lie in the sun, without your clothes. Why don't you?" said the mother.

"When I am fit to do so, I will. Do you want to kill me?" Juliet flew at her.

"To kill you, no! Only to do you good."

"For God's sake, leave off wanting to do me good."

The mother at last was so hurt and incensed, she departed.

The sea went white—and then invisible. Pouring rain fell. It was cold, in the house built for the sun.

Again a morning when the sun lifted himself naked and molten, sparkling over the sea's rim. The house faced south-west. Juliet lay in her bed and watched him rise. It was as if she had never seen the sun rise before. She had never seen the naked sun stand up pure upon the sea-line, shaking the night off himself.

So the desire sprang secretly in her to go naked in the sun. She cherished her desire like a secret.

But she wanted to go away from the house—away from people. And it is not easy, in a country where every olive tree has eyes, and every slope is seen from afar, to go hidden.

But she found a place: a rocky bluff, shoved out to the sea and sun and overgrown with large cactus, the flat-leaved cactus called prickly pear. Out of this blue-grey knoll of cactus rose one cypress tree, with a pallid, thick trunk, and a tip that leaned over, flexible, up in the blue. It stood like a guardian looking to sea; or a low, silvery candle whose huge flame was darkness against light: earth sending up her proud tongue of gloom.

Juliet sat down by the cypress trees and took off her clothes. The contorted cactus made a forest, hideous yet fascinating, about her. She sat and offered her bosom to the sun, sighing, even now, with a certain hard pain, against the cruelty of having to give herself.

But the sun marched in blue heaven and sent down his rays as he went. She felt the soft air of the sea on her breasts, that seemed as if they would never ripen. But she hardly felt the sun. Fruits that would wither and not mature, her breasts.

Soon, however, she felt the sun inside them, warmer than ever love had been, warmer than milk or the hands of her baby. At last, at last her breasts were like long white grapes in the hot sun.

She slid off all her clothes and lay naked in the sun, and as she lay she looked up through her fingers at the central sun, his blue pulsing roundness, whose outer edges streamed brilliance. Pulsing with marvellous blue, and alive, and streaming white fire from his edges, the sun! He faced down to her with his look of blue fire, and enveloped her breasts and her face, her throat, her tired belly, her knees, her thighs and her feet.

She lay with shut eyes, the colour of rosy flame through her lids. It was too much. She reached and put leaves over her eyes. Then she lay again, like a long white gourd in the sun, that must ripen to gold.

She could feel the sun penetrating even into her bones; nay, farther, even into her emotions and her thoughts. The dark tensions of her emotion began to give way, the cold dark clots of her thoughts began to dissolve. She was beginning to feel warm right through. Turning over, she let her shoulders dissolve in the sun, her loins, the backs of her thighs, even her heels. And she lay half stunned with wonder at the thing that was happening to her. Her weary, chilled heart was melting, and, in melting, evaporating.

When she was dressed again she lay once more and looked up at the cypress tree, whose crest, a flexible filament, fell this way and that in the breeze. Meanwhile, she was conscious of the great sun roaming in heaven.

So, dazed, she went home, only half-seeing, sun-blinded and sun-dazed. And her blindness was like a richness to her, and her dim, warm, heavy half-consciousness was like wealth.

"Mummy! Mummy!" her child came running toward her, calling in that peculiar bird-like little anguish of want, always wanting her. She was surprised that her drowsed heart for once felt none of the anxious love-anguish in return. She caught the child up in her arms, but she thought: He should not be such a lump! If he were in the sun, he would spring up.

She resented, rather, his little hands clutching at her, especially at her neck. She pulled her throat away. She did not want to be touched. She put the child gently down.

"Run!" she said. "Run in the sun!"

And there and then she took off his clothes and set him naked on the warm terrace.

"Play in the sun!" she said.

He was frightened and wanted to cry. But she, in the warm indolence of her body, and the complete indifference of her heart, rolled him an orange across the red tiles, and with his soft, unformed little body he toddled after it. Then immediately he had it, he dropped it because it felt strange against his flesh. And he looked back at her, querulous, wrinkling his face to cry, frightened because he was stark.

"Bring me the orange," she said, amazed at her own deep indifference to his trepidation. "Bring Mummy the orange."

"He shall not grow up like his father," she said to herself. "Like a worm that the sun has never seen."

II

She had had the child so much on her mind, in a torment of responsibility, as if, having borne him, she had to answer for his whole existence. Even if his nose were running, it had been repulsive and a goad in her vitals, as if she must say to herself: Look at the thing you brought forth!

Now a change took place. She was no longer vitally interested in the child, she took the strain of her anxiety and her will from off him. And he thrived all the more for it.

She was thinking inside herself, of the sun in his splendour, and her mating with him. Her life was now a whole ritual. She lay always awake, before dawn, watching for the grey to colour to pale gold, to know if cloud lay on the sea's edge. Her joy was when he rose all molten in his nakedness, and threw off blue-white fire, into the tender heaven.

But sometimes he came ruddy, like a big, shy creature. And sometimes slow and crimson red, with a look of anger, slowly pushing and shouldering. Sometimes again she could not see him, only the level cloud threw down gold and scarlet from above, as he moved behind the wall.

She was fortunate. Weeks went by, and though the dawn was sometimes clouded, and afternoon was sometimes grey, never a day passed sunless, and most days, winter though it was, streamed radiant. Then thin little wild crocuses came up mauve and striped, the wild narcissi hung their winter stars.

Every day she went down to the cypress tree, among the cactus grove on the knoll with yellowish cliffs at the foot. She was wiser and subtler now, wearing only a dove-grey wrapper, and sandals. So that in an instant, in any hidden niche, she was naked to the sun. And the moment she was covered again she was grey and invisible.

Every day, in the morning towards noon, she lay at the foot of the powerful, silver-pawed cypress tree, while the sun rode jovial in heaven. By now she knew the sun in every thread of her body, there was not a cold shadow left. And her heart, that anxious, straining heart, had disappeared altogether, like a flower that falls in the sun, and leaves only a ripe seed-case.

She knew the sun in heaven, blue-molten with his white fire edges, throwing off fire. And though he shone on all the world, when she lay unclothed he focussed on her. It was one of the wonders of the sun, he could shine on a million people and still be the radiant, splendid, unique sun, focussed on her alone.

With her knowledge of the sun, and her conviction that

the sun *knew* her, in the cosmic carnal sense of the word, came over her a feeling of detachment from people, and a certain contempt for human beings altogther. They were so un-elemental, so unsunned. They were so like graveyard worms.

Even the peasants passing up the rocky, ancient little road with their donkeys, sun-blackened as they were, were not sunned right through. There was a little soft white core of fear, like a snail in a shell, where the soul of the men cowered in fear of death, and in fear of the natural blaze of life. He dared not quite emerge: always innerly cowed. All men were like that.

Why admit men!

With her indifference to people, to men, she was not now so cautious about being unseen. She had told Marinina, who went shopping for her in the village, that the doctor had ordered sun-baths. Let that suffice.

Marinina was a woman over sixty, tall, thin, erect, with curling dark grey hair, and dark grey eyes that had the shrewdness of thousands of years in them, with the laugh that underlies all long experience. Tragedy is lack of experience.

"It must be beautiful to go unclothed in the sun," said Marinina, with a shrewd laugh in her eyes, as she looked keenly at the other woman. Juliet's fair, bobbed hair curled in a little cloud at her temple. Marinina was a woman of Magna Græcia, and had far memories. She looked again at Juliet. "But you have to be beautiful yourself, if you're not going to give offence to the sun? Isn't it so?" she added, with that queer, breathless little laugh of the women of the past.

"Who knows if I am beautiful!" said Juliet.

But beautiful or not, she felt that by the sun she was appreciated. Which is the same.

When, out of the sun at noon, sometimes she stole down over the rocks and past the cliff-edge, down to the deep gully where the lemons hung in cool eternal shadow, and in the silence slipped off her wrapper to wash herself quickly at one of the deep, clear green basins, she would notice, in the bare green twilight under the lemon leaves, that all her body was rosy, rosy and turning to gold. She was like another person. She was another person.

So she remembered that the Greeks had said, a white, un-sunned body was fishy and unhealthy.

And she would rub a little olive oil in her skin, and wander a moment in the dark underworld of the lemons, balancing a lemon flower in her navel, laughing to herself. There was just a chance some peasant might see her. But if he did he would be more afraid of her than she of him. She knew the white core of fear in the clothed bodies of men.

She knew it even in her little son. How he mistrusted her, now that she laughed at him, with the sun in her face! She insisted on his toddling naked in the sunshine every day. And now his little body was pink, too, his blond hair was pushed thick from his brow, his cheeks had a pomegranate scarlet, in the delicate gold of the sunny skin. He was bonny and healthy, and the servants, loving his red and gold and blue, called him an angel from heaven.

But he mistrusted his mother: she laughed at him. And she saw in his wide blue eyes, under the little frown, that centre of fear, misgiving, which she believed was at the centre of all male eyes now. She called it fear of the sun.

"He fears the sun," she would say to herself, looking down into the eyes of the child.

And as she watched him toddling, swaying, tumbling in the sunshine, making his little, bird-like noises, she saw that he held himself tight and hidden from the sun, inside himself. His spirit was like a snail in a shell, in a damp, cold crevice inside himself. It made her think of his father. She wished she could make him come forth, break out in a gesture of recklessness and salutation.

She determined to take him with her, down to the cypress tree among the cactus. She would have to watch him, because of the thorns. But surely in that place he would come forth from that little shell, deep inside him. That little civilised tension would disappear off his brow.

She spread a rug for him and sat him down. Then she slid off her wrapper and lay down herself, watching a hawk high in the blue, and the tip of the cypress hanging over.

The boy played with stones on the rug. When he got up to toddle away, she sat up too. He turned and looked at her. Almost, from his blue eyes, it was the challenging, warm look of the true male. And he was handsome, with the scarlet in the golden blond of his skin. He was not really white. His skin was gold-dusky.

"Mind the thorns, darling," she said.

"Thorns!" re-echoed the child, in a birdy chirp, still look-ing at her over his shoulder, like some naked cherub in a picture, doubtful.

"Nasty prickly thorns."

"'Ickly thorns!'"

He staggered in his little sandals over the stones, pulling at the dry, wild mint. She was quick as a serpent, leaping to him, when he was going to fall against the prickles. It sur-prised even herself. "What a wild cat I am, really!" she said to herself.

She brought him every day, when the sun shone, to the cypress tree.

"Come!" she said. "Let us go to the cypress tree."

And if there was a cloudy day, with the tramontana blow-ing, so that she could not go down, the child would chirp incessantly: "Cypress tree! Cypress tree!"

He missed it as much as she did.

It was not just taking sunbaths. It was much more than that. Something deep inside her unfolded and relaxed, and she was given. By some mysterious power inside her, deeper than her known consciousness and will, she was put into con-nection with the sun, and the stream flowed of itself, from her womb. She herself, her conscious self, was secondary, a secondary person, almost an onlooker. The true Juliet was this dark flow from her deep body to the sun.

She had always been mistress of herself, aware of what she was doing, and held tense for her own power. Now she felt inside her quite another sort of power, something greater than herself, flowing by itself. Now she was vague, but she had a power beyond herself.

III

The end of February was suddenly very hot. Almond blossom was falling like pink snow, in the touch of the smallest breeze. The mauve, silky little anemones were out, the asphodels tall in bud, and the sea was cornflower blue.

Juliet had ceased to trouble about anything. Now, most of the day, she and the child were naked in the sun, and it was all she wanted. Sometimes she went down to the sea to bathe: often she wandered in the gullies where the sun shone in, and she was out of sight. Sometimes she saw a peasant

with an ass, and he saw her. But she went so simply and
quietly with her child; and the fame of the sun's healing
power, for the soul as well as for the body, had already
spread among the people; so that there was no excitement.

The child and she were now both tanned with a rosy-
golden tan all over. "I am another being!" she said to herself, as she looked at her red-gold breasts and thighs.

The child, too, was another creature, with a peculiar,
quiet, sun-darkened absorption. Now he played by himself
in silence, and she hardly need notice him. He seemed no
longer to know when he was alone.

There was a breeze, and the sea was ultramarine. She
sat by the great silver paw of the cypress tree, drowsed in the
sun, but her breasts alert, full of sap. She was becoming
aware that an activity was rousing in her, an activity which
would carry her into a new way of life. Still she did not
want to be aware. She knew well enough the vast cold
apparatus of civilisation, so difficult to evade.

The child had gone a few yards down the rocky path,
round the great sprawling of a cactus. She had seen him, a
real gold-brown infant of the winds, with burnt gold hair and
red cheeks, collecting the speckled pitcher-flowers and laying
them in rows. He could balance now, and was quick for his
own emergencies, like an absorbed young animal playing
silent.

Suddenly she heard him speaking: *"Look, Mummy!
Mummy, look!"* A note in his bird-like voice made her lean
forward sharply.

Her heart stood still. He was looking over his naked little
shoulder at her, and pointing with a loose little hand at a
snake which had reared itself up a yard away from him, and
was opening its mouth so that its forked, soft tongue flickered
black like a shadow, uttering a short hiss.

"Look, Mummy!"

"Yes, darling, it's a snake!" came the slow, deep voice.

He looked at her, his wide blue eyes uncertain whether to
be afraid or not. Some stillness of the sun in her reassured
him.

"Snake!" he chirped.

"Yes, darling! Don't touch it, it can bite."

The snake had sunk down, and was reaching away from
the coils in which it had been basking asleep, and slowly was

easing its long, gold-brown body into the rocks, with slow curves. The boy turned and watched it in silence. Then he said:

"Snake going!"

"Yes! Let it go. It likes to be alone."

He still watched the slow, easing length as the creature drew itself apathetic out of sight.

"Snake gone back," he said.

"Yes, it's gone back. Come to Mummy a moment."

He came and sat with his plump, naked little body on her naked lap, and she smoothed his burnt, bright hair. She said nothing, feeling that everything was passed. The curious soothing power of the sun filled her, filled the whole place like a charm, and the snake was part of the place, along with her and the child.

Another day, in the dry stone wall of one of the olive terraces, she saw a black snake horizontally creeping.

"Marinina," she said, "I saw a black snake. Are they harmful?"

"Ah, the black snakes, no! But the yellow ones, yes! If the yellow ones bite you, you die. But they frighten me, they frighten me, even the black ones, when I see one."

Juliet still went to the cypress tree with the child. But she always looked carefully round before she sat down, examining everywhere where the child might go. Then she would lie and turn to the sun again, her tanned, pear-shaped breasts pointing up. She would take no thought for the morrow. She refused to think outside her garden, and she could not write letters. She would tell the nurse to write.

IV

It was March, and the sun was growing very powerful. In the hot hours she would lie in the shade of the trees, or she would even go down to the depths of the cool lemon grove. The child ran in the distance, like a young animal absorbed in life.

One day she was sitting in the sun on the steep slope of the gully, having bathed in one of the great tanks. Below, under the lemons, the child was wading among the yellow oxalis flowers of the shadow, gathering fallen lemons, pass-

ing with his tanned little body into flecks of light, moving all
dappled.

Suddenly, high over the land's edge, against the full-lit pale
blue sky, Marinina appeared, a black cloth tied round her
head, calling quietly: *"Signora! Signora Giulietta!"*

Juliet faced round, standing up. Marinina paused a
moment, seeing the naked woman standing alert, her sun-
faded fair hair in a little cloud. Then the swift old woman
came on down the slant of the steep track.

She stood a few steps, erect, in front of the sun-coloured
woman, and eyed her shrewdly.

"But how beautiful you are, you!" she said coolly, almost
cynically. "There is your husband."

"My husband!" cried Juliet.

The old woman gave a shrewd bark of a little laugh, the
mockery of the women of the past.

"Haven't you got one, a husband, you?" she taunted.

"But where is he?" cried Juliet.

The old woman glanced over her shoulder.

"He was following me," she said. "But he will not have
found the path." And she gave another little bark of a laugh.

The paths were all grown high with grass and flowers and
nepitella, till they were like bird-trails in an eternally wild
place. Strange, the vivid wildness of the old places of civilisation, a wildness that is not gaunt.

Juliet looked at her serving-woman with meditating eyes.

"Oh, very well!" she said at last. "Let him come."

"Let him come here? Now?" asked Marinina, her laughing, smoke-grey eyes looking with mockery into Juliet's. Then
she gave a little jerk of her shoulders.

"All right, as you wish. But for him it is a rare one!"

She opened her mouth in a laugh of noiseless joy. Then she
pointed down to the child, who was heaping lemons against
his little chest. "Look how beautiful the child is! That,
certainly, will please him, poor thing. Then I'll bring him."

"Bring him," said Juliet.

The old woman scrambled rapidly up the track again.
Maurice was standing grey-faced, in his grey felt hat and his
dark grey suit, at a loss among the vine terraces. He looked
pathetically out of place, in that resplendent sunshine and the
grace of the old Greek world; like a blot of ink on the pale,
sun-glowing slope.

"Come!" said Marinina to him. "She is down here."

And swiftly she led the way, striding with a rapid stride, making her way through the grasses. Suddenly she stopped on the brow of the slope. The tops of the lemon trees were dark, away below.

"You, you go down here," she said to him, and he thanked her, looking up at her swiftly.

He was a man of forty, clean-shaven, grey-faced, very quiet and really shy. He managed his own business carefully, without startling success, but efficiently. And he confided in nobody. The old woman of Magna Græcia saw him at a glance: he is good, she said to herself, but not a man, poor thing.

"Down there is the Signora!" said Marinina, pointing like one of the Fates.

And again he said "Thank you! Thank you!" without a twinkle, and stepped carefully into the track. Marinina lifted her chin with a joyful wickedness. Then she strode off towards the house.

Maurice was watching his step through the tangle of Mediterranean herbage, so he did not catch sight of his wife till he came round a little bend, quite near her. She was standing erect and nude by the jutting rock, glistening with the sun and with warm life. Her breasts seemed to be lifting up, alert, to listen, her thighs looked brown and fleet. Her glance on him, as he came like ink on blotting-paper, was swift and nervous.

Maurice, poor fellow, hesitated, and glanced away from her. He turned his face aside.

"Hello, Julie!" he said, with a little nervous cough—"Splendid! Splendid!"

He advanced with his face averted, shooting further glances at her, as she stood with the peculiar satiny gleam of the sun on her tanned skin. Somehow she did not seem so terribly naked. It was the golden-rose tan of the sun that clothed her.

"Hello, Maurice!" she said, hanging back from him. "I wasn't expecting you so soon."

"No," he said. "No! I managed to slip away a little earlier."

And again he coughed awkwardly.

They stood several yards away from one another, and there was silence.

"Well!" he said, "er—this is splendid, splendid! You are—
er—splendid! Where is the boy?"

"There he is," she said, pointing down to where a naked
urchin in the deep shade was piling fallen lemons together.

The father gave an odd little laugh.

"Ah, yes, there he is! So there's the little man! Fine!"
he said. He really was thrilled in his suppressed nervous soul.
"Hello, Johnny!" he called, and it sounded rather feeble.
"Hello, Johnny!"

The child looked up, spilling lemons from his chubby arms,
but did not respond.

"I guess we'll go down to him," said Juliet, as she turned
and went striding down the path. Her husband followed,
watching the rosy, fleet-looking lifting and sinking of her
quick hips, as she swayed a little in the socket of her waist.
He was dazed with admiration, but also, at a deadly loss.
What should he do with himself? He was utterly out of the
picture, in his dark grey suit and pale grey hat, and his grey,
monastic face of a shy business man.

"He looks all right, doesn't he," said Juliet, as they came
through the deep sea of yellow-flowering oxalis, under the
lemon trees.

"Ah!—yes! yes! Splendid! Splendid! Hello, Johnny!
Do you know Daddy? Do you know Daddy, Johnny?"

He crouched down and held out his hands.

"Lemons!" said the child, birdily chirping. "Two lemons!"

"Two lemons!" replied the father. "Lots of lemons."

The infant came and put a lemon in each of his father's
open hands. Then he stood back to look.

"Two lemons!" repeated the father. "Come, Johnny!
Come and say 'Hello' to Daddy."

"Daddy going back?" said the child.

"Going back? Well—well—not to-day."

And he gathered his son in his arms.

"Take a coat off! Daddy take a coat off!" said the boy,
squirming debonair away from the cloth.

"All right, son! Daddy take a coat off!"

He took off his coat and laid it carefully aside, then again
took his son in his arms. The naked woman looked down at
the naked infant in the arms of the man in his shirt-sleeves.
The boy had pulled off the father's hat, and Juliet looked at
the sleek, black-and-grey hair of her husband, not a hair out

of place. And utterly, utterly indoors. She was silent for a long time, while the father talked to the child, who was fond of his Daddy.

"What are you going to do about it, Maurice?" she said suddenly.

He looked at her swiftly, sideways.

"Er—about what, Julie?"

"Oh, everything! About this! I can't go back into East Forty-Seventh."

"Er——" he hesitated, "no, I suppose not—not just now at least."

"Never," she said, and there was a silence.

"Well—er—I don't know," he said.

"Do you think you can come out here?" she said.

"Yes, I can stay for a month. I think I can manage a month," he hesitated. Then he ventured a complicated, shy peep at her, and hid his face again.

She looked down at him, her alert breasts lifted with a sigh, as if a breeze of impatience shook them.

"I can't go back," she said slowly. "I can't go back on this sun. If you can't come here——"

She ended on an open note. He glanced at her again and again, furtively, but with growing admiration and lessening confusion.

"No!" he said. "This kind of thing suits you. You are splendid! No, I don't think you can go back."

He was thinking of her in the New York flat, pale, silent, oppressing him terribly. He was the soul of gentle timidity, in his human relations, and her silent, awful hostility after the baby was born, had frightened him deeply. Because he had realised she couldn't help it. Women were like that. Their feelings took a reverse direction, even against their own selves, and it was awful—awful! Awful, awful to live in the house with a woman like that, whose feelings were reversed even against herself! He had felt himself ground down under the millstone of her helpless enmity. She had ground even herself down to the quick, and the child as well. No, anything rather than that.

"But what about *you?*" she asked.

"I? Oh, I! I can carry on the business, and—er—come over here for the holidays—as long as you like to stay. You stay as long as you wish." He looked a long time down at the earth, then glanced up at her with a touch of supplication in his uneasy eyes.

"Even for ever?"

"Well—er—yes, if you like. For ever is a long time. One can't set a date."

"And I can do anything I like?" She looked him straight in the eyes, challenging. And he was powerless against her rosy, wind-hardened nakedness.

"Er—yes! I suppose so! So long as you don't make yourself unhappy—or the boy."

Again he looked up at her with a complicated, uneasy appeal—thinking of the child, but hoping for himself.

"I won't," she said quickly.

"No!" he said. "No! I don't think you will."

There was a pause. The bells of the village were hastily clanging midday. That meant lunch.

She slipped into her grey crêpe kimono, and fastened a broad green sash round her waist. Then she slipped a little blue shirt over the boy's head, and they went up to the house.

At table she watched her husband, his grey city face, his fixed, black-grey hair, his very precise table manners, and his extreme moderation in eating and drinking. Sometimes he glanced at her, furtively, from under his black lashes. He had the gold-grey eyes of an animal that has been caught young, and reared completely in captivity.

They went on to the balcony for coffee. Below, beyond, on the next podere across the steep little gully, a peasant and his wife were sitting under an almond tree, near the green wheat, eating their midday meal from a little white cloth spread on the ground. There was a huge piece of bread, and glasses with dark wine.

Juliet put her husband with his back to this picture; she sat facing. Because, the moment she and Maurice had come out on the balcony, the peasant had glanced up.

V

She knew him, in the distance, perfectly. He was a rather fat, very broad fellow of about thirty-five, and he chewed large mouthfuls of bread. His wife was stiff and dark-faced, handsome, sombre. They had no children. So much Juliet had learned.

The peasant worked a great deal alone, on the opposite podere. His clothes were always very clean and cared-for, white trousers and a coloured shirt, and an old straw hat. Both he and his wife had that air of quiet superiority which belongs to individuals, not to a class.

His attraction was in his vitality, the peculiar quick energy which gave a charm to his movements, stout and broad as he was. In the early days before she took to the sun, Juliet had met him suddenly, among the rocks, when she had scrambled over to the next podere. He had been aware of her before she saw him, so that when she did look up, he took off his hat, gazing at her with shyness and pride, from his big blue eyes. His face was broad, sunburnt, he had a cropped brown moustache, and thick brown eyebrows, nearly as thick as his moustache, meeting under his low, wide brow.

"Oh!" she said. "Can I walk here?"

"Surely!" he replied, with that peculiar hot haste which characterised his movement. "My padrone would wish you to walk wherever you like on his land."

And he pressed back his head in the quick, vivid, shy generosity of his nature. She had gone on quickly. But instantly she had recognised the violent generosity of his blood, and the equally violent *farouche* shyness.

Since then she had seen him in the distance every day, and she came to realise that he was one who lived a good deal to himself, like a quick animal, and that his wife loved him intensely, with a jealousy that was almost hate; because, probably, he wanted to give himself still, still further, beyond where she could take him.

One day, when a group of peasants sat under a tree, she had seen him dancing quick and gay with a child—his wife watching darkly.

Gradually Juliet and he had become intimate, across the distance. They were aware of one another. She knew, in the morning, the moment he arrived with his ass. And the moment she went out on the balcony he turned to look. But they never saluted. Yet she missed him when he did not come to work on the podere.

Once, in the hot morning when she had been walking naked, deep in the gully between the two estates, she had came upon him, as he was bending down, with his powerful shoulders, picking up wood to pile on his motionless, waiting donkey. He saw her as he lifted his flushed face, and she was backing away. A flame went over his eyes, and a flame flew over her body, melting her bones. But she backed away behind the bushes, silently, and retreated whence she had come. And she wondered a little resentfully over the silence in which he could work, hidden in the bushy places. He had that wild animal faculty.

Since then there had been a definite pain of consciousness in the body of each of them, though neither would admit it, and they gave no sign of recognition. But the man's wife was instinctively aware.

And Juliet had thought: Why shouldn't I meet this man for an hour, and bear his child? Why should I have to identify my life with a man's life? Why not meet him for an hour, as long as the desire lasts, and no more? There is already the spark between us.

But she had never made any sign. And now she saw him looking up, from where he sat by the white cloth, opposite his black-clad wife, looking up at Maurice. The wife turned and looked, too, saturnine.

And Juliet felt a grudge come over her. She would have to bear Maurice's child again. She had seen it in her husband's eyes. And she knew it from his answer, when she spoke to him.

"Will you walk about in the sun, too, without your clothes?" she asked him.

"Why—er—yes! Yes, I should like to, while I'm here—I suppose it's quite private?"

There was a gleam in his eyes, a desperate kind of courage of his desire, and a glance at the alert lifting of her breasts in her wrapper. In this way, he was a man, too, he faced the world and was not entirely quenched in his male courage. He would dare to walk in the sun, even ridiculously.

But he smelled of the world, and all its fetters and its mongrel cowering. He was branded with the brand that is not a hall-mark.

Ripe now, and brown-rosy all over with the sun, and with a heart like a fallen rose, she had wanted to go down to the hot, shy peasant and bear his child. Her sentiments had fallen like petals. She had seen the flushed blood in the burnt face, and the flame in the southern blue eyes, and the answer in her had been a gush of fire. He would have been a pro-creative sun-bath to her, and she wanted it.

Nevertheless, her next child would be Maurice's. The fatal chain of continuity would cause it.

THE WOMAN WHO RODE AWAY

I

SHE had thought that this marriage, of all marriages, would be an adventure. Not that the man himself was exactly magical to her. A little, wiry, twisted fellow, twenty years older than herself, with brown eyes and greying hair, who had come to America a scrap of a wastrel, from Holland, years ago, as a tiny boy, and from the gold-mines of the west had been kicked south into Mexico, and now was more or less rich, owning silver-mines in the wilds of the Sierra Madre: it was obvious that the adventure lay in his circumstances, rather than his person. But he was still a little dynamo of energy, in spite of accidents survived, and what he had accomplished he had accomplished alone. One of those human oddments there is no accounting for.

When she actually *saw* what he had accomplished, her heart quailed. Great green-covered, unbroken mountain-hills, and in the midst of the lifeless isolation, the sharp pinkish mounds of the dried mud from the silver-works. Under the nakedness of the works, the walled-in, one-storey adobe house, with its garden inside, and its deep inner veranda with tropical climbers on the sides. And when you looked up from this shut-in flowered patio, you saw the huge pink cone of the silver-mud refuse, and the machinery of the extracting plant against heaven above. No more.

To be sure, the great wooden doors were often open. And then she could stand outside, in the vast open world. And see great, void, tree-clad hills piling behind one another, from nowhere into nowhere. They were green in autumn-time. For the rest, pinkish, stark dry and abstract.

And in his battered Ford car her husband would take her into the dead, thrice-dead little Spanish town forgotten among the mountains. The great, sun-dried dead church, the dead portales, the hopeless covered market-place, where, the first time she went, she saw a dead dog lying between the meat-stalls and the vegetable array, stretched out as if for

546

ever, nobody troubling to throw it away. Deadness within deadness.

Everybody feebly talking silver, and showing bits of ore. But silver was at a standstill. The great war came and went. Silver was a dead market. Her husband's mines were closed down. But she and he lived on in the adobe house under the works, among the flowers that were never very flowery to her.

She had two children, a boy and a girl. And her eldest, the boy, was nearly ten years old before she aroused from her stupor of subjected amazement. She was now thirty-three, a large, blue-eyed, dazed woman, beginning to grow stout. Her little, wiry, tough, twisted, brown-eyed husband was fifty-three, a man as tough as wire, tenacious as wire, still full of energy, but dimmed by the lapse of silver from the market, and by some curious inaccessibility on his wife's part.

He was a man of principles, and a good husband. In a way, he doted on her. He never quite got over his dazzled admiration of her. But essentially, he was still a bachelor. He had been thrown out on the world, a little bachelor, at the age of ten. When he married he was over forty, and had enough money to marry on. But his capital was all a bachelor's. He was boss of his own works, and marriage was the last and most intimate bit of his own works.

He admired his wife to extinction, he admired her body, all her points. And she was to him always the rather dazzling Californian girl from Berkeley, whom he had first known. Like any sheikh, he kept her guarded among those mountains of Chihuahua. He was jealous of her as he was of his silver-mine: and that is saying a lot.

At thirty-three she really was still the girl from Berkeley, in all but physique. Her conscious development had stopped mysteriously with her marriage, completely arrested. Her husband had never become real to her, neither mentally nor physically. In spite of his late sort of passion for her, he never meant anything to her, physically. Only morally he swayed her, downed her, kept her in an invincible slavery.

So the years went by, in the adobe house strung round the sunny patio, with the silver-works overhead. Her husband was never still. When the silver went dead, he ran a ranch lower down, some twenty miles away, and raised pure-bred

K

hogs, splendid creatures. At the same time, he hated pigs. He was a squeamish waif of an idealist, and really hated the physical side of life. He loved work, work, work, and making things. His marriage, his children, were something he was making, part of his business, but with a sentimental income this time.

Gradually her nerves began to go wrong: she must get out. She must get out. So he took her to El Paso for three months. And at least it was the United States.

But he kept his spell over her. The three months ended: back she was, just the same, in her adobe house among those eternal green or pinky-brown hills, void as only the undiscovered is void. She taught her children, she supervised the Mexican boys who were her servants. And sometimes her husband brought visitors, Spaniards or Mexicans or occasionally white men.

He really loved to have white men staying on the place. Yet he had not a moment's peace when they were there. It was as if his wife were some peculiar secret vein of ore in his mines, which no one must be aware of except himself. And she was fascinated by the young gentlemen, mining engineers, who were his guests at times. He, too, was fascinated by a real gentleman. But he was an old-timer miner with a wife, and if a gentleman looked at his wife, he felt as if his mine were being looted, the secrets of it pried out.

It was one of these young gentlemen who put the idea into her mind. They were all standing outside the great wooden doors of the patio, looking at the outer world. The eternal, motionless hills were all green, it was September, after the rains. There was no sign of anything, save the deserted mine, the deserted works, and a bunch of half-deserted miners' dwellings.

"I wonder," said the young man, "what there is behind those great blank hills."

"More hills," said Lederman. "If you go that way, Sonora and the coast. This way is the desert—you came from there —and the other way, hills and mountains."

"Yes, but what *lives* in the hills and the mountains? *Surely* there is something wonderful? It looks *so* like nowhere on earth: like being on the moon."

"There's plenty of game, if you want to shoot. And Indians, if you call *them* wonderful."

"Wild ones?"

"Wild enough."

"But friendly?"

"It depends. Some of them are quite wild, and they don't let anybody near. They kill a missionary at sight. And where a missionary can't get, nobody can."

"But what does the government say?"

"They're so far from everywhere, the government leaves 'em alone. And they're wily; if they think there'll be trouble, they send a delegation to Chihuahua and make a formal submission. The government is glad to leave it at that."

"And do they live quite wild, with their own savage customs and religion?"

"Oh yes. They use nothing but bows and arrows. I've seen them in town, in the Plaza, with funny sort of hats with flowers round them, and a bow in one hand, quite naked except for a sort of shirt, even in cold weather—striding round with their savage's bare legs."

"But don't you suppose it's wonderful, up there in their secret villages?"

"No. What would there be wonderful about it? Savages are savages, and all savages behave more or less alike: rather low-down and dirty, unsanitary, with a few cunning tricks, and struggling to get enough to eat."

"But surely they have old, old religions and mysteries—it *must* be wonderful, surely it must."

"I don't know about mysteries—howling and heathen practices, more or less indecent. No, I see nothing wonderful in that kind of stuff. And I wonder that you should, when you have lived in London or Paris or New York——"

"Ah, *everybody* lives in London or Paris or New York"— said the young man, as if this were an argument.

And this particular vague enthusiasm for unknown Indians found a full echo in the woman's heart. She was overcome by a foolish romanticism more unreal than a girl's. She felt it was her destiny to wander into the secret haunts of these timeless, mysterious, marvellous Indians of the mountains.

She kept her secret. The young man was departing, her husband was going with him down to Torreon, on business: would be away for some days. But before the departure, she made her husband talk about the Indians: about the wandering tribes, resembling the Navajo, who were still wandering free; and the Yaquis of Sonora: and the different groups in the different valleys of Chihuahua State.

There was supposed to be one tribe, the Chilchuis, living in a high valley to the south, who were the sacred tribe of all the Indians. The descendants of Montezuma and the old Aztec or Totonac kings still lived among them, and the old priests still kept up the ancient religion, and offered human sacrifices—so it was said. Some scientists had been to the Chilchui country, and had come back gaunt and exhausted with hunger and bitter privation, bringing various curious, barbaric objects of worship, but having seen nothing extraordinary in the hungry, stark village of savages.

Though Lederman talked in this off-hand way, it was obvious he felt some of the vulgar excitement at the idea of ancient and mysterious savages.

"How far away are they?" she asked.

"Oh—three days on horseback—past Cuchitee and a little lake there is up there."

Her husband and the young man departed. The woman made her crazy plans. Of late, to break the monotony of her life, she had harassed her husband into letting her go riding with him, occasionally, on horseback. She was never allowed to go out alone. The country truly was not safe, lawless and crude.

But she had her own horse, and she dreamed of being free as she had been as a girl, among the hills of California.

Her daughter, nine years old, was now in a tiny convent in the little half-deserted Spanish mining-town five miles away.

"Manuel," said the woman to her house-servant, "I'm going to ride to the convent to see Margarita, and take her a few things. Perhaps I shall stay the night in the convent. You look after Freddy and see everything is all right till I come back."

"Shall I ride with you on the master's horse, or shall Juan?" asked the servant.

"Neither of you. I shall go alone."

The young man looked her in the eyes, in protest. Absolutely impossible that the woman should ride alone!

"I shall go alone," repeated the large, placid-seeming, fair-complexioned woman, with peculiar overbearing emphasis. And the man silently, unhappily yielded.

"Why are you going alone, mother?" asked her son, as she made up parcels of food.

"Am I *never* to be let alone? Not one moment of my life?" she cried, with sudden explosion of energy. And the child, like the servant, shrank into silence.

She set off without a qualm, riding astride on her strong roan horse, and wearing a riding-suit of coarse linen, a riding-skirt over her linen breeches, a scarlet neck-tie over her white blouse, and a black felt hat on her head. She had food in her saddle-bags, an army canteen with water, and a large, native blanket tied on behind the saddle. Peering into the distance, she set off from her home. Manuel and the little boy stood in the gateway to watch her go. She did not even turn to wave them farewell.

But when she had ridden about a mile, she left the wild road and took a small trail to the right, that led into another valley, over steep places and past great trees, and through another deserted mining settlement. It was September, the water was running freely in the little stream that had fed the now-abandoned mine. She got down to drink, and let the horse drink too.

She saw natives coming through the trees, away up the slope. They had seen her, and were watching her closely. She watched in turn. The three people, two women and a youth, were making a wide detour, so as not to come too close to her. She did not care. Mounting, she trotted ahead up the silent valley, beyond the silver-works, beyond any trace of mining. There was still a rough trail that led over rocks and loose stones into the valley beyond. This trail she had already ridden, with her husband. Beyond that she knew she must go south.

Curiously she was not afraid, although it was a frightening country, the silent, fatal-seeming mountain slopes, the occasional distant, suspicious, elusive natives among the trees, the great carrion birds occasionally hovering, like great flies, in the distance, over some carrion or some ranch-house or some group of huts.

As she climbed, the trees shrank and the trail ran through a thorny scrub, that was trailed over with blue convolvulus and an occasional pink creeper. Then these flowers lapsed. She was nearing the pine trees.

She was over the crest, and before her another silent, void,

green-clad valley. It was past midday. Her horse turned to a
little runlet of water, so she got down to eat her midday meal
She sat in silence looking at the motionless unliving valley,
and at the sharp-peaked hills, rising higher to rock and pine
trees, southwards. She rested two hours in the heat of the
day, while the horse cropped around her.

Curious that she was neither afraid nor lonely. Indeed, the
loneliness was like a drink of cold water to one who is very
thirsty. And a strange elation sustained her from within.

She travelled on, and camped at night in a valley beside a
stream, deep among the bushes. She had seen cattle and had
crossed several trails. There must be a ranch not far off. She
heard the strange wailing shriek of a mountain-lion, and the
answer of dogs. But she sat by her small camp-fire in a secret
hollow place and was not really afraid. She was buoyed up
always by the curious, bubbling elation within her.

It was very cold before dawn. She lay wrapped in her
blanket looking at the stars, listening to her horse shivering,
and feeling like a woman who has died and passed beyond.
She was not sure that she had not heard, during the night, a
great crash at the centre of herself, which was the crash of
her own death. Or else it was a crash at the centre of the
earth, and meant something big and mysterious.

With the first peep of light she got up, numb with cold,
and made a fire. She ate hastily, gave her horse some pieces
of oil-seed cake, and set off again. She avoided any meeting—
and since she met nobody, it was evident that she in turn
was avoided. She came at last in sight of the village of
Cuchitee, with its black houses with their reddish roofs, a
sombre, dreary little cluster below another silent, long-
abandoned mine. And beyond, a long, great mountain-side,
rising up green and light to the darker, shaggier green of pine
trees. And beyond the pine trees stretches of naked rock
against the sky, rock slashed already and brindled with white
stripes of snow. High up, the new snow had already begun
to fall.

And now, as she neared, more or less, her destination, she
began to go vague and disheartened. She had passed the little
lake among yellowing aspen trees whose white trunks were
round and suave like the white round arms of some woman.
What a lovely place! In California she would have raved
about it. But here she looked and saw that it was lovely, but

she didn't care. She was weary and spent with her two nights in the open, afraid of the coming night. She didn't know where she was going, or what she was going for. Her horse plodded dejectedly on, towards that immense and forbidding mountain-slope, following a stony little trail. And if she had had any will of her own left, she would have turned back, to the village, to be protected and sent home to her husband.

But she had no will of her own. Her horse splashed through a brook, and turned up a valley, under immense yellowing cottonwood trees. She must have been near nine thousand feet above sea-level, and her head was light with the altitude and with weariness. Beyond the cottonwood trees she could see, on each side, the steep sides of mountain-slopes hemming her in, sharp-plumaged with overlapping aspen, and, higher up, with sprouting, pointed spruce and pine tree. Her horse went on automatically. In this tight valley, on this slight trail, there was nowhere to go but ahead, climbing.

Suddenly her horse jumped, and three men in dark blankets were on the trail before her.

"Adios!" came the greeting, in the full, restrained Indian voice.

"Adios!" she replied, in her assured, American woman's voice.

"Where are you going?" came the quiet question, in Spanish.

The men in the dark sarapes had come closer, and were looking up at her.

"On ahead," she replied coolly, in her hard, Saxon Spanish.

These were just natives to her: dark-faced, strongly-built men in dark sarapes and straw hats. They would have been the same as the men who worked for her husband, except, strangely, for the long black hair that fell over their shoulders. She noted this long black hair with a certain distaste. These must be the wild Indians she had come to see.

"Where do you come from?" the same man asked. It was always the one man who spoke. He was young, with quick, large, bright black eyes that glanced sideways at her. He had a soft black moustache on his dark face, and a sparse tuft of beard, loose hairs on his chin. His long black hair, full of life, hung unrestrained on his shoulders. Dark as he was, he did not look as if he had washed lately.

His two companions were the same, but older men, powerful and silent. One had a thin black line of moustache, but was beardless. The other had the smooth cheeks and the sparse dark hairs marking the lines of his chin with the beard characteristic of the Indians.

"I come from far away," she replied, with half-jocular evasion.

This was received in silence.

"But where do you live?" asked the young man, with that same quiet insistence.

"In the north," she replied airily.

Again there was a moment's silence. The young man conversed quietly, in Indian, with his two companions.

"Where do you want to go, up this way?" he asked suddenly, with challenge and authority, pointing briefly up the trail.

"To the Chilchui Indians," answered the woman laconically.

The young man looked at her. His eyes were quick and black, and inhuman. He saw, in the full evening light, the faint sub-smile of assurance on her rather large, calm, fresh-complexioned face; the weary, bluish lines under her large blue eyes; and in her eyes, as she looked down at him, a half-childish, half-arrogant confidence in her own female power. But in her eyes also, a curious look of trance.

"*Usted es Señora?* You are a lady?" the Indian asked her.

"Yes, I am a lady," she replied complacently.

"With a family?"

"With a husband and two children, boy and girl," she said.

The Indian turned to his companion and translated, in the low, gurgling speech, like hidden water running. They were evidently at a loss.

"Where is your husband?" asked the young man.

"Who knows?" she replied airily. "He has gone away on business for a week."

The black eyes watched her shrewdly. She, for all her weariness, smiled faintly in the pride of her own adventure and the assurance of her own womanhood, and the spell of the madness that was on her.

"And what do *you* want to do?" the Indian asked her.

"I want to visit the Chilchui Indians—to see their houses and to know their gods," she replied.

The young man turned and translated quickly, and there

was a silence almost of consternation. The grave elder men were glancing at her sideways, with strange looks, from under their decorated hats. And they said something to the young man, in deep chest voices.

The latter still hesitated. Then he turned to the woman.

"Good!" he said. "Let us go. But we cannot arrive until to-morrow. We shall have to make a camp to-night."

"Good!" she said. "I can make a camp."

Without more ado, they set off at a good speed up the stony trail. The young Indian ran alongside her horse's head, the other two ran behind. One of them had taken a thick stick, and occasionally he struck her horse a resounding blow on the haunch, to urge him forward. This made the horse jump, and threw her back in the saddle, which, tired as she was, made her angry.

"Don't do that!" she cried, looking round angrily at the fellow. She met his black, large, bright eyes, and for the first time her spirit really quailed. The man's eyes were not human to her, and they did not see her as a beautiful white woman. He looked at her with a black, bright inhuman look, and saw no woman in her at all. As if she were some strange, unaccountable *thing*, incomprehensible to him, but inimical. She sat in her saddle in wonder, feeling once more as if she had died. And again he struck her horse, and jerked her badly in the saddle.

All the passionate anger of the spoilt white woman rose in her. She pulled her horse to a standstill, and turned with blazing eyes to the man at her bridle.

"Tell that fellow not to touch my horse again," she cried.

She met the eyes of the young man, and in their bright black inscrutability she saw a fine spark, as in a snake's eye, of derision. He spoke to his companion in the rear, in the low tones of the Indian. The man with the stick listened without looking. Then, giving a strange low cry to the horse, he struck it again on the rear, so that it leaped forward spasmodically up the stony trail, scattering the stones, pitching the weary woman in her seat.

The anger flew like a madness into her eyes, she went white at the gills. Fiercely she reined in her horse. But before she could turn, the young Indian had caught the reins under the horse's throat, jerked them forward, and was trotting ahead rapidly, leading the horse.

L

The woman was powerless. And along with her supreme anger there came a slight thrill of exultation. She knew she was dead.

The sun was setting, a great yellow light flooded the last of the aspens, flared on the trunks of the pine trees, the pine needles bristled and stood out with dark lustre, the rocks glowed with unearthly glamour. And through the effulgence the Indian at her horse's head trotted unweariedly on, his dark blanket swinging, his bare legs glowing with a strange transfigured ruddiness in the powerful light, and his straw hat with its half-absurd decorations of flowers and feathers shining showily above his river of long black hair. At times he would utter a low call to the horse, and then the other Indian, behind, would fetch the beast a whack with the stick.

The wonder-light faded off the mountains, the world began to grow dark, a cold air breathed down. In the sky, half a moon was struggling against the glow in the west. Huge shadows came down from steep rocky slopes. Water was rushing. The woman was conscious only of her fatigue, her unspeakable fatigue, and the cold wind from the heights. She was not aware how moonlight replaced daylight. It happened while she travelled unconscious with weariness.

For some hours they travelled by moonlight. Then suddenly they came to a standstill. The men conversed in low tones for a moment.

"We camp here," said the young man.

She waited for him to help her down. He merely stood holding the horse's bridle. She almost fell from the saddle, so fatigued.

They had chosen a place at the foot of rocks that still gave off a little warmth of the sun. One man cut pine boughs, another erected little screens of pine boughs against the rock for shelter, and put boughs of balsam pine for beds. The third made a small fire, to heat tortillas. They worked in silence.

The woman drank water. She did not want to eat—only to lie down.

"Where do I sleep?" she asked.

The young man pointed to one of the shelters. She crept in and lay inert. She did not care what happened to her, she was so weary, and so beyond everything. Through the twigs of spruce she could see the three men squatting round the fire on their hams, chewing the tortillas they picked from the

ashes with their dark fingers, and drinking water from a
gourd. They talked in low, muttering tones, with long
intervals of silence. Her saddle and saddle-bags lay not far
from the fire, unopened, untouched. The men were not
interested in her nor her belongings. There they squatted
with their hats on their heads, eating, eating mechanically,
like animals, the dark sarape with its fringe falling to the
ground before and behind, the powerful dark legs naked and
squatting like an animal's showing the dirty white shirt and
the sort of loin-cloth which was the only other garment,
underneath. And they showed no more sign of interest in her
than if she had been a piece of venison they were bringing
home from the hunt, and had hung inside a shelter.

After a while they carefully extinguished the fire, and went
inside their own shelter. Watching through the screen of
boughs, she had a moment's thrill of fear and anxiety, seeing the dark forms cross and pass silently in the moonlight.
Would they attack her now?

But no! They were as if oblivious to her. Her horse was
hobbled; she could hear it hopping wearily. All was silent,
mountain-silent, cold, deathly. She slept and woke and slept
in a semi-conscious numbness of cold and fatigue. A long,
long night, icy and eternal, and she aware that she had died.

II

Yet when there was a stirring, and a clink of flint and steel,
and the form of a man crouching like a dog over a bone, at
a red splutter of fire, and she knew it was morning coming, it
seemed to her the night had passed too soon.

When the fire was going, she came out of her shelter with
one real desire left: for coffee. The men were warming more
tortillas.

"Can we make coffee?" she asked.

The young man looked at her, and she imagined the same
faint spark of derision in his eyes. He shook his head.

"We don't take it," he said. "There is no time."

And the elder men, squatting on their haunches, look up at
her in the terrible paling dawn, and there was not even
derision in their eyes. Only that intense, yet remote, inhuman
glitter which was terrible to her. They were inaccessible.
They could not see her as a woman at all. As if she *were* not

a woman. As if, perhaps, her whiteness took away all her womanhood, and left her as some giant, female white ant. That was all they could see in her.

Before the sun was up, she was in the saddle again, and they were climbing steeply, in the icy air. The sun came, and soon she was very hot, exposed to the glare in the bare places. It seemed to her they were climbing to the roof of the world. Beyond against heaven were slashes of snow.

During the course of the morning, they came to a place where the horse could not go farther. They rested for a time with a great slant of living rock in front of them, like the glossy breast of some earth-beast. Across this rock, along a wavering crack, they had to go. It seemed to her that for hours she went in torment, on her hands and knees, from crack to crevice, along the slanting face of this pure rock-mountain. An Indian in front and an Indian behind walked slowly erect, shod with sandals of braided leather. But she in her riding-boots dared not stand erect.

Yet what she wondered, all the time, was why she persisted in clinging and crawling along these mile-long sheets of rock. Why she did not hurl herself down, and have done! The world was below her.

When they emerged at last on a stony slope, she looked back, and saw the third Indian coming carrying her saddle and saddle-bags on his back, the whole hung from a band across his forehead. And he had his hat in his hand, as he stepped slowly, with the slow, soft, heavy tread of the Indian, unwavering in the chinks of rock, as if along a scratch in the mountain's iron shield.

The stony slope led downwards. The Indians seemed to grow excited. One ran ahead at a slow trot, disappearing round the curve of stones. And the track curved round and down, till at last in the full blaze of the mid-morning sun, they could see a valley below them, between walls of rock, as in a great wide chasm let in the mountains. A green valley, with a river, and trees, and clusters of low flat sparkling houses. It was all tiny and perfect, three thousand feet below. Even the flat bridge over the stream, and the square with the houses around it, the bigger buildings piled up at opposite ends of the square, the tall cottonwood trees, the pastures and stretches of yellow-sere maize, the patches of brown sheep or goats in the distance, on the slopes, the railed enclosures by the stream-side. There it was, all small and perfect, looking magical, as any place will look magical, seen from the mountains above. The unusual thing was that the low houses glittered white, white-washed, looking like crystals of salt, or silver. This frightened her.

They began the long, winding descent at the head of the barranca, following the stream that rushed and fell. At first it was all rocks; then the pine trees began, and soon, the silver-limbed aspens. The flowers of autumn, big daisy-like flowers, and white ones, and many yellow flowers, were in profusion. But she had to sit down and rest, she was so weary. And she saw the bright flowers shadowily, as pale shadows hovering, as one who is dead must see them.

At length came grass and pasture-slopes between mingled aspen and pine trees. A shepherd, naked in the sun save for his hat and his cotton loin-cloth, was driving his brown sheep away. In a grove of trees they sat and waited, she and the young Indian. The one with the saddle had also gone forward.

They heard a sound of someone coming. It was three men, in fine sarapes of red and orange and yellow and black, and with brilliant feather head-dresses. The oldest had his grey hair braided with fur, and his red and orange-yellow sarape was covered with curious black markings, like a leopard-skin. The other two were not grey-haired, but they were elders too. Their blankets were in stripes, and their head-dresses not so elaborate.

The young Indian addressed the elders in a few quiet words. They listened without answering or looking at him or at the woman, keeping their faces averted and their eyes turned to the ground, only listening. And at length they turned and looked at the woman.

The old chief, or medicine-man, whatever he was, had a deeply wrinkled and lined face of dark bronze, with a few sparse grey hairs round the mouth. Two long braids of grey hair, braided with fur and coloured feather, hung on his shoulders. And yet, it was only his eyes that mattered. They were black and of extraordinary piercing strength, without a qualm of misgiving in their demonish, dauntless power. He looked into the eyes of the white woman with a long piercing look, seeking she knew not what. She summoned all her strength to meet his eyes and keep up her guard. But it was no good. He was not looking at her as one human being looks at another. He never even perceived her resistance or her challenge, but looked past them both, into she knew not what.

She could see it was hopeless to expect a human communication with this old being.

He turned and said a few words to the young Indian.

"He asks what do you seek here?" said the young man in Spanish.

"I? Nothing! I only came to see what it was like."

This was again translated, and the old man turned his eyes on her once more. Then he spoke again, in his low muttering tone, to the young Indian.

"He says, why does she leave her house with the white men? Does she want to bring the white man's God to the Chilchui?"

"No," she replied, foolhardy. "I came away from the white man's God myself. I came to look for the God of the Chilchui."

Profound silence followed, when this was translated. Then the old man spoke again, in a small voice almost of weariness.

"Does the white woman seek the gods of the Chilchui because she is weary of her own God?" came the question.

"Yes, she does. She is tired of the white man's God," she replied, thinking that was what they wanted her to say. She would like to serve the gods of the Chilchui.

She was aware of an extraordinary thrill of triumph and exultance passing through the Indians, in the tense silence that followed when this was translated. Then they all looked at her with piercing black eyes, in which a steely covetous intent glittered incomprehensible. She was the more puzzled, as there was nothing sensual or sexual in the look. It had a terrible glittering purity that was beyond her. She was afraid, she would have been paralysed with fear, had not something died within her, leaving her with a cold, watchful wonder only.

The elders talked a little while, then the two went away, leaving her with the young man and the oldest chief. The old man now looked at her with a certain solicitude.

"He says are you tired?" asked the young man.

"Very tired," she said.

"The men will bring you a carriage," said the young Indian.

The carriage, when it came, proved to be a litter consisting of a sort of hammock of dark woollen frieze, slung on to a pole which was borne on the shoulders of two long-haired Indians. The woollen hammock was spread on the ground, she sat down on it, and the two men raised the pole to their shoulders. Swinging rather as if she were in a sack, she was carried out of the grove of trees, following the old chief, whose leopard-spotted blanket moved curiously in the sunlight.

They had emerged in the valley-head. Just in front were the maize-fields, with ripe ears of maize. The corn was not very tall, in this high altitude. The well-worn path went between it, and all she could see was the erect form of the old chief, in the flame and black sarape, stepping soft and heavy and swift, his head forward, looking neither to right nor left. Her bearers followed, stepping rhythmically, the long blue-black hair glistening like a river down the naked shoulders of the man in front.

They passed the maize, and came to a big wall or earthwork made of earth and adobe bricks. The wooden doors were open. Passing on, they were in a network of small gardens, full of flowers and herbs and fruit trees, each garden watered by a tiny ditch of running water. Among each cluster of trees and flowers was a small, glittering white house, windowless, and with closed door. The place was a network of little paths, small streams, and little bridges among square, flowering gardens.

Following the broadest path—a soft narrow track between leaves and grass, a path worn smooth by centuries of human feet, no hoof of horse nor any wheel to disfigure it—they came to the little river of swift bright water, and crossed on a log bridge. Everything was silent—there was not a human being anywhere. The road went on under magnificent cottonwood trees. It emerged suddenly outside the central plaza or square of the village.

This was a long oblong of low white houses with flat roofs, and two bigger buildings, having as it were little square huts piled on top of bigger long huts, stood at either end of the oblong, facing each other rather askew. Every little house was a dazzling white, save for the great round beam-ends which projected under the flat eaves, and for the flat roofs. Round each of the bigger buildings, on the outside of the square, was a stockyard fence, inside which was garden with trees and flowers, and various small houses.

Not a soul was in sight. They passed silently between the houses into the central square. This was quite bare and arid, the earth trodden smooth by endless generations of passing feet, passing across from door to door. All the doors of the windowless houses gave on to this blank square, but all doors were closed. The firewood lay near the threshold, a clay oven was still smoking, but there was no sign of moving life.

The old man walked straight across the square to the big house at the end, where the two upper storeys, as in a house of toy bricks, stood each on smaller than the lower one. A stone staircase, outside, led up to the roof of the first storey.

At the foot of this staircase the litter-bearers stood still, and lowered the woman to the ground.

"You will come up," said the young Indian who spoke Spanish.

She mounted the stone stairs to the earthen roof of the first house, which formed a platform round the wall of the second storey. She followed around this platform to the back of the big house. There they descended again, into the garden at the rear.

So far they had seen no one. But now two men appeared, bare-headed, with long braided hair, and wearing a sort of white shirt gathered into a loin-cloth. These went along with the three newcomers, across the garden where red flowers and yellow flowers were blooming, to a long, low white house. There they entered without knocking.

It was dark inside. There was a low murmur of men's voices. Several men were present, their white shirts showing in the gloom, their dark faces invisible. They were sitting on a great log of smooth old wood, that lay along the far wall. And save for this log, the room seemed empty. But no, in the dark at one end was a couch, a sort of bed, and someone lying there, covered with furs.

The old Indian in the spotted sarape, who had accompanied the women, now took off his hat and his blanket and his sandals. Laying them aside, he approached the couch, and spoke in a low voice. For some moments there was no answer. Then an old man with the snow-white hair hanging round his darkly-visible face, roused himself like a vision, and leaned on one elbow, looking vaguely at the company, in tense silence.

The grey-haired Indian spoke again, and then the young Indian, taking the woman's hand, led her forward. In her linen riding-habit, and black boots and hat, and her pathetic bit of a red tie, she stood there beside the fur-covered bed of the old, old man, who sat reared up, leaning on one elbow, remote as a ghost, his white hair streaming in disorder, his face almost black, yet with a far-off intentness, not of this world, leaning forward to look at her.

His face was so old, it was like dark glass, and the few curling hairs that sprang white from his lips and chin were quite incredible. The long white locks fell unbraided and disorderly on either side of the glassy dark face. And under a faint powder of white eyebrows, the black eyes of the old chief looked at her as if from the far, far dead, seeing something that was never to be seen.

At last he spoke a few deep, hollow words, as if to the dark air.

"He says, do you bring your heart to the god of the Chilchui?" translated the young Indian.

"Tell him yes," she said, automatically.

There was a pause. The old Indian spoke again, as if to the air. One of the men present went out. There was a silence as if of eternity in the dim room that was lighted only through the open door.

The woman looked round. Four old men with grey hair sat on the log by the wall facing the door. Two other men, powerful and impassive, stood near the door. They all had long hair, and wore white shirts gathered into a loin-cloth. Their powerful legs were naked and dark. There was a silence like eternity.

At length the man returned, with white and dark clothing on his arm. The young Indian took them, and holding them in front of the woman, said:

"You must take off your clothes, and put these on."

"If all you men will go out," she said.

"No one will hurt you," he said quietly.

"Not while you men are here," she said.

He looked at the two men by the door. They came quickly forward, and suddenly gripped her arms as she stood, without hurting her, but with great power. Then two of the old men came, and with curious skill slit her boots down with keen knives, and drew them off, and slit her clothing so that it came away from her. In a few moments she stood there white and uncovered. The old man on the bed spoke, and they turned her round for him to see. He spoke again, and the young Indian deftly took the pins and comb from her fair hair, so that it fell over her shoulders in a bunchy tangle.

Then the old man spoke again. The Indian led her to the bedside. The white-haired, glassy-dark old man moistened his finger-tips at his mouth, and most delicately touched her on the breasts and on the body, then on the back. And she winced strangely each time, as the finger-tips drew along her skin, as if Death itself were touching her.

And she wondered, almost sadly, why she did not feel shamed in her nakedness. She only felt sad and lost. Because nobody felt ashamed. The elder men were all dark and tense with some other deep, gloomy, incomprehensible emotion, which suspended all her agitation, while the young Indian had a strange look of ecstasy on his face. And she, she was only utterly strange and beyond herself, as if her body were not her own.

They gave her the new clothing: a long white cotton shift, that came to her knees: then a tunic of thick blue woollen stuff, embroidered with scarlet and green flowers. It was fastened over one shoulder only, and belted with a braid sash of scarlet and black wool.

When she was thus dressed, they took her away, barefoot, to a little house in the stockaded garden. The young Indian told her she might have what she wanted. She asked for water to wash herself. He brought it in a jar, together with a long wooden bowl. Then he fastened the gate-door of her house, and left her a prisoner. She could see through the bars of the gate-door of her house, the red flowers of the garden, and a humming-bird. Then from the roof of the big house she heard the long, heavy sound of a drum, unearthly to her in its summons, and an uplifted voice calling from the house-top in a strange language, with a far-away emotionless intonation, delivering some speech or message. And she listened as if from the dead.

But she was very tired. She lay down on a couch of skins, pulling over her the blanket of dark wool, and she slept, giving up everything.

When she woke it was late afternoon, and the young Indian

was entering with a basket-tray containing food, tortillas, and corn-mush with bits of meat, probably mutton, and a drink made of honey, and some fresh plums. He brought her also a long garland of red and yellow flowers with knots of blue buds at the end. He sprinkled the garland with water from a jar, then offered it to her, with a smile. He seemed very gentle and thoughtful, and on his face and in his dark eyes was a curious look of triumph and ecstasy, that frightened her a little. The glitter had gone from the black eyes, with their curving dark lashes, and he would look at her with this strange soft glow of ecstasy that was not quite human, and terribly impersonal, and which made her uneasy.

"Is there anything you want?" he said, in his low, slow, melodious voice, that always seemed withheld, as if he were speaking aside to somebody else, or as if he did not want to let the sound come out to her.

"Am I going to be kept a prisoner here?" she asked.

"No, you can walk in the garden to-morrow," he said softly. Always this curious solicitude.

"Do you like that drink?" he said, offering her a little earthenware cup. "It is very refreshing."

She sipped the liquor curiously. It was made with herbs and sweetened with honey, and had a strange, lingering flavour. The young man watched her with gratification.

"It has a peculiar taste," she said.

"It is very refreshing," he replied, his black eyes resting on her always with that look of gratified ecstasy. Then he went away. And presently she began to be sick, and to vomit violently, as if she had no control over herself.

Afterwards she felt a great soothing languor steal over her, her limbs felt strong and loose and full of languor, and she lay on her couch listening to the sounds of the village, watching the yellowing sky, smelling the scent of burning cedar wood, or pine wood. So distinctly she heard the yapping of tiny dogs, the shuffle of far-off feet, the murmur of voices, so keenly she detected the smell of smoke, and flowers, and evening falling, so vividly she saw the one bright star infinitely remote, stirring above the sunset, that she felt as if all her senses were diffused on the air, that she could distinguish the sound of evening flowers unfolding, and the actual crystal sound of the heavens, as the vast belts of the world-atmosphere slid past one another, and as if the moisture ascending and the moisture descending in the air resounded like some harp in the cosmos.

She was a prisoner in her house, and in the stockaded garden, but she scarcely minded. And it was days before she realised that she never saw another woman. Only the men, the elderly men of the big house, that she imagined must be some sort of temple, and the men priests of some sort. For they always had the same colours, red, orange, yellow, and black, and the same grave, abstracted demeanour.

Sometimes an old man would come and sit in her room with her, in absolute silence. None spoke any language but Indian, save the one younger man. The older men would smile at her, and sit with her for an hour at a time, sometimes smiling at her when she spoke in Spanish, but never answering save with this slow, benevolent-seeming smile. And they gave off a feeling of almost fatherly solicitude. Yet their dark eyes, brooding over her, had something away in their depths that was awesomely ferocious and relentless. They would cover it with a smile, at once, if they felt her looking. But she had seen it.

Always they treated her with this curious impersonal solicitude, this utterly impersonal gentleness, as an old man treats a child. But underneath it she felt there was something else, something terrible. When her old visitor had gone away, in his silent, insidious, fatherly fashion, a shock of fear would come over her; though of what she knew not.

The young Indian would sit and talk with her freely, as if with great candour. But with him, too, she felt that everything real was unsaid. Perhaps it was unspeakable. His big dark eyes would rest on her almost cherishingly, touched with ecstasy, and his beautiful, slow, languorous voice would trail out its simple, ungrammatical Spanish. He told her he was the grandson of the old, old man, son of the man in the spotted sarape: and they were caciques, kings from the old, old days, before even the Spaniards came. But he himself had been in Mexico City, and also in the United States. He had worked as a labourer, building the roads in Los Angeles. He had travelled as far as Chicago.

"Don't you speak English, then?" she asked.

His eyes rested on her with a curious look of duplicity and conflict, and he mutely shook his head.

"What did you do with your long hair, when you were in

the United States?" she asked. "Did you cut it off?"

Again, with the look of torment in his eyes, he shook his head.

"No," he said, in a low, subdued voice, "I wore a hat, and a handkerchief tied round my head."

And he relapsed into silence, as if of tormented memories.

"Are you the only man of your people who has been to the United States?" she asked him.

"Yes. I am the only one who has been away from here for a long time. The others come back soon, in one week. They don't stay away. The old men don't let them."

"And why did you go?"

"The old men want me to go—because I shall be the cacique——"

He talked always with the same naïveté, and almost childish candour. But she felt that this was perhaps just the effect of his Spanish. Or perhaps speech altogether was un-real to him. Anyhow, she felt that all the real things were kept back.

He came and sat with her a good deal—sometimes more than she wished—as if he wanted to be near her. She asked him if he was married. He said he was—with two children.

"I should like to see your children," she said.

But he answered only with that smile, a sweet, almost ecstatic smile, above which the dark eyes hardly change from their enigmatic abstraction.

It was curious, he would sit with her by the hour, without ever making her self-conscious, or sex-conscious. He seemed to have no sex, as he sat there so still and gentle and apparently submissive with his head bent a little forward, and the river of glistening black hair streaming maidenly over his shoulders.

Yet when she looked again, she saw his shoulders broad and powerful, his eyebrows black and level, the short, curved, obstinate black lashes over his lowered eyes, the small, fur-like line of moustache above his blackish, heavy lips, and the strong chin, and she knew that in some other mysterious way he was darkly and powerfully male. And he, feeling her watching him, would glance up at her swiftly with a dark lurking look in his eyes, which immediately he veiled with that half-sad smile.

The days and the weeks went by, in a vague kind of contentment. She was uneasy sometimes, feeling she had lost the power over herself. She was not in her own power, she was under the spell of some other control. And at times she had moments of terror and horror. But then these Indians would come and sit with her, casting their insidious spell over her by their very silent presence, their silent, sexless, powerful physical presence. As they sat they seemed to take her will away, and leaving her will-less and victim to her own indifference. And the young man would bring her sweetened drink, often the same emetic drink, but sometimes other kinds. And after drinking, the languor filled her heavy limbs, her senses seemed to float in the air, listening, hearing. They had brought her a little female dog, which she called Flora. And once, in the trance of her senses, she felt she *heard* the little dog conceive, in her tiny womb, and begin to be complex, with young. And another day she could hear the vast sound of the earth going round, like some immense arrow-string booming.

But as the days grew shorter and colder, when she was cold, she would get a sudden revival of her will, and a desire to go out, to go away. And she insisted to the young man, she wanted to go out.

So one day, they let her climb to the topmost roof of the big house where she was, and look down the square. It was the day of the big dance, but not everybody was dancing. Women with babies in their arms stood in their doorways, watching. Opposite, at the other end of the square, there was a throng before the other big house, and a small, brilliant group on the terrace roof of the first storey, in front of wide open doors of the upper storey. Through these wide open doors she could see fire glinting in darkness and priests in head-dresses of black and yellow and scarlet feathers, wearing robe-like blankets of black and red and yellow, with long green fringes, were moving about. A big drum was beating slowly and regularly, in the dense, Indian silence. The crowd below waited.

Then a drum started on a high beat, and there came the deep, powerful burst of men singing a heavy, savage music, like a wind roaring in some timeless forest, many mature men singing in one breath, like the wind; and long lines of dancers walked out from under the big house. Men with naked, golden-bronze bodies and streaming black hair, tufts of red and yellow feathers on their arms, and kilts of white frieze with a bar of heavy red and black and green embroidery round their waists, bending slightly forward and stamping the earth in their absorbed, monotonous stamp of the dance. a fox-fur, hung by the nose from their belt behind, swaying with the sumptuous swaying of a beautiful fox-fur, the tip of the tail writhing above the dancer's heels. And after each man, a woman with a strange elaborate head-dress of feathers and sea-shells, and wearing a short black tunic, moving erect, holding up tufts of feathers in each hand, swaying her wrists rythmically and subtly beating the earth with her bare feet.

So, the long line of the dance unfurling from the big house opposite. And from the big house beneath her, strange scent of incense, strange tense silence, then the answering burst of inhuman male singing, and the long line of the dance unfurling.

It went on all day, the insistence of the drum, the cavernous, roaring, storm-like sound of male singing, the incessant swinging of the fox-skins behind the powerful, gold-bronze, stamping legs of the men, the autumn sun from a perfect blue heaven pouring on the rivers of black hair, men's and women's, the valley all still, the walls of rock beyond, the awful huge bulking of the mountain against the pure sky, its snow seething with sheer whiteness.

For hours and hours she watched, spellbound, and as if drugged. And in all the terrible persistence of the drumming and the primeval, rushing deep singing, and the endless stamping of the dance of fox-tailed men, the tread of heavy, bird-erect women in their black tunics, she seemed at last to feel her own death; her own obliteration. As if she were to be obliterated from the field of life again. In the strange towering symbols on the heads of the changeless, absorbed women she seemed to read once more the *Mene Mene Tekel Upharsin*. Her kind of womanhood, intensely personal and individual, was to be obliterated again, and the great primeval symbols were to tower once more over the fallen individual independence of woman. The sharpness and the quivering nervous consciousness of the highly-bred white woman was to be destroyed again, womanhood was to be cast once more into the great stream of impersonal sex and impersonal passion. Strangely, as if clairvoyant, she saw the immense sacrifice prepared. And she went back to her little house in a trance of agony.

After this, there was always a certain agony when she heard the drums at evening, and the strange uplifted savage sound of men singing round the drum, like wild creatures howling to the invisible gods of the moon and the vanished sun. Something of the chuckling, sobbing cry of the coyote, something of the exultant bark of the fox, the far-off wild melancholy exultance of the howling wolf, the torment of the puma's scream, and the insistence of the ancient fierce human male, with his lapses of tenderness and his abiding ferocity.

Sometimes she would climb the high roof after nightfall, and listen to the dim cluster of young men round the drum on the bridge just beyond the square, singing by the hour. Sometimes there would be a fire, and in the fire-glow, men in their white shirts or naked save for a loin-cloth, would be dancing and stamping like spectres, hour after hour in the dark cold air, within the fire-glow, forever dancing and stamping like turkeys, or dropping squatting by the fire to rest, throwing their blankets round them.

"Why do you all have the same colours?" she asked the young Indian. "Why do you all have red and yellow and black, over your white shirts? And the women have black tunics?"

He looked into her eyes, curiously, and the faint, evasive smile came on to his face. Behind the smile lay a soft, strange malignancy.

"Because our men are the fire and the day-time, and our women are the spaces between the stars at night," he said.

"Aren't the women even stars?" she said.

"No. We say they are the spaces between the stars, that keep the stars apart."

He looked at her oddly, and again the touch of derision came into his eyes.

"White people," he said, "they know nothing. They are like children, always with toys. We know the sun, and we know the moon. And we say, when a white woman sacrifice herself to our gods, then our gods will begin to make the world again, and the white man's gods will fall to pieces."

"How sacrifice herself?" she asked quickly.

And he, as quickly covered, covered himself with a subtle smile.

"She sacrifice her own gods and come to our gods, I mean that," he said soothingly.

But she was not reassured. An icy pang of fear and certainty was at her heart.

"The sun he is alive at one end of the sky," he continued, "and the moon lives at the other end. And the man all the time have to keep the sun happy in his side of the sky, and the woman have to keep the moon quiet at her side of the sky. All the time she have to work at this. And the sun can't ever go into the house of the moon, and the moon can't ever go into the house of the sun, in the sky. So the woman, she asks the moon to come into her cave, inside her. And the man, he draws the sun down till he has the power of the sun. All the time he do this. Then when the man gets a woman, the sun goes into the cave of the moon, and that is how everything in the world starts."

She listened, watching him closely, as one enemy watches another who is speaking with double meaning.

"Then," she said, "why aren't you Indians masters of the white men?"

"Because," he said, "the Indian got weak, and lost his power with the sun, so the white men stole the sun. But they can't keep him—they don't know how. They got him, but they don't know what to do with him, like a boy who catch a big grizzly bear, and can't kill him, and can't run away from him. The grizzly bear eats the boy that catch him, when he want to run away from him. White men don't know what they are doing with the sun, and white women don't know what they do with the moon. The moon she got angry with white women, like a puma when someone kills her little ones. The moon, she bites white women—here inside," and he pressed his side. "The moon, she is angry in a white woman's cave. The Indian can see it. And soon," he added, "the Indian women get the moon back and keep her quiet in their house. And the Indian men get the sun, and the power over all the world. White men don't know what the sun is. They never know."

He subsided into a curious exultant silence.

"But," she faltered, "why do you hate us so? Why do you hate me?"

He looked up suddenly with a light on his face, and a startling flame of a smile.

"No, we don't hate," he said softly, looking with a curious glitter into her face.

"You do," she said, forlorn and hopeless.

And after a moment's silence, he rose and went away.

III

Winter had now come, in the high valley, with snow that melted in the day's sun, and nights that were bitter cold. She lived on, in a kind of daze, feeling her power ebbing more and more away from her, as if her will were leaving her. She felt always in the same relaxed, confused, victimised state, unless the sweetened herb drink would numb her mind altogether, and release her senses into a sort of heightened, mystic acuteness and a feeling as if she were diffusing out deliciously into the harmony of things. This at length became the only state of consciousness she really recognised : this exquisite sense of bleeding out into the higher beauty and harmony of things. Then she could actually hear the great stars in heaven, which she saw through her door, speaking from their motion and brightness, saying things perfectly to the cosmos, as they trod in perfect ripples, like bells on the floor of heaven, passing one another and grouping in the timeless dance, with the spaces of dark between. And she could hear the snow on a cold, cloudy day twittering and faintly whistling in the sky, like birds that flock and fly away in autumn, suddenly calling farewell to the invisible moon, and slipping out of the plains of the air, releasing peaceful warmth. She herself would call to the arrested snow to fall from the upper air. She would call to the unseen moon to cease to be angry, to make peace again with the unseen sun like a woman who ceases to be angry in her house. And she would smell the sweetness of the moon relaxing to the sun in the wintry heaven, when the snow fell in a faint, cold-perfumed relaxation, as the peace of the sun mingled again in a sort of unison with the peace of the moon.

She was aware too of the sort of shadow that was on the Indians of the valley, a deep stoical disconsolation, almost religious in its depth.

"We have lost our power over the sun, and we are trying to get him back. But he is wild with us, and shy like a horse that has got away. We have to go through a lot." So the young Indian said to her, looking into her eyes with a strained meaning. And she, as if bewitched, replied:

"I hope you will get him back."

The smile of triumph flew over his face.

"Do you hope it?" he said.

"I do," she answered fatally.

"Then all right," he said. "We shall get him."

And he went away in exultance.

She felt she was drifting on some consummation, which she had no will to avoid, yet which seemed heavy and finally terrible to her.

It must have been almost December, for the days were short when she was taken again before the aged man, and stripped of her clothing, and touched with the old finger-tips.

The aged cacique looked her in the eyes, with his eyes of lonely, far-off, black intentness, and murmured something to her.

"He wants you to make the sign of peace," the young man translated, showing her the gesture. "Peace and farewell to him."

She was fascinated by the black, glass-like, intent eyes of the old cacique, that watched her without blinking, like a basilisk's, overpowering her. In their depths also she saw a certain fatherly compassion, and pleading. She put her hand before her face, in the required manner, making the sign of peace and farewell. He made the sign of peace back again to her, then sank among his furs. She thought he was going to die, and that he knew it.

There followed a day of ceremonial, when she was brought out before all the people, in a blue blanket with white fringe, and holding blue feathers in her hands. Before an altar of one house she was perfumed with incense and sprinkled with ash. Before the altar of the opposite house she was fumigated again with incense by the gorgeous, terrifying priests in yellow and scarlet and black, their faces painted with scarlet paint. And then they threw water on her. Meanwhile she was faintly aware of the fire on the altar, the heavy, heavy sound of a drum, the heavy sound of men beginning powerfully, deeply, savagely to sing, the swaying of the crowd of faces in the plaza below, and the formation for a sacred dance.

But at this time her commonplace consciousness was numb, she was aware of her immediate surroundings as shadows, almost immaterial. With refined and heightened senses she could hear the sound of the earth winging on its journey, like a shot arrow, the ripple-rustling of the air, and the boom of the great arrow-string. And it seemed to her there were two great influences in the upper air, one golden towards the sun, and one invisible silver; the first travelling like rain ascending to the gold presence sunwards, the second like rain silverily descending the ladders of space towards the hovering, lurking clouds over the snowy mountain-top. Then between them, another presence, waiting to shake himself free of moisture, of heavy white snow that had mysteriously collected about him. And in summer, like a scorched eagle, he would wait to shake himself clear of the weight of heavy sunbeams. And he was coloured like fire. And he was always shaking himself clear, of snow or of heavy heat, like an eagle rustling.

Then there was a still stranger presence, standing watching from the blue distance, always watching. Sometimes running in upon the wind, or shimmering in the heat-waves. The blue wind itself, rushing, as it were, out of the holes into the sky, rushing out of the sky down upon the earth. The blue wind, the go-between, the invisible ghost that belonged to two worlds, that played upon the ascending and the descending chords of the rains.

More and more her ordinary personal consciousness had left her, she had gone into that other state of passional cosmic consciousness, like one who is drugged. The Indians, with there heavily religious natures, had made her succumb to their vision.

Only one personal question she asked the young Indian:

"Why am I the only one that wears blue?"

"It is the colour of the wind. It is the colour of what goes away and is never coming back, but which is always here, waiting like death among us. It is the colour of the dead. And it is the colour that stands away off, looking at us from the distance, that cannot come near to us. When we go near, it goes farther. It can't be near. We are all brown and yellow and black hair, and white teeth and red blood. We are the ones that are here. You with blue eyes, you are the messengers from the far-away, you cannot stay, and now it is time for you to go back."

"Where to?" she asked.

"To the way-off things like the sun and the blue mother of

rain, and tell them that we are the people on the world again, and we can bring the sun to the moon again, like a red horse to a blue mare; we are the people. The white women have driven back the moon in the sky, won't let her come to the sun. So the sun is angry. And the Indian must give the moon to the sun."

"How?" she said.

"The white woman got to die and go like a wind to the sun, tell him the Indians will open the gate to him. And the Indian women will open the gate to the moon. The white women don't let the moon come down out of the blue coral. The moon used to come down among the Indian women, like a white goat among the flowers. And the sun want to come down to the Indian men, like an eagle to the pine trees. The sun, he is shut out behind the white man, and the moon she is shut out behind the white woman, and they can't get away. They are angry, everything in the world gets angrier. The Indian says he will give the white woman to the sun, so the sun will leap over the white man and come to the Indian again. And the moon will be surprised, she will see the gate open, and she not know which way to go. But the Indian woman will call to the moon: *Come! Come! Come back into my grasslands. The wicked white woman can't harm you any more.* Then the sun will look over the heads of the white men, and see the moon in the pastures of our women, with the Red Men standing around like pine trees. Then he will leap over the heads of the white men, and come running past to the Indians through the spruce trees. And we, who are red and black and yellow, we who stay, we shall have the sun on our right hand and the moon on our left. So we can bring the rain down out of the blue meadows, and up out of the black; and we can call the wind that tells the corn to grow, when we ask him, and we shall make the clouds to break, and the sheep to have twin lambs. And we shall be full of power, like a spring day. But the white people will be a hard winter, without snow——"

"But," said the white woman, "I don't shut out the moon—how can I?"

"Yes," he said, "you shut the gate, and then laugh, think you have it all your own way."

She could never quite understand the way he looked at her. He was always so curiously gentle, and his smile was so soft.

Yet there was such a glitter in his eyes, and an unrelenting sort of hate came out of his words, a strange, profound, impersonal hate. Personally he liked her, she was sure. He was gentle with her, attracted by her in some strange, soft, passionless way. But impersonally he hated her with a mystic hatred. He would smile at her, winningly. Yet if, the next moment, she glanced round at him unawares, she would catch that gleam of pure after-hate in his eyes.

"Have I got to die and be given to the sun?" she asked.

"Some time," he said, laughing evasively. "Some time we all die."

They were gentle with her, and very considerate with her. Strange men, the old priests and the young cacique alike, they watched over her and cared for her like women. In their soft, insidious understanding, there was something womanly. Yet their eyes, with that strange glitter, and their dark, shut mouths that would open to the broad jaw, the small, strong, white teeth, had something very primitively male and cruel.

One wintry day, when snow was falling, they took her to a great dark chamber in the big house. The fire was burning in a corner on a high raised dais under a sort of hood or canopy of adobe-work. She saw in the fire-glow the glowing bodies of the almost naked priests, and strange symbols on the roof and walls of the chamber. There was no door or window in the chamber, they had descended by a ladder, from the roof. And the fire of pinewood danced continually, showing walls painted with strange devices, which she could not understand, and a ceiling of poles making a curious pattern of black and red and yellow, and alcoves or niches in which were curious objects she could not discern.

The older priests were going through some ceremony near the fire, in silence, intense Indian silence. She was seated on a low projection of the wall, opposite the fire, two men seated beside her. Presently they gave her a drink from a cup, which she took gladly, because of the semi-trance it would induce.

In the darkness and in the silence she was accurately aware of everything that happened to her: how they took off her clothes, and, standing her before a great, weird device on the wall, coloured blue and white and black, washed her all over with water and the amole infusion; washed even her hair, softly, carefully, and dried it on white cloths, till it was soft and glistening. Then they laid her on a couch under another great indecipherable image of red and black and yellow, and now rubbed all her body with sweet-scented oil, and massaged all her limbs, and her back, and her sides, with a long, strange, hypnotic massage. Their dark hands were incredibly powerful, yet soft with a watery softness she could not understand. And the dark faces, leaning near her white body, she saw were darkened with red pigment, with lines of yellow round the cheeks. And the dark eyes glittered absorbed, as the hands worked upon the soft white body of the woman.

They were so impersonal, absorbed in something that was beyond her. They never saw her as a personal woman: she could tell that. She was some mystic object to them, some vehicle of passions too remote for her to grasp. Herself in a state of trance, she watched their faces bending over her, dark, strangely glistening with the transparent red paint, and lined with bars of yellow. And in this weird, luminous-dark mask of living face, the eyes were fixed with an unchanging steadfast gleam, and the purplish-pigmented lips were closed in a full, sinister, sad grimness. The immense fundamental sadness, the grimness of ultimate decision, the fixity of revenge, and the nascent exultance of those that are going to triumph—these things she could read in their faces, as she lay and was rubbed into a misty glow by their uncanny dark hands. Her limbs, her flesh, her very bones at last seemed to be diffusing into a roseate sort of mist, in which her consciousness hovered like some sun-gleam in a flushed cloud.

She knew the gleam would fade, the cloud would go grey. But at present she did not believe it. She knew she was a victim; that all this elaborate work upon her was the work of victimising her. But she did not mind. She wanted it.

Later, they put a short blue tunic on her and took her to the upper terrace, and presented her to the people. She saw the plaza below her full of dark faces and of glittering eyes. There was no pity: only the curious hard exultance. The people gave a subdued cry when they saw her, and she shuddered. But she hardly cared.

Next day was the last. She slept in a chamber of the big house. At dawn they put on her a big blue blanket with a fringe, and led her out into the plaza, among the throng of silent, dark-blanketed people. There was pure white snow on the ground, and the dark people in their dark-brown blankets looked like inhabitants of another world.

A large drum was slowly pounding, and an old priest was declaiming from a house-top. But it was not till noon that a litter came forth, and the people gave that low, animal cry which was so moving. In the sack-like litter sat the old, old cacique, his white hair braided with black braid and large turquoise stones. His face was like a piece of obsidian. He lifted his hand in token, and the litter stopped in front of her. Fixing her with his old eyes, he spoke to her for a few moments, in his hollow voice. No one translated.

Another litter came, and she was placed in it. Four priests moved ahead, in their scarlet and yellow and black, with plumed head-dresses. Then came the litter of the old cacique. Then the light drums began, and two groups of singers burst simultaneously into song, male and wild. And the golden-red, almost naked men, adorned with ceremonial feathers and kilts, the rivers of black hair down their backs, formed into two files and began to tread the dance. So they threaded out of the snowy plaza, in two long, sumptuous lines of dark red-gold and black and fur, swaying with a faint tinkle of bits of shell and flint, winding over the snow between the two bee-clusters of men who sang around the drums.

Slowly they moved out, and her litter, with its attendance of feathered, lurid dancing priests, moved after. Everybody danced the tread of the dance-step, even, subtly, the litter-bearers. And out of the plaza they went, past smoking ovens, on the trail to the great cottonwood trees, that stood like grey-silver lace against the blue sky, bare and exquisite above the snow. The river, diminished, rushed among fangs of ice. The chequer-squares of gardens within fences were all snowy, and the white houses now looked yellowish.

The whole valley glittered intolerably with pure snow, away to the walls of the standing rock. And across the flat cradle of snow-bed wound the long thread of the dance, shaking slowly and sumptuously in its orange and black motion. The high drums thudded quickly, and on the crystalline frozen air the swell and roar of the chant of savages was like an obsession.

She sat looking out of her litter with big, transfixed blue eyes, under which were the wan markings of her drugged weariness. She knew she was going to die, among the glisten of this snow, at the hands of this savage, sumptuous people. And as she stared at the blaze of the blue sky above the slashed and ponderous mountain, she thought: "I am dead already. What difference does it make, the transition from the dead I am to the dead I shall be, very soon!" Yet her soul sickened and felt wan.

The strange procession trailed on, in perpetual dance, slowly across the plain of snow, and then entered the slopes between the pine trees. She saw the copper-dark men dancing the dance-tread, onwards, between the copper-pale tree trunks. And at last, she, too, in her swaying litter, entered the pine trees.

They were travelling on and on, upwards, across the snow under the trees, past superb shafts of pale, flaked copper, the rustle and shake and tread of the threading dance, penetrating into the forest, into the mountain. They were following a stream-bed: but the stream was dry, like summer, dried up by the frozenness of the head-waters. There were dark, red-bronze willow bushes with wattles like wild hair, and pallid aspen trees looking cold flesh again the snow. Then jutting dark rocks.

At last she could tell that the dancers were moving forward no more. Nearer and nearer she came upon the drums, as to a lair of mysterious animals. Then through the bushes she emerged into a strange amphitheatre. Facing was a great wall of hollow rock, down the front of which hung a great, dripping, fang-like spoke of ice. The ice came pouring over the rock from the precipice above, and then stood arrested, dripping out of high heaven, almost down to the hollow stones where the stream-pool should be below. But the pool was dry.

On either side the dry pool the lines of dancers had formed, and the dance was continuing without intermission, against a background of bushes.

But what she felt was that fanged inverted pinnacle of ice, hanging from the lip of the dark precipice above. And behind the great rope of ice she saw the leopard-like figures of priests climbing the hollow cliff face, to the cave that like a dark socket bored a cavity, an orifice, half-way up the crag.

Before she could realise, her litter-bearers were staggering in the footholds, climbing the rock. She, too, was behind the ice. There it hung, like a curtain that is not spread, but hangs like a great fang. And near above her was the orifice of the cave sinking dark into the rock. She watched it as she swayed upwards.

On the platform of the cave stood the priests, waiting in all their gorgeousness of feathers and fringed robes, watching her ascent. Two of them stooped to help her litter-bearer. And at length she was on the platform of the cave, far in behind the shaft of ice, above the hollow amphitheatre among the bushes below, where men were dancing, and the whole populace of the village was clustered in silence.

The sun was sloping down the afternoon sky, on the left. She knew that this was the shortest day of the year, and the last day of her life. They stood her facing the iridescent column of ice, which fell down marvellously arrested, away in front of her.

Some signal was given, and the dance below stopped. There was now absolute silence. She was given a little to drink, then two priests took off her mantle and her tunic, and in her strange pallor she stood there, between the lurid robes of the priests, beyond the pillar of ice, beyond and above the dark-faced people. The throng below gave the low, wild cry. Then the priest turned her round, so she stood with her back to the open world, her long blonde hair to the people below. And they cried again.

She was facing the cave, inwards. A fire was burning and flickering in the depths. Four priests had taken off their robes, and were almost as naked as she was. They were powerful men in the prime of life, and they kept their dark, painted faces lowered.

From the fire came the old, old priest, with an incense-pan. He was naked and in a state of barbaric esctasy. He fumigated his victim, reciting at the same time in a hollow voice. Behind him came another robeless priest, with two flint knives.

When she was fumigated, they laid her on a large flat stone, the four powerful men holding her by the outstretched arms and legs. Behind stood the aged man, like a skeleton covered with dark glass, holding a knife and transfixedly watching the sun; and behind him again was another naked priest, with a knife.

She felt little sensation, though she knew all that was happening. Turning to the sky, she looked at the yellow sun. It was sinking. The shaft of ice was like a shadow between her and it. And she realised that the yellow rays were filling half the cave, though they had not reached the altar where the fire was, at the far end of the funnel-shaped cavity.

Yes, the rays were creeping round slowly. As they grew ruddier, they penetrated farther. When the red sun was about to sink, he would shine full through the shaft of ice deep into the hollow of the cave, to the innermost.

She understood now that this was what the men were waiting for. Even those that held her down were bent and twisted round, their black eyes watching the sun with a glittering eagerness, and awe, and craving. The black eyes of the aged cacique were fixed like black mirrors on the sun, as if sightless, yet containing some terrible answer to the reddening winter planet. And all the eyes of the priests were fixed and glittering on the sinking orb, in the reddening, icy silence of the winter afternoon.

They were anxious, terribly anxious, and fierce. Their ferocity wanted something, and they were waiting the moment. And their ferocity was ready to leap out into a mystic exultance, of triumph. But they were anxious.

Only the eyes of the oldest man were not anxious. Black, and fixed, and as if sightless, they watched the sun, seeing beyond the sun. And in their black, empty concentration there was power, power intensely abstract and remote, but deep, deep to the heart of the earth, and the heart of the sun. In absolute motionlessness he watched till the red sun should send his ray through the column of ice. Then the old man would strike, and strike home, accomplish the sacrifice and achieve the power.

The mastery that man must hold, and that passes from race to race.

SMILE

HE had decided to sit up all night, as a kind of penance. The telegram had simply said: "Ophelia's condition critical." He felt, under the circumstances, that to go to bed in the *wagon-lit* would be frivolous. So he sat wearily in the first-class compartment as night fell over France.

He ought, of course, to be sitting by Ophelia's bedside. But Ophelia didn't want him. So he sat up in the train.

Deep inside him was a black and ponderous weight: like some tumour filled with sheer gloom, weighing down his vitals. He had always taken life seriously. Seriousness now overwhelmed him. His dark, handsome, clean-shaven face would have done for Christ on the Cross, with the thick black eyebrows tilted in the dazed agony.

The night in the train was like an inferno: nothing was real. Two elderly Englishwomen opposite him had died long ago, perhaps even before he had. Because, of course, he was dead himself.

Slow, grey dawn came in the mountains of the frontier, and he watched it with unseeing eyes. But his mind repeated:

> "And when the dawn came, dim and sad
> And chill with early showers,
> Her quiet eyelids closed: she had
> Another morn than ours."

And his monk's changeless, tormented face showed no trace of the contempt he felt, even self-contempt, for this bathos, as his critical mind judged it.

He was in Italy: he looked at the country with faint aversion. Not capable of much feeling any more, he had only a tinge of aversion as he saw the olives and the sea. A sort of poetic swindle.

It was night again when he reached the home of the Blue Sisters, where Ophelia had chosen to retreat. He was ushered into the Mother Superior's room, in the palace. She rose and bowed to him in silence, looking at him along her nose. Then she said in French:

"It pains me to tell you. She died this afternoon."

He stood stupefied, not feeling much, anyhow, but gazing at nothingness from his handsome, strong-featured monk's face.

The Mother Superior softly put her white, handsome hand on his arm and gazed up into his face, leaning to him.

"Courage!" she said softly. "Courage, no?"

He stepped back. He was always scared when a woman leaned at him like that. In her voluminous skirts, the Mother Superior was very womanly.

"Quite!" he replied in English. "Can I see her?"

The Mother Superior rang a bell, and a young sister appeared. She was rather pale, but there was something naïve and mischievous in her hazel eyes. The elder woman murmured an introduction, the young woman demurely made a slight reverence. But Matthew held out his hand, like a man reaching for the last straw. The young nun unfolded her white hands and shyly slid one into his, passive as a sleeping bird.

And out of the fathomless Hades of his gloom he thought: "What a nice hand!"

They went along a handsome but cold corridor, and tapped at a door. Matthew, walking in far-off Hades, still was aware of the soft, fine voluminousness of the women's black skirts, moving with soft, fluttered haste in front of him.

He was terrified when the door opened, and he saw the candles burning round the white bed, in the lofty, noble room. A sister sat beside the candles, her face dark and primitive, in the white coif, as she looked up from her breviary. Then she rose, a sturdy woman, and made a little bow, and Matthew was aware of creamy-dusky hands twisting a black rosary, against the rich, blue silk of her bosom.

The three sisters flocked silent, yet fluttered and very feminine, in their volumes of silky black skirts, to the bed-head. The Mother Superior leaned, and with utmost delicacy lifted the veil of white lawn from the dead face.

Matthew saw the dead, beautiful composure of his wife's face, and instantly, something leaped like laughter in the depths of him, he gave a little grunt, and an extraordinary smile came over his face.

The three nuns, in the candle glow that quivered warm and quick like a Christmas tree, were looking at him with heavily compassionate eyes, from under their coif-bands. They were like a mirror. Six eyes suddenly started with a little fear, then changed, puzzled, into wonder. And over the three nuns' faces, helplessly facing him in the candle-glow, a strange, involuntary smile began to come. In the three faces, the same smile growing so differently, like three subtle flowers opening. In the pale young nun, it was almost pain, with a touch of mischievous ecstasy. But the dark Ligurian face of the watching sister, a mature, level-browed woman, curled with a pagan smile, slow, infinitely subtle in its archaic humour. It was the Etruscan smile, subtle and unabashed, and unanswerable.

The Mother Superior, who had a large-featured face something like Matthew's own, tried hard not to smile. But he kept his humorous, malevolent chin uplifted at her, and she lowered her face as the smile grew, grew and grew over her face.

The young, pale sister suddenly covered her face with her sleeve, her body shaking. The Mother Superior put her arm over the girl's shoulder, murmuring with Italian emotion: "Poor little thing! Weep, then, poor little thing!" But the chuckle was still there, under the emotion. The sturdy dark sister stood unchanging, clutching the black beads, but the noiseless smile immovable.

Matthew suddenly turned to the bed, to see if his dead wife had observed him. It was a movement of fear.

Ophelia lay so pretty and so touching, with her peaked, dead little nose sticking up, and her face of an obstinate child fixed in the final obstinacy. The smile went away from Matthew, and the look of super-martyrdom took its place. He did not weep: he just gazed without meaning. Only, on his face deepened the look: I knew this martyrdom was in store for me!

She was so pretty, so childlike, so clever, so obstinate, so worn—and so dead! He felt so blank about it all.

They had been married ten years. He himself had not been perfect—no, no, not by any means! But Ophelia had always wanted her own will. She had loved him, and grown obstinate, and left him, and grown wistful, or contemptuous, or angry, a dozen times, and a dozen times come back to him.

They had no children. And he, sentimentally, had always wanted children. He felt very largely sad.

Now she would never come back to him. This was the thirteenth time, and she was gone for ever.

But was she? Even as he thought it, he felt her nudging him somewhere in the ribs, to make him smile. He writhed a little, and an angry frown came on his brow. He was not *going* to smile! He set his square, naked jaw, and bared his big teeth, as he looked down at the infinitely provoking dead woman. "At it again!"—he wanted to say to her, like the man in Dickens.

He himself had not been perfect. He was going to dwell on his own imperfections.

He turned suddenly to the three women, who had faded backwards beyond the candles, and now hovered, in the white frames of their coifs, between him and nowhere. His eyes glared, and he bared his teeth.

"*Mea culpa! Mea culpa!*" he snarled.

"*Macchè!*" exclaimed the daunted Mother Superior, and her two hands flew apart, then together again, in the density of the sleeves, like birds nesting in couples.

Matthew ducked his head and peered round, prepared to bolt. The Mother Superior, in the background, softly intoned a Pater Noster, and her beads dangled. The pale young sister faded farther back. But the black eyes of the sturdy, black-avised sister twinkled like eternally humorous stars upon him, and he felt the smile digging him in the ribs again.

"Look here!" he said to the women, in expostulation, "I'm awfully upset. I'd better go."

They hovered in fascinating bewilderment. He ducked for the door. But even as he went, the smile began to come on his face, caught by the tail of the sturdy sister's black eye, with its everlasting twink. And, he was secretly thinking, he wished he could hold both her creamy-dusky hands, that were folded like mating birds, voluptuously.

But he insisted on dwelling upon his own imperfections. *Mea culpa!* he howled at himself. And even as he howled it, he felt something nudge him in the ribs, saying to him: *Smile!*

The three women left behind in the lofty room looked at one another, and their hands flew up for a moment, like six birds flying suddenly out of the foliage, then settling again.

"Poor thing!" said the Mother Superior, compassionately.

"Yes! Yes! Poor thing!" cried the young sister, with naïve, shrill impulsiveness.

"*Già!*" said the dark-avised sister.

The Mother Superior noiselessly moved to the bed, and leaned over the dead face.

"She seems to know, poor soul!" she murmured. "Don't you think so?"

The three coifed heads leaned together. And for the first time they saw the faint ironical curl at the corners of Ophelia's mouth. They looked in fluttering wonder.

"She has seen him!" whispered the thrilling young sister.

The Mother Superior delicately laid the fine-worked veil over the cold face. Then they murmured a prayer for the anima, fingering their beads. Then the Mother Superior set two of the candles straight upon their spikes, clenching the thick candle with firm, soft grip, and pressing it down.

The dark-faced, sturdy sister sat down again with her little holy book. The other two rustled softly to the door, and out into the great white corridor. There softly, noiselessly sailing in all their dark drapery, like dark swans down a river, they suddenly hesitated. Together they had seen a forlorn man's figure, in a melancholy overcoat, loitering in the cold distance at the corridor's end. The Mother Superior suddenly pressed her pace into an appearance of speed.

Matthew saw them bearing down on him, these voluminous figures with framed faces and lost hands. The young sister trailed a little behind.

"*Pardon, ma Mère!*" he said, as if in the street. "I left my hat somewhere. . . ."

He made a desperate, moving sweep with his arm, and never was man more utterly smileless.